Prai … *els*

"If you like alpha heroes, wild rides, and pages that sizzle in your hand, you're going to love [Angela Knight]!"

—J. R. Ward, #1 *New York Times* bestselling author

"Chills, thrills, and a super hero and heroine will have readers racing through this sexy tale. Take note, time-travel fans, the future belongs to Knight!"

—Emma Holly, *USA Today* bestselling author

"Sexy and unique."

—*Romance Reader at Heart*

"A wonderful science fiction romantic suspense."

—*Genre Go Round Reviews*

"The character chemistry is gorgeous; the sex is searing hot; the world fascinating and a joy to explore. All in all, a great book!"

—*Errant Dreams Reviews*

"Solid writing . . . sexy love scenes, and likable characters. I look forward to [Knight's] next book."

—*All About Romance*

"Nicely written, quickly paced, and definitely on the erotic side."

—*Library Journal*

"The sex scenes were explosive and should have come with a warning for the reader to have a fire extinguisher handy during reading."

—*Euro-Reviews*

"Delicious . . . Wonderfully crafted . . . Angela Knight brings such life to her characters."

—*Romance Reviews Today*

Titles by Angela Knight

Mageverse Series

MASTER OF THE NIGHT
MASTER OF THE MOON
MASTER OF WOLVES
MASTER OF SWORDS
MASTER OF DRAGONS
MASTER OF FIRE
MASTER OF SMOKE
MASTER OF SHADOWS
MASTER OF DARKNESS

The Time Hunters Series

JANE'S WARLORD
WARRIOR
GUARDIAN

CAPTIVE DREAMS
(with Diane Whiteside)

MERCENARIES

WICKED GAMES

LOVE BITES

Specials

MOON DANCE

Anthologies

HOT BLOODED
(with Christine Feehan, Maggie Shayne, and Emma Holly)

BITE
(with Laurell K. Hamilton, Charlaine Harris, MaryJanice Davidson, and Vickie Taylor)

KICK ASS
(with Maggie Shayne, MaryJanice Davidson, and Jacey Ford)

OVER THE MOON
(with MaryJanice Davidson, Virginia Kantra, and Sunny)

BEYOND THE DARK
(with Emma Holly, Lora Leigh, and Diane Whiteside)

SHIFTER
(with Lora Leigh, Alyssa Day, and Virginia Kantra)

HOT FOR THE HOLIDAYS
(with Lora Leigh, Anya Bast, and Allyson James)

BURNING UP
(with Nalini Singh, Virginia Kantra, and Meljean Brook)

LOVE BITES

Angela Knight

BERKLEY SENSATION, NEW YORK

THE BERKLEY PUBLISHING GROUP
Published by the Penguin Group
Penguin Group (USA) LLC
375 Hudson Street, New York, New York 10014

USA • Canada • UK • Ireland • Australia • New Zealand • India • South Africa • China

penguin.com

A Penguin Random House Company

This book is an original publication of The Berkley Publishing Group.

Library of Congress Cataloging-in-Publication Data

Knight, Angela.
Love bites / Angela Knight.—Berkley Sensation trade paperback edition.
pages cm
ISBN 978-0-425-25491-2
1. Vampires—Fiction. I. Title.
PS3611.N557L68 2014
813'.6—dc23
2014020314

PUBLISHING HISTORY
Berkley Sensation trade paperback edition / September 2014

PRINTED IN THE UNITED STATES OF AMERICA

10 9 8 7 6 5 4 3 2 1

Cover photo © coka/Shutterstock Images.
Cover design by Rita Frangie.
Interior text design by Laura K. Corless.

ACKNOWLEDGMENTS

I'm very fortunate to have wonderful beta readers and critique partners willing to read my work and give me comments with heroic speed in order to accommodate my deadlines.

My newest crit partner, Joey W. Hill, writes truly delicious erotic romance. As with Arthur and Gwen's story, "The Once and Future Lover," in *Wicked Games*, Joey's invaluable suggestions helped me deepen the romance in "Oath of Service."

For years now, a group of terrific writers has been reading my books and giving me pointers about improving them. If you'd like to read something hot enough to singe your eyebrows off, look no further than the work of my good friends Shelby Morgen, Kate Douglas, Diane Whiteside, Camille Anthony, and Marteeka Karland.

Virginia Ettel, aka Bookdragon, is not a writer, but I trust and value her unflinching honesty and perception. Virginia, with Diane, also moderates my Yahoo loop, which I deeply appreciate. Like Diane, Shelby, Kate, Camille, Marteeka, and Joey, she's a dear friend I'm lucky to have.

And as always, I want to thank my endlessly patient editor, Cindy Hwang; her assistant, Kristine Swartz; and Berkley's production team.

CONTENTS

FOREWORD

Be warned: this anthology is quite a bit hotter than my other Mageverse books. All three stories in *Love Bites* deal with themes of domination and submission, featuring bondage, spanking, and kinky sex. If you don't like those things, you probably won't like this book.

Besides kink, the stories all involve vampires, though they're set in different universes with different rules. The first of them, "Oath of Service" is a novella of the Mageverse, in which the Knights of the Round Table are vamps—or Magi—and their ladies are witches called Majae. I've published nine previous books and several novellas set in the Mageverse; you can learn more about them at my website, angelasknights.com. But even if you've never read any of the rest of the series, "Oath of Service" is written to be a stand-alone story.

"Oath" is a novel-length present-day tale about the romance between the witch Morgana le Fay and Sir Percival, dominant and Knight of the Round Table. Morgana often drives the action in my Mageverse novels with her cool manipulation. She finally meets her match in Percival, who doms her ruthlessly with a little help from his partner knights, Cador and Marrok.

The following short, "Be Careful What You Wish For," was penned for the entertainment of my Yahoo group some years ago. Previously unpublished, it features Amanda Carlton, Beau Gabriel, and Jim Decker, a trio of vampires who appeared in several unpublished stories. In the Mageverse, women become witches rather than vampires, but that's not the case in Amanda's universe. When she and her male companions clash with an evil wizard, things get extremely kinky.

The third short, "The Bloodslave," is a futuristic story about three vampire mercenaries who capture a pretty virgin warrior they consider the answer to their kinky prayers. Previously published in an e-book called *Bodice Rippers* in 2001, it's always been a favorite of mine, so I'm offering it here.

Finally, I'm including a sample chapter of my next book, a romantic suspense. Cops Frank Murphy and Alex Rogers attempt to balance their mutual taste for BDSM with the demands of being sheriff's deputies in a conservative Southern town. To make their lives even more complicated, they find themselves the target of a cop killer who doesn't approve of their kinky love affair.

If you have a taste for fanged dominants and the ladies who love them, I hope you'll enjoy my *Love Bites*.

LOVE BITES

OATH OF SERVICE

ONE

The bald leather-clad man hauled the plump, pretty blonde across his lap and flipped up her short PVC skirt to reveal lacy stockings, a garter belt, and no panties at all. Growling, he gave her a dozen ruthless swats that made her yelp and buck. When he finished, the blonde collapsed over his thighs with a moaning sigh that sounded far more like pleasure than pain.

A flare of longing flashed through Morgana le Fay, and she looked hastily away from the sated sub. It was far too easy to imagine herself draped across a man's lap. Not the bald dominant's, but *his*.

Keep your mind on the job, witch, she told herself firmly, forcing her thoughts away from the knight who'd been an obsession for too long. *Somebody's murdering these people, and using magic to do it. You don't have time for kinky fantasies if you want to stop the killer.*

And it would be far too easy to get distracted in a place like Club Penitent, which seemed designed to rouse the forbidden needs she fought so desperately to ignore.

Especially tonight, on a day her ghosts paced and moaned, tormenting her until she had no business going out on any mission at all.

The only thing more unacceptable was to allow her team to go into battle without her. No other witch could protect them as well as she could, because no other witch had her raw power.

Just keep your mind on the job, Morgana. Stop the bastard. Concentrate on that. Forget everything else. Ignore everything else. All the ghosts. All the need. None of it matters but the team and the killer's victims.

She swept another glance over her surroundings. Club Penitent was one of New York's most exclusive nightclubs, whether devoted to Bondage, Domination and Sadomasochism—the erotic lifestyle called BDSM—or to more vanilla activities. The membership leaned toward upwardly mobile, if kinky, professionals: doctors, lawyers, bankers, stockbrokers, even a celebrity or two.

The place accordingly had an air of expensive seduction, between the long, massive bar and the surrounding tables and chairs, all of them dark walnut carved with gothic crosses to go with the club's Spanish Inquisition theme. The bar area was surrounded by a ring of smaller "dungeon" rooms equipped with St. Andrew's Crosses, spanking benches, and other assorted gear designed for tying people up and doing painfully erotic things to them. The overall result was an air of sensual menace, rather as if the fifteenth-century Grand Inquisitor Torquemada had decided to run a bordello between torturing alleged witches.

Gregorian chants filled the air with deep masculine voices instead of the usual deafening rock du jour of other clubs. Given Morgana's sensitive Maja ears, she approved, though the reminder of the Church's witch-torturing history made her twitch.

She'd come entirely too close to getting hanged by a fanatical priest once. It hadn't been erotic at all.

Though if Percival was doing the torturing . . . *Stop that.*

Involuntarily, her gaze flashed across the bar to the rear booth where her team sat. The three men looked ready for battle at a moment's notice, between their holstered 9mm SIGs and the long swords they wore diagonally across their backs. Illegal weapons, of course, but also invisible to mortal eyes, thanks to the spells Morgana had cast.

While the club's Masters wore everything from monk's robes to biker leathers, her teammates needed no special regalia to look like dominants. Instead they'd chosen clothing that would allow them to blend without hampering their ability to fight: leather vests over bare chests, faded jeans and tooled leather boots, perfectly broken in.

Looking at them lounging in their booth like a trio of lions on the veldt, Morgana couldn't deny their effect on her. But then, if a woman didn't feel a tingle at the sight of Percival, Cador, and Marrok looking ready to break all Ten Commandments, she needed to check her pulse.

Someone who didn't know them would probably register Marrok first. He appeared the most menacing of the three, being six-five and brawny as a bull, with a lantern jaw, deep-set brown eyes, and a lazily sensual mouth. His crooked nose had been repeatedly broken during childhood by his abusive prick of a father. Despite the air of brutishness, he was a laughing, genial soul who often played peacemaker between his hot-tempered teammates.

Which made what happened if you managed to truly anger him all the more shocking. His berserker rages could make even King Arthur Pendragon step softly. He'd been known to cut through enemy forces like a plow through a wheat field, leaving broken bodies and barren earth in his wake.

Then there was Cador. At six feet, he was shorter than the others, but that only made him look more like a muscular male wall. Which was something of a natural result given that all three spent hours a day swinging battle-axes and broadswords.

In contrast to Marrok's short dark hair, Cador wore his long, braided tightly for combat. At the moment, though, it tumbled past his shoulders in a curling mane. The eye-catching effect was intensified by its color, a rich, dark auburn, glossy as a fox's pelt.

His features looked as if God had calculated every angle for maximum impact on anyone with estrogen in her veins. Thick auburn brows dipped over laughing eyes the striking turquoise blue of the Caribbean. His nose was straight and knife-blade narrow, while his wide, mobile mouth was prone toward deceptively charming smiles.

Deceptive, because Cador had a sadistic streak as broad as the Thames. He was not the kind of man you wanted to meet in combat, particularly if you'd done something to piss him off. He and Morgana often locked horns; he had a cutting, cynical sense of humor she found irritating. For his part, he called Morgana arrogant, though she preferred to think of it as natural self-confidence.

All right, she supposed she was a little arrogant.

Last—but hardly least, since he was the trio's leader—there was Percival. At six-three, he was a bit leaner than the others, with all the muscular power, explosive speed, and hypnotic grace of a puma. His broad-shouldered, elegant body was marked here and there by scars from spears, arrows, and swords—reminders of his mortal life fighting King Arthur's wars.

As if to emphasize all that stark masculinity, Percival had the kind of face that called ancient gladiators to mind: angular, square-jawed, with a flaring swoop of a nose that just missed being too long, and a pugnacious cleft chin. The overall effect was softened by a wide, lush mouth that Morgana had hungered to kiss for a very long time. His deep-set gray eyes were cool and watchful, heated by flashes of erotic cruelty she wished she didn't find so intriguing. One of his blond brows was bisected by a thin scar, a reminder of a wound that had almost cost him his right eye. He wore his thick, honey-gold hair just barely long enough to curl. Morgana longed to run her fingers through it, but it wasn't a good idea to give into temptation where Percival was concerned. He'd take ruthless advantage of any weakness she handed him.

Percival wanted her. Had wanted her for years—centuries—though she doubted the desire he felt was anything more than physical. If she wasn't damned careful, Morgana knew she'd end up the latest in his parade of hapless submissives. The really galling thing was that she'd probably love every minute of her subjugation—until he moved on to the next sub, leaving her heart in ruins. Dangerous ruins.

The kind with nuclear land mines.

Yet sometimes when she gazed into those demanding gray eyes, Morgana wanted to confess all the secrets she'd kept so long. She knew better, though. She didn't dare let Percival discover that she teetered on the edge—or how far she had to fall.

She'd been skating along that precipice for fifteen hundred years, since becoming one of the immortals tasked with protecting mankind. That was when the wizard Merlin and his enchantress lover Nimue had appeared at King Arthur's Camelot court, where Morgana had been a Druid healer.

Merlin had told the king those who drank from his enchanted Grail would gain immortality and vast power—*if* they could pass the couple's tests. For the knights, that meant duels to prove their strength and courage.

For Camelot's ladies, the challenge was mental rather than physical. Nimue's psychic spells forced each woman to confront her worst fears, while giving her the illusion of vast magical powers. The enchantress then evaluated her response to determine whether she could be trusted with real magic.

But when it was Morgana's turn, even Nimue was astonished at the results . . .

Morgana balanced on a stool on the tips of her toes, her rope-burned, bloodless wrists bound in front of her, dark spots dancing before her eyes. She couldn't draw breath for the pressure of the noose around her neck, its taut rope looped over the hook in the cottage's ceiling.

A little boy screamed, his voice ringing high with terror. Morgana's blood chilled as a man in a priest's robes dragged the struggling dark-haired child into the room. "Mamma!" the boy shrieked. "Mamma, help me!"

"I can give you the power to save your son—and yourself," *a bodiless voice whispered in her mind.* "Will you accept?"

Desperately fighting to suck in a breath past the strangling noose, Morgana wheezed, "Yes. Horned God, yes!"

Energy poured into her, a flaming wave of it that seared its way up her spine. Magic such as she'd never known, effortless and blazing. It made the power she was used to wielding feel like a feeble trickle.

She sent that blaze shooting down to her bound wrists and up to the noose around her neck. When her new power hit the loops of rope, it burned them instantly to floating flecks of ash. Sucking down a relieved whoop of air, Morgana fell off her tiptoes, rocking back down onto her heels so suddenly she almost toppled off the stool.

As the sensation of suffocation lifted, she looked down at the priest who'd just forced her shrieking son to the floor. Rage flooded her with the blind need to kill. Her hands began to burn, casting a furious yellow light over the dark, dirty little cottage with its stink of piss and terror. "Now, you bastard," she hissed. "Now you'll pay."

The priest stared up at her, his eyes widening at the sight of her blazing hands.

She stepped off the stool. Bennett leaped to his feet and backed away, his watery blue eyes darting beneath his balding pate, his thin lips peeled back from yellowed, crooked teeth. "Witch! Damned creature, you will not touch me, or you'll know God's justice!"

"I'll do more than touch you." Morgana's hands shot out, seized the sides of his face and jerked him close. "And if anyone should know divine justice, it's you."

The old man jerked against her grip, fighting like a rabid fox in a wolf trap, yelping in terror.

"Enough!" she snapped. "Be still!" Her will blasted him, paralyzing him where he stood and locking his terrorized mind in winter ice. The need to kill lashed within her like a flaming snake. He deserved it for what he'd done to her, to Mordred.

And yet . . . killing left a stain on the soul. He'd taught her that. Better to leave the bastard alive—but make damned sure he never did to anyone else what he'd done to them.

But more, he needed to suffer for his crimes, share the pain and terror of his victims, feel the weight of his betrayal of his God and his flock.

Morgana's will slashed Bennett like a steel-tipped flail, forcing him to experience the full horror of his sins. By the time she was done with him, she knew he'd never harm another innocent as long as he drew breath.

"You are not like the others."

Morgana opened her eyes to find Merlin's witch lover studying her, a frown on her too-young face. Nimue looked fifteen at most—a delicate nymph with waist-length blonde hair and eyes as black as a night sky. Eyes too ancient and wise to belong to any mortal, much less a fifteen-year-old child.

"You don't seem to have the magical limitations the others do," Nimue told her thoughtfully. "That could be dangerous; the human mind is not equipped to deal with power without limit. And yet . . ." Her gaze flicked as if studying something in the distance, and she paused, appeared to debate herself.

At last the enchantress shrugged. "But your power is needed, despite the risk. You will simply have to take care."

The girl gestured, and the Grail appeared, a delicate filigreed silver cup. The potion it held glowed and bubbled gently, misted by shimmering tendrils of blue smoke. "Will you drink from the Grail and become an immortal witch? Will you use your skills to safeguard humanity, even from itself?"

"Yes," Morgana said.

Accepting the cup, she swallowed liquid fire.

It had been fifteen centuries since that night. Morgana had never told anyone of the potential she had for power greater than what any other witch could claim.

And yet . . . when Percival looked at her in that way he sometimes had, her heart insisted, *You could give him control. You could trust him. He would never betray you.*

No, her fear hissed. *Stop it, Morgana. You can't take the chance.*

Not with her demons.

A Celtic-pale redhead strutted past, clamps swinging from her generous breasts. They looked damned painful, judging by the swollen red nipples they gripped. Heat rushed into Percival's groin at the thought of capturing another woman's nipples in such clamps . . .

"God, I'd love to put a pair of those on Morgana," Marrok murmured, saying exactly what Percival was thinking.

Snorting, Cador took a swig of his Coke. "She'd geld you with a fireball."

"Yeah, but it'd be worth it."

As the clamped girl jiggled past Morgana, the witch's eyes slid to the girl's bare breasts, then directly to Percival's face. Her spring-green eyes darkened with need. His cock hardened to its full length in a searing liquid rush.

In the middle of a fucking mission to keep a werewolf from eating more women.

And it hadn't even been the first time tonight. The raw eroticism of the club's atmosphere had obviously shot Morgana's concentration all to hell. Even worse, the effect was contagious. He and his knights seemed to be suffering too. Except in their case, the focus was Morgana herself.

Which wasn't surprising. During the years they'd worked together, Morgana had been equal parts temptation and frustrating pain in the arse.

True, most of the time she was an invaluable addition on any mission. Percival, Marrok, and Cador had worked with a number of witches over the centuries, but Morgana was the most powerful of them all.

She was also as fearless as any male warrior, and damned near as good with a sword as one of the Knights of the Round Table.

What's more, Morgana never admitted defeat. She'd do whatever it took to succeed, refusing to yield to physical or mental exhaustion. She pushed herself so hard that she'd won the respect of all three knights, even Cador, who personally disliked her. Percival had seen her keep casting spells to defend the team when she was so badly wounded he was surprised she was even conscious. Again and again, she'd proven she was willing to die for them—as they, in turn, would die for her.

Which didn't mean she couldn't royally piss them all off.

For one thing, Morgana only went on the most tricky and dangerous missions, and insisted on leading most of those. She steadfastly refused to bow to any authority but her own. If Percival tried to assume control, usually because things had gone to hell, her reaction was often bitchy in the extreme.

That wouldn't drive him half as mad as it did, except his dominant instincts insisted she was hiding a submissive streak. At times she seemed to be deliberately bratting—the BDSM term when a submissive tried to earn a punishment from her dominant by acting out like a bratty child.

Except in Morgana's case, it was worse than obnoxious behavior, because she sometimes gave him and his team painful magical jolts.

The powers given to witches and vampires complemented each other; vampires couldn't work magic beyond self-healing and shape-shifting, while Majae weren't as physically powerful as their counterparts. That meant a vampire couldn't overpower a witch's spells, just as she couldn't overpower his strength.

A Maja could, however, use her abilities to give a vampire a nasty jolt if he forgot himself and tried to take her blood by force. Most

Majae were careful not to abuse that power, but Morgana never seemed to hesitate. Percival had sworn he'd one day give her bare arse a swat for every zap she'd dealt him and his team.

A woman cried out from one of Club Penitent's dungeon rooms, her voice spiraling high with a blend of arousal, pain, and pleasure. Perhaps from the application of nipple clamps or a riding crop or a demanding kiss.

For the second time in less than a minute, Morgana's gaze slid back to the three knights.

Percival's temper began to steam, burning all the hotter because he was as angry at himself as he was at her.

Passing his thumb over the heavy gold enchanted ring on his right hand, he activated the spell that allowed them to communicate during missions. "*Get your head out of your cunt and on the fucking job, Morgana. If one of these women dies because of you, I swear to Merlin I will bend you over the Round Table and flog you with a buggy whip!*"

"*You forget yourself, Lord Percival,*" she replied in that cool contralto voice of hers. "I *lead this mission.*"

"*Then lead it,*" Percival snarled, "*and quit turning it into fucking amateur hour.*"

A white-hot stiletto of agony stabbed between his eyes, so savagely intense it almost tore a gasp of pain from his mouth. He bit it back.

"*Goddammit Morgana!*" Cador growled in the link, "'*Rok and I didn't do anything. Why hit us?*" Morgana's spell must've caught the pair as it traveled through their mission rings. Morgana made no reply; she'd evidently closed communications.

"Sorry," Percival growled.

Cador grunted and took another deep swallow of his Coke, auburn brows dipping in a frown. "I don't like the way this is going. I've never seen Morgana so far off her game." He glowered. "I'm beginning to wonder if we should work with her again. We may have reached the point of diminishing returns."

"Bullshit." Marrok glowered at him. "Name one witch with as much raw power as Morgana le Fay. I'll admit she can be a pain in the arse . . ."

Cador smirked. "Sometimes literally."

". . . But we've never failed to achieve a mission objective when we worked with Morgana. That's not always a given when we work with other witches."

"You know, it doesn't have to be just one Maja," Cador pointed out. "Two or even three . . ."

"Might be equivalent to Morgana's power, but they wouldn't have her experience or skill in magical combat strategy." Percival rattled the ice in his glass impatiently. "Nobody is as good in a magical fight as Morg. Except maybe Kel, and he's a dragon."

Cador pursed his lips, considering. "Gwen's pretty damn good."

"True, but Arthur is hardly going to let us have Gwen, is he?" Marrok leaned in, his jaw taking on a familiar stubborn jut.

As the two knights began arguing about which Maja would make a better addition to their partnership, Percival's gaze drifted back to Morgana. He'd known the witch fifteen centuries now, years of desperate combat, furious arguments, and steely friendship. She'd been driving him insane for most of that time.

Centuries ago, the four of them had been among the first twenty-four people to drink from Merlin's Grail. The potion it contained had magically transformed them all. King Arthur and his Knights of the Round Table had become Magi—vampires, in other words. The twelve ladies of Camelot's court, including Morgana and Queen Guinevere, became witches, or Majae.

In the centuries since, those twenty-four had become ten thousand, as their descendants joined them in the battle to protect humanity against its own self-destructive impulses. Collectively they were called the Magekind, sworn to use their impressive abilities to hunt those like the magical killer who was their target tonight.

Today they all lived in Avalon, an enchanted city of immortals located in the Mageverse, a parallel universe where magic was a universal force like gravity or electromagnetism. Which was why that universe's version of Earth was inhabited by everything from fairies to dragons.

This Earth, meanwhile, was home to werewolves like the one they were hunting today.

Though most werewolves were basically decent, this one was a thoroughly nasty bastard. Over the past two months, seventeen women had vanished from nightclubs around the country, only to be found the next day as piles of gnawed bone. He'd evidently *eaten* them.

The mortal authorities had yet to realize what was actually going on. Because the victims' bodies had been reduced to skeletal remains so quickly, law enforcement had assumed they'd been dead much longer than they actually had been. This made identification basically impossible. Police needed some idea who a victim might be in order to obtain dental records to compare skulls to, and they'd excluded anyone who'd been missing less than a month.

Unlike the police, however, Percival and his team had Morgana. Last night the witch had a vision that some kind of magical predator was abducting, murdering, and eating women. Women who'd been taken from nightclubs. Merlin's Grimoire—an enchanted talking book that was the magical equivalent of a supercomputer—had produced articles from newspapers around the country dealing with skeletal remains said to be the victims of animal attacks. When Morgana described an image from her vision—a hand holding a whip outlined in red neon—Grim had identified it as the logo for Club Penitent.

Which explained why the most powerful witch on the planet was dressed in a red corset, matching thong, lacy stockings, and high heels. The costume displayed every gorgeous inch of her elegant body, long, toned legs, and full breasts—and made Percival's dick sit up and beg.

She also looked like just the sort of submissive the killer liked to hunt. Morgana played bait the way she did everything else: to the hilt, prancing around on those crimson stilettos, drawing the eyes of every straight man in the place, whether dominant or sub.

Percival couldn't blame them for drooling. The witch had a long-boned, elegant face with a narrow nose, full lips, and delicately chiseled cheekbones. Her large eyes were a green so vivid, they reminded him of spring leaves, and her black hair fell in a silken waterfall of ebony curls to the small of her back.

All in all, an irresistible target for the killer.

Which was why the three knights were undercover as sexual dominants. If the killer was a werewolf, as Morgana believed, she'd need the backup. Werewolves were not only eight feet of fangs, fur, and claws, they were invulnerable to magical attacks. That would leave her with no way of defending herself; she'd be almost as helpless as the mortal victims had been.

True, Morgana was stronger than a human, not to mention good with a sword—given fifteen hundred years of experience, she should be—but that might not be enough to let her fight off a monster. Percival, Marrok, and Cador, with their vampire strength, would more than balance the scales. Considering what the killer had done to those seventeen women, the fuzzy fuck deserved everything they could dish out.

The bastard couldn't even claim to be a victim of animal instinct. Unlike the movie version, real werewolves were no more driven to murder than real vampires. This prick was just a serial killer, fanged and furry or not.

"Morg's got another nibble," Marrok said.

Percival tensed as the strange dominant approached Morgana. He was a handsome man, tall and blond, with blue eyes so piercing the color was evident all the way across the room. Dressed in black jeans and a navy blue polo shirt, he looked broad shouldered and muscular as he loomed over the witch, though she was not a short woman. Percival figured he must be six-one or six-two. Just her type; Morg liked them tall. He leaned down to speak to her, his expression hooded, sensual.

Under the table, Percival's hands curled into fists.

Morgana looked up at the man, sweeping an assessing look from feet to face. She said something and turned away, her body language dismissive.

The big man froze, going expressionless. Then he nodded stiffly and walked off.

"Aaaaand another one goes down in a rain of flaming wreckage." Cador flashed a cynical grin and lifted his Coke in a mock toast. "Morgana le Fay—body of a Victoria's Secret model, personality of a rabid polar bear."

The witch glanced toward their table, then quickly away again. Her cheeks darkened.

Percival knew why, too. Normally Morgana could watch an orgy without turning a hair, but in a place like this, given the submissive streak he suspected? He'd be willing to bet if he came up behind her, stroked a hand down the delicate curve of her back, put his lips to her nape and caressed her with his fangs . . . she'd cream that pretty thong. Which explained why her cheeks had been going cherry red all night.

The woman would be the death of him yet.

Cador straightened, eyes narrowing as Morgana glanced hastily away. "Did she just blush?"

"Appeared that way to me," Marrok drawled.

Both men turned and looked at Percival, who glowered back. "What?"

Cador put down his glass with a thump. "You know what. Percival, you need to do something about this thing you've got going with her."

"There is no 'thing.'" Percival gritted his teeth so hard, they creaked.

"Don't play stupid," Cador snapped. "You can't pull it off."

Marrok leaned forward and directed a cool, level gaze his way. "She wants you, Percival. She's wanted you almost as long as you've wanted her. And it's time you quit fucking around and claim her for the sake of our collective sanity."

"Morgana doesn't want me—she wants a bloody giant lizard." Percival curled a lip and sipped his drink, only to grimace as he realized it was nothing but half-melted ice. He gestured their waitress over, wishing he could order something with a bit more kick; by law, New York BDSM clubs could only serve soft drinks. "I'm afraid I don't measure up."

"Soren's not her lover." Cador sprawled back in the booth, eyeing him. "Soren's just her scaly, shape-shifting fuck buddy, and well you know it." He was also Dragonkind's ambassador to Avalon. The pair had been on-again, off-again lovers for the better part of a decade.

Yet Percival would bet his enchanted sword she'd never submitted to her dragon lover. Or, for that matter, any of the others she'd dallied with, even knights like Galahad. Certainly not the way she'd always seemed to tremble on the edge of yielding to Percival.

One day, he swore, he'd push her right over—and catch her when she fell.

TWO

Morgana wished Percival would stop watching her with his eyes burning with that hooded heat. She wasn't sure if the emotion was lust, or anger over that jolt she'd given them.

Either way, she really shouldn't have zapped them. It was a blatant misuse of her power, even if the spell did nothing worse than give the knights headaches. It was no more acceptable for her to hurt them with her magic than for them to misuse their vampire strength against her.

In fifteen centuries, she'd never seen Percival turn his power against an innocent, not before he'd become a vampire, and not since. His sense of honor wouldn't permit it. He'd sworn to protect the helpless, and that's exactly what he did.

Morgana, though . . . Whenever she felt backed into a corner, it was if a switch would flip somewhere in her brain, and her ghosts rose again to torment her into doing something she'd regret.

Even today, after so many centuries, she heard Mordred's voice breathe low and deep with that chilling, stomach-churning note of seduction. "*When Arthur's dead, you'll be at my mercy. No one will care what I do to you. They'll be too busy seeking my favor . . .*"

"*Stop it!*"

"*I'll do everything I ever fantasized about, and you'll be helpless . . .*"

"*Stop it stop it STOP IT!*"

"*It's no more than you deserve. After all, you let that priest do it to me, didn't you?*"

Gritting her teeth, Morgana forced away the memory of big hands clamping around her arms with bruising force, the hard crack of a fist against her cheek, the explosion of light in her head, her own high-pitched cry of pain.

Another man's face rose in her memory, twisted with lust, fevered eyes glittering in sick excitement. Father Bennett spoke in a voice pitched higher than her son's velvet baritone, but edged in the same vicious malice. "*You may as well admit your crimes, witch. We all know what you are, what black perversion you hide beneath your beauty. Confess, and seek my mercy!*"

Stop it! They're dead. They're both dead. They've been *dead.*

She'd worked so hard to slay her demons. Yes, it had been bad the first three or four decades, but as she'd put her first century behind her, she'd learned to ignore those black memories. She'd often gone years without thinking of either of them, though Mordred's birthday could bring it all back.

But then things had . . . changed. The last decade had been a difficult one for the Magekind, as they'd found themselves fighting everything from demons to dragons to werewolves who were immune to magic.

And Morgana, who'd thought she had everything under control, found she controlled nothing at all. Especially not herself. As her control frayed, it became all too tempting to strike out with her magic against anyone with the bad luck to rouse her ghosts. Including Percival and his team.

That lack of control, of honor, was one of the things she most despised about herself. Especially since she was surrounded by those whose sense of honor was so acute.

For fifteen centuries, the Knights of the Round Table had been considered the very embodiment of honor, even by those mortal storytellers who knew nothing of who they truly were. The same bards portrayed Morgana as the villain of the tale. In their songs, she was the witch who'd given birth to Mordred after an incestuous union with Arthur. Mordred, in turn, had led a rebellion against the king that plunged Britain into the Dark Ages. The songs the mortals sung bore little resemblance to reality, yet the bones of the truth were there.

The poets had been right when they'd said Mordred was Morgana's son with the High King from an incestuous union. What they hadn't known was that Morgana and Arthur had been teenagers when the boy was conceived, chance-met strangers. It was only much later that Merlin told them Arthur's father, King Uther Pendragon, had raped Morgana's mother, a Druid priestess.

In retrospect, that revelation had explained a great deal Morgana had never understood about her childhood. Her mother had always treated Morgana with a certain frigid distance. Duana, a Druid priestess, had only shown any interest in her daughter at all when it became obvious the child had a natural talent for healing. Even then, Duana had subjected her to constant stinging criticism of her attempts to master Druid herbal lore.

Morgana had never understood why her mother treated her so coldly, until Merlin's revelation. Duana was a tall blonde whose lovely face was a soft oval, while dark-haired Morgana's features were a more delicate version of Arthur's strong, angular face.

And Arthur, she'd been told, looked exactly like his father.

Every time she looked at Morgana, Duana must have been reminded of Uther Pendragon. Yet her mother had never told Morgana she was a product of rape, probably because of the cold pride that was so much a part of the Druid priestess's character. If she had, history would have followed a very different course, for Morgana would have never knowingly slept with her half-brother.

As it was, when Morgana was nineteen, Arthur fought a battle not far from the temple. Morgana was one of the healers called out to tend the wounded, and ended up treating Arthur's best friend, Lancelot. She'd saved his life—and Arthur, who at seventeen had already been a skilled seducer, had taken her to bed.

When she'd returned, her mother had taken one look at her and known—probably thanks to the Sight—that she was pregnant. Duana had demanded the father's identity. When Morgana told her, she'd recoiled in revulsion and driven her daughter from the temple that was the only home she'd ever known. "Take the contents of your cursed womb, and get from my sight!"

But she hadn't said why, not even when Morgana had tearfully begged to know. Penniless, the girl had ended up taking shelter in a village not far away.

Which, tragically, had proven to be the home of a certain Father Bennett. After Bennett's death, the village's elders had sheltered mother and son—possibly out of guilt as much as anything else—until Mordred was ten. That was when Morgana decided to travel to Camelot to seek the position of royal healer.

Arthur had taken one look at Mordred and promptly realized he was his son. The childless royal couple greeted them with open arms.

After nine years as Arthur's heir, learning he was the product of incest was the final straw for Mordred. From then on, he'd seemed to see himself as cursed, even evil. It was as if the knowledge gave him permission to ignore any sense of honor and decency Morgana, Arthur, and Guinevere had ever taught him.

But then, maybe he'd always felt that way since suffering the less-than-tender attentions of Father Bennett. In any case, her sweet, sunny little boy had grown up to be a twisted, vicious man.

"I'll do everything I ever fantasized about, and you'll be helpless . . ."

Just as the poets wrote, Mordred had gone on to lead a failed rebellion against Arthur. The king had ultimately been forced to kill him. Morgana had felt only relief at her son's death; he would have destroyed them all.

Today, on what would have been his birthday, the memory of Mordred paced at the edges of Morgana's mind like some bloody Shakespearean ghost. Her cheek seemed to sting from the spectral weight of his fist, just as his remembered threats made her stomach twist in revulsion.

She'd known today would be bad the moment she woke this morning. *Maybe I should have stayed home.*

But no. The team needed her.

Percival needed her.

She started to glance toward him, only to freeze as she sensed a wave of dark, boiling magic rolling through the bar toward her. Morgana's eyes narrowed as she went on high alert. Reinforcing her magical shields, she cast a probing spell. Something was definitely coming, something that felt almost oily in the weight and texture of its evil. There was no doubt about it: Their quarry was here . . . or something just as bad.

Pivoting, Morgana swept her gaze across the bar just as a wave of force hit her, vicious and alien, almost punching through her magical shields. She had to catch the edge of the bar to keep from being knocked right off her stilettos. With an effort, she shook off the effects of that dark attack and focused her attention on the club's entrance.

It seemed the murdering werewolf had arrived. Now they just had to kill the furry bastard . . .

Except . . .

Morgana frowned in puzzlement. She knew the feel of werewolf magic from painful experience. *Claws raked across her skin as the wolves closed in, their eyes glowing orange with bloodlust . . .*

The taste of this creature's power was different, much stronger than anything she'd felt before from any other wolf. A tsunami of malice and magic that was both alien and all too familiar.

"That's not *a werewolf,"* Percival said over the mission link, echoing the thought that had made her heart skip in dread. *"That's a dragon."*

"Oh," Morrak groaned, *"we're so fucked."*

They were both right. Heart pounding, Morgana started toward the club's entrance, pushing through the laughing, dancing crowd, grimly determined to intercept the killer.

The creature who strode into the bar a moment later didn't look like a murderous shape-shifting dragon. He was just tall enough to draw a woman's eye in a crowd, lean and muscular as an Olympic swimmer in a well-cut gray suit that suggested its wearer had both money and taste. Morgana could see how an unwary woman might follow him to her death, deceived by his smoldering GQ looks and artfully tousled black hair.

But the gaze he swept over the crowd was so intensely predatory, so cruel, that Morgana found herself jolting toward him, desperate to divert him before he picked out some mortal woman to victimize.

"Morgana, watch your cover," Percival murmured through their enchanted mission rings.

She caught herself, camouflaging her alarm with a seductive smile and her best hip-rolling, leggy stride. As she sauntered over, the dragon's gaze flicked to meet hers, piercingly blue and cold enough to inflict frostbite. The creature smiled, his lips taking on a sensual curve. "Why, hello," he purred, his voice deep and rumbling as he extended his hand.

Quickly reinforcing her magical shields, Morgana reached to accept the offered handshake, even as she prepared a spell blast. "And hello to you. I . . ."

Inhumanly powerful fingers clamped around hers hard enough to grind bone on bone. A wave of psychic force rolled from his hand to hers, blasting through her attempt to shield as if it were tissue paper. The dragon's attack slammed into her mind hard enough to buckle her knees.

"Morgana!" Percival's furious mental bark sounded distant as she fought to shake off the dragon's attack.

Though her thoughts felt swathed in cotton, she realized she was lucky she'd shielded, even if the psychic barrier hadn't protected her completely. *Otherwise I'd be dead now.*

Blinking at the spots that filled her vision, she caught herself against a barstool. Marrok appeared at her elbow to slide an arm around her waist. "Are you all right?" the big knight demanded, lifting her to her feet and steadying her when she swayed. His tone sharpened. "Morgana, answer me. Are you okay?"

"I'm fine." Scanning the crowd, Morgana realized the dragon was nowhere to be seen. Neither were Percival and Cador. Oh, hell, she must have lost consciousness, or damned close to it. "Where's the team?"

"Tracking our scaly friend through the club, trying to make sure he doesn't kidnap anybody. He headed for the scene rooms as you went down. Percival told me to make sure you were okay." His dark gaze searched her features, his worry evident. "Are you?"

"I'm *fine*, dammit. Where did they go?"

"This way." Marrok turned and bulled through the crowd, half-carrying her as the other patrons stumbled back from his overwhelming strength.

The last of the fog from the dragon's attack lifted, and she realized just how bad the situation was. If they weren't damned careful—and lucky—everyone in Club Penitent could end up dead. Especially if the bastard shifted.

Forty feet of dragon in the middle of a nightclub was a prescription for tragedy.

Another thing: if somebody got cell phone video of an honest-to-*Lord of the Rings* dragon and posted it to Facebook, the paranormal cat would be out of the bag. Discovering magic actually existed would change human society in ways no one could predict.

Morgana shuddered. She'd been through witch hunts before. She had no desire to experience the twenty-first-century version.

We have got to lure him outside if we want to get this clusterfuck back under control.

Luckily, Morgana could shift too. She'd been practicing draconic combat techniques with both Kel and her lover, Soren. She was reasonably sure she could handle herself in a fight with the dragon—*if* she could lure him away from the club and its potential hostages.

What would be preferable was if she could enlist Kel and Soren's help. Both shifters were veterans of draconic combat who'd be far more capable of taking out the killer than she was.

And they don't have to worry about losing control.

Though Soren might have to worry about the political implications. True, Cachamwri, the elemental the Dragonkind worshipped as a god, had let it be known he would no longer tolerate his people treating the Magekind as enemies. Unfortunately, that still didn't mean Soren could take the Magekind's side against another dragon, not without proof the creature actually was the serial killer who'd been eating women. Soren would probably do it anyway, but the political repercussions could be highly unpleasant for him. There were still a great many dragons who hated humans, just on general principles. Morgana didn't want to put her lover in that position unless she had absolutely no choice.

Fortunately her other option was a Knight of the Round Table; Morgana could definitely call on Kel. Arthur had made the big shapeshifter one of his elite knights after Kel helped save the Magekind from a demonic magic user. And he was literally the Round Table's biggest big gun. Morgana had an ugly feeling she was going to need him.

Unfortunately, she soon learned she wasn't going to get him, at least not right away.

"Nineva and I are butt-deep in a firefight, Morgana," Kel informed her via their enchanted iPhones when she reached him minutes later. Somewhere nearby, someone fired what sounded like an AK-47 in a thunderous rolling volley. "Bloody terrorists. Look, can you keep the dragon occupied for a half-hour or so?" Something went *WHOMP*, followed by the sound of debris raining down on the ground. Kel swore. "Nineva, grab that kid before someone shoots her! Morg, if Nineva and I can get these children evacuated, I should be able to come roast the monster for you. Just keep him busy until I get there."

Morgana's heart sank as Kel cut the link, presumably so he could concentrate on rescuing the school full of hostages he and his wife were trying to save.

Normally, she'd stack her team up against any other three Knights of the Round Table, including Lancelot, Galahad, and Arthur himself. But skilled as they were, leading Percival, Marrok, and Cador against a dragon could well get them all killed. Vampires could take a hell of a lot of damage, but not the kind of injuries inflicted by a fire-breathing lizard the size of Air Force One.

She'd be damned if she'd put them in that position. Especially not Percival.

"Morgana, Marrok, where the fuck are you?" Percival demanded through the mission link.

"Coming. Where are you?"

"Alley behind the club. When we caught up with him, we found the bastard had put some kind of spell on two girls. He gated off with them." His tone turned grim. *"But before he left, he threatened to eat them."*

The alley between Club Penitent and the deli next door smelled of rotting garbage and cat urine. Something scuttled in the shadows, claws skittering audibly over the sound of late-night traffic rumbling past. The brick walls wore looping lines of spray paint, the efforts of neighborhood taggers marking gang territory.

Percival watched in frustrated worry as Morgana stood in the center of the spell circle she'd cast in an effort to track the dragon. Normally she would have been able to sense the monster's destination, but because she hadn't been present when he'd cast his dimensional gate, she had to do things the hard way.

Frowning, the knight studied her in the illumination of the alley's security light. She'd conjured full armor for them all—chain mail and enchanted plate, camouflaged by a spell to make it all look like jeans and T-shirts to mortal passersby. Normally using that much magic wouldn't faze Morgana, but she looked too pale, and there was a faint line between her winging dark brows that he knew meant she was in pain. Probably a lingering effect from the dragon's spell blast.

Percival didn't like the looks of any of it. His gut told him to abort the mission, but he couldn't, not with the pair of female hostages.

In all the centuries he'd known the witch, she'd never let personal shit bother her—not even during her son's rebellion. Something was sure as hell bothering her now, though. Something beyond the lizard's attack.

"I've got it," Morgana said finally. "It doesn't seem he's taken the women back to the Dragonlands, though they're definitely somewhere in the Mageverse. Probably out in the middle of nowhere, if I had to guess."

"Good. Let's gate, then." Percival drew his sword as Cador and Marrok moved in, preparing to step through the dimensional gate as soon as she got it open.

The witch lifted both hands in a gesture he'd seen a thousand times before. Magic streamed from her delicate fingers to splash in midair, forming a wavering oval window on the moonlit forests beyond. Judging by the constellations overhead,the gate opened on Mageverse Earth.

Then a sound rang through the gate: a woman's scream, high-pitched with utter terror. They all tensed.

Morgana's gaze met Percival's as her delicate jaw set, her brows lowering in an expression he knew too well. It meant he wasn't going to like whatever high-handed stunt she was about to pull. She shrugged. "Sorry." She stepped through her gate.

Before they could follow, it collapsed behind her. Percival stopped in mid-step, gaping at the fading point of her gate as it disappeared.

"Did that little bitch just leave us?" Cador demanded in astonishment.

"Couldn't have." Morrak sounded bewildered. "She wouldn't do that."

Except that was exactly what she'd done. "'*Sorry*'? You're going to be 'sorry' when I get done with you, witch." Cursing steadily, Percival pulled the iPhone off his belt.

No cell phone company had service to the Mageverse, of course, but the phones had been enchanted to send messages to headquarters. They were definitely needed; a lot of agents were always on duty on the two earths, working cases involving everything from wars to natural disasters.

To make matters worse, the Magekind were desperately shorthanded. Over the past decade, Avalon had fought a series of battles with aliens, demons, and werewolves, resulting in the deaths of hundreds of agents. Even the dozen Knights of the Round Table were down a man; there were currently only eleven of them.

Fortunately Galahad and his wife were on call tonight, rather than some less experienced team, though Percival did wish Kel had been available. He felt grimly relieved when the pair stepped through Caroline's conjured gate.

They were a handsome couple. Galahad had that distinctive broad-shouldered swordsman's build, with long sable hair and blue eyes. His wife had the lush, sexy body of the cheerleader she'd once been, with dark hair that complemented her big brown eyes and girl-next-door looks.

All of which was in stark contrast to the enchanted plate armor she and Galahad wore. Caroline looked tense, while her husband wore a dark frown, his hand lingering on the hilt of his sword.

While Caro went to work on the same tracking spell Morgana had just performed—Percival was definitely going to kick Morgana's arse—the knights could only cool their heels.

"You went out on a mission with Morgana *today*?" Leaning against the club's alley door, Galahad gave them a dubious shake of the head.

Percival eyed the other knight. A hundred years ago, Galahad and Morgana had spent a decade as lovers. Apparently, he knew something Percival didn't. "What do you mean?"

"Well, it's February third."

"Yeah. So?"

"Mordred's birthday?"

"Oh, that's right," Marrok said. "She always gets depressed on the anniversary."

Percival frowned. "That was today?"

"Why the hell would that matter? It's been fifteen centuries," Cador said.

"Jesus, Cador, he was her son," Galahad growled.

"He was a murdering son of a bitch."

"She was still his mother."

"I never noticed she got all that worked up about it."

"That's because you're a self-absorbed prick, and you never liked her anyway."

Cador glared at Galahad. "Aren't you married, not to mention Truebonded?"

"Drop it," Percival growled.

Cador, for once, decided to obey.

Percival watched as Caroline chanted the words of her spell, trying to ignore the sick tension gathering in the pit of his stomach. A fight could go bad in the space of seconds—in the space of a single heartbeat.

It had been minutes since Morgana had gated out. Was she even still alive? Were the hostages? *Morgana,* he thought, *I'm going to kick your arse so hard . . .*

He only hoped to have the chance to do it.

At long last, the gate swelled into existence, a hole in the air that danced like heat streaming up from a summer sidewalk, revealing moonlit forests beyond. As usual, Marrok was the first one to step through; he was so damn big, he gave most attackers pause. The rest of them followed, swords lifted, wary and ready.

They almost stepped on the victims.

Percival cursed as the knights twisted and jumped aside, avoiding the still, bloodied forms that lay in a tangle of arms and legs and torn fabric.

"They're already dead," Marrok growled in that deep, barely human rumble that meant he was halfway to losing it. "The son of a bitch butchered them."

"No." Caroline dropped to her knees beside the pitiful bodies, magic pouring from her hands to sweep across the still forms. "They're not dead, not yet. Keep Lizard Boy off me long enough, I may be able to heal them."

"Oh, that bastard is going to be far too busy to even glance in your . . ." A thunderous crash cut Galahad off. Something roared so loudly the ground shook under their feet.

"Fuck," Percival spat as fear stabbed his heart. "Morgana!" Whirling toward the sound, he saw a trail of fallen trees and crushed undergrowth that led toward a thick stand of oaks. It looked as if something huge had forced its way through.

"Well, I don't think we're going to need a bloodhound to track the bastard," Cador drawled.

Rather than walking along the trail the dragon had broken—that could too easily be a trap—the knights moved through the woods parallel to it in a crouching rush, swords drawn, dodging stumps, broken tree trunks, and crushed vegetation. Only to freeze in appalled awe at what they saw there.

Two dragons fought in a writhing tangle of whipping tails and snaking necks, ripping at one another with claws and teeth. Percival recognized the smaller of the two, with its sleek, elegant head and black scales shimmering with iridescent blues and greens.

"Morgana, you idiot," he snarled. "It's one thing to shift to dragon form to fuck Soren. But that doesn't mean you can *duel* one of them!"

THREE

"That's the biggest bloody dragon I've ever seen," Marrok whispered, appalled.

He was right. The beast Morgana fought was at least twice her size, a good sixty feet of scarlet-scaled killer. The dragon was massively built, with a head longer than Percival was tall, more teeth than he'd ever seen in one place, and claws the length of Excalibur.

Morgana reared over her huge opponent and breathed out a gust of fire that splashed off the creature's hemispherical shield. Before she could withdraw, the dragon lunged, clamping its jaws around her throat. Blood flew, and Morgana cried out, a high draconic squeal of pain. Her body lashed as she fought to writhe free from the dragon's vicious grip. Struggling to draw in a breath, she wheezed, jolting Percival out of his appalled fascination with the sight of battling giants. "Bastard's choking her!"

"Come on!" he roared to his fellow knights as he ran toward the entangled dragons, his mind working desperately as he tried to figure out a way to attack the monster that would have more effect than a mosquito bite. Those damned scales were harder to cut than enchanted plate armor—he knew that much from fighting alongside the Dragonkind against the demonic alien invaders called the Dark Ones a few years back. Hacking at the dragon would only piss it off.

Something wet glistened, catching his eye. Blood ran from a raking wound where the killer's muscled neck met its back. Morgana had gotten in at least one good bite. The trick was reaching it. *"There!"* he snapped through the mission ring link at his fellow knights. *"That wound on the neck. See it?"*

"Percival, no!" With a wheezing, gagging cry, Morgana whipped her head, clawing at her captor's crocodilian muzzle with one foreleg. The dragon clamped down harder on her throat. *"Get out of here! Get Kel!"*

"Little damned late for that, Morgana." Gathering himself as he ran, he flung himself upward in a leap for the bloody wound. He sailed through the air in a fifteen-foot bound, sword raised overhead in both hands as he roared a battle cry. The scaled flexing wall that was the dragon's shoulder shot toward his face. At the apex of his leap, he slammed his sword forward with all his vampire strength. The blade thunked deep into the bloody wound, and his body jerked to a sickening, swinging halt as he dangled from its hilt.

The killer squealed in rage and pain, so deafening and high-pitched, it sliced into his ears like a blade.

Catching a glimpse of Marrok flying past overhead, Percival heard the big knight bellow as he landed on the dragon's back. Just as he was about to swing upward and try for the beast's shoulder, Marrok's huge palm appeared in front of his face. He let go of the sword with one hand and grabbed it, allowing his friend to pull him upward as he clung to the blade with the other hand. His booted feet found a purchase on a ridge of thick muscle.

A clawed forepaw shot toward his face too fast to dodge. He instantly realized it would knock him off his perch, and Marrok would be pulled off with him. They'd lose the blade he'd managed to bury in the dragon's wound. He let go of both the sword and his friend's hand.

Brilliant white light exploded in his head as the dragon hit him like an eighteen-wheeler slamming into a deer with the shrieking crunch of enchanted armor.

"Percival!" Marrok bellowed.

He had a wild, whirling view of starry sky and moonlit forest. A volley of fireworks exploded in his skull as he hit the ground with bone-crushing force. His armor rattled and clanked as he rolled, spending the force of the fall as he'd been trained. He tried to flip to his feet, but he was going too fast, and his body kept helplessly tumbling. A tree flew at his face . . .

CRUNCH. He tasted blood.

Everything went dark.

Percival!" Morgana roared as the knight slammed face-first into an oak and collapsed in a senseless heap of bloody armor.

Sick, frantic rage exploded through her, but the dragon still gripped her throat, choking her. She lashed her head back and forth, fighting the creature's hold in a desperate effort to reach her knight, but the monster refused to release her.

Magic sang in the darkness, a hypnotic song of temptation and destruction. Magic she knew—*knew*—would be enough to free her, and let her destroy her enemy.

But at what cost? *I could end up a greater threat than the fucking dragon.* Yet Percival was down, and she had to do something. *He's not dead,* she told herself fiercely. She'd know if he was dead. A quick scan with her magical senses told her he was injured, but nothing he couldn't heal by shifting to wolf form.

Unfortunately, at the moment he was badly concussed and unconscious, so he had no way to shift. She could heal him with a spell—if she could only get free from the damned dragon long enough.

There was nothing she wouldn't do to save Percival, even if it meant courting madness. Even if it meant becoming something the rest of the Magekind would have to destroy.

Lips drawing off a mouthful of razor-sharp draconic teeth, she reached for the power. Magic surged through her, bringing strength with it. Strength enough to let her tear out of the dragon's grip and coil around its huge body in a stranglehold. It fought her grip, hissing and roaring, but she only called more magic and bore down.

Euphoria hit her with a wild sense of freedom. There was nothing she couldn't do with the kind of power she could pull from the Mageverse. If she chose, she could tear the dragon apart like a chicken in the jaws of a fox.

But at what cost? whispered the dying ghosts of her judgment and self-control. The rest of her didn't give a shit, too hungry for magic, for the death of the enemy who'd hurt Percival.

Which was when she felt the knight wake up in the mission link.

Oh, she thought, letting her eyes close in an instant's prayer of gratitude, *thank the goddess.*

But that lizard is still going to pay.

Big.

Dazed, Percival opened his eyes and blinked at the stars overhead. His head pounded with a deep, vicious throbbing beat, and his stomach twisted, threatening to heave its contents.

Where the hell am I? Something hit me . . .

"Percival! Percival, get the fuck up!" Cador's voice bellowed through the mission link.

Pain rolled over him, burning waves of it that tore a scream from his lips before he could bite it back.

"PERCIVAL!" Morgana and Cador in a shouted chorus flavored with a note of—was that *fear? "Shift!"*

"I'm up, I'm up!" But when he made a drunken attempt to roll to

his feet, pain shot through him with such searing brutality, Percival realized he'd broken both legs. *Among other things,* he thought, looking down through his bent and battered visor. Blood pumped through long rips in his cuirass and one armored thigh that looked as if he'd lost a fight to the death with a can *opener.*

"Percival, damn you, shift!" Now Morgana's voice had gone cool and controlled—too much so—in that tone she reserved for utter fucking disasters.

Got to help, he realized. *I've got to help, got to get back up there on that dragon.* Though God knew it was the last thing he wanted to do just now.

He reached for his magic and sent it whirling around his broken body. The world exploded into gold sparks before coalescing into the alien colors, textures, and smells his senses delivered when he was in wolf form.

But the pain, thank Merlin, was gone. As always, shifting to his wolf form had healed his injuries. Which had been so extensive, a mortal would probably have died. He'd certainly suffered a nasty concussion and God knew how many broken bones and internal injuries. *That scaly bastard can hit.*

Now he had to get back to the fight. Had to help Morgana before she got herself killed. Which, given the current situation, was all too likely.

"Percival, you need to do something about this thing you've got going with her." Tonight's little adventure had demonstrated Cador had a point about his obsession with Morgana, but this wasn't the time to worry about it. But once the dragon was dead and she was safe . . . Well, Morgana was going to discover the rules had changed. Percival was, by God, going to change them.

Glancing around, he spotted a writhing knot of tails and wings and snaking necks amid meaty thunks and ear-shattering roars. Percival shot off toward the battling creatures on four swift paws.

Shifting back to human form in midstride, he found his bloody armor was still bent and mangled around him; when a vampire transformed, whatever he was wearing changed with him. His transformation had done nothing for the damaged plate, of course. Ignoring the pain of torn metal digging into the healed flesh beneath, he scanned the dragon's neck for a place to land.

The monster had evidently given up on choking Morgana, who now coiled around her foe like a boa constrictor, pinning his forelegs with her own as she held on grimly, keeping him from throwing his attackers off or batting them with his massive tail.

Marrok had gone berserk, as he tended to do when one of the team was hurt. Morgana had evidently turned his sword into a battle-ax, and he was putting it to frenzied use, hacking at the dragon's wounded neck as he balanced on its heaving back.

The other two knights chopped away brutally as they all fought to behead the creature. Galahad was armed with an ax, but Cador had two long swords, having apparently appropriated the one Percival had left jammed in the wound. He swung the blades in bloody alternating arcs.

"Cador!" Aiming for a spot beside his teammate, Percival leaped. This time he made it, grabbing one of the dragon's jutting spines and hauling himself up beside the other knight.

Cador paused long enough to throw him his sword and growl through his mission ring, *"This dragon-slaying thing is not for pussies."*

Percival grunted, took aim with his sword, and swung at the dragon's neck as if he were trying to cut down a sequoia.

As his blade bit into the deepening wound, the dragon convulsed, heaving free of Morgana's coiled grip as the beast reared, clawing for the sky with a roar of pain and fury.

Goddammit, not again, Percival thought, as he tumbled off the creature's back.

At least he landed better this time, going into a neat, controlled roll that ended with him on his feet. Not for nothing did the knights spend as much time practicing throws and tumbles as they did swordplay.

Before he could congratulate himself, a massive downdraft

flattened him as the dragon took to the sky, wings beating furiously. Galahad leaped clear barely in time, followed by Cador, who grabbed Marrok and dragged him, howling in rage, to safety.

Cursing viciously, Marrok swung his battle-ax at the dragon's retreating belly, though it was well out of range now. The big knight hurled his weapon. The ax sailed skyward, higher and higher and . . .

Hit the top of its arc and plummeted. Right for Marrok, still raging directly beneath.

Percival tackled the big knight in a deafening clash of armor hitting armor. The impact barely carried them clear before the battle-ax hit the ground, its blade biting deep into the churned, torn earth.

Something rammed the side of Percival's head. He saw stars *again*, but he held on, both arms wrapped around Marrok's powerful thighs as the big knight fought him, so lost to bloodlust he saw Percival only as an enemy. "Marrok, Marrok, it's me! It's Percival. You're all right. It's all right!"

Marrok's only reply was a frenzied howl of fury.

Cursing, Cador piled on to help, Galahad joining them a moment later as all three tried to pin Marrok and calm him down. Still the huge knight raged and bucked, his massive fists and feet slamming into them whenever they lost their grip.

A gauntleted feminine hand shot into the milling knot of armored flesh and locked around Marrok's visor. Magic flared in a spill of golden light. "Enough! Quit it with the 'Hulk Smash!'" Caroline snapped.

Marrok froze. "Wha'?" He sounded groggy, voice slurred. "Wha' happened?"

"Thank Christ," Cador grunted. "Dammit, Marrok, I've had horses give me gentler kicks in the head."

Disentangling himself from his friend, Percival climbed wearily to his feet and gave Marrok a hand up. "Thanks, Caro."

Her face looked pale as she eyed the big knight. "He's a scary sucker when he gets going, isn't he? His rage when I touched his mind . . ."

"Yeah. Marrok has . . . issues." Percival steadied Cador, who staggered, giving his head a shake. The knight evidently hadn't been kidding about that kick to the head, but a quick shift would probably heal any damage. Percival looked around at Caro. "How are the dragon's victims?"

But the Maja was locked in Galahad's arms, in the midst of a fierce hug and a blazing kiss. By the time she came up for air, she looked a little dazed. "Ummmm. What was the question?"

Percival's lips twitched. "The girls?"

"Oh. Uh. They're much better now. It was touch and go for a while; I was afraid I was going to lose them." Caroline shook her head. "He'd damned near bitten that one girl in half. I only just now got them healed and asleep. Sorry I wasn't able to join the fight with that Smaug rip-off."

Galahad snorted. "I'm not."

Percival couldn't blame him; he wouldn't want the woman he loved fighting a dragon either.

Speaking of . . . He looked toward Morgana, realizing she hadn't shifted back. "Morg?" She lay on the ground in a heap of wings and long reptilian neck. She wasn't moving. Fear stabbed him. "Morgana!" She didn't even twitch a wing.

"Shit!" Cador spat, as they all started toward the unmoving black-scaled form.

"Oh, hell, she's hurt. Bad." Caroline broke into a run.

"How bad?" Percival raced after her.

"Shhhh!" She slapped both hands over the nearest draconic foreleg and closed her eyes as she began to chant, her tone urgent.

The knights gathered around, tense and anxious as they waited.

"She seriously needs her arse kicked for leaving us back in that alley," Cador muttered. "She damned near got herself killed—along with those girls."

"Yeah, I'm fully aware of that," Percival growled. "And yes, I *will* see to that arse kicking." As soon as she was conscious. He stared at her crumpled draconic form in worry.

* * *

In the distance, a child cried.

Morgana balanced on a stool on the tips of her toes, her hands bound in front of her, spots dancing in front of her eyes. She couldn't draw breath for the pressure of the noose around her neck . . .

"Morgana!"

The magical voice cut through her nightmare, followed by a wave of energy that healed her injuries and forced her to shift back to human form.

Panicked by the alien magical presence, she came off the ground with her instincts howling.

A deep voice jerked her out of the nightmare before she could attack the source of that magic. "Morgana."

At the sound of Percival's familiar baritone, full consciousness hit her. She blinked, realizing she was staring into the knight's face with magic boiling around her hands. Beside him stood Caroline, looking startled, healing magic fading from her own hands.

Percival's gray eyes flicked pointedly to the murderous energy globes Morgana still held at the ready. *Oh, Merlin's Cup!* She'd damned near shot him. "Sorry." She banished the magic, trying to remember what was going on.

He glowered at her. "You want to tell me what the hell you thought you were doing?"

She licked her dry lips, still wracking her desperate memory. "Uh . . . When?"

He exploded. "When you fucking left us in that fucking alley to go fight a fucking dragon fucking *solo*! Were you *trying* to kill yourself?"

Any time Percival stared using the "F" word multiple times in the same sentence, you had transgressed. The more "fucks" there were, the more you'd pissed him off. Four was a record.

Morgana winced as the events of the last hour flooded back, replacing the sticky remnants of the hanging dream. "I . . ."

"Save it!" he snapped. "I do not want to hear any fucking rationalizations!"

Only one fuck that time. At least he was calming down.

W*ell, I screwed that up,* Morgana thought two hours later as she paced the corridor's gleaming black marble floor, shooting anxious glances at the door of the Round Table Chamber. They'd gated directly to the towering stone Great Hall in the magical city of Avalon, home of the Magekind. Percival's team had promptly closeted themselves with Arthur Pendragon to make a formal complaint.

She had never seen Percival so furious. The other two men wouldn't speak to her at all.

Even Kel had frowned at her when he and Nineva sought her out to apologize for not being able to come to the rescue. It had all been over by the time the couple had fought off the terrorists and gotten the children to safety.

In human form, Kel was a big, powerfully built man as tall as Marrok, with shoulder-length blue hair and eyes the color of rubies. His wife Nineva was as small and delicately lush as he was huge, with white-blonde hair and the pointed ears of her half-Sidhe heritage. Both wore bloody armor and swords at their belts. A pair of Heckler & Koch G36 assault rifles hung over their shoulders.

The dragon knight gave her a frustrated glower. "Morg, what the hell were you thinking? You're lucky you didn't wind up Purina Dragon Chow."

"I was thinking I didn't want my team to end up as the lizard kibble." She raked a hand through her hair. "Look, the killer got away. Do you think you can get the Dragonkind to help bring him to justice?"

"I'll give it a shot." He shrugged. "Though I think it's only fair to warn you, there are a lot of dragons who are still pretty hostile to the Magekind. I don't know how much cooperation we'll get."

"Ask Soren. I'm sure he'd help search. He may also be able to persuade other dragons to assist."

"It's certainly worth a try. In any case, I think bringing this creature down is a task for dragons, not Magekind." Kel shot her a stern look. "Even shape-shifting Magekind."

"So go catch him," Morgana said. "Hopefully before he kills anybody else."

Kel flashed a grim smile. "We'll do our best." His gaze turned thoughtful. "In fact, I think I'll head to the Dragonlands now and see what I can find out."

Gesturing, he opened a dimensional gate and stepped through it. Nineva gave Morgana a sympathetic look before following her husband. "Good luck, Morgana."

"Thanks." *From the sound of things, I'll need it.*

Almost against her will, her thoughts slipped back in time to the night she'd first seen—really *seen*—who and what Percival was. The first time she'd felt the primal male power he could command.

Camelot, 500 CE

Morgana paused outside the room that belonged to Sir Percival and paused, swallowing nervously. Percival had defeated three other warriors the day before for the right to drink from Merlin's Grail.

That one sip of the magical potion knocked him unconscious while it transformed his body, making him into an immortal blood drinker.

After a full day out cold, Percival had regained consciousness. Now he'd need to feed for the first time. The problem was that when the Magi first woke from the Grail Sleep, their starving brains were barely capable of speech, much less complex thought.

But they were more than capable of sex and seduction.

Nimue had warned Morgana that Percival might not recognize her at all, but he would want to drink from her, as well as satisfy the raging sexual arousal that was a side effect of Merlin's spell.

The idea of experiencing Percival's passion didn't strike Morgana as particularly frightening. She'd known the big, blond knight for years, and had always found him intelligent, honorable, and capable—as well as handsome and intriguing. She was more than happy to fulfill any needs he had.

Unlocking his chamber door with a flick of her will, Morgana moved inside. It was dark in the small room, and she gestured, sending a wave of magic to light the lamp that hung from a chain by the bed. She smiled with pleasure at the easy way the power had leaped to her command.

Powerful hands seized her, snatching her off her feet. She hit a muscled body with a startled, breathless *woof*! Instinct almost drove her to hit her attacker with a fireball. *Percival,* she realized belatedly. *It's Percival!*

Her eyes widened as she realized the knight was naked.

Very, very naked.

Tall, his bare chest broad, powerful, and furred in gold, his handsome head was surrounded by a disordered fall of blond hair. His gray eyes stared hungrily at her, his nostrils flaring at her scent. Her gaze tracked down the length of his torso to his erection. She blinked at the sight of it—the long, thick shaft with its ruddy head, the balls covered in blond curls. "Oh," she said in a hoarse voice. She cleared her throat. "My."

He licked his sensual lips, the tips of his fangs just visible between them. His hard body pressed against her, hot and powerful, making her intensely aware of her femininity. Something in his possessive male gaze sent heat flooding her sex until she instinctively pressed her thighs together in rising need.

"Want you." His voice sounded impossibly deep and hot. And incredibly seductive. "Now."

Morgana licked her dry lips and swallowed as she glanced up, meeting Percival's pale eyes in the dim light. She'd come in here fully intending to give him her throat, but somehow she hadn't counted on the intimidating intensity of his hunger. "Sir Knight, I . . ."

He looked her over, dominance and demand in his gaze. "Need you," he growled. One big hand stroked down the length of her back. Despite her instinctive alarm at his predatory hunger, her body simultaneously tightened and heated in response to his delicious sensuality. She knew she could hit him with a blast of magic, force him to release her. Escape. Yet she had no desire to go. She wanted to experience his dark hunger, the feeling of his cock in her sex, his fangs in her throat. Wanted to satisfy the hot female curiosity he'd inspired in her since the day she'd met him. Just the thought of making love to him flooded her sex with cream.

Percival studied her with that animal hunger in his eyes. He smiled in satisfaction at what he saw and said, his voice rumbling low and deep, a sound she felt in her chest as much as heard. "Taking you *now*."

He dropped her to the bed in a rustle of dried grass mattress and pounced, his hands grabbing the cord belt that bound her filmy white tunic closed. Stripping it off and tossing it aside, he jerked the tunic off over her head.

The knight braced over her on powerful arms, staring down at her nudity, his gaze glittering on the tight peaks of her breasts. One hand came up, finding the right nipple, tugging and twisting it until she squirmed at the liquid heat rolling through her. Sensing her helpless need, he stroked a big forefinger of his free hand between her slick vaginal lips. The combination of his lupine stare and his skillfully stroking fingers soon had her shuddering in helpless need. He teased her breasts with one hand and her sex with the other until her hips began to pump, her teeth sinking into her lower lip. "Oh, Horned God, Percival, please!"

With a satisfied growl, he slid his fingers from her pussy to close both hands over the round globes of her breasts, plumping the soft flesh as he lowered his blond head. His fangs bit deep into the soft flesh on either side of her nipple.

Morgana convulsed in shock at the sharp, stinging bite, "Percival!"

She shoved at his powerful shoulders, only to find herself unable to budge his muscled weight as he pinned her to the bed. "That hurts!"

He crooned to her, keeping her pinned, drinking in deep swallows, his tongue swirling and stroking, drawing patterns around the hard little nubbin. Every drawing tug of his mouth worked her breast with such wicked skill. Wrapped in his powerful arms, Morgana found herself yielding to his vampire strength as the pain faded and pleasure started to rise. She gasped, her eyes sliding closed. It made no sense at all, yet somehow the sting of his teeth intensified the pleasure of his suckling. She'd never experienced anything like it before, but the pleasure/pain was too strong to be denied. Too intense. Too dark. Too delicious. Too much.

Morgana writhed as the wicked pleasure of the moment sent her body's arousal leaping higher and hotter. Her desire grew as he continued to feed, taking the blood his newly transformed body needed. "Horned God, Percival!" she gasped in his ear, her hips rolling helplessly against his, seeking stimulation from his thick cock-stand. Her nails dug into his muscled arse, trying to pull him closer so she could grind her clit against his sword-hard shaft.

Dragging his fangs from her breast with a low growl of lust, the knight moved up between her thighs and speared his cock deep in one ruthless thrust. Morgana cried out, writhing as he filled her, his cock feeling as if it extended well past her navel. "Perrrrrrcivaaaaaal!"

He growled back at her, the sound rough and animal. Lunging hard, stroking deep, he fucked her with such force their bodies jolted together with loud slaps. So hard it should have hurt, probably would have hurt if he hadn't aroused her so savagely, so quickly. Her pleasure grew, spiraling in a searing corkscrew so intense it seemed to glow behind her closed lids.

Bucking and screaming, Morgana came as he roared, the sound of his completion almost deafening her. The blinding delight of her climax pulsed deep in her belly, throbbing on and on, longer than any orgasm she'd ever had, fierce and sweet and merciless.

At last she collapsed back onto the bed, sweating, breathing with heaving effort, her heart beating so hard, it made her breasts bounce and judder. Percival panted just as hard as he held her close.

She listened to the deep, hard strokes of his heart, still feeling stunned by the force of her peak. It had almost seemed as if the pain of his feeding had spurred her pleasure. That made no sense—why would the sting of those fangs intensify her climax? And yet it had.

Finally he stirred against her, drawing back. The gray eyes that met hers now held a man's intelligence as they probed hers. Guinevere had told her that once the Magus had taken enough blood on waking, his mind would return to normal. It seemed the queen had been right.

Percival's gaze searched hers, narrow, fierce with demand. "You're mine now. You hear me, Morgana?"

Her heart seemed to simply . . . stop. The thought of belonging to this beautiful man was incredibly seductive, incredibly tempting.

Morgana had never considered herself a weak-willed person. She was too stubborn to be easily led. But as she looked up into Percival's fierce, handsome face, felt the hard strength of those massive arms, she realized she wanted to be his. Wanted to belong to him, as she'd never belonged to anyone before. "What . . . what do you mean?"

"I mean I've wanted you since you came to court, but you never even looked at me. Now I've *got* you." His mouth came down on hers in a kiss that demanded her utter surrender. She melted against him with a soft moan. But as he kissed her, drawing her tight, fear rose in the back of her mind, an icy shaft that stabbed through her heat. Yes, he wanted her now, against all logic, all reason. But that need couldn't be real. What happened when he decided he didn't want her any longer?

And that day would come. Everyone she'd ever loved had turned on her. Her mother had. Her son had. What happened when Percival, too, betrayed her? She remembered the fury she'd felt when Mordred threatened her with rape. If she'd had the power then that she did now, what would she have done to her son in the grip of that dark rage?

What would she do to Percival?

In her rising fear of that inevitable rejection, her first instinct was to scream at him, rant until she drove him away. She instantly realized that was exactly the wrong approach to take with a Knight of the Round Table. She had to be cool, rigidly controlled, or he would counter-attack, probe the cause of her panic. She couldn't bear that. Not now, when she felt so vulnerable to his intoxicating passion.

"No," Morgana snapped, her voice icy to her own ears. "Get off me, Percival!" A flick of her magic picked the knight up and threw him against the wall of the chamber with stunning force. "I do not want you, sir knight. And you will *not* have me—not now and not ever."

She heard his shout of rage and pain as he tumbled to the floor, but she was already rolling off the bed and running for the door. Jerking it open, she snapped over her shoulder, "Stay the hell away from me, Lord Percival, or I will not be responsible for what I do!"

FOUR

It hadn't taken Morgana long to think better of demanding that Percival keep his distance. He and his team were too skilled, as she learned when they were forced to work together despite her initial resistance. Morgana wasn't stupid enough to deprive herself of such invaluable help. She'd compensated by maintaining a careful emotional distance during their missions, not letting Percival get too close, despite the way his big, sensual body tempted her. Fortunately, he hadn't pushed the point, though there'd been times his gray gaze had lingered on hers, hooded and hot. As a result of her careful self-control, the missions they'd worked together had always been successful.

At least until today.

The Table Chamber's massive carved oak door swung silently wide. Percival, Marrok, and Cador stalked out, still in their bloodied armor. None of them said a word as they strode past. Morgana had never been so thoroughly ignored. "Percival!"

He kept walking, refusing to even give her a glance. Only Marrok looked back at her. His expression was so cold, the sick knots in her stomach tightened even more. If even 'Rok was that pissed, she was in serious trouble. Because of his issues with anger management, the knight usually cultivated a deliberately sunny attitude, or at least the pretense of one.

Arthur's deep voice rumbled from inside the chamber. "Step in, Morgana. And close the door." Judging by that icy tone, he was in one of his Pendragon rages.

Merlin's balls, this is going to be nasty. Swallowing, she obeyed.

Entering the great circular chamber, she found Arthur sitting in his seat at the Round Table, the muscles of his jaw working, his black eyes cold and narrow with rage. She took her usual seat at the massive gleaming circular table with its chairs carved with images of knights and ladies. Straightening her shoulders, she stubbornly refused to cower.

He stared at her through an uncomfortable, weighted silence. Arthur wasn't a tall man, but he had a thickly muscled build that made him look lethally intimidating. Black hair fell to his shoulders, and a short, dark beard framed his wide mouth. "What the fuck did you think you were doing?"

"I hate to mention this, but we're equals now, Arthur. As Liege of the Majae, I don't answer to you." She was responsible for assigning witches to teams, just as the former king directed which vampires worked with whom on what. Both of them had recently been reelected by their respective constituencies yet again; she'd lost count of the number of times it had been now.

"You answer to me if you almost get three of my men killed," Arthur growled. "To say nothing of the two girls you almost got eaten."

She lifted a brow. "You've never had a mission go off the rails, Arthur?"

He snorted. "You know better than that. *Everybody's* had missions go off the rails. Which is why you analyze where you fucked up and determine how to avoid it the next time. In this case, I strongly suspect it has something to do with Percival's calling you on your sexual arousal in that fucking bar."

Mortified heat flooded her face. "That had nothing to do with it."

"Bullshit." He sat forward in his chair, hunching his massive shoulders. "You got your arse on your shoulders, decided you had a point to prove, and *stranded* your team in that alley. They lost fifteen crucial minutes contacting the next team on call, waiting while Caroline retraced the steps you'd already taken, then gated them all to the scene. It's pure luck you and those girls weren't halfway down that dragon's throat by the time they got there."

Morgana glared at him, refusing to be cowed . . . or admit he had a point. "If I'd taken the men with me, they might have been the ones on the receiving end of the teeth."

"That's their damned job, Morgana! Besides which, I'll remind you that *they* rescued *you*."

"After I brought the dragon down! If we'd all gated there first, the killer would have done exactly what he did when I arrived—gone airborne. What the hell was the team going to do with him flying around three hundred feet over their heads? I had to shift and go after him, which is what I knew I was going to have to do to start with! Kel had told me if I could stall the dragon for a half hour, he'd be able to come help me fry the bastard."

"Yeah, assuming you could survive that long. Given the fucker was twice your size, I seriously doubt you'd have been able to make it a half hour. Face it—you and those girls would have ended up eaten if the team hadn't arrived when they did."

"I had it handled, Arthur!"

"Bullshit! You had no business playing Lone Ranger with the scaly bastard." His face turned grim. "Especially not today. Your judgment has always sucked on February third." He smiled, but it had the quality of a grimace. "Not that I blame you. Mordred could warp anybody."

She blew out a breath, staring sightlessly at one of the tapestries that lined the chamber. This one depicted battling knights fighting with sword and spear during the Battle of Camlann, when Arthur had killed Mordred, their murderous son. "Yeah, but I should be over it by now. I thought I was, dammit. I thought I'd banished my ghosts, but I'm still having nightmares."

"Kiddo, unlike mortals, we never forget a fuckin' thing. Makes it tough to get objective distance." He drummed his fingers on Excalibur's hilt where the big sword hung at his hip. "Which is why these postmortems are so important, even if they do sting like a motherfucker. You should have called in *more* backup, not left the backup you had cooling their heels on Mortal Earth."

Really, what could she say to that? He was right. "All right, maybe I miscalculated. I'll remind you, it's not like I make a habit of it. It won't happen again."

Arthur was silent so long, Morgana had to look at him again. She found him studying her with such calculation in his dark eyes, she instantly had to wonder what the hell he was thinking. "Unfortunately," he said at last, "I don't think that's the case."

"What do you mean by that?" She glared at him.

Being Arthur, he didn't look away. "I mean it's going to happen again unless you address the root cause of this mess: the sexual tension between you and your team that's interfering with your ability to assess situations coolly and unemotionally."

"My sex life is not your business, Arthur."

"I will repeat: it is when it interferes with the mission. You're arrogant, Morgana. You have a deadly habit of underestimating your foes and overestimating yourself." His ebony eyes narrowed in a calculating expression she didn't like a bit. "Your team might be just the ones to give you the lesson in humility you so desperately need."

She gritted her teeth. "All I need from those three is their sword arms."

"And if you mean to keep them, you'll offer Percival your Oath of Service."

Morgana stared at him in horrified shock for a heartbeat before she thought to wipe the reaction from her face. "If you think I'll willingly become the next thing to Percival's sex slave for the next year, you've taken too many blows to the head."

Arthur studied her, and she suddenly remembered why he'd been England's greatest king. He knew how to read people with an accuracy that was terrifying. "You're afraid you're going to fall in love with him."

Her heart seemed to stop beating as the shot sank home with a sniper's unerring accuracy. She forced a scornful laugh. "That's absurd."

His deep voice lowered to a dark male purr. "So you're telling me you feel nothing at the thought of being bound hand and foot while he rides you like a mare?"

"You're being crude, Arthur. It doesn't suit you." As Morgana's mouth went dry, she looked away before she remembered herself and jerked her eyes back to his. She couldn't afford to show him any weakness at all.

"And you didn't answer the question." There was an unyielding note in his voice that told her she'd better damned well answer.

Panic stung her. *Oh, God, what was the question?* She mentally rewound the conversation. "No, there's nothing sexual between Percival and me."

Arthur lifted a brow as one corner of his mouth quirked. "Vampires have a keen sense of smell."

Morgana felt herself blush scarlet as she realized what he meant. He'd scented the arousal that had flooded her sex from the moment he'd mentioned giving Percival her Oath. She gritted her teeth. "You can be quite the bastard, Arthur."

"Yes, and you'd do well to keep that in mind. Because if you refuse to offer Percival your Oath, I'm going to reassign his team. You'll need to pick which of your witches to assign to them. You'll be with Lamorak and Baldulf."

Morgana jolted. "No! They wouldn't be able to . . ." At the last moment, she managed to bite the sentence off. Arthur didn't need to know why she needed the team so desperately. If he ever guessed she could become a greater danger than some of the monsters they fought—that she only trusted Percival and his team to control her . . .

He frowned. "Lamorak and Baldulf are Knights of the Round Table, Morgana. They're hardly second-stringers."

"That's not the issue. I've spent centuries learning to work with Percival and his team. We're so good at reading each other's minds in combat, we're practically Truebonded. I wouldn't be as effective with anyone else."

"Unfortunately, at the moment you're not effective at all. You and Percival and his boys have too much baggage. It's getting in the way of doing the job. One way or the other, I'm putting a stop to it before you get somebody killed."

She stared at him, barely breathing. His black gaze was unwavering, fierce. It was his King Arthur face, the expression that said you'd better damned well do what he wanted, or you'd regret it.

He means it. Her stomach sank. She was going to lose them if she didn't do something.

"All right, you high-handed bastard." Morgana rose to her feet and glared across the Round Table at him. "I'll offer Percival my damned Oath."

Maddeningly unruffled, Arthur lounged back in his chair. "He has to accept it, or the deal's off, and you go to Lamorak and Baldulf."

"Fine. I'll convince him." She spun on her heel and stalked out.

Morgana strode along the cobblestone street, trying to ignore the incendiary combination of sexual heat and anxiety in the pit of her stomach. She'd told Arthur she could convince Percival to accept her Oath.

But now she'd started to imagine what it would actually be like being the knight's Oath Servant. She wasn't sure what disturbed her more: her arousal at the idea, or the deeper feelings for the knight she'd felt since the night she'd fed him for the first time.

Either way, she was vulnerable to Percival in ways she couldn't afford to encourage. Fortunately, she could think of at least one way to make that dangerous vulnerability a little less acute.

It was three A.M. or so. The moon rode high in the sky over the magical city of Avalon with its eclectic array of architectural styles—everything from thoroughly modern American townhouses to Scottish castles and Roman villas. No matter what the style, all of them had been erected with magic rather than mortal construction techniques. The Majae—a notoriously competitive lot of witches—vied to see who could produce the most elaborate and elegant homes for themselves. In general, the more powerful you were, the more gorgeous your residence. Which was why the homes of single vampires tended to be more modest than those of their Maja counterparts. Part of that was because the Magi were generally too focused on going on missions to care where they slept between them. But more than that, they had to convince some Maja to build their homes for them.

Morgana's team lived in a trio of homes on adjoining lots in Avalon's oldest neighborhood. None of the three houses were anywhere near that old, of course, since she made a point of building them new places to live every century or so, whether they asked for them or not. She usually told the men it was a matter of personal pride on her part, but the truth was, she liked making sure they had somewhere comfortable to live.

Percival's place was a brooding gray stone pile that bore a strong resemblance to a gothic castle. Its stained glass windows depicted interwoven Celtic knots in vivid colors. The colored glass wasn't just beautiful; it also protected sleeping vampires from the sunlight that could inflict nasty burns.

Morgana climbed the stone steps, refusing to let herself falter. She might have to do this, but that didn't mean she had to do it the way Arthur dictated.

Offering her Oath to Percival alone wasn't an option. That would be too intimate, make her too vulnerable. If she gave him that kind of opening, Merlin alone knew what he'd do with it.

"So you're telling me you feel nothing at the thought of being bound hand and foot while he rides you like a mare?"

Oh, she felt something, all right. And that was exactly why she wasn't going to put herself in that position. At least, not the way Arthur intended.

Morgana swept through the front door without knocking; she had the ugly suspicion Percival wouldn't have let her in if she had.

She found the three men sprawled in the house's lower level, where a fully stocked bar and an impressive flat-screen shared space with an enormous navy blue sectional. The couch formed a U-shape around a massive oak coffee table with a black marble top.

"Save your breath," Percival told her, as he emerged from behind the bar carrying a bottle of Jack Daniels and sauntered over to his teammates. All three of them had shed their bloodied, dented armor in favor of jeans, boots, and knit shirts. "We're not going to ask Arthur to change his mind."

"I'm not asking you to." She managed a cool smile despite her clawing nerves. "Arthur has already given me another option."

Percival hesitated a moment before he sat down and topped off the glass Cador extended to him. "Not interested."

Morgana ignored his effort to shut her down, instead dropping to her knees. In rolling, formal tones, she said, "Percival, Cador, and Marrok, I wish to offer you my Oath of Service. If you accept my offer, for the next year I vow to serve your desires, whether for sex or blood, in whatever way you choose." Bowing her head, she waited, watching them through her lowered lashes. Her heart pounded furiously in anxious arousal.

Marrok's dark brows shot up. Cador straightened; if he'd been in wolf form, his ears would have pricked in interest.

But it was Percival who spoke. "No."

Morgana stiffened in shock. She'd been utterly sure he'd jump at the chance to make her his Oath Servant. "What do you mean, no?"

He shrugged and dropped onto one side of the couch's U, swinging his long legs up and crossing his booted ankles. He gave her a cool, emotionless stare. "For one thing, I doubt your sincerity," he drawled, his gaze sliding over her, as heated as his bare palms. "That's not how an Oath Servant dresses for her Masters."

She firmed her lips. It was a challenge, but more than that, that hard look sent a quiver right down between her legs. She had to make this work. She had to. Reaching into the Mageverse, Morgana drew on the simmering reservoir of power there. Ignoring the magic's seductive offer of omnipotence, she let the magic spill down her body, transforming the elegant red suit she wore into a negligee of thin scarlet lace. "Is this closer to what you had in mind?"

Still kneeling, acutely aware of the nipples so boldly visible through the red lace, she looked at them from beneath her lashes. To her satisfaction, lust flared in the eyes of all three men.

Percival was the first to sit back as his gaze shuttered, that handsome mouth taking a cruel set. "Just shows how desperate you are, Morgana. Answer's still no. I've had it. We're no longer effective together."

Marrok nodded, though at least there was longing in his eyes as he contemplated her near-nudity. "We've been discussing this for a while now. I'd always argued in your favor, but what happened today has changed my mind. There's too much emotional shit with you, Morgana. It's a problem."

Her temper began to steam, almost drowning out her panic. "There isn't a witch in Avalon with the power I have, and you know it!"

"That's not the point, Morgana." Percival paused to down a slug of his drink. "Raw power doesn't mean a damn thing if we can't trust you not to misuse it the way you did tonight. Or have you forgotten those two women almost died?"

"The dragon hurt them before I even arrived, Percival! I cast that locator spell as quickly as I could, but . . ."

"*You left us.*" He looked up at her over his glass, his narrowed gray eyes blazing. "You stranded us in that bloody alley so you could go off and fight that dragon by yourself. We had to call Caroline to find out where you were and transport us there. What if those women had died while we did all that utterly unnecessary fucking around?"

"And what would have happened if I'd wasted precious time calling in reinforcements before we gated? I'll tell you—he'd have *eaten* those girls, just the way he did the seventeen others who'd come before."

"Not if we'd gated when you did and held him at bay while you made the call. Instead, you damned near ended up dead with them. It was only the luck of the draw that we got there in time to save your arse. If a less-powerful Maja than Caroline had been on call, or someone who didn't know how to do that kind of tracking spell, the delay could have been fatal to all three of you."

"The whole thing was inexcusable, Morgana." Marrok's jaw jutted as his thick brows lowered over hot black eyes. "What the hell were you thinking?"

"She was thinking Percival had pissed her off when he called her on her focus issues, and she decided to show us the error of our ways." Cador gave her that nasty smile that made her want to hit him. "Didn't work out that way, did it, baby?"

"Cador." Percival gave him a look. Yeah, he was as pissed as any of them, and he'd intentionally cut her pride with the taunt to make her change clothes, but they all knew more was involved than that. "Morgana, you should have been honest with us about the way Mordred's birthday would affect you today, and how it would fuck up your thinking process. You owed us that, but you didn't say a word."

"Everyone makes mistakes. It's not like I make a habit out of it." She stalked behind the bar and grabbed herself a glass, then scanned the liquor until she spotted a bottle of eighteen-year-old Glenlivet. Splashing two fingers into the glass—and ignoring Marrok's wince at her mistreatment of the expensive liquor—Morgana tossed it back in a single searing swallow. She banged the glass down and glowered at the three knights. "I've saved every one of you bastards a dozen times . . ."

Percival picked up the bottle of Jack off the coffee table and poured himself a deliberate refill. "As we've saved you."

". . . and the whole bloody planet at least twice. You could cut me a damned break. In fifteen hundred years, I've never given anyone my Oath . . ."

"Because nobody was dumb enough to take it."

"Fuck you too, Cador." Morgana splashed more scotch into her glass. Damned if she was going to do this sober. "It's not an offer I make casually."

"And the first time one of us really tried to dom you, you'd burn our balls good with one of those nasty jolts you love dishing out." Cador curled his lip. "Not my idea of happy fun time."

She stiffened and glared. "If you accept my Oath, I'll bloody well keep it."

"Yeah, right."

The skepticism on Cador's face was to be expected. What stung was the way Marrok's mirrored it. Worst of all was the wintery disbelief in Percival's gaze.

I'm losing them. I can't lose them—they're the only ones who can do what needs doing if my control fails. "Fine. How about this, then." Pointing at the coffee table before the knights, Morgana gestured, spilling a stream of sparks from her fingertips as she called the conjuration from her worktable. More sparks spilled as it materialized on the coffee table in front of Percival. "I've been working on this for months—

it was a bitch to pull off, but I finally completed it a couple of weeks ago. Luckily we haven't had a need for it yet, but the time will come."

Percival leaned back, frowning down at the metal circlet with its intricate swirl of magical symbols. "A collar." He looked up at her with a dismissive flick of his gaze. "Very pretty."

"It's far more than pretty, Percival. That collar is designed to block a Maja's access to her powers." She tilted her chin, mustered her most challenging smile. "If you accept my Oath and collar me, I'd effectively be powerless unless you chose to deactivate it for missions. I'll be completely at your mercy."

Percival froze. And swallowed.

Morgana stood before them, her lushly beautiful body barely clad in a red lace corset that clearly displayed her perfect breasts and hard nipples. A catlike smile curved her lips as she tilted her head, sending her waist-length black curls shifting around her creamy shoulders.

He silently cursed the erection swelling behind the fly of his jeans. Leaning forward, Percival braced his elbows on his knees, hoping to keep those sharp green eyes of hers from spotting his cock-stand and going for the kill.

The witch had always known how to make a man sit up and beg. Then she'd curl those long red fingernails around his balls and tie them in a knot.

Marrok frowned and asked the question Percival hadn't managed to think of, not with all his blood headed to his cock. "Something like that would be a piece of major magic. What the hell would be the point?"

"It's a way to control new Majae with Mageverse Fever," Morgana explained, picking up the collar in her long, elegant fingers. She was talking about the ugly tendency of new witches to be driven mad by suddenly gaining the raw power of the Mageverse. "It prevents them from being able to draw on their full magic. A Court Seducer could collar the girl before sleeping with her the third time, so when Merlin's Gift triggered, she wouldn't be able to commit mayhem if she went insane. That's not a minor consideration, given the number of Court Seducers who've been slain by insane Majae over the years. Not to mention the girls themselves." Something grim slid through her green eyes. "I am tired of killing those children for something that isn't their fault."

"Doesn't that only delay the inevitable?" Percival asked. "You can't cure Mageverse Fever; it's their own power that drives those women insane. Unless you kept the Maja collared for the rest of her life . . ."

Cador smirked. "Much as that might be interesting . . ."

Percival ignored him. ". . . She'd try to destroy everything around her the moment you took the collar off."

Morgana leaned forward, her eyes going bright with enthusiasm. "But what if it's the immediate onslaught of the Mageverse that drives the girls insane? What if the collar could let them have the power a bit at a time, allowing them to learn how to manage it? Perhaps that would keep them from going mad."

Marrok eyed her, then reached for the bottle of Jack and refilled his glass. "You're not contemplating some kind of experiment—like giving someone the Gift when you suspect they might go insane?"

Was that a flicker of hurt in those vivid eyes? "Do you seriously think I'd do something like that?"

"Would you?" Cador lifted a cinnamon brow.

"No, damn you." Morgana turned and began to pace restlessly, gesturing as she spoke. She evidently didn't notice the way they watched her long legs stride in those sheer red stockings and four-inch crimson fuck-me heels. And God, her arse . . . Percival's hands itched to grab those pert cheeks and spread them so he could see the plump curves of her labia, the tight pucker of her anus . . .

When she turned, there was a shadow of genuine hurt in her eyes.

It distracted him from his lust, made him realize just how rough they were being on her. He was surprised by the stab of guilt he felt.

Maybe he was being a little too hasty in rejecting her Oath. Could this really be the way to finally resolve the sexual issues between them? Not that he'd ever let himself become too vulnerable to Morgana—that would be asking for trouble. His gaze lingered on her practically naked body, and he felt his cock harden even more. A sideways glance confirmed his partners were just as aroused.

Percival frowned. They'd shared women before, of course. Most of the time the team went on missions with one Maja, two at the most. Any time a job went for longer than a few hours, there was usually the opportunity for a little sex, and one thing would lead to another. Knights of the Round Table never had a problem getting laid. Besides, Percival and his team had acquired a certain reputation among the Majae; the women were always eager to experience a night with the three of them.

But sharing Morgana . . . that was something else again. He didn't like that idea one bit. Unfortunately, having her to himself didn't seem to be on the table. If he wanted her at all—and God knew he did—then he was going to have to ignore his possessive instincts and share her with Marrok and Cador.

Unaware of his thoughts, Morgana was still explaining the theory behind the collar. "No matter how carefully we screen the candidates or how well-trained our Court Seducers are in accessing them, a percentage of our Latents always go insane." Pivoting, she paced the other way. "If we collared all of them before that third time, even the stable women wouldn't suffer the psychic storm of gaining their full power at one time. We could ease them all into becoming Majae, especially the unstable ones. If they didn't develop full-blown Mageverse Fever, killing them wouldn't be necessary."

"God knows that's a worthy goal." His thoughts went to Clarice.

Fifteen years ago, Lancelot had been forced to kill Percival's only daughter to keep her from murdering Morgana's granddaughter, Grace. Percival hadn't even known about Clarice's existence until she'd been identified as a candidate for the Gift. Which, unfortunately, was one of the hazards of siring illegitimate children.

Percival had been impressed with Clarice in the brief time he'd known her; she was an intelligent, idealistic woman who volunteered in her local soup kitchen and was passionately involved in environmental causes.

Then she was dead, all her bright potential lost with her. Though he'd barely known the girl, he'd grieved her passing. Especially since she'd died during an attempt to kill sixteen-year-old Grace Morgan. In her right mind, Clarice would have been horrified at the idea of doing something like that to a child.

Watching Morgana gesture, eyes alight with passion as she talked about the problem of Mageverse Fever, Percival realized she sincerely wanted to find a way to save those girls. He wasn't surprised: though the Liege of the Majae had a well-deserved reputation for cool ruthlessness, she was also deeply protective when it came to innocents.

"I've had to put mad girls down far too many times over my life." Morgana turned to face them, pain in her green eyes. "If at all possible, I never want to do it again."

"Yeah, I get that," Cador said. "But there's a hell of a long way between creating something to keep women from going insane and wearing that collar yourself. You're actually willing to let us collar you and strip you of your magic?"

She tilted her chin in regal defiance. "Yes." Just like that. Flat. Assured. Definite.

"You sure about that?" Percival growled. He grimaced at the sound of his own voice; it sounded low and rough with lust even to his own ears. His cock throbbed like a sore tooth. "As you said, you'd be completely at our mercy."

Cador grinned, his eyes hungry. "And I assure you, we wouldn't have any."

FIVE

I would expect nothing less," Morgana said coolly. "But the collar does need testing. We have to discover whether it will burn out, or somehow harm its wearer."

Percival glowered. "If you aren't sure, you don't need to be wearing it."

She shrugged, causing arousing movement of her lush, thinly veiled breasts. "Better me testing it than some child." Not that the girls they Gifted were actually children, but compared to Morgana's centuries, they might as well be.

"So in other words, by collaring you and stripping you of your powers, we'd be performing a public service." Cador's eyes gleamed as his gaze flicked hungrily from the collar to her face, then down again to her nipples. His smile took on the twist that meant he was contemplating doing something sadistic to whatever female who was presently in his sights. Except this time, his target was Morgana.

Percival's hands curled into fists.

"I don't think this is a good idea." Marrok's deep voice broke into his jealous preoccupation. "How do we know that it won't do something to you? Strip you of your powers permanently?"

Morgana glowered at him. "I know what I'm doing, Marrok. The collar's effects are strictly temporary."

"And you know that how?" Percival demanded, eyeing her suspiciously.

"I've worn it. As soon as I removed it, my abilities came back, just as powerful as always."

"Goddammit, Morgana!" Merlin's balls, sometimes the woman had no sense at all. "What if the collar had depowered you permanently?"

She shrugged, evidently secure in her own infallibility. *That, or she doesn't give a fuck.* With Morgana, it could go either way. "Gwen would have reversed the spell. Or Kel. But the point is the collar worked exactly as it was supposed to. It's perfectly safe."

"I still don't like it," Marrok growled.

Cador grinned. "I do."

"That's because you're a prick."

"Enough," Percival growled. His gaze dropped to the collar and lingered there as he shifted restlessly in his seat. Flashes of fantasy licked across his consciousness, hot as a sword in a blacksmith's flame. *Morgana, mine to do with as I please. To punish and fuck however it suits me.*

As she'd been that one night centuries ago, when she'd fed him her blood. He'd never known why she'd run from him. But if he accepted her Oath of Service, she *couldn't* run. She'd belong to him.

A cooler, saner part of his brain sent up a blast of alarm at the steaming lust that roared through him at that thought. *This is definitely not a good idea.* He needed to talk her out of it. And knowing Morgana, he knew how. He gave her a deliberately nasty smile. "You might want to consider rescinding your Oath, Morgana. If we do this, you'll be punished for what you did today. And you're not going to enjoy it." He let some of his darker fantasies show in his smile. "But *we* will."

Her gaze flicked down to the thick bulge behind his fly as he sprawled back on the couch. "Yes, I can tell."

The heat in him took on an angry simmer. "The first thing we'd do is break you of that arrogance. An Oath Servant doesn't talk to her Masters with such insolence."

Cador gave her the smile that had been known to make hardcore mortal submissives run screaming from the BDSM clubs the team frequented. "We'll make you scream in pain—and pleasure. You'll come again and again as we fuck you in that smart mouth, that tight, creamy pussy." His voice deepened into a purring rumble. "In that snug, hot arse. You won't be allowed to deny us any part of your lovely body."

Percival flashed his own variation on Cador's evil smile. "We'll own you for the next year. You'll beg for mercy—and we won't give a damn."

Morgana stared at him. Her beautiful green eyes widened as her lips parted. Percival's sensitive vampire nose picked up the unmistakable scent of arousal.

In the ticking silence, he realized Marrok and Cador had frozen with the same kind of predatory hunger he felt—and *he* could drive nails with his dick. "Well?" he demanded.

The witch angled her chin up in a gesture he knew far too well, a glitter of defiant determination in her eyes. "I've offered you my Oath, gentleman. The only question is, are you going to take me on?" She curled a lip. "Unless you're afraid you're not up to the task. . . ."

That, of course, aroused an entirely predictable reaction from Cador. He lounged back on the couch in a sprawl that called blatant attention to his massive erection. "Oh, darling, I can assure you, I'm definitely up to the task of putting you in your place." One hand cupped his balls as his grin took on a carnivorous edge.

"We need to discuss this," Marrok said, a muscle rolling in his broad jaw. "Give us a minute, Morgana."

"Of course." She angled her head in a courteous little nod, then turned with a roll of lush hips and sauntered out. A gesture had the door closing behind her, propelled by a rolling wave of golden sparks.

"Oh, God, that arse . . ." Cador moaned. "I can't wait to flog it a nice rosy pink before I give it a grinding fuck. You know Morgana le Fay has never let anybody touch her anal cherry. I'll bet it's tight as a miser's purse."

"I'm sure it is," Percival growled, shooting him a glance of narrow-eyed warning. "I'm also sure you're not going to be the first to claim it."

Marrok shot off the couch and began to pace. "Which is exactly why accepting her Oath is such a piss-poor idea. You two are going to end up fighting over that bloody witch like two stallions with one mare. No bit of pussy is worth wrecking the team."

Stung, Percival stared at his friend. "Of course we're not going to wreck the team. We've shared women before, and it's never been a problem."

Marrok met his gaze with a level stare. "Those women were bed-sport. You always cared for their needs as a dom's duty demands, but they weren't more to you than that." He shrugged. "True, you weren't any more than that to the women, either. But still."

Percival curled a lip. "Are you suggesting I'm in love with Morgana le Fay?"

Cador snorted and stretched his long legs out, propping them on the coffee table's granite top. "Yeah, right. Because he has such a weakness for flaming bitches."

"As to that," Percival growled, "I believe we can break her of that particular character defect."

"Clamps on her nipples would probably be highly effective." Cador grinned and licked his lips.

Marrok stared at him, then scrubbed a hand over his face with a groan, his massive shoulders slumping. "I'm wasting my fucking breath. You've already made up your minds." He glanced at Cador. "Both of you. I'm outvoted."

"Christ, Marrok, are you kidding?" Cador demanded. "Think of all those little zaps every time we went out with her the past few years. Think of the way she always insisted on leading missions, though Percival has more field experience." His lip curled. "Personally, I think the bitch witch just gets off on giving us orders and watching us jump."

Marrok smiled reluctantly. "I wouldn't put it past her."

"Now we have a chance to put a collar on her and get a little of our own back." Cador's mouth curled into a dark smile. "And I, for one, am looking forward to it."

God, so was Percival. Maybe too much. His cock ached with the stark need to do everything Cador had mentioned. Flog that delicious arse, fuck it.

Fuck *her*.

Unfortunately, Marrok had a point. He didn't like the idea of Cador touching her, sadistic bastard that he was. His friend would hurt her. Carefully, with precise self-control, but he'd still hurt her. And he'd like it.

Never mind that Percival would do the same thing. He still hated the idea of either of his friends touching that ridiculously lush, tempting body. Hearing her breathy moans. Fencing with her as she used that sarcastic, biting wit. Making her bend that stiff neck to their dominance.

Holding her in the aftermath, listening to her breathe, to the deep thump of her slowing heartbeat . . .

Oh, hell. Hell, no. Not Morgana le Fay. Despite her carefully camouflaged compassion, the witch was manipulative, arrogant, and generally in desperate need of several painful lessons in humility.

This would be nothing more than sex and revenge. He wouldn't let it be anything else. Especially not anything that would damage his relationship with the two men he'd fight and die for. His brothers in all but blood.

Yeah, he'd collar her. He'd get her out of his system by fucking her in every way he'd ever dreamed of in his darkest, most frustrated fantasies. He'd do everything he'd ever jerked off thinking about, no matter how humiliating it would be to her.

He'd bring her to her knees—and make her suck his cock while she was down there. He'd even share her with his brothers and watch while they fucked her. He'd ignore his instinctive possessiveness, force himself to endure it just as he'd learned to endure the pain of sword wounds in order to win battles in Arthur's service.

"Are we agreed then?" he demanded.

"No," Marrok growled. "But that point is basically . . ." Suddenly he stiffened, and his eyes narrowed. "You know," he said slowly, "I have no problem believing Arthur would order Morgana to offer Percival her Oath. What I have trouble with is that he'd tell her to offer it to all three of us."

"Oh, come on, Marrok . . ." Cador began.

"No, *you* come on. Stop thinking with your dick and consider the implications. How much stress would sharing her put on the team?"

Cador opened his mouth, only to immediately close it again. "You're right," he admitted reluctantly, grimacing as if at the taste of something foul. "We'd be fighting over who got to fuck her, how, when, and where."

Marrok nodded grimly. "Exactly. Would Arthur do that to us?"

"No." Cador shot Percival a speculative glance. "But I could easily see him ordering Morgana to offer *Percival* her Oath."

Fury swirled through Percival, and he curled his hands into fists. "And I could see Morgana disobeying his exact orders out of a desire to play us against each other." He rose from the couch, aware of Cador doing the same. "Morgana?"

She entered with that lazy, seductive stride, her expression politely enquiring. If she felt any anxiety over the outcome of their discussion, it didn't show—but then, she'd always been a damned good actress. "Yes?"

He stalked toward her and stopped, aware of Cador and Marrok moving up behind him to watch. "Did Arthur tell you to offer your Oath to all three of us, or just to me?"

Her gaze flickered, but she angled her chin upward. She knew better than to lie outright to a vampire who could smell deception. "To you alone."

He ground his teeth. "Why did you disobey him?"

She shrugged gracefully. "He didn't tell me *not* to offer it to the three of you."

"Did you intend to destroy the team?"

Her eyes widened, and panic flashed across her face. "No! I wouldn't do that . . ."

"Wouldn't you?" Percival stared at her with narrow eyes. "What do you think would happen if the three of us disagreed about which of us is to fuck you, or whose orders you should obey?"

She hesitated, only to sigh. "All right, I can see how that could cause friction. But it wasn't my intention to create it deliberately."

"I'm sure that would have been a huge comfort if the team cracked wide open because you were *fucking playing games*."

Morgana angled her chin upward in a familiar gesture of defiance. "You would have done what you always do, Percival. You'd have led, and they'd have followed."

"Maybe," Percival growled. "But when you throw sex in the mix, things get complicated."

Marrok huffed. "That's the damned truth."

Cador rocked back on his heels and gave Morgana a flat, cold stare. "I have no interest in accepting your Oath. Not when it's so obvious you can't be trusted."

Marrok bared his teeth in a snarl. "Neither do I."

"I, however, will happily accept your Oath." Percival smiled. He knew it wasn't a pretty smile by any means. "By the time I get done with you, it's safe to say you won't dare lie to me again, whether by implication or otherwise." He lifted a blond brow. "Unless you'd care to rescind your offer, of course."

She swallowed. "But if I rescind it, Arthur will reassign me."

He shrugged. "Probably."

Morgana raised her chin, an edge of defiance in her gaze. "Then, no, I will not rescind it."

Suddenly Marrok spoke up. "I would like a moment with you, Morgana."

Percival frowned. He recognized the hard jut of his friend's jaw. "Marrok . . ."

"I think she needs my input before she makes a final decision."

She hesitated, giving the big knight a long look before she nodded slowly. "All right." Turning, she led him into the next room.

"What the hell was that about?" Percival growled.

"No idea." Cador said. "But I'm sure it's something he thinks she needs to hear."

Percival glowered. *I swear to God, if 'Rok talks her out of this, I'll kill him.*

Morgana followed Marrok's massive back down the corridor. When he turned to face her, her stomach tightened at the cold lack of expression in his eyes. It wasn't the sort of look she was used to getting from the big knight, who was usually such a warm, friendly man.

He eyed her, letting the tension build, before he finally asked, "Do you know what it's like when I go mad in battle?"

Morgana blinked. Of all the questions he could have asked, that wasn't the one she'd expected. "I . . . no."

"It starts with rage, of course. And the fear. But then when I sink into it, the fury quickly turns to euphoria. I feel . . . exalted, like a saint with a vision."

Morgana blinked, feeling a sudden sense of kinship with him. She'd often experienced that same wild joy herself.

Claws raked across her skin as the wolves closed in, their eyes glowing orange with bloodlust . . . Terrified, she reached for the power, let it roll over her, bringing with it a wild exhilaration . . .

"But the vision I see isn't some saint's dream of angels and God," Marrok continued in a low, too-controlled voice. "It's the bright pattern my sword weaves. And the blood." His eyes drifted shut, and his nostrils flared as if at a delicious memory. "Jesu, the *blood*. The smell of it, the taste of it when it hits my face. I love that taste."

"Well," she managed faintly, "You *are* a vampire."

He opened his eyes to meet her gaze again with an expression that chilled her. "My enemies fight, but I fear no fear, no rage. Just the sweet joy of the sword, the parry and thrust, the thud of the blade hitting home, the vibration in my bones. I hear Percival's voice through the mission ring, making sure I don't kill allies and innocents . . ."

Morgana knew how that felt too—the icy fear of killing the innocent and those she loved.

He fell silent, glancing away, his eyes seeming to gaze into some distant vision. Abruptly his attention returned to her, his expression hardening. When he spoke again, his voice took on a biting edge. "But then he wakes me, and I see what I've done."

Morgana swallowed, remembering battlefields strewn with corpses. Not all of them killed by Marrok, of course, though many had been. He always struck so quickly, so mercilessly, there was a kind of elegance in his brutality. Even the werewolves hadn't had a chance.

"When the bodies have been hacked into nothing more than meat, I can't tell who I've slain," he said with that terrifying lack of emotion. "And for a moment, I always wonder: is this Percival? Cador? Arthur? You? It's not until Percival reassures me that I'm sure they were all enemies. And every single time, I wonder: If something happened to him, would I have stopped? *Could* I have stopped?"

"Arthur could stop you." Arthur might have been almost a foot shorter than Marrok, but he was still Arthur. To use the modern parlance, he was *the* alpha of the collection of alpha males he'd assembled.

"Maybe. Or maybe not. I'd rather not take the chance of waking surrounded by the corpses of my dearest friends." His eyes focused on her face with a frigidity that iced the blood in her veins. "So I beg you to believe me when I say that if you fuck with my team, if you drive a wedge between us, you'd better be prepared to kill me." His voice lowered to a rumble like distant thunder warning of a hurricane. "Otherwise, I'll kill you. And that, my dove, is not an idle threat."

Morgana swallowed. Her mouth felt as if she'd stuffed her jaws with cotton. "I know. And believe me, I have no interest in sabotaging the team."

For one thing, she needed them every bit as much as he needed Percival—and for basically the same reason. He wasn't the only one capable of lethal destruction.

But that wasn't something she could tell Marrok.

He studied her for a long moment before nodding stiffly. "See that you don't."

Marrok stalked past her, a rigid set to his massive shoulders. Once again, she followed him.

When they returned to the room, Percival, sprawled on the sectional, studied Marrok. "You done?"

The big knight shot Morgana a cool, warning glance that made Percival wonder what the two had talked about. Marrok shrugged. "Yes."

Percival turned to Morgana. "Are you going to call it off?"

She met his gaze, her own calm, sure. "Hardly."

Relieved, Percival lifted the collar off the coffee table where she'd left it. "Then get over here and kneel."

Now a flicker of anxiety did show in Morgana's eyes, but she still didn't hesitate as she approached him without appearing to hurry, the peignoir fluttering around her long legs. Her breasts swayed, full, yet beautifully shaped. The tight points of her nipples were clearly visible through the thin lace of her corset.

His eye dropped to the dark delta between her thighs. The scent of her arousal filled the air, maddening and delicious.

God, he couldn't wait to taste her. Fuck her. Drink that rich, sweet blood.

Percival stood and moved out from behind the coffee table as she sank gracefully to her knees in a puddle of lace. He had to drag his eyes away from the lush curves of her breasts the red lace corset displayed. Turning his attention to the collar in his hands, he examined it. The two ends were open, waiting to be slipped around that delicate throat. The sooner he collared her, the sooner he could have her.

Fantasies spun through his brain. *Morgana, chained with arms and legs spread wide while he wielded a deer-hide flogger across the beautiful curves of her arse. Morgana, naked, bound hand and foot while he fucked her hard, admiring the stripes.* "How do you activate the spell on this?" His voice sounded hoarse.

Morgana looked up at him, her eyes very green and a little nervous. She would have looked downright terrified if she'd known what he was thinking. "Simply by locking it around my throat."

Percival nodded as he prepared to snap the clasp closed. "Do you, Morgana le Fay, swear to obey all my commands without question or hesitation, yielding your body to serve my needs for the next year, whether for sex or for blood?"

"I, Morgana le Fay, Liege of the Majae, do swear to obey you in all your commands without question or hesitation, yielding my body to serve your needs, whether for sex or for blood, for the next year." Morgana's voice was steady, clear, despite the unease in those vivid eyes.

"I, Sir Percival, Knight of the Round Table, hereby accept your Oath of Service." He pressed the collar's ends together with a soft click. Magic spilled out of the thin silver band in a glittering wave, rolling to the top of her head and the bottom of her feet with a quiet hiss.

She sighed, her eyes sliding closed, her expression smoothing. Percival would have expected regret at the loss of her power, perhaps even fear at her sudden vulnerability. Instead he saw only . . . was that relief?

Why relief, for God's sake?

Marrok eyed her, frowning. "Did it work?"

Moving with smooth vampire speed, Cador stepped forward, snaked an arm down and caught one of her erect nipples in a sharp pinch. Morgana jolted, eyes flying wide in startled outrage as she flicked her fingers at him in a familiar gesture. Percival braced for the sting of pain burning through their mission rings.

Nothing happened.

Cador grinned at him like a devil. "It worked."

Her lovely green eyes widened. *Now* it hit her how vulnerable she was without her powers.

Still Percival frowned, remembering that moment of relief. Almost like someone who'd carried a friend halfway across a desert, finally putting him down beside the blue relief of an oasis. Why had she looked like that? What did it mean?

Who gives a fuck? snarled a dark mental voice. *She's mine now by her own oath.* Hunger clawed at him, heat pooling in his balls, making them feel heavy, swollen. *Mine to take in whatever way suits me. Starting now.*

He didn't even recognize his own voice when he spoke. "Turn around and bend over. I want to see your pussy and arse."

Morgana shot him a wide-eyed, vulnerable look, which had the effect of making him even harder. "What?" Her voice sounded hoarse.

"You heard the man," Cador told her, giving her a nasty grin. "Turn around and show him your pussy."

She licked her lips, anxiety flickering through her eyes. Then she met his gaze with that cool, defiant determination Percival knew too well.

He grabbed her by one arm and hauled her over to the couch, then sat down and pulled her across his lap, ignoring her instinctive yelp of protest.

Lifting one hand, he brought it down hard on the beautiful curve of her arse with a juicy smack.

SIX

Nice." Cador prowled around them for a better view as Percival prepared to give her arse another swat. "She's needed that for a very long time."

"Pull up the robe," Marrok suggested, joining him. "Please. I'd love a better view."

Morgana muttered a curse and latched onto his leg, steadying herself in her head-down position.

With a chuckle, Percival obeyed, flipping the peignoir out of the way to discover that she wore a lace thong that bared her cheeks. One of them already showed the rosy imprint of his palm. With a growl of lust, he lifted his hand again and brought it down with carefully regulated strength. Morgana yelped once, though her tone suggested offended shock more than actual pain. She gripped his thigh as she hung head-down, her long nails digging in, though his jeans protected his skin.

Percival almost broke off to ask if he'd hurt her. *Of course I didn't hurt her,* he told himself impatiently. *I've dommed enough women to know what I'm doing.*

Though none of them had been Morgana. None of them ever gave him a hard-on up to his navel, until he was holding on to his self-control by his fingernails.

Smack followed smack, five of them, making her cheeks jiggle and redden.

Lifting her off his lap, he rose and put her down on her high heels, then grabbed a handful of her silky black hair. Pulling her head back, he growled in her ear, "I want to see your cunt and arse. I do not give orders twice."

Morgana turned and bent over slowly, stiffly, as if fighting her own instinct to tell him to bugger off. Again, the robe blocked his view, and he reached out to sweep it aside, draping it over her right hip. He grabbed the scrap of lace that was the thong, twisted, and jerked, shredding it.

She gasped. His cock hardened even more, bucking against the fly of his jeans with a hunger so dark and feral, it was all he could do not to unzip and just ram into her like a beast in rut. "Over all the way. Grab your ankles."

He braced to spank her again—he couldn't believe she'd simply obey him—but Morgana bent, though with a shivering hesitation that stoked the burn of his lust. A delicious, tantalizing scent wafted from her cunt.

"Smell that?" he said to his brothers in a rough growl.

Cador grinned at him wickedly. "Wet cunt."

"She's got a pretty arse." Marrok sounded hoarse. He shifted restlessly. Percival forced himself not to send the other men from the room so he could devour her in greedy solitude, drinking from her throat between fucking and buggering her.

Liege or not, I'm going to kick Arthur's arse for putting me in this position—after *I finish fucking her until she can't stand up.*

Morgana had never been so aroused in all her long life. Gripping her ankles in white-knuckled hands, she fought not to pant. She'd had fantasies like this. Wanton daydreams after particularly difficult missions, when she knew the team had headed off to one of their perverted mortal clubs to punish and fuck whatever lucky submissives fell into their hands.

Now here she was at last, bent and spread.

"Wider," Percival said in that rumbling growl. Sliding an arm around her waist, he lifted her onto her toes and kicked her spiked heels further apart, then lowered her to her feet again.

Percival parted her vaginal lips with big, warm fingers. As if he owned her, as if she were a slave and not just an Oath Servant. "Merlin's balls, she really is wet." He slid a broad forefinger into her pussy in an endless, seductive stroke and pumped.

For an electric, humiliating moment, she listened to the juicy evidence of her own arousal. Morgana watched upside down through her wide-spread thighs as the three men stared hungrily at her glistening pussy.

"Why, Morgana, you kinky little tart," Cador drawled. "This *is* turning you on, isn't it?"

Her face blazed with the heat of a furious blush. She wanted to deny it, but she'd done enough lying for one night. She was on thin ice with Percival as it was.

"Fuck me," Marrok breathed. "Look at that. So wet. She's so damned wet."

"And so fucking helpless," Cador added in a wicked male purr. "No magic at all. No way to keep Percival from doing any damned thing he wants with her. Lucky bastard."

God, her mouth was dry. Her heart pounded so hard, she knew the three vampires must hear it. Did it make them hungry?

"You're shaking," Percival rumbled. "Are you afraid, Morgana?"

The words came out of her mouth by sheer unthinking reflex. "Don't be absurd."

"What?" Percival snarled.

Morgana, you idiot, she thought, as her heart sank, remembering belatedly that she'd just thought she'd lied to Percival enough for one night.

A hand fisted in her hair and jerked her upright, forcing her to stare up into Percival's furious gray glare. "The next time you lie to me, I will consider it an invitation to give your arse the pounding you've needed for a very long time. First with my hand, then with my dick deep in that tiny hole of yours. Are we clear on that?"

She swallowed and gasped out, "Yes sir!" And felt herself grow hotter, wetter, as she pictured him carrying out that deliciously brutal threat.

Percival's grin chilled her blood, suggesting that he was imaging it just as vividly. He stared into Morgana's eyes, his gaze hard and feral. "Gentlemen, perhaps you wouldn't mind leaving me alone with my new Oath Servant."

"What, you want us to leave now?" Cador protested. "Just when it's getting good?"

Marrok thumped a big hand on his shoulder. "Of course we wouldn't mind, Percival."

"Lying bastard," Cador grumbled, and jerked his shoulder, dodging Marrok's second swat. "All right, all right. Have fun, Percival."

Percival laughed, the sound more than a bit sinister. "Oh, don't worry." He bared his fangs at her. "I intend to."

The door closed behind the two men. Dry-mouthed, Morgana stared at Percival as the two knights climbed the stairs, Marrok's laughter booming over the sound of whatever wicked remark Cador had just made.

The distilled male menace of Percival's gaze sent a wave of ice across her skin. "Now, witch, you and I are going to have a word."

The ice turned to heat when he grabbed the hem of his blue knit shirt and dragged it off over his head. She sucked in a breath, then hoped he hadn't noticed.

"I get hot when I work." He tossed the shirt across the back of the couch without breaking the intent focus of his gaze. Morgana longed to look away, only to find herself frozen like a rabbit in a combination of fear and erotic anticipation.

He was . . . incredible. She'd seen Percival without a shirt before, of course, but there was a world of difference between seeing him shirtless during laughing horseplay and . . . this. Knowing he owned her now, that she'd taken an oath to obey him, fuck him, however he wanted. So she stared, listening to her heart's frantic thump.

All that sculpted brawn, the swells and hollows of muscle groups clearly defined, the branching veins snaking down his biceps, his triceps. Body hair formed a silken golden cloud on his chest, narrowing into a fine line down his belly and pointing the way toward the massive bulge behind his fly.

Oh, goddess . . .

He took a step forward, and she bit back a scream as he swept her off the floor the way an angry man would pick up a bag of frozen peas. Whirling, he took three long paces and banged her back against the nearest wall.

Despite her best efforts to suppress it, a startled yelp escaped Morgana's lips as he pinned her there with the hot, hard weight of his body. "Now," he growled, "let's discuss this habit you have of lying to me."

"You might want to remember I'll get my powers back." She winced the minute the words were out of her mouth. *Stupid, stupid, stupid.*

Percival smiled. Someone who didn't know him well might have thought it a pleasant expression. Morgana, however, recognized the carefully throttled rage in the tight curve of his handsome mouth.

"But you don't have those powers now, do you?" Leaning in, he whispered the words in her ear, each syllable a warm puff against her sensitive flesh. "And I have all of mine." He cupped her breast through the thin lace gown she'd stupidly worn to tempt the three knights.

She licked her dry lips. "You won't hurt me."

"Won't I?"

"You don't hurt women, Percival."

"Lord Percival," he gritted.

"What?" She was too close to real terror to grasp his point.

"You will address me with respect. Lord Percival, Sir Percival, or my lord." He bared his fangs. "Not. Percival."

She swallowed, staring at those lupine teeth inches from her face. "Yes, Lord Percival."

"That's better." A tight smile of satisfaction lit his starkly handsome face. "Both arms over your head, wrists crossed."

"Why do . . . ?"

His eyes narrowed. She hastily obeyed. "Thank you." He caught her wrists in one big, warm hand, pinning them against the wall. She knew without trying that she'd be utterly unable to break his implacable grip.

Stepping back, he gave her body the kind of long, insulting up-and-down scan no Magus had ever given her. Then he met her eyes again, silently daring her to protest.

She kept her mouth shut. Nobody had ever said Morgana le Fay was stupid.

That smile flashed again as he wrapped his free hand in her lace robe. Fisted it. And ripped, shredding the peignoir as easily as if he were tearing down a cobweb. She couldn't seem to bite back her gasp. Still holding her gaze, he hooked a finger in her corset and gave it a slow tug. The laces popped like cotton thread, leaving her clad in only a lace garter belt, stockings, and heels.

She stared up at him, her mouth dry. When she'd tested the collar in the past, just to control her powers, she'd felt relief at its success, but wearing it for Percival was something else again. It felt more profound somehow. In handing over control to Percival, knowing she was at his mercy, she felt an even deeper sense of . . . letting go.

Percival looked her over, scanning her naked body. "Nice." His voice sounded hoarse. He cleared his throat. "Very nice."

She licked her desperately dry lips. Why in the hell was she getting so wet? Nothing about this ruthless domination should be so intensely arousing.

And yet it was. Merlin help her, it was.

Morgana opened her mouth for some bit of acid sarcasm to make him let her go so she wouldn't feel so bloody vulnerable. Perhaps "*I'm delighted you approve,*" or "*You always did have a bard's way with a compliment,*" delivered in a suitably icy tone.

Before she could get either line out of her mouth, his eyes narrowed. She snapped her teeth closed so fast, she almost bit her tongue.

"I've always loved your tits, Morgana." The words may have been flirtatious, but the cold warning in his tone was anything but. "I'm going to like being able to do any damned thing I want to them."

For the sweet sake of the Lady, that was a threat, Morgana told her idiot cunt. It kept growing slicker anyway, responding to . . . something. His eyes, his dark velvet voice, the white points of the fangs that flashed when he spoke. His sheer, fucking size . . . Gods, he was *dangling* her by her arms, yet her feet were still well clear of the floor.

His nostrils flared, and one corner of his lip lifted in a carnal cross between a sneer and a smile. Reaching between her legs, Percival stroked a finger between her labia and deep into her sex. "Ohhh, yesssss. You are creamy, aren't you? And how can anybody who regularly fucks a forty-foot lizard be so bloody tight?"

"Obviously, I shape-shift," she gritted.

"That would help." He added a second finger, pumped deep again, and flicked his thumb over her clit. She jerked at the knife-sharp delight.

Percival grinned. "Liked that, did you? Too bad. I'm afraid you're being punished for today's tactical goat-fuck, so you won't be coming. I will, though. I intend to enjoy you thoroughly."

The fingers withdrew from her traitorous pussy and reached for her right breast. The knight's big, warm hand gave it a squeezing stroke before tugging and twisting its aching nipple. Milking her, he watched her face in erotic calculation.

Morgana dropped her eyes, unable to hold his gaze, not with him beaming raw dominance at her with the intensity of a laser. That proved to be a mistake; when she looked down, her gaze fell on the bulge behind his fly.

Horned God, it was *huge*.

Percival laughed, a dark chuckle, and stepped against her again, pinning her against the wall. Pressing his face against her throat, he inhaled as if dragging her scent deep into his lungs. "You smell delicious." His lips moved against her skin with every word, a warm, sensual tease. "My two favorite things: pussy and blood."

"Percival . . ." When he stiffened, she corrected herself. "My lord Percival . . ."

"Can you keep your mouth shut, or would you prefer a ball gag?" He scraped the tips of his fangs over her helplessly banging pulse. "I don't care to be interrupted while I'm eating."

Which triggered another humiliating gush of cream into her sex.

With a growl, he sank his fangs deep, the sudden hot sting startling a gasp from her throat. She'd known he was going to bite her, but somehow she hadn't expected it just now. Morgana bucked, jerking against his grip, but he had her pinned too thoroughly. She couldn't move at all.

His hand abandoned her breast to seek out her crotch, his forefinger skating between slick labia to slide into her opening. He made a sound against her throat at what he found there, a triumphant growl that deepened to a rumble as he pumped deep, in and out, keeping the pace slow—goddess, far too slow as he drank in hot swallows.

Letting her head fall back against the wall, she moaned in helpless lust. The moan became a gasp as he added a second finger, thumb strumming her clit like a lute string. His body rolled against hers, branding the feel of hot, hard strength against every inch of her smaller, softer one.

This was why she'd always preferred bottling her blood. Feeding a vampire directly from her throat was too damned seductive, too much an arousing act of submission.

But Percival didn't give a damn what she preferred. He just took her, like prey, like a mortal woman he was using, fingering her cunt as he drank, shooting her toward her peak with his erotic brutality until she . . .

But just as her climax began to pulse, he jerked his hand away. The orgasm drained away, leaving her body aching with vibrating, helpless need. Morgana cried out in frustrated protest.

He chuckled against her throat.

Her temper sparked. "Percival, you . . ." Remembering herself, she bit off the rest.

Too late. He growled, a savage rumble that vibrated against her throat. His hand slapped against her cunt, thumb and forefinger finding her clit to pinch to the verge of pain, less a punishment than a stark reminder of what he could do if she really pissed him off. She arched in shock. "I'm sorry!"

The growl deepened, the fingers tightened until, squirming in pain, she remembered his title. "Milord! I'm sorry, milord!"

Another growl, this one sounding satisfied. How could he communicate so much with such a primitive sound?

He took his hand away from her cunt and went right on feeding, until she was grateful she'd kept forgetting to bottle her blood the past few weeks. His fingers found her breast again, tugging idly at her nipple, intensifying her helpless desire. Tugging, drinking, until she planted one high heel against the wall for leverage as she ground against his rock-muscled body. She tried to bite back her moans, hoping to avoid having him deny her again.

At last his hungry swallows ceased, and he drew his fangs from her throat. For a moment she hung in his grip as he lazily tormented one nipple. "Delicious," he purred in her ear. "But then, I knew you would be." His voice dropped to a growl. "I still remember the way you taste."

"You should," she managed. "You must have drunk from me a dozen times." But except for the first time, it had always been in emergencies, when Percival was badly injured, and usually she'd only given him her wrist. Anything else was too intimate. She was too vulnerable to him as it was.

"But not like this. And that first time, I was basically out of my head." He rolled his hips, making her aware of his hard-on, his overwhelming strength and size against her own utter helplessness. "And speaking of things I've been aching to do for far, far too long . . ."

A heartbeat later, she was cradled in his arms and moving in a dizzying swoop and a couple of long strides. He dropped down on the sectional and stood her up between his thighs, only to start bending her over.

Realizing belatedly what he intended, Morgana started to struggle, more as a matter of instinct than anything else. But there was no way in hell she was going to win a wrestling match with Percival.

In a flash, her legs were trapped in the clamp of his thighs, her wrists pinned at the small of her back in one of his big hands . . .

And her bare rump was at the vampire's mercy.

Percival gazed down at Morgana's pale, round arse.

"Percival!" she gasped. "What the hell are you . . ."

His palm hit her backside with a loud *SLAP!* "How do you address your Master?" he thundered.

"Lord Percival!" She gasped, her voice shaking, sounding both frightened and aroused. "Sir, why are you . . . ?"

"Because it fucking pleases me, Oath Servant." *SLAP.* "And because you damned near got two innocents, yourself, and all of us killed with your games." SLAP. Her backside jiggled and reddened under his hand, an effect rendered even more tempting by the way she bucked and struggled. He paused to caress the silky curves, traced one finger along the shadowed cleft. "Because you're arrogant and manipulative, and I should have put you over my knee fifteen centuries ago to teach you humility."

"I was trying to keep you alive!" Morgana burst out, as if unable to keep her mouth shut any longer. "At least I could take dragon form, fight him with magic. You're the best knights I've ever worked with, but I feared the dragon would kill you. I didn't want . . ."

SMACK! "Maybe you didn't notice, but we did more damage to that thing than you did, Morgana!" Furious, insulted, he laid into her arse in a rain of stinging smacks that soon had her yelping, her feet snapping out in kicks.

"I couldn't lose you!" she cried.

The anguish in her voice brought him up short. She meant that; sincerity rang in her voice, along with a need and pain that didn't sound like the controlled, arrogant woman he knew.

Percival felt a stab of yearning for something more than the collar and the kink—a desire for an emotional connection to Morgana, the woman who had been his obsession for so very long.

Instantly, his instincts for self-preservation revolted at the idea. Damned if he was going to give Morgana le Fay an opening like that.

Again, he started smacking her round, tempting arse until she bucked and squealed.

God, he loved spanking a beautiful woman, particularly one who had submissive tendencies she'd never acknowledged. A single-tail might be more frightening when used with skill, paddles might deliver more sting, crops and canes might inflict more painful marks the girl would remember for days. Chaining a sub might render her more intensely helpless than simply holding her wrists pinned.

But nothing beat putting a woman over your knee if you wanted to make her aware of your greater size and strength, of the fact that you had her and there was absolutely nothing she could do about it.

Then there was the potential for giving the sub a really great head-fuck as you forced her to realize that being held helpless aroused her. Too, there was the interesting fact that if you really knew what you were doing, you could make a sub come with a skillful spanking.

Percival knew what he was doing.

But while he was at it, he was going to make damned sure the head-fuck only went one way. He was most definitely not going to let Morgana under his skin. This was about sex and revenge and teaching a certain arrogant witch humility.

Percival lowered his aim to come up under her arse, so the impact vibrated right through her bum to her cunt and clit. He gave her five carefully measured smacks, just hard enough to make her shudder and writhe.

"Ooh! *Lord Percival . . . !*"

Yeah, she'd definitely felt *that,* all right.

He stopped spanking her in favor of tracing his fingertips over her round, pink arse, enjoying the heat building beneath her skin. Licking the blood off his fangs, he savored its hot flavor, so rich and seductive. Morgana tasted delicious, shimmering with magic despite the collar. Evidently the device only kept her from accessing her power, for it was definitely still there. Mageverse energy burned in her blood with an intensity that made the Jack he'd had earlier seem like a white wine spritzer by comparison.

No mortal tasted so rich. Hell, few Majae had blood that shimmered with the kind of power Morgana le Fay had. Some of it was her age; the older a witch was, the stronger her magic, as if she stored it up like a battery to feed the lucky bastard who sank his fangs into her delicate throat.

Bottled blood just didn't give the same kick. It sure as hell never gave him a raging cock-stand. Percival had rarely been so hard in his life. Some of it was the way she looked at him, with those pretty green eyes so wide and helpless. Anxious with a kind of erotic edge that made his balls draw hot and heavy.

God, he wanted to fuck her. Just throw her down on her back and cram his cock into that juicy pussy, pump hard and deep until he blew his load and filled her full.

No, he told his clawing lust. *I've been waiting for this too damned long. I'm not going to rush it. I'm going to savor every last thrust, every last second of bringing her to her knees. By the time dawn rolls around, she's going to know who she belongs to. She'll call me 'my lord' and* mean it. *She'll* beg . . .

God, the thought of Morgana le Fay begging him made his cock jerk and buck against his zipper until he wanted to free it from its uncomfortable prison in his jeans.

Instead he started spanking her again, varying the force and speed, pausing in between swats to make sure the nerves had time to recover instead of losing sensitivity. Morgana squirmed, tried to kick, but he had her thighs clamped between his, her arse raised high, a perfect, juicy target, so he could stimulate her clit with each blow.

And it was working. Every breath he took smelled of wet pussy. Percival grinned, watching her body's helpless, shamed writhing.

God, he'd never done anything so hot in his life.

Dammit, he's spanking me like a child, Morgana thought, panting, as her rump stung savagely from the blows of Percival's relentless palm. *I shouldn't be getting so wet.*

But the furious mental lecture did no good at all. Pleasure reverberated through her nerves despite the hot pain blistering her arse. She tried to suppress her jerking bucks, but her body absolutely refused to obey.

While Percival loved every flinch and quiver.

There could be no doubt he thoroughly enjoyed her helpless struggles, not considering the size of the bulge pressed into her hip. The man felt as hard as a broadsword.

Finally he paused in those merciless, measured swats. "If I didn't know better," Percival drawled, "I'd think you were enjoying this spanking almost as much as I am." Sliding one finger into her pussy, he purred in pleasure at what he found. "God, you are wet." He added a second finger. "Why, Morgana le Fay—do you have a streak of masochism buried beneath all that arrogance and ice?"

Her face burning in a furious blush, she made no answer.

His hand hit her rump in a blow so hard, it wasn't even remotely erotic. She shouted in startled protest.

"Your Oath Master asked you a question, servant," Percival snarled. "Are you hiding a streak of masochism beneath that arrogance?"

"No!" she cried. But it was less a denial than a desperate prayer.

"I warned you not to lie to me, witch," he snapped, and cut loose in a furious rain of swats that had her kicking and squirming in the prison of his thighs. When he finally stopped again, shamed tears ran down her face, and her cunt was swollen and hot with helpless lust.

"Now, once more," Percival asked in that icy tone that meant you'd better not push him one inch further. "Are you a masochist, Morgana?"

"Yes!" The word burst from her, leaving her dumbfounded. Where the hell had *that* come from?

"Good." Percival sank two fingers into her pussy, pumped deep. "Because I am most definitely a sadist where you're concerned." And he found her anus with his cream-slicked finger and slid it deep, stretching her ruthlessly.

SEVEN

Morgana jerked in helpless reaction to the forefinger thrusting deep in her arse. "Ahhh! Per . . . Lord Percival!"

"Very nice. Very tight." He added the second finger, scissored them apart, tormenting the snug channel. She gasped at the hot sting. "If I didn't know better, I'd think you were a virgin. I'm going to have a very good time fucking this. And I'll make sure it hurts."

Morgana shivered, picturing it: Percival's big body pinning hers as he forced his thick cock deep in her rectum, grinding in ruthlessly. *Oh, Merlin's balls,* she realized, appalled. *He's right—I do have a masochistic streak.*

She'd always recognized the edge of cruelty in Percival. He usually controlled it with ruthless discipline, but if an enemy pissed him off enough, he'd make the poor bastard wish he'd never been whelped. Marrok might be bigger, might flare into berserker rages, Cador might be mean as hell, but it was Percival who really scared the shit out of her.

Percival could break her. Make her lose control. She couldn't afford that, because her control of herself was the key to controlling her power. If she lost that, everyone might end up paying the price.

And yet, she needed him. Needed him even though he seemed

ruthlessly determined to crack her open like an egg. She needed him because she knew he and his team would do whatever was necessary if she did lose it.

He released the clamp of his thighs around hers and pushed her off his lap, releasing her wrists and dumping her onto the floor. Some remnant of chivalry had him catching her shoulders before she would have crashed to her knees.

Percival came to his feet in a towering male rush, looming over her. Breath caught, Morgana watched as he unzipped his jeans and shoved his black boxers down to free his erect cock. Horned God, it looked huge—ruddy and thick and pearled with a bead of pre-cum.

"Open your mouth," he snapped. "You're about to get your face fucked."

She licked her lips, automatically reaching for him. She'd always loved giving blow jobs, had prided herself on her ability to drive her lover insane.

"Did I tell you that you could use your hands? Put them behind your back." When she hesitated, startled, he snapped, "Now, Morgana!"

Hesitantly, she obeyed, just as he grabbed a fistful of her hair and aimed his cock at her lips. "Open."

Dazed, she obeyed, and he filled her mouth in a rush of stone-hard flesh. He hadn't been kidding about fucking her face; he gave her no chance to use her skills, rolling his hips in ruthless thrusts that made her gag more than once, eyes tearing in helpless reaction.

If she'd thought she could get away with it, she'd have knocked him on his arse, mounted him, and impaled herself on that thick shaft.

She'd never been so hot in her life.

Percival knew he was being an utter bastard. This was not how a Knight of the Round Table was supposed to act, even with an Oath Servant who'd pissed him off as thoroughly as Morgana had.

Yet when Percival looked down, watched his big shaft sliding in and out of her helplessly open mouth, felt her lips and tongue caressing him, the wet cavern of her throat stroking his length—he didn't give a damn about chivalry. All he wanted was to go on fucking Morgana's face.

Especially with those green eyes turned up to his. The emotion in her gaze wasn't mere submission; it had a feral edge, as if he'd somehow triggered something primal and animal in her, something that called to the dominant beast in him.

"That's right, suck your lord's dick," he growled, scarcely aware of what he said. "Use your tongue and lips to please me well enough, and maybe I'll let you come." He drove in a deliberately hard thrust to make her gag. "Or maybe I won't."

Percival hoped she didn't realize the hand he'd wrapped in her hair was shaking. *Who, exactly, is being taught a lesson in this particular scene?*

He was going to ream her so hard she'd walk bowlegged for the next week.

Heat began to pulse in his balls, and he knew he was about to spill. For a moment he considered pulling out and shooting all over her face and glorious tits . . .

But no. He wanted to come inside her, to claim her so deep she'd never get him out again.

"Swallow," he growled, as the climax boiled up the length of his cock. "You drink it all down, witch."

He came so hard his knees almost buckled at the shuddering hot pulses. Staring down at her, he drank in the sight of Morgana kneeling at his feet and suckling his jerking shaft like something out of his darkest fantasies.

When he was finished, he felt hollow, as if he'd blown the contents of his very soul into her.

And worse, she knew it.

There was a look in her eyes, as though she'd beaten him, even if her arse was red and swollen from the spanking he'd given her, and frustrated arousal wafted from her pink, glistening pussy. Despite everything he'd done, those sharp green eyes had spotted the moment his knees had almost given way.

Oh, fuck that. It did him no good to put a collar on the little bitch if he let her top him through his own damned dick.

Percival was damned if he'd fail the mission Arthur had given him. He'd served the man long enough to have a fair idea what his Liege had intended when he'd ordered the witch to give him her Oath.

Percival was supposed to make damned sure that Morgana le Fay quit playing stupid games with the lives of those who followed her. Which meant that by the time the sun was up, he'd better make sure he was her Master.

And that she bloody well knew it.

Lamb's wool formed a thick, soft padding inside the wristbands' tough black leather. Gleaming steel D rings jingled every time she moved her arm. He'd attached chains to the cuffs that led to a rather sinister hook in the ceiling, but he hadn't drawn them taut yet.

"Is that too tight?" Percival asked, eyeing the cuffs critically.

"No." She swallowed, acutely conscious of her own nudity. She wore only her collar, cuffs, stockings, and stilettos—plus, of course, the shackles clipped to the eyelets in the stone floor. The steel rings were more than shoulder-width apart, forcing her to stand with her high-heeled feet spread wide. Given that, and the fact that he obviously intended to chain her with her arms over her head, she didn't believe it was a pose she could hold for long.

Unfortunately, she wasn't sure he'd care. Morgana knew she'd pissed him off by showing her triumph in the aftermath of that blowjob.

Brainless. Absolutely brainless. Because now he obviously intended to demonstrate who was the bottom here—and it sure as hell wasn't him.

It looked as if he had more than enough equipment to give that demonstration. He'd marched her down the stairs to the honest-to-God dungeon in the basement. She wondered who'd conjured it for him, since it wasn't her work: stone walls illuminated by torches that cast light over gleaming cherry spanking benches and a Saint Andrew's Cross. Not to mention assorted attachment points for chains.

And then there was his toy rack.

Despite her best intentions, Morgana's gaze skittered over to the back wall yet again. Floor to ceiling cherry shelves held crops, canes, floggers, and a single-tail. There were all sorts of nipple clamps, a selection of dildos and vibrators ranging from size small to *no-way-in-hell*, butt-plugs in the same range of dimensions, and a number of other sinister objects whose purpose stumped her completely.

Morgana knew better than to voice the question this display triggered, but she couldn't seem to help herself.

"What the hell is all this? I know you're not bringing your mortal submissives here."

"What makes you think all my submissives are mortal?" He grabbed the end of the chain that bound her wrists and dragged it downward, pulling her bound wrists over her head before using a steel carabineer to clip it into position. The tension on the chain stretched her body into a tight, straining line, though her feet didn't leave the ground—quite. The position drew her back into an arch, though, forcing her bare breasts outward, so that their swollen, jutting peaks seemed to beg for a dominant's sadistic attentions.

Her dominant's attentions.

Her knees were shaking. God, she was wet. Morgana could smell herself, the nakedly erotic scent filling her nose, revealing just how aroused she was.

Meeting her eyes, Percival gave her a slow, feral smile that revealed the points of his fangs. "You have very pretty nipples, Morgana," he purred. "They look . . . edible."

I really shouldn't have pissed him off. Morgana licked her dry lips as she watched Percival contemplate her helpless nipples with predatory interest. She remembered the first time he'd bitten her there, an act she'd never allowed any of her other lovers. But Percival wasn't one of her lovers. He was her dominant. Her Master.

Morgana heard herself start to babble, but she couldn't seem to control her runaway tongue. "Don't dominants and submissives do some kind of negotiations in those clubs?"

"Of course. I'd never play with a sub otherwise." He shrugged. "I ask about any physical limitations, what she will and will not do, fantasies and fears. Her safeword." His gaze hardened. "But you're not a submissive. The oath you swore lets me do as I damned well choose with you, while you gave up the right to set limits." His grin was downright nasty as he eyed her hard nipples. "Oath Servants don't get a safeword."

She considered telling him he was a bastard, but judging by the glint in those cold gray eyes, he was just waiting for her to give him an excuse. *Sorry, Percival, I'm not quite that dumb.*

When she managed to resist the urge to say something inflammatory, he walked over to the shelves and started plucking out assorted objects, including a pair of clamps, a flogger, a riding crop, a butt-plug, and a tube of lube. He arranged the toys on a tall wheeled wooden table he then rolled to within easy reach.

As Morgana contemplated the table uneasily, Percival stepped over to her until his bare chest almost touched her naked nipples. Her eyes jerked up to his as he crossed his massive arms and proceeded to loom.

Morgana swallowed, entirely too aware of the sheer size of the man—his height, the way his chest seemed to fill her field of vision like a wall, the chiseled shapes of hard muscle and snaking veins. A lock of blond hair fell over his eyes as he stared down at her, giving him a hint of softness at odds with the inhuman hunger in his gaze.

He looks so strong, so indomitable. As if he could solve any problem. She wished he could solve hers. Wished she could tell him everything.

She'd come so close to confessing everything to him so many times over the years, but in the end she'd held her silence. Yet now, wearing his collar, utterly vulnerable, she had the remarkable thought that maybe she could trust him. That unlike everyone else she'd loved, he wouldn't reject her, wouldn't turn his back.

Not now, her libido hummed. *I'll tell him later, deal with his rage later. Right now I want his passion.*

Her gaze dropped without her conscious intention down to his groin in the soft, well-washed jeans. His erection jutted boldly against the fabric, so brutally long and thick that she shifted uneasily on her high heels.

Yes, later would be soon enough.

"You look delicious like that," he said in a dark, deep rasp. "All strung up and helpless, with those long rose nipples just begging for my teeth. God, I want to bite you."

She forced herself to lift her chin and met his gaze. "You've always been something of a sadistic bastard."

The humor vanished from his eyes, and he snagged her chin between thumb and forefinger. "That is not the way an Oath Servant speaks to her Master. You would do well to beg my pardon."

Morgana, you idiot. You had to go and push. Despite the cool fear breathing down her spine, she met his gaze, refusing to let her own falter. "I will not beg your pardon when I speak nothing but the truth."

She expected him to explode in the kind of furious male rant that would hand her a psychological victory, no matter how Pyrrhic in terms of her reddened arse. Instead he smiled, revealing the sharp points of his fangs. "Yeah, I figured it wouldn't be long before you had to see how far you could push me." He stroked his thumb along the length of her jawline to the frantically throbbing carotid. "The answer is, of course, not very fucking far."

Wrapping his fist in her hair, Percival jerked her mouth up into his kiss. There was nothing sweet or tender about it. It was a furious male conquest of a kiss, all teeth and thrusting tongue, forcing her jaws wide, a rough reminder of the way he'd used his cock. One fang scratched her lower lip, and he drew it into his mouth, sucking the blood from the tiny, stinging wound.

By the time Percival drew back, she was shaking, the chains jingling, as if mocking her attempt at defiance. His hard gaze bored into hers, daring her to drop her eyes as he slowly bent toward her arched breasts.

Finally he transferred that potent attention to her right nipple. He contemplated it for a long moment as her heartbeat filled her ears and her breath rasped in and out.

Morgana felt suspended between lust and terror, swinging back and forth like an erotic pendulum. Just as she was about to babble something insulting to goad him into action, he leaned in and gave the taut peak a lick.

Slow. Wet. Hot. The sensation was so intense, it was all she could do not to squirm. Another lick, a burning spiral around her desperately hard nipple. "Mmmmm," he rumbled. "I knew you'd be delicious." His palm cupped her, warm and sword-calloused and impossibly arousing. Thumb and forefinger caught the lush peak. Tugged slowly, twisting, sending hot curls of raw pleasure from nipple to sex. "You taste like magic and pussy."

Half-mindless, she reached up and gripped the chains that stretched her body out so helplessly.

He scooped up one of the clamps. She flinched, but there was nowhere she could go as the padded jaws closed over the jutting peak.

"Horned God, Percival!" Morgana gasped. "That hurts!"

The knight looked up at her and smiled darkly. "It's supposed to, darling."

As she panted, trying to breathe through the pain lancing from her abused nipple, he started licking and sucking the other breast. "The idea," he told her between licks, "is that the clamp closes off the blood supply. Then when you take it off, the blood rushes back." He paused to suckle her in a deep, hot draw. She pulled upward on the chain, pulling herself off her feet with her Maja strength. Scooping up the other clamp, he applied it. She sucked in a breath at the vicious sting, throwing her head back. "That, of course, is when I'll *bite*."

"Jesu, Percival!"

"Yes, well, you did offer me your Oath, Morgana." He stepped back a few paces and cocked his head as if admiring the sight of her, all strung out in her bonds, the clamps biting her tits. Turning to the table and its collection of evil toys, he picked up the deer-hide flogger. "And you can't claim you don't have it coming. You've been a right bitch for entirely too long." He studied her as he gave the flogger a sharp, experimental flick, making it swish. "And I wonder why that is, Morgana? Are you trying to keep us at a distance? Are you afraid we'll get to you if we get too close? Don't you trust yourself?"

Hell, no. But he was working his way too close to the one secret she had to keep, so she went on the defensive. "Do you want to psychoanalyze me, or do you want to fuck?"

"Actually," he drawled, his eyes kindling with temper, "I thought I'd flog those luscious tits until you scream."

Morgana braced herself, expecting him to tear into her with the whip. But once again, she'd underestimated his skill as a dominant.

Percival began to walk around her, flicking the flogger across her bare breasts. She was surprised at how soft the whip's deerskin falls felt in his skilled hand.

Morgana watched him, feeling half-drugged, suspended in sensual amber honey.

A flogger is a short-range weapon, and so he paced less than an arms-length away. Again she was conscious of his size, the width of his shoulders, the thick brawn of his bare arms, muscle rolling and working as he sent the flogger sweeping out to strike her naked skin. Instead of the sharp pain she'd expected, the blows felt almost lazy, gentle, a deerskin massage that fell with soft plops rather than sharp whip cracks.

Slowly, he picked up the pace and force of his blows until they began to sting. It was an oddly pleasant sensation. A light sweat broke out over his skin, less from effort than pure erotic heat. Morgana had never met a man who appeared so divinely built for sexual dominance—or one who made her ache to submit with such helpless intensity.

As he strolled in catlike circles around her bound body, he rotated his wrist in figure eights and loops, striking her breasts, her waist, her hips, and her sex, first from one direction, then the other, painting blushing impacts along her body like an artist with a brush.

But it was his stare that truly ignited her helpless lust. She'd always thought his gray eyes cool, but they burned now from beneath his thick blond brows. Torchlight sketched shadows beneath the hard, handsome angles of his face, emphasizing the feral intensity of his expression, the stark animal lust in his gaze. His sensual lips parted as he stalked before her, revealing the sharp white tips of his fangs.

When he circled around behind her, it was all she could do not to beg him to come back where she could see him. Watch him. She craved the sight of his darkly seductive strength, his sadistic grace as he wielded the flogger. But she was not in control here, was she? And so, she kept her tongue between her teeth and listened to the pad of his boots passing behind her.

His steps paused. It seemed she could almost feel the heat of his breath on the back of her neck, and she wondered if he was going to bite her again. Her nipples hardened in the grip of the clamps, and she felt her labia swell with another wave of lust.

As if sensing her arousal, Percival sent the flogger licking out to strike her up between her thighs, the soft falls stimulating her hard clit and thumping against her spread pussy. She squirmed helplessly and fought the need to beg.

The heat he'd been building in her pussy intensified as he beat her slowly, every impact of the flogger stoking it steadily into a licking, savage fire that owed more to lust than pain.

Teeth gritted against the need to plead for his cock, Morgana clung to the chains as the flogger hit her ass in soft, hot strokes.

Jesu, flogging Morgana le Fay was the hottest thing Percival had ever done in his very long life. Yet this was hardly his first scene; he'd been seriously exploring the intersection of pain and pleasure for years.

He'd always been dominant, of course, all the way back to his human days. He adored tying a woman up to enhance her sexual desire as well as his own. But when it came to erotic discipline, he'd never used anything but his hands, belt, or the occasional riding crop until twenty years ago.

That was when mortals began actively codifying the rules and skills of their elaborate BDSM games in clubs, play parties, and munches. He, Cador, and Marrok had first begun playing with D/s out of curiosity—and a certain boredom with plain vanilla sex.

It hadn't taken them long to realize just how powerful those erotic techniques could be, or how deliciously satisfying they were. Percival loved nothing more than chaining a beautiful woman and tormenting her as he taught her things about her own body she'd never known.

This time, though, it wasn't just any woman writhing under his flogger.

How many times had he jerked off thinking about getting Morgana le Fay naked and helpless under his whip? He'd lost count of the number of times he'd woken from dreams of her with come on his belly and the memory of her dream moans in his ears.

But Merlin's Balls, those fantasies had never done her justice. Her breasts were ripe and round on her lean torso, her nipples dark red in the grip of the clamps. She was nobody's idea of brawny, but long muscle curved in her arms and wide-spread legs, an elegant female strength built in combat, both during the daily practice sessions and actual bloody fights with everything from mortals to axe-wielding Dark Ones. Yes, magic was her preferred weapon, but she knew how to use a sword, if a considerably lighter weapon than the ones the knights favored. Her efforts with it had given her body a long, feminine elegance, a graceful strength.

And Jesu, those legs. Veiled in lace, spread wide in crimson spike heels, muscles working under her silken skin every time his flogger teased her thighs.

He burned to fuck her. Now. Forget the foreplay, forget whatever punishment she'd earned with today's idiocy. He'd waited fifteen centuries to sink his dick into that tight pink pussy again, and damned if he wanted to wait any longer.

Percival set his teeth and fought down the furious lust as he turned back to the table, put down the flogger, and picked up his favorite crop.

As much as he wanted to fuck her blind, sometimes a dominant had to ignore his own needs in favor of serving his submissive. Even if that service took the form of beating her ridiculously tempting arse.

He walked up behind her, his possessive gaze on the anxiously flexing muscle of her cheeks. For a moment he pictured spreading them, seeking out the tight rosebud of her anus and oiling it up with the lube he had sitting so conveniently at hand. He thought about watching his cock sink into that tiny hole, forcing it to spread, listening to her breathy moans as he worked his way deep, millimeter by millimeter. His cock bucked behind his fly at the searing fantasy image.

Not yet. He drew in a hard breath between his teeth. If his years as a dominant had taught Percival anything, it was that a climax was all the sweeter when you delayed it as long as you could.

So instead he sent the crop in his hand licking out at one of those tempting female cheeks. Morgana jerked with a startled shout. His cock jerked again.

Smiling a trifle grimly, Percival started working her over in earnest, planting wicked blows across her gorgeous rump as she jerked and struggled in her bonds. He couldn't blame her. He'd been the recipient of the crop himself, and he knew it stung like a bitch.

He wasn't a submissive by any stretch of the imagination, but you couldn't use a tool properly until you'd had it used on you. Years ago, he'd sought out a very pretty domme to teach him the erotic use of the cane, flogger, and single-tail whip. She'd been so damned good with her toys, he'd even managed to fly—carried into erotic euphoria by a blend of endorphins and adrenaline. He'd promptly broken the chains and fucked the domme silly with his fangs buried in her throat.

Submission wasn't really his thing.

Though the domme hadn't been unwilling, she'd eyed him warily afterward, despite the spell Morgana had used to make sure she didn't remember the more supernatural aspects of their encounter. Apparently she wasn't a sub either.

Morgana was. And he meant to drive her to her knees—and keep her there.

Biting back a scream, Morgana writhed as Percival's crop cut another line of fire across her arse. She wanted to curse, toss a fireball at his head—hell, punch him in that handsome, arrogant nose. But she couldn't do any of that because he was her Oath Master, and she'd given him the right to punish her in whatever way suited him.

But the thing that truly infuriated her was the arousal that burned in her blood like a flame following a trail of spilled brandy. She'd bedded some of the most skilled and passionate lovers in Avalon, men who were so gorgeous and fiercely sexy, other women eyed her with naked envy. Hell, she'd had Arthur himself before he'd met and married Guinevere.

Yet none of them had made her want to beg for cock like a cat in heat. The savagery of her need was humiliating. The only bright spot in this whole ordeal was that she hadn't actually lost control enough to beg Percival to fuck her.

But Horned God, she'd wanted to.

Somehow the flogger's thudding impacts had stimulated her clit and anus, not to mention deeper pleasure centers in her sex. To make matters even worse, her pussy had swollen from the flogging, so that every time she writhed or struggled, she ended up stimulating her hungry cunt even more.

But it wasn't just his skill with a dominant's toys that got to her. It was the way his dominance seemed to fit her submission as if they'd been designed that way. She'd long sensed that possibility, which was why she'd always feared yielding to Percival's overwhelming sensuality.

But the real danger he posed had nothing to do with sex. It was the way he made her feel safe. Morgana hadn't felt safe since her own son had abused her.

WHAP!

She jolted as the riding crop cut a flaming swath across her arse, blasting every other thought right out of her head. Unlike the session with the flogger, there was no doubt he intended this beating as punishment for her behavior during the fight with the dragon.

Morgana writhed in time with each *whish* the crop cut across her tormented rear cheeks like a knife blade. She was surprised she wasn't bleeding, but her skin was wet with nothing more than sweat. Which was an act of obvious mercy on Percival's part; she knew he could have cut her up like a sheet of tissue paper.

The crop ceased its fiery strikes, and he moved away. She heard a door open and close; it sounded like the small dorm-sized refrigerator against the wall.

Morgana braced herself, breathing hard, expecting him to start in again. He'd often paused, apparently to let her pain receptors recover for the next blow. So when a broad, warm hand stroked over her hot arse cheeks, she jumped, startled. "That pale skin of yours marks up well," he said in a dark velvet rumble. "The healer is going to find the view rather . . . provocative in the morning."

Morgana licked her dry lips, wishing fiercely she could conjure a bottle of water. "I don't need a healer."

His fingers tightened painfully on her right cheek as he leaned in. "Yet," he growled in her ear, stepping up against her bare back. "You may think differently by the time I'm finished with you."

EIGHT

One hand wrapped possessively in her hair, Percival pulled her head back to rest on his shoulder. To her surprise, he lifted a bottle of water to her lips. Must have been what he'd gotten out of the fridge, Morgana thought as she drank thirstily. She probably shouldn't have been surprised at his sensitivity to her needs. Percival had always taken his responsibilities to those under his command very seriously.

Apparently that care extended to Oath Servants.

At his urging, she drained the bottle before he took it away and sent it sailing into a nearby trashcan with a ringing rattle.

"Thank you."

"You may want to save those thanks." Turning back to her, Percival stepped up against her back. Making her feel him, his size, his hard muscle and animal warmth. "I still have an appetite," he murmured in her ear. She felt her nipples tighten at the deep rasp of his voice. "By the time I get done milking those pretty tits, you're going to need a medic."

Morgana shuddered in reaction. She wanted to get angry, more as a reaction to her own too-responsive nipples than Percival's sensual threat. She couldn't seem to manage it. "You *are* a bastard, aren't you?"

"Definitely." Releasing her arse, he slid that hand around her hip to cup her between her legs. Morgana caught her breath as he slid a forefinger between her wet, swollen labia. Percival chuckled. "Somebody enjoyed her flogging. I guess this answers the masochism question." Stroking two fingers between her labia, he tormented her plump, erect clit between them.

Morgana gasped at the intense sensations that boiled up between her thighs in time to the juicy sounds of his thrusting fingers. She was intensely aware of his massive erection pressing against her cheeks. "I'm not the only one who enjoyed it, judging from the size of that cock-stand."

"Oh, I loved every minute of beating your gorgeous arse. Just as I intend to enjoy this . . ." Tightening his grip on her hair, he pulled her face around as he stood behind her and took her mouth. The kiss was fierce, hot, and slow, with deep, swirling thrusts of his tongue he matched with rolling pumps of his hips against her backside.

At first Morgana stiffened. She'd expected the cock pumping against her rump, the fingers driving deep into her sex, but not the passion in his kiss, the tenderness as well as lust in the way he drank at her mouth, eyes closed, fist tight in her hair. Unable to resist—even knowing she should—Morgana melted back against him. His body felt hot and powerful against her spine.

And that cock, rigid as a length of pipe against her arse, both threat and promise as his fingers teased her pussy until she moaned into his mouth.

Finally he drew away from her, releasing his grip on her hair. "God, I adore the taste of your mouth." His gray eyes dipped to her lips. "So sweet. So hot." He gave her a slow, carnivorous smile. "Almost as hot as that tight pussy I can't wait to fuck."

He dropped to one knee and went to work unbuckling the thick leather cuff around first one ankle, then the other. Morgana sighed in relief and waited for him to free her chained wrists, suddenly aware of how they ached from being bound over her head.

Instead he rose and stalked around in front of her, then stepped in close. Catching one of the clamps gripping her nipples, he opened the tiny rubber jaws and threw the clamp aside.

Morgana sucked in a breath at the pain that instantly stabbed into the tight-drawn peak. "Oh, fuck, Percival!" she gasped. When his brow lifted icily, she added hastily. "*Lord* Percival."

"You'd better get in the habit of using that title, or you're going to wish you had." Giving her that lupine smile again, he unzipped his jeans and pulled his thick, rigid cock out of the opening of his boxers. "Fortunately for you, I'm in the mood to fuck you instead of punishing you as you so richly deserve."

"What do you call what you've been doing for the past hour?" Morgana demanded, damned if she'd be cowed into silence.

He grinned savagely. "Entertainment."

One hand scooped under her swollen, red arse, pulling her off her feet as he used the other to aim his thick cock at her pussy. Morgana caught her breath, grabbing the chains to steady herself as the round mushroom head of his shaft nosed the swollen lips of her sex.

He entered slowly, working his way in by tormenting fractions. Morgana caught her breath at the hot sensation of being so gradually, ruthlessly stuffed.

Oh, Horned God, it felt so sweet. She'd dreamed of this, dreamed of knowing his cock again, so thick and long and hot.

He watched her face as he filled her, his gray eyes intent, his lush upper lip lifted enough to reveal the points of his fangs. Morgana stared back, utterly unable to do anything else. Hypnotized and helpless, like a rabbit in the deceptively gentle grip of a puma.

Just before he flashed those teeth . . .

Despite her clamoring instincts, her lids slid closed, the better to savor the sensation of that long, smooth, thick cock slowly working its way to the root. *At last.* At last Percival was inside her, where she'd wanted him so fucking long.

Morgana thought of all those lonely dreams she'd had, only to wake restless in an empty bed. Needing. Not only needing cock—though Merlin knew she did—but needing *him*. Percival, her handsome, arrogant knight, with his fierce tactical intelligence and hard warrior's body. Courageous, yes, but with the wit not to be stupidly brave. Good with a sword or a combat knife or a Desert Eagle. Cool-eyed as an assassin, even when it got bloody and hot. The kind of man other men would follow into hell's teeth, because they knew he wouldn't lead them there unless there was absolutely no choice about the destination.

But Horned God, the man also had a cock that was downright menacing in its width and length. You'd think she wouldn't find that such a surprise, since she'd made love to him once before. But that had been centuries ago. True, Merlin knew she'd seen him with a hard-on any number of time since then, but there was a difference between the way a dick looked behind a man's fly and how it felt buried halfway to your rib cage. Jeans made it easier to convince yourself there wasn't really all that much of him, that the denim made him look bigger.

Nope.

He was in to the balls now. She could feel them resting like velvet weights against her arse cheeks.

"There now," he said, and she thought again of that puma, purring. "There we go."

He shifted his hold on her, one hand going around her arse, the other around her waist to support the length of her back. The chains around her wrists held her arms in the air. The resulting pose wasn't one a human man could have held for long, even if he'd been as fit as Percival.

But vampire muscle did make a difference, so he was able to support her weight even with it thrown forward at that awkward angle. Concerned for his back, she wrapped both legs around his waist . . . which had the pleasant effect of pulling him in even deeper.

Morgana sighed in sensuous pleasure, enjoying the sensation of every inch of her being filled with every inch of him.

"Mmmmmm." He purred it. There was no other way to describe that deep male rumble.

Gathering her even closer, Percival began to roll his strong hips, pulling that endless cock out and pushing it deep again. Slow. Slooooow and delicious and Horned God, just incredible.

Clinging to him as he fucked her, Morgana belatedly realized his head was just at the level of her breasts. He gave her bare nipple a thoughtful lick, then engulfed it for a deep suckle. She inhaled sharply at the pleasure, her eyes drifting closed again with a helpless shiver of delight.

God, the way he felt. Pure sex and sin packed in six feet, three inches of vampire muscle and bone. So good. So bloody *good*, with his hips rolling and his mouth suckling her long nipple.

So when he turned his head and caught the clamp on the other nipple in his teeth, she didn't see it coming. Didn't anticipate that fiery blaze of heat when the blood rushed back into the tortured nipple. She jerked, barely aware of the clatter as he spat the clamp onto the floor.

Sharp fangs sank into the curve of her breast while she was still dealing with the merciless burn of returning circulation.

"Percival!" she cried out as he drank and fucked, her fingers clawing helplessly at the chains. Swinging in her bonds while he took her in short, quick thrusts as he drank her magical blood. Feeding and fucking while she shivered in his arms.

Morgana le Fay had never felt so helpless in her life.

It was something of a surprise when she came in a furious, racking storm a heartbeat later, bucking in his ruthless arms. Impaled on his fangs and his dick. Utterly helpless. And loving it entirely too much.

Percival shuddered in helpless reaction to the feeling of Morgana's slick sex clamping rhythmically around his shaft, triggering pulses of delight. Eyes shuttering, he swallowed, drinking her rich blood, the taste of magic foaming on his tongue. The pleasure was so intoxicating, he wondered if he'd ever know the likes of it again.

Oh, I'll know it again, he thought, swallowing another heated mouthful. *I've got her for the next year.* The possessive anticipation in that thought made him grin against the smooth, delicate flesh of her breast, hands cradling her delightful arse as he pumped between her slim thighs.

His. She was his at last.

At last the hard pulses died away, leaving his knees weak. He eased out of her slick body reluctantly, though some part of him wanted only to keep her in his arms. As he slid his jeans and boxers back into place over his hips and zipped his fly, Percival met her gaze. He was gratified by the dazed look in those beautiful green eyes as she hung limp in her bonds.

"That was . . ." She paused and swallowed." . . . Interesting."

He grinned and went to work unbuckling the cuffs around her wrists. "I thought so."

For a moment, Percival considered sweeping Morgana into his arms and carrying her upstairs. He wanted to sleep wrapped around her so he could drink in the scent of her curling dark hair and the warmth of her soft skin.

A wave of tenderness took him by surprise.

No. Oh, no. This was Morgana le Fay here. If he let her sense any vulnerability, any weakness she could exploit, she'd tie his balls in a knot, magic or no magic.

Jaw firming, he knelt to jerk open the ankle cuffs and set her free. She swayed, and he looked up and registered how pale and dazed she looked. Percival frowned, remembering how hard he'd just fed.

Oh, to hell with it. He stood and swept her into his arms, then started up the stairs with her.

"Percival," she said, sounding a bit slurred. He really had fed too deeply. "Where are you taking me, my lord?"

"To bed. Shush."

To his surprise, Morgana obeyed, her eyes sliding closed, her head dropping to rest on his shoulder. He frowned, afraid for a moment she'd passed out. But no, her heartbeat was strong and steady. In fact, he realized it probably sounded better than it had before he'd fed. He wondered whether she'd been putting off donating blood too long again, something he knew she had a habit of doing. Majae needed to donate frequently or risk strokes from high blood pressure.

But still, she did look pale. He frowned. Reaching his bedroom, Percival carried her inside. He put her down by the bed just long enough to flip the covers down. "In you go."

She muttered something, still sounding slurred—which might be a product of exhaustion as much as the blood he'd taken, now that he thought about it. She'd fought a bloody dragon today, after all, throwing around a hell of a lot of magic to do it. Then there'd been the confrontation with Arthur, followed by the one with him and his team. And of course, the way he'd fucked and fed on her.

Morgana crawled into the big bed and curled up on her side, falling asleep almost instantly. He joined her, flipping the dark-blue bedspread over on top of both of them. Pulling her back into his arms, he let himself relax.

Her hair smelled of jasmine, tempting him into ducking his head close and inhaling deeply, savoring the sweet scent of woman and sex. She felt warm and soft and deliciously tempting. Not at all like the cool, controlled woman he knew.

The sun would rise soon, bringing the Daysleep with it and stealing his consciousness away. He stared toward the pair of stained glass windows across the room, though there wasn't enough light to see the knight and his lady the colored glass depicted. Percival let his thoughts float, remembering the pleasure he'd found in dominating Morgana and imagining what he might try next. He had a long list . . .

"No. No, don't. Please don't . . ."

Stiffening, he looked down at the woman in his arms as Morgana stirred. Her voice was a breathy whisper, thin and high, growing louder, higher, as she began to struggle, fighting his hold. "Morgana?"

"No, you can't . . ."

He stroked one hand up and down her arm, trying to soothe her out of the nightmare that obviously had her in its grip. "Morgana, you're okay. You're dreaming . . ."

"I'm your mother!" She jerked upright, dragging herself out of his arms. *"You don't touch me like that!"*

Reacting instinctively to the horrified revulsion in her tone, he jerked his hands away from her. "Morgana?"

She blinked, coming awake. "Percival?" Her voice sounded thin, unsure.

"Yeah, it's me." He turned and flicked on the bedside lamp, knowing she needed the light to reassure her she was finally awake. "Sounded like you were having a nightmare."

And what a nightmare. *"You don't touch me like that?"* Oh, shit. His stomach twisted. Mordred had been a big man—inches taller than Arthur, with a bull-like build. He frowned, remembering bruises that had made the king once say he suspected Morgana had an abusive lover. But what if the man who'd beaten her had been Mordred? And what if beating her hadn't been all he'd done? *"You don't touch me like that!"* God, what a horrific thought. He frowned. Was that why she'd rejected him so furiously after he'd fed from her those centuries ago? Had Mordred's treatment left her gun-shy?

"A nightmare." Morgana huffed a sound that might have been a laugh except for its utter lack of humor. "Yeah, you could say that." She sat forward and buried her face in shaking hands.

"It sounded like you were dreaming about Mordred," Percival told her carefully.

She shrugged and dropped her hands and looked away. "Yesterday would have been his birthday. I tend to dream about him on his birthday."

"He's been dead a long time."

"I was his mother."

"Yeah." He decided to take the bull by the horns. Maybe he'd just gotten the wrong impression. Hell, he hoped he had, because the alternative . . . "Did he treat you like his mother?"

She stared at him, and her face went pale. Her gaze slid away from his. "I'm going to need something to wear home. I can't conjure anything with this collar." Morgana slid out of bed and headed toward his bureau. "Mind if I borrow something of yours?"

"Feel free." He watched her. "That reminds me—see a healer. Since your magic is blocked, your body won't be able to repair the blood loss with any speed."

She ignored him pointedly, opening and closing drawers as she searched for something to wear. Locating one of his black T-shirts, she pulled it on. It hung on her to mid-thigh, the fit putting him in mind of a sack and reminding him uncomfortably how much smaller she was compared to him.

Or Mordred.

"Don't touch me like that!"

It's been fifteen hundred years, he reminded himself. *Even if he did abuse her, that's a long time. Surely she'd be over it by now.* Assuming you ever got over something like that.

I need to find out exactly what happened. If he hurt her so badly she's still having nightmares about it fifteen centuries later, that could explain a lot.

"How do you feel?" Percival asked, his voice low and rough to his own ears. "I took you pretty hard. Including your blood."

"I'm fine." She closed a drawer a bit harder than was strictly necessary.

Percival grappled for patience. "I'm going to ask this again. And this time I don't want any bullshit. Are you feeling weak? Can you walk home, or do I need to call a healer now?"

She shot him a look over one shoulder. "The sun's about to come up, Percival."

"I know what fucking time it is. *Are you feeling dizzy?*"

"You didn't take *that* much blood."

"It was easily a pint and a half."

"I'm a Maja, Percival, not a mortal. A pint and a half donation is not going to make me pass out."

"Not normally, perhaps, but without your magic . . ."

She swung on him, anger in her eyes, her delicate jaw tight. "Look, my lord, I'm a big witch now. I can donate a couple of pints without keeling over. Especially considering it's been more than a month since I donated." Jerking a pair of sweats out of the drawer, she pulled them on, balancing on her high heels.

He frowned, wishing she could turn them into a pair of Nikes for the trek back to her place. The pants hung on her, their hems flopping around her feet in another silent reminder of the difference in their sizes. "Go to the damned healer, Morgana."

"I don't need a healer!" she spat.

"Your Oath Master just gave you an order, Servant!" he snapped back, in no mood for her stubbornness. "See a healer!" He was seriously tempted to order her to stay, even if he had to chain her to the foot of his bed to keep her there.

Something deep within him growled at the thought of letting her leave him even during the Daysleep, when he wouldn't be conscious. *Don't be a possessive ass,* he told himself. *It's enough to make sure she's back by the time I wake.* "And then you'd better be back here at sunset," he told her in his best inflexible dom voice. "I have plans for you tomorrow night, and I do not want to wait to carry them out."

She shot him a glittering look. "Why?"

"Why do you think?" He gave her a darkly suggestive grin, though in reality, he was at least as motivated by a desire to make sure she was all right.

Nightmare or no nightmare, son or no son, he had no intention of showing Morgana le Fay that kind of weakness.

Anger and shame clawing at her, Morgana whirled and opened her mouth to retort to this latest high-handed demand.

Before she could get a word out of her mouth, Percival's eyes slid shut, his expression smoothing with the magical sleep that descended on Magi the moment the sun rose.

The Daysleep had begun.

Morgana's shoulders slumped as she realized she no longer had to put up an invulnerable front for him. Good thing. Given that nightmare, she wouldn't have had the energy for it much longer.

Her stilettos teetered under her, and she decided they had to go. No way was she up to negotiating Avalon's cobblestone streets in heels, not after giving him close to two pints. And yes, judging by the way her head seemed to be floating on her neck, it was closer to two pints than the pint and a half she'd claimed, though damned if she'd admit as much to him.

Locating a pair of flip flops in the back of Percival's closet, she changed out of the heels, and headed for home with the shoes' straps hooked over her fingers. Now that she could no longer conjure anything she needed with a moment's thought, she needed to hang on to every bit of clothing she could. Especially since Percival seemed to like ripping it all off her.

As she walked, her mind drifted back to the nightmare. She shuddered. It had been fifteen centuries, yet she still remembered the bruising grip of her son's hands the night before his duel with Arthur. Mordred hadn't raped her, but if the king had fallen to him during the fight for Merlin's Grail, she was very much afraid he would have done exactly what he'd threatened.

There'd been something broken in her son, ever since he'd fallen into Bennett's hands as a five-year-old. He'd certainly seemed to blame her for it. And he'd had a point.

Bennett had hated Morgana with such virulence because she'd used Druid techniques to save a child the priest had tried—and failed—to heal. He'd been convinced her abilities owed more to Satan than to Druid magic. When she'd refused to name Mordred's father despite Bennett's relentless questioning—she could hardly accuse the king—the priest decided the boy must be the devil's own son.

Remembering the week she'd been the priest's "guest" as he'd questioned, threatened, and beaten her, Morgana's hands drew into white-knuckled fists. She'd made sure Bennett would never hurt anyone else, but she hadn't done it soon enough. Not for herself, and certainly not for Mordred.

Years later, Mordred had fallen to Arthur's blade at Camlann. He'd been only nineteen.

They're both dead, Morgana told herself. Now if only she could forget them.

As Morgana walked along listening to the *flap flap flap* of her flip-flops hitting her heels, she watched the sun climb over Avalon's glorious skyline. The light painted the clouds in rose, orange, and violet, and cast a golden glow over the immortal city's palaces, castles, and little brick bungalows.

The most striking of all the homes lay just ahead of her, a sprawling French château complete with elaborate gardens and bronze statuary. Really, the thing was ridiculous, especially as a residence for one person.

But a rational use of magic wasn't the point. The point was to establish oneself in the minds of everyone else as a witch of great power. Morgana's château made certain everyone knew she was the city's most powerful witch.

The irony was that in the collar, she had less power than the youngest, least powerful Maja in the city.

With a tired sigh, Morgana wound her way through the elaborate garden, opened the mansion's great double-doors, and stepped into the imposing foyer.

"Horned God," she murmured, looking around the two-story entryway with its gleaming black-and-white marble tile. Statues of gods and goddesses posed serenely in niches in the wainscoted walls between paintings by Renaissance masters. Shaking her head, she sighed. "I'm so bloody shallow."

Luckily the house remained solid, despite her current lack of power. Objects given form from the energy of the Mageverse retained that solidity.

Exhaustion weighing at her feet, she headed through the foyer to the great marble floating staircase that curved to the second floor.

At least her bedroom wasn't as bloody pretentious as the house's first floor. A king-sized bed sprawled in the center of the room under a thick tapestry comforter Morgana had embroidered herself. If the knight the spread depicted resembled Percival, that was nobody's business but her own. She'd always been able to use her magic to change the spread's appearance if she needed to keep a lover from seeing it.

A big floor-length mirror occupied one corner, near an oak armoire large enough to accommodate an entire Broadway show's costume wardrobe. A comfortable armchair sat opposite the mirror, next to a floor lamp and a bookshelf stuffed three-deep with paperbacks.

Brilliant oils lined the walls, depicting images of brawny nude gods and graceful goddesses. Fifteen centuries had given Morgana a lot of time to learn to paint, and she'd gotten reasonably good at it. She had an art studio just down the hall; the smell of oil and linseed filled the floor, the scent pleasant to Morgana's artist's nose.

Now, though, she needed sleep. With a weary sigh, she pulled off Percival's ridiculously loose pants and crawled into bed.

NINE

Teeth ripped into Morgana's scaled hide with the savage sensation of tearing flesh and raw agony. She cried out at the stark pain; her voice sounded deep, bestial—a dragon's roar.

It had her. *The dragon killer had her again, and he meant to eat her, the way he'd ripped into those girls.*

I'm going to die!

Morgana threw herself skyward, her wings beating desperately as she tried to tear herself from the fanged grip of her draconic foe. He roared, wrapping his massive body around her, squeezing and suffocating her with his merciless grip.

She wasn't strong enough to get away.

Desperately, she reached for the magic of the Mageverse, dragging pure power into her body. More and more and MORE, *until her very consciousness seemed to blaze.*

Twisting in the dragon's grip, she opened her jaws and let magic boil out in a savage blast of power. Her enemy squealed in agony . . .

And began to burn.

As he convulsed, she threw herself upward, flinging herself from his grip. Wings beating as she shot upward, she threw a glance downward.

The dragon blazed, shrieking, writhing, his body twisting as her magic seared him, but she felt no pity.

All she felt was the bright euphoria she felt whenever she drank in the Mageverse's power. She felt drunk on the sense that she could do anything. Nobody could stop her. The proof was that enemy dragon, dying a well-deserved death in the flaming grip of her power.

Victorious, Morgana soared over the battlefield, roaring in triumph as her foe burned. Swooping downward, she swept her gaze over the scene, determined to make sure the dragon had no more allies.

And that she had no more enemies.

Three men stared up at her, their expressions fierce, determined, weapons raised. Anger flashed through her. How dare they oppose her? She, who had suffered, fought, bled. Morgana opened her jaws . . .

And Percival died, screaming in pain as her fire boiled over him, Cador and Marrok blazing and howling at his side.

Morgana jerked awake to the sound of her own horrified shriek. She collapsed back against the pile of pillows, shaking with the sickening aftereffects of her nightmare. Sucking in a deep breath, she scrubbed her trembling hands over her sweating face.

Knowing sleep was a lost cause after her second ugly nightmare of the day—though a glance at the bedside clock revealed it was barely noon—Morgana started to roll out of bed. She stopped dead with a gasp as her sore muscles complained bitterly at the attempt to move so quickly. Definitely *not* a good idea.

Morgana worked her way out of bed until she could plant both bare feet on the floor. Limping over to the full-length mirror, she lifted the hem of Percival's T-shirt and raised it over her shoulders. Turning around, she studied her reflection.

And blinked. Her arse looked better than she'd half-expected based on her flinching body's aching protests. True, there were a few long bruises from the crop, but other than that, he hadn't done much damage. Except, perhaps, for the bite on one breast where he'd fed.

Studying the crop marks, she was surprised to feel her nipples draw into tight points. The way he'd paced around her, so deliciously sexy, so dominant. So hot . . .

Her fingers lifted without her conscious intent to brush the engraved metal of her collar, heavy and cool around her throat.

Staring at her bare, peaked nipple with its fang mark, she remembered Percival's deep, heavy thrusts as he drank. Remembered heat rolled over her, and she closed her eyes. *Percival died, screaming in pain as her fire boiled over him, Cador and Marrok blazing and howling at his side.*

Morgana's eyes flew open as she felt that sickening dip in her stomach again. Horned God, she hoped that wasn't a vision. *Let it only be a nightmare, Mother Goddess.*

Feeling a bit sick, Morgana dropped the hem of her T-shirt and let the soft, loose cotton slip down over her shoulders to her hips.

It wasn't the first time she'd had a nightmare about killing Percival and his team, though the details had differed over the years. But in every one of those dreams, the three knights fought back hard. Sometimes they died in the attempt, but other times Morgana fell to them in her bitter madness.

The dream means nothing, she told herself firmly. *Just because I fear something, that doesn't mean it's going to happen.* Otherwise the details of the dream would be the same every time. She'd had enough genuine visions to know that much.

Shaking off the nightmare's sticky mental aftermath, Morgana pulled open the armoire and began to search for something to wear. Unfortunately, the pickings were pretty slim: a wool dress too hot for the weather, a pair of jeans a size too big, a couple of ratty T-shirts.

When you could conjure anything you wanted on a whim, you tended not to keep the clothing you made.

She was digging in the matching chest of drawers when she heard a brisk knock at the front door.

Well, it wasn't Percival or one of his knights; the sun was still up. Which left a Maja, though Morgana wasn't exactly overwhelmed with friends. She trotted downstairs to find out who'd dropped by. Pulling the hem of Percival's shirt down over her bare thighs, Morgana opened the massive front door.

Guinevere Pendragon gave her a sunny smile. "Hi, Morgana."

"Uh . . . hi." When the former queen looked at her expectantly, she stepped back. "Come in!" *Tea. Do I have any tea I can serve?*

"Thanks." The pretty blonde strode in, slim and lovely in jeans and a striped pink polo shirt. The whole outfit just screamed "soccer mom" in a marked contrast to the regal High Queen of Britain Guinevere had once been.

The witch's clever blue eyes swept over her, taking in the too-big T-shirt and bare feet. Her gaze lingered on the power nullification collar with its thick Celtic engraving. "How was your night?"

"Ummm . . ." Morgana considered and discarded several responses as she turned and led the way into the elaborate sitting room to the right of the foyer. The room was dominated by a marble and gold fireplace with flanking Greek goddesses. A pair of graceful settees, both in a deep, verdantly green velvet, stoodflanked by antique tables.

Morgana seated herself gingerly on one of the couches, biting her lip as her bruised backside and thighs complained. As Gwen sat down beside her, she said dryly, "Well, it's safe to say it was a bit . . . intense."

"Yeah, I expected as much, after my idiot husband told me about the ultimatum he gave you." Reaching out, she started to brush her fingers over the collar, then jerked her hand back as if it had burned her. "That thing has a bite, doesn't it? But then, it would have to, to strip *you* of your powers."

She frowned. "How did you know about the collar? Arthur just told me to offer Percival my Oath of Service. I added the collar because he would have refused otherwise."

Gwen grimaced. "I had a vision. Saw that collar of yours and knew what you'd done. You twit."

Morgana studied her uneasily. To give her hands something to do, she reached for the crystal decanter on the sideboard and poured each of them a glass of wine. "What did you see?" If a witch had a vision about something, the implications were usually pretty grim.

Guinevere's gaze flickered uneasily. "To be honest, I'm not really sure. I saw . . . fire. And a dragon—I think it was the one you fought last night. And you and your team, but none of it made a hell of a lot of sense. But that collar . . ." She frowned. "I think you need to get rid of it, Morgana. I think it's going to be a problem."

She stiffened. "No."

"Morgana, you . . ."

"If I got rid of the collar, Percival would consider it a violation of my Oath. Besides, he's the only one who can take the thing off, so I'm basically stuck with it anyway."

Guinevere's expression went flat and cool. "I could remove it."

Of course she could. After all, Morgana had always intended her as a failsafe if something went wrong with the collar. She sighed and admitted reluctantly, "I don't want it off, Gwen."

Her friend scowled. "Dammit, Morgana . . ."

Morgana's fingers brushed over the cool metal circlet, taking reassurance from it. "I need this."

Percival died, screaming in pain as her fire boiled over him, Cador and Marrok blazing and shrieking at his side . . .

As long as she wore the collar, they were safe.

Her old friend studied her face with that unnerving perception that had made her such a formidable queen. "You mean you need Percival."

Morgana found she couldn't quite hold Gwen's gaze. "Him and his team, certainly."

"Uh, huh." Gwen gave her a long look. "So how much damage did Percival do to your backside? And don't bother denying it, because I watched you sit down like there were pins in this overstuffed monstrosity of a settee."

Caught, Morgana could only laugh. "Yeah, okay, he plays pretty hard."

"There's a shock. Take off the shirt, Morgana."

Modesty was a waste of time after the years they'd spent together. She rose and stripped off the shirt.

Gwen inhaled sharply, reaching out to run a hand delicately down the length of her back. "He did enjoy himself, didn't he?"

Morgana felt her cheeks heat. "I suppose."

Her friend snorted and passed a hand along her spine again, but this time Morgana felt the bubbling heat of magic rolling from her fingertips. Instantly, the ache and pain of her bruises began to fade, vanishing completely a heartbeat later. "And he drank deep." Her tone chilled. "Almost too deep."

Morgana met her friend's gaze. "Yes."

Gwen closed her eyes, flattening her palm between her shoulders. Again, Morgana felt the rise and heat of her magic.

"So," the former queen said, opening her eyes and giving her an incisive glance, "it's obvious he enjoyed himself. But did you?"

"I . . ." Morgana took a deep breath and owned up, both to her friend and herself. "Yes. I did enjoy it."

Gwen lifted a blonde brow. "But you're not sure you should have."

"Well, let's face it, Gwen. He flogged my arse, fucked me silly, and milked me like Bessie. And it hurt."

Her friend gave her a slow, wicked grin. "And you loved every minute of it."

She laughed, a trifle uncomfortably. "I did."

"Of course you did. Percival's hotter than hell."

Morgana shot her a mock-scandalized glance. "Why, Guinevere Pendragon! Shame on you, lusting after one of Arthur's knights . . ."

"And after I confess my evil thoughts, I assure you Arthur will make me pay dearly." Gwen settled back in her seat, one corner of her lip quirking up. "And he uses a single-tail."

"Does he?" Morgana blinked. She'd had her suspicions about her half-brother's tastes, but Gwen had never come right out and admitted it. "You don't sound particularly worried."

"Probably because I'm looking forward to it. In the meantime . . ." Her eyes narrowed. ". . . let's tend to your wardrobe issues—and your larder. I doubt there's a loaf of bread in this entire mausoleum you call a house. Let's start with the closet."

Morgana could only shake her head as she rose and led the way upstairs. "You do know me entirely too well."

"After all these centuries?" Gwen snorted. "I damned well should."

"Guess so." Morgana crossed her bedroom to swing the armoire door open. "And you're right. I do feel a little uncomfortable about enjoying Percival's . . . games. It seems wrong somehow, finding pleasure in being flogged."

Her friend hesitated, as if considering what to say as she swept a glance into the wardrobe. "My God, this thing is so empty, it practically echoes." She gestured, beginning to conjure pairs of jeans in a variety of shades and styles. Every one of which would no doubt fit Morgana like a coat of paint. Shooting her a sidelong glance, Gwen continued, "And you sound like one of those medieval priests, convinced that pleasure is somehow sinful."

She snorted. "It's been my experience that priests were only concerned about the sins of other people. Their own evidently didn't count."

"Not all priests are like Father Bennett, Morgana. In fact, the majority of them were every bit as devout as they appeared." Gwen flicked her fingers, sending out a stream of magic to become blouses and tops. "But we're getting off the subject. My point is that there's nothing wrong with anything that you and your partner both enjoy, so long as it doesn't inflict real damage on either of you. Or hurt anyone else, for that matter."

"But I'm Liege of the Majae, Gwen. I'm not supposed to . . ."

"Who said?" Guinevere retorted, propping both hands on her hips. "Because if there's a contract somewhere that says a Liege isn't supposed to be kinky, Arthur's in violation."

"Arthur's a dominant."

"And you're a submissive. None of which has a damn thing to do with your ability to do your respective jobs."

"Granted, but . . . Look, Gwen, I suppose what I'm trying to say is that it's a little frightening, giving up control to Percival like that. All my life, I've had to be in control. And when I wasn't . . ." She shrugged. "Bad things happened, either to me or innocent people."

"And that's exactly why giving up control to Percival feels so good." Gwen gestured at the band circling Morgana's throat. "In that collar, you don't have to worry about controlling anything, not even your own magic. It's all in Percival's hands. And you can relax, because he's the kind of man who can be trusted to take care of the burdens you've put down, if only temporarily."

"Yes," Morgana admitted slowly. "He does give that impression."

"Darling, it's not just an impression. I have never known of Percival to drop the ball on anything. And I've known him even longer than you have." She started conjuring pairs of shoes—boots, stilettoes, pumps, all in a rainbow of colors. "You've been carrying the weight of your responsibilities for a very long time. It's not a sin to leave them in Percival's capable hands for a few hours so you can . . . rest."

Morgana snorted. "Or something."

"Speaking of Percival's hands," Gwen added wickedly, "let's talk sexy underwear. Does he prefer you in lace, silk, or rubber?"

Morgana couldn't help it. She roared with laughter.

* * *

Morgana had disobeyed.

Percival stalked into the top floor of his mansion, a sword in one hand, a shield in the other. The gym was the biggest room in the house of necessity, between the running track, free weights, assorted weight machines, and the huge ring padded with sawdust he and his brothers used to practice their combat skills first thing every evening.

He was certainly in the mood to kick some arse at the moment. Good thing Marrok and Cador were already present, ragging one another about the submissive they'd shared after leaving Percival and Morgana the night before.

Evidently the thought of Morg as an Oath Servant had turned them on as much as it had him.

As always, Percival had woken precisely at sunset, a wicked grin curling his mouth, expecting to see Morgana waiting for him as he'd ordered. His cock had instantly hardened at the thought of the wet swirl of her tongue, the tight, liquid clasp of her cunt.

The even tighter grip of the arse he hadn't gotten around to breaching last night.

And that was just the beginning of what he intended to do. He'd had years of fantasies about Morgana—of forcing her to admit the submissive needs he'd always suspected. About what it would be like when she finally yielded to his dominance.

Last night he'd found, to his immense satisfaction, that he'd been right: she was indeed a submissive. She'd yielded deliciously, responding with hot need even when he'd tested her with the crop.

He wanted more.

He wanted to claim that tight, exquisite arse, listen to her cries of surrender as he again drank deep of her blood.

And held her in the aftermath, listening to the sound of her heartbeat, the sigh of her breathing . . .

Which was why he was so pissed when she'd been nowhere to be seen. Not in his bedroom, not in his living room. Not even in the dungeon, where the bitch damn well should present herself if she knew what was good for her. All greased up and ready for punishment.

So much for her Oath.

Unless something had prevented her from obeying his order. Frowning, he remembered the nightmare she'd had about her son. *"Don't touch me like that!"*

She'd felt so fragile in his arms. Which was a surprise, since fragility was not a word he'd ever associated with Morgana le Fay.

Bad dreams or not, I gave her an order, Percival thought. *She was supposed to be here at sunset, and she wasn't.*

She'd given him her Oath just yesterday. He was damned if he was going to let her get away with flouting him this soon. The minute he finished with combat practice, he was going to track her down and teach her a badly needed lesson.

"Enough chat," he growled at his friends, interrupting their argument about who'd banged last night's Morgana substitute harder. "Let's fight." Glowering at Marrok and Cador, Percival fell into guard, lifting his backup shield into position. His primary armor and weapons had been beaten and clawed all to hell in the fight with the dragon, and Morgana hadn't repaired them before accepting the collar that had stripped her of her powers. They were going to have to find some other Maja to repair the damage.

Morgana bloody well wasn't going to get her powers back any time soon. Not if Percival had anything to say about it.

"So how was the witch?" Marrok asked, as he raised his own shield and sidestepped into a warrior's crouch. "I trust you striped that sweet arse red . . ."

". . . And fucked it just as hard," Cador threw in, his teeth flashing white as he circled in the opposite direction.

Percival's only reply was a snarl as he leaped at Marrok, his sword swinging wide around his shield to slam into the big man's blade. Marrok jumped back out of range with an oath. Percival pursued him, only to be forced into retreat himself when Cador attacked in a flurry of sword-strokes. Swords rang on shields, and Cador swore as Percival's blade sliced across his shoulder, the wound shallow but painful.

The bitter scent of vampire blood filled the air, making Percival's fangs twinge as he went after his friends at just short of full speed.

How dare she ignore a direct order? Furious, he probed Marrok's defenses again, trying to find a way past the big vampire's guard. *Does your Oath mean nothing to you, Morgana? Well, this will be the last time you'll disobey an order of mine. I'll flog you bloody . . .*

Unless she'd been unable to obey. He had fed pretty deep last night. What if he'd taken too much, and she was lying unconscious somewhere, without the magic to heal herself—or even summon a healer?

The thought sent a wave of ice rolling over his skin, a chilly terror so distracting, he didn't even see Marrok's sword coming until an explosion of stars lit his skull.

He went down like a felled ox.

"Hey." A hand the size of a turkey breast slapped his cheek once, then twice. "Hey, Percival. Rouse and rise, my friend."

He caught the thick wrist before the man could hit him a third time. "Stop that." His voice sounded slurred, and he struggled to remember where they were and what they were doing. It must have been one hell of a hit. But who had done the honors?

The dragon . . . Percival jerked upright amid the thick sawdust of the practice ring.

"You're lucky Marrok struck you with the flat of his blade instead of the edge." Cador studied him, frowning.

"Fortunately, I noticed how damned distracted you were," Marrok growled, concern in his dark eyes as he knelt by Percival's side. "What the hell is going on? First you're going after us like it's actual combat instead of practice. Then you damned near *nod off* right in the middle of an engagement. What the fuck is your problem?"

Cador snorted. "I can tell you that—and her name is Morgana le Fay."

Marrok's thick brows lowered as Percival reeled to his feet and brushed the sawdust off his practice leathers. "That right, Percival? I thought the whole idea was to get the witch *out* of your system, not let her burrow in deeper."

Percival felt his cheeks heat as his two friends eyed him. "Morgana is my concern, not yours," he snapped at Cador. "I'll handle her as I see fit."

"Yeeeah, riiiiiight," the other knight drawled. "Because you're obviously doing such a good job of handling her right now."

"Fuck off." A chill slid over him again as he remembered the fear that had so distracted him during that weapons pass.

Was Morgana all right?

He bent to pick his sword up out of the sawdust, flicked off a few clinging wood chips, and sheathed it with the speed of long practice. Without another word to either of his friends, he headed toward the gym door.

She'd better be all right. But if she was, he was going to teach her the error of her ways.

Frowning, Marrok watched Percival stalk out, the set of his shoulders rigid with rage. "I don't like the looks of this. She's getting to him."

"We knew she would. She's good at that." One corner of Cador's lip lifted. "Women generally are."

Marrok grunted. What few people knew was that Cador was actually a disillusioned romantic. As the second son of a minor king centuries ago, he'd been the prey of every plotting pretty woman in his father's court. Cador had been only about fifteen or sixteen at the time, young enough to be easily seduced—and even more easily hurt. Again and again, he'd fall in love to discover the object of his affections was only using him to get to his brother, the king's heir.

Apparently those women had been pretty vicious in their scorn for Cador's gullibility.

When sixteen-year-old King Arthur had come through recruiting warriors to join his fight to reconquer his father's fractured territories, Cador had been glad to join him and leave the scene of his repeated humiliation behind.

Like Marrok, he'd quickly fallen into Percival's charismatic orbit. The three men—actually, boys at the time—had soon learned to fight as a lethal unit. It hadn't been long before Arthur had made all three of them Knights of the Round Table.

Then Morgana had come along, and promptly become Percival's obsession.

"Not that I can blame Percival for wanting to put the little bitch on her knees," Cador said. "I'd kill to get a piece of that myself."

"Who wouldn't?" Marrok agreed. "That woman could give a corpse a cock-stand."

"The question is how are we going to keep her from gutting Percival while he's distracted by all the blood leaving his head for his dick?"

"By doing the only thing we can do: keep a damned close eye on them." Marrok bared his teeth. "And be ready to shut her down cold before she can do any real damage."

Percival found Morgana lying on her bed on a pile of fur, the sable a gorgeous contrast to her creamy skin. For a moment, he stared at her, caught between relief and worry; she lay unmoving. Hell, she barely even seemed to be breathing.

He moved around the bed until he could see her naked back. He'd flogged subs before, and he knew the effects of the kind of erotic beating he'd given her. There should have been at least a few long, slashing bruises across her arse and thighs, but the lush skin was unmarked. Bending his head as he stood over her, he listened with his vampire hearing and was promptly reassured by the steady, strong thump of her heartbeat.

She may not have obeyed him when it came to presenting herself to him at sunset, but at least she'd had the sense to call a healer.

Percival found himself wishing he could have stayed with her in the aftermath of her punishment. He'd always enjoyed giving his submissives aftercare—the affection and cossetting that was as much a part of BDSM as the discipline itself. Such play had a way of stripping away a sub's emotional shields, leaving her painfully vulnerable. It was a top's responsibility to help his bottom deal with those emotions.

He wanted to see Morgana like that—stripped of those formidable defenses. Open to him in every sense, not just sexually. Staring down at her, Percival was abruptly aware of a wave of need that darkened even as he gazed at her pale, lovely curves. She looked almost innocent as she lay curled there, though he knew she was anything but. Still, the effect sharpened his hunger into a ruthless craving.

Her arse was beautiful. He stared at the sweet, lush curves of her backside with its peach cleft, so deliciously tempting. His cock jerked in raw lust as he imagined the tight pucker between those pretty cheeks. What a delicious punishment that would be. Forcing his big dick into that tiny channel, grinding deep, listening to her moaning gasps as he buggered her mercilessly . . .

He grinned, feeling his fangs lengthen as his cock hardened at the thought of everything he was going to do to Morgana le Fay.

TEN

A big hand wrapped around her jaw and dragged her head back. "Comfortable, Morgana?" Percival growled, his deep voice rumbling in her ear. "The sun has been down for fifty minutes, and I find you *still in fucking bed.*"

Panic splashed over her like an ice water bath, and she jolted awake, eyes flaring wide. Instinctively, she tried to roll out of bed, only to feel brawny arms drag her back against a big body. Half-awake, she tried to fight—but that, of course, did her no good at all, given that Percival was easily six inches taller and a hundred pounds heavier. Being a Maja made Morgana stronger than a human male her size, but nowhere near strong enough to match all that vampire muscle.

"I'm sorry," she gasped. "Gwen healed me, and I just meant to lie down for a moment, but I don't have an alarm clock and . . ."

"Are you giving me *excuses?*"

She swallowed as her brain belatedly came on line. "No, my Lord Percival."

He grunted. "At least you remembered my title this time."

"Does that disappoint you?" She instantly wished she'd kept her mouth shut. It was definitely not the time for sarcasm.

The big hand tightened around her throat, his grip almost ruthless enough to make her choke. Almost. "I don't need an excuse to beat your tempting arse, my dear." He licked the curve of her throat, making her shiver. "I can do it just because I'm bored."

Powerful thighs wrapped around hers, tightening as one arm slid under hers, pulling her torso into an arch that forced her breasts out. A wide, warm palm covered a curving mound, long fingers plucking and twisting its peak. The sensation made her shudder and catch her breath. He teased her breasts slowly, first one and then the other, before sliding his hand down between her thighs. His fingers teased her erect clit and skated in her heating cream.

God, it felt good. So nakedly erotic. So maddening. "Percival . . ." she whimpered.

"Lord Percival."

Her tongue couldn't seem to manage the extra syllable. She could only groan and shiver as he tormented her with a sadist's skill. "Like that?" he demanded, all black velvet heat.

"Ooooh," she whimpered, unable to manage any reply more coherent than that.

He laughed, a dark male growl of satisfaction, and rolled her over on her stomach. Morgana opened her mouth to protest, only to freeze as he plucked a pair of leather cuffs from a gym bag on the bedside table. She realized he must have brought it with him.

Damned if she'd just lie there and submit. Morgana bucked against his merciless grip as he began buckling on the restraints. "Stop that!" he snapped in an unyielding tone. His broad male hand descended on her backside with a loud SWAT that sent an explosion of hot pain through her cheeks. Startled by the intensity of the sting, Morgana screeched. Ignoring her, Percival calmly finished fastening the cuffs and clipped them together behind her back. When he reached for her ankles, she gave him an instinctive kick. "Percival, you . . ."

"Don't you think you've pushed me far enough?" he growled, clamping her thighs together between his own. Morgana fought—she couldn't help herself—but it was like being caught in an industrial vise. There was absolutely no way to break Percival's grip as he deliberately paused, spinning out the wait as he contemplated her bare arse.

Morgana felt her face go hot under that fierce stare.

He lifted his hand, paused an agonizing second, and brought it down with a meaty smack that made her arse jiggle. Heat instantly flushed through her dancing flesh. "Very nice. How does it feel knowing I can do anything I want to you?"

She swallowed. Her heart hammered so hard she could feel it in her throat.

"I asked you a question." That hand came down again in another fiery blow. "How does it feel knowing I can beat your little rump until it's pretty and pink? How does it feel knowing my cock is going up your tight little arse—and there's absolutely nothing you can do to stop me?"

"I can say no," she gasped.

"You could," he retorted. "If you don't mind violating your Oath. I'd even stop." The hand rose and fell and rose again, each swat more painfully intense than the ones he'd given her before. "And then I'll get up and walk out, and you will *never* go on another mission with my team again."

Morgana swallowed. She couldn't let that happen, no matter what he chose to do to her.

By the time he flipped her back onto the bed, her rump was red hot and her teeth were set against threatening tears. He cuffed her ankles and attached them to a spreader bar he pulled from that bag of his. She lay there, blinking hard against the sting in her eyes, as he produced a length of chain he looped around the foot of the bed.

The most humiliating thing about the whole experience was how wet her pussy was. Something about being spanked and chained triggered a fierce arousal such as she'd never felt before.

Her pride stung almost as much as her arse cheeks. Panting, Morgana glowered at Percival and growled, "You're such a prick."

"You're really pushing it with that insolence." He grinned, flashing fangs in a display that made her wonder whether he was more pissed or aroused. With vampires, it could be either.

With Percival, it was probably both.

Rolling off the bed, he started to strip out of his combat leathers. He dropped his scabbarded sword with a clatter at the foot of the bed, then shucked off his boots, leather jacket, and pants.

Her mouth went dry as she contemplated his towering strength, all cut, brawny muscularity.

And that dick. It jutted at her, looking every bit as thick as her wrist, with its ruddy head and heavy balls. Pre-cum pearled on its slit as he stared at her with hot, possessive gray-wolf eyes.

"I've been waiting a long time for this, Morgana," he told her, his voice low, rough. "I can't tell you how many times I've jerked off thinking about doing this to you." As she watched, he delved in the black gym bag before pulling out a tube of lubricant. Squeezing it out in his palm, he started slicking it slowly over his cock, his eyes fixed on hers with an intensity that seemed to burn. "I trust you realize this is going to be more than a bit painful." He bared his teeth. "But then, you have it coming."

"What do *you* have coming?"

Percival's smile was slow and thoroughly menacing as his hand caressed the length of his cock. She had no idea why that savage expression made her nipples tighten and her pussy clench. "Let's find out, shall we?"

He picked up a pillow and stuffed it under her hips to lift her arse before kneeling astride her thighs. Morgana tensed, turning her head to watch him nervously. He grinned as he settled down over her, mantling her in thick muscle, his heavy cock pressing against her cheeks.

"Now," he murmured in her ear, "how shall I break you of this habit of insolence?" He licked her carotid slowly in another of those erotic threats he did so well. "And then there's the tardiness and lazy streak."

Despite the sadism evident in his hold, her sense of humor kicked in. "I'll admit to the insolence and tardiness, but I am *not* lazy."

"Were you or were you not *asleep* when your Master had commanded your presence?" He rolled his hips against her rump in a slow, deliberate grind. "That sounds lazy to me, Oath Servant."

"I didn't oversleep deliberately, my lord."

"Do you really think I give a damn?" Sliding a hand under her, he traced his fingers between her labia and then thrust deep into her pussy. He growled in pleasure at her wet, tight grip. "I must admit you don't seem to feel much dread at the prospect of your punishment . . . Though I'm afraid you may find what I have in mind a bit more painful than you expect."

"You do menace well, sir, but you're wasting your breath. I don't fear you."

"No." The vampire raked the tips of his fangs along the frantically thumping carotid that belied her bold words. "But you really should." He chuckled in an evil male rumble. "And before I'm done with you, you will."

She closed her eyes at the rush of hot, wet heat that pumped through her veins. "Do your worst." *Please.*

"Oh, I intend to." He sat back, kneeling astride her thighs as he contemplated her bottom with blatant lust as he reached for the tube of lube and squeezed a generous amount into his palm.

He took his time greasing her anus, stroking two fingers deep, stretching her mercilessly. "Ooh, yes," he purred. "You're going to be a delicious fuck. And I'm going to bugger you hard."

Morgana shuddered helplessly at the sensation of those big fingers readying her for his cock. She felt unspeakably aroused, even knowing how painful this was likely to be. She was no anal virgin, but the last time she'd attempted it had been a few decades back, and even then, her partner hadn't had Percival's savage size.

He was right: this was going to hurt.

And she didn't give a damn. The idea of being taken by her knight in this dark way, submitting to his dominance as she'd always secretly yearned to do . . . Morgana closed her eyes and shuddered. Horned God, she'd never been so hot in her life. Never felt so raw, so eager to fuck, to feel the deep thrusts of a man's cock in her arse.

And not just any cock, but Percival's. She hungered for his possession with a deep, helpless yearning. Even if it hurt.

Maybe especially if it hurt.

"There now." He contemplated her well-greased ass with satisfaction. "I think you're ready for your lesson in obedience."

The vampire knight mounted her, and Morgana tensed, arousal burning through her blood. Bracing himself on one arm, he positioned his cock. Hot, smooth skin brushed the tight, tiny pucker. "Now, look up."

She raised her eyes and saw that at some point he'd moved her big full-length mirror so that it reflected the bed. Her reflected face looked pale and anxious. Percival's looked predatory.

"Really, my lord?" She forced a superior smile. "Isn't voyeurism beneath you?"

"No." He leaned closer until she felt the heat of each word breathed against her ear. "I want to watch your face while I stuff your arse full of cock. Do *not* close your eyes, and do not look away." He paused to taste the skin of her throat just above her collar in a way that suggested he was trying to decide where to bite. "I want you to watch your face in the mirror while you get it."

Her eyes looked huge and anxious, her reflected face white as he covered her. He was so much larger than she was, his biceps and upper arms looking massive holding her down. She'd never seen herself as delicate, or particularly feminine, but she felt like a doll held in Percival's merciless grip.

Instinctively, she tightened down as he began to press his way inside, though she knew it was exactly the wrong thing to do. She just couldn't seem to stop herself.

Her anus began to sting ferociously around his merciless cock, the sensation building to a hot ache as it opened under the ruthless pressure. In the mirror, her green eyes widened even more as he circled his hips, screwing his way past the tight inner muscles one blazing inch at a time.

Morgana bit her lip, fighting the impulse to plead. She knew her Oath Master wasn't in the mood to listen.

"Mmmm," Percival rumbled as he slowly, sloooowly, entered her arse. "Very nice. I love the way you're gripping my cock like a fist." Bracing himself on his elbows as he forced another fraction deeper and lowered his head until he could whisper in her ear. "I'll bet that hurrrrrts."

"You're a bastard," she gasped.

"I certainly am." The knight licked her ear and wrapped his hand around the front of her throat. "And you've got a delicious arse that just begs for reaming. I don't mind telling you, this is my favorite kind of punishment, especially with such a delightfully snug victim."

The fire built, the ache growing hotter and hotter as he rocked his hips and forced her arse to spread.

Finally his heavy balls nestled against her bottom, and he rumbled in possessive satisfaction. "In to the balls. How does that feel?"

Biting her lip, she refused to answer until he ground in with sadistic skill, tormenting the delicate inner tissues into a blaze of pain. "I asked you a question."

"Ahhh! It hurts, you . . ." Stopping, she belatedly corrected herself. "It hurts, my lord. As you very well know."

He laughed. "A good punishment is supposed to hurt." Circling his hips, he gave her another hard grind. "And you've got it coming, don't you?"

Teeth clenched, she made no answer.

He lifted his head, so that his gaze impaled hers in the mirror, narrow and cold in stark contrast to the heat of his possession. "*You have it coming, don't you?*"

"Yes, my lord." She looked away.

"Eyes on me, Morgana!" he rapped out, and her head snapped up to meet his stare again. "For the record," he growled, "I'm not talking about the petty, nasty shit you've done to me over the past fifteen hundred years."

He reared over her, deepening the penetration another brutal fraction until there wasn't room enough for a hair between them. She gasped.

"I'm talking about what you did to my brothers just because you fucking could. The casual jolts and magical cruelties you inflicted on men who couldn't defend themselves—men who then had to fight and defend you because you were their teammate, and that was their duty. All that shit was beneath you, Morgana, and you know it."

Her eyes stung as she stared into those hot, contemptuous eyes. "Yes, my lord."

"'Yes, my lord,' what?"

"Yes, using my power against them was beneath me, my lord," Morgana admitted, feeling the bite of shame more acutely even than the pain of his possession.

And he was right. She'd had no business hitting them with those ugly magical zaps—spells designed to humiliate as much as hurt as a way of forcing them to submit to her. She'd known that by rights, she should have been following Percival rather than the other way around.

The thing was, Morgana had feared yielding to him, feared surrender. But it had never really been Percival she'd feared. It had been herself.

She didn't trust her own reaction if he rejected her. She wasn't sure she'd be able to manage the pain and rage she knew she'd feel. It was just too damned dangerous.

But Percival, of course, knew none of that.

"And when I decide to trust you with your powers again—or when your year at my hands is up—you'll remember what it's like to be the target of casual cruelty, and you'll resist the fucking impulse." He pulled out a fraction and shoved back in hard enough to wrench a gasp from her lips. "Won't you?"

"Yes, my lord." Blinking, she stared into his savage eyes and managed not to quail.

"'Yes, my lord,' what? Spell it out, witch."

"Yes, my lord, I vow never again to misuse my powers against you or your brothers."

He lifted his upper lip in a snarl, flashing his fangs at her in the mirror. "*Especially* not my brothers."

"Especially not Cador and Marrok," she managed.

His gaze in the mirror softened not one jot at her submission. Instead he began drawing his cock out of her arse.

And Morgana caught her breath in surprise at the sudden astonishing pleasure of the sensation. It was a complex, alien sensation compared to the feeling of being fucked more conventionally, but it was no less intense. Perhaps even more so. "Oh!"

"Yeah," he grunted. "'Oh.' There are a great many pleasure receptors in a woman's rectum—almost as many as in her clit. So if a man knows what he's doing, he can play all kinds of interesting games." Percival paused and gave her a very dark smile. "I *definitely* know what I'm doing."

The only response she could manage was a helpless moan—which spiraled into a startled yelp when he slid two fingers into her empty cunt and curled them, stroking along the knot of nerves that was her G-spot. "And there. How do you like that?"

He'd pulled out until only the head of his cock remained inside her, then began pushing deep, rocking his hips to inflict that eye-watering torment again. Except this time, he teased her G-spot to blend pleasure and pain with erotic artistry.

Soon she was writhing at the combination of ruthless delight. He picked up the pace, fucking in and out faster and faster. Horned God, it was overwhelming—the pulsing blasts of raw sensation, so intense that she shook with it.

And the whole time he fucked her, she was conscious of his gray, possessive gaze watching her reactions in the mirror. Relishing every gasp and whimper with predatory delight.

Right up until he leaned over her carotid and sank his fangs deep.

She came with a helpless shriek, twisting in his ruthless hold as his cock probed her anus and his soft lips sealed over the wounds his fangs inflicted. Stiffening, he climaxed with a low, animal growl of pleasure. Morgana could only gasp, shuddering as he pumped her arse full of his come in deep, hard pulses.

Percival freed her from the wrist cuffs and spreader bar, gave her a bottle of water and ordered her to drink it, then started getting dressed.

Lying in a naked heap, Morgana watched him clothe that magnificent body of his, feeling dazed, her arse and punctured throat stinging from his use.

Without looking around at her, he told her, "This Sunday is the Super Bowl . . ."

Morgana frowned. She thought that was some kind of sporting event involving the American version of football. "Why would you care?"

He turned to give her a steady look. "Because Arthur is of the opinion that we need to be familiar with contemporary culture if we're to understand the people we serve."

She shrugged, shifting uncomfortably and longing for the hot shower she meant to take as soon as he left. "Of course." Arthur's position had always been that they needed to have a solid understanding of as many human cultures as possible. That, however, didn't answer the question of why the sudden fascination with this particular sporting event, out of all the thousands that obsessed mortals.

"I intend to invite my brothers over to watch the game. You may not be aware of the finer details of this tradition, but one is expected to serve food to one's guests." He gave her a slow, toothy grin. "Which is where you come in."

Morgana stiffened. "What?"

He lifted a blond brow. "I'll be serving you to my brothers, Morgana. As I said, after all the years you've spent tormenting us, they deserve the chance to make you pay."

She licked her lips. "When you say serving . . ."

"I mean sexually." His gaze was distinctly predatory. "Among other things."

The Lord's Club was located in an elegant brick Georgian that had the decor of a Victorian men's club, between its dark, carved wainscoting, stained glass windows, and impressive bar stocked with glittering crystal bottles of expensive liquor. Massive chairs upholstered in oxblood leather sat around circular tables of dark walnut.

Those tables were crowded tonight, between Knights of the Round Table, assorted national champions, and other vampires drinking, laughing, and telling lies, either about the women they'd fucked or the fights they'd had.

Percival found himself a solitary corner table where he sat down to start working his way steadily through a bottle of Jack Daniels. No matter how he tried, he couldn't seem to pry his mind away from memories of his possession of Morgana earlier in the night.

God, it had been sweet. The grip of the witch's delicious anus as he'd fucked her deep—just as deep as he'd fantasized about in all those frustrated wet dreams. And the taste of her blood had been exquisite.

But after you fed from a Maja, you had to lick the punctures to encourage them to seal quickly, or she could lose too much blood. So he'd held her and tongued that soft, smooth throat, enjoying the intoxicating taste of magic fizzing on his tongue.

And she'd felt delicious in his arms. So soft, so warm and curving and female. Nothing like he'd have expected from such a cool-eyed, aloof woman.

The thought of letting any other man touch her made him grind his teeth. Even his brothers. Yeah, he'd happily give his life for Cador and Marrok, but a primitive part of him growled like a wolf at the thought of them fucking her. Never mind that they had a right to punish her for what she'd spent years doing to them. He'd meant what he said: there was no excuse for the way she'd treated them with such casual cruelty.

None of that meant a damn thing to the possessive wolf inside him.

"Mind if I join you?"

Percival glanced up to see Galahad standing beside the table, holding a glass and a bottle of Johnnie Walker. The big man wore jeans and a sports coat over an Oxford cloth shirt in pale blue. He gave his fellow Knight of the Round Table a nod. "Have a seat."

"Thank you." The big knight sank into the chair opposite him and poured himself a glass, then lifted the bottle at him in question.

"Thanks, but I think I'll stick with Gentleman Jack."

Galahad took a sip of the liquor, studying him over the rim of his glass, his gaze probing and entirely too perceptive. "I gather congratulations are in order."

Percival frowned. "For what?"

"Word is Arthur ordered Morgana to offer you her Oath of Service, and you accepted." He lifted a dark brow. "Even provided you with a collar to nullify her powers. Which means you've pretty much got her at your mercy. When the word gets around, half the men in Avalon will be jealous as hell."

Percival swore. "I am going to kick Cador's arse." Marrok would never have blabbed something like that; his sense of honor was too acute.

"Actually, Gwen told Caroline when she got worried about not seeing Morg after the fight." Reaching into a breast pocket of his jacket, he withdrew a gold case and flipped it open, offering Percival one of the thick, hand-rolled Cuban cigars inside. "She was afraid Morgana had taken some kind of magical injury during the fight she didn't detect."

Choosing a cigar, Percival lit it from the thin gold lighter Galahad offered next. "Thank you."

The knight selected a cigar of his own from the case, then lit it and took a few contemplative puffs. "So anyway, Gwen spilled the beans."

And of course, with a Truebonded couple, what one knew, they both knew. All of which was why it was so damned difficult to keep a secret in Avalon, especially if you were a Knight of the Round Table. Fucking *everybody* knew your business.

Percival shrugged. "Yeah, I accepted Morgana's Oath. Not entirely sure what the congratulations are for." There were knights who disliked Morgana enough to congratulate Percival on the chance to punish her, but Galahad wasn't on that list.

Actually, a punch in the teeth would have been more in character from the dark knight, especially if he'd known the way Percival had just buggered the hell out of Morgana. Galahad might be Truebonded to Caroline now, but Percival suspected he'd truly loved Morgana once. He'd certainly seemed wounded when it ended all those years ago.

Galahad hesitated a long moment before he said, "I was referring to the chance to finally get it right. Which had started looking pretty fucking remote."

Percival eyed him narrowly. "Get what right?"

The knight blew a gust of blue smoke in his direction. "You. Her. You're such a stubborn bastard, I was starting to think it would never happen. Luckily, Arthur must have gotten as frustrated as the rest of us who actually give a shit, and decided to play matchmaker."

"Matchmaker? Arthur Pendragon?" Percival started to laugh.

Galahad's flat stare sucked the humor right out of the idea. "I think you should know—if she were a different kind of woman, you're the last son of a bitch I'd want anywhere near her."

Percival eyed the knight as his temper began to steam. "Are you sure you're Truebonded?"

Galahad exhaled the smoke directly into his face this time. "Morg and my wife are friends."

And God knew Morgana didn't have many.

For the first time, Galahad looked away. "Everybody knows you like to play rough. So does Morgana. I . . ." He paused a long moment. "I never did. Tried it when we were together, but I couldn't give her what she needed."

Given that he was Lancelot du Lac's son—the man who'd basically invented chivalry—this was not a surprise. The surprise was that Galahad had once loved Morgana enough to even make the attempt.

The dark-haired knight turned to meet his gaze with a cool, level expression. "But the real reason Morg and I didn't make it was I'm not you."

He stubbed out his cigar in the crystal ashtray that sat on their table. "So you've got a chance. Don't fuck it up."

Dumbfounded, Percival watched Sir Galahad get up and walk away.

ELEVEN

"He's serving you to his partners as a *party platter?*" Gwen shook her head, laughing. "Jesu, that's kinky."

After Percival had left her lying dazed and sore—if sated—after her punishment, Morgana had showered, dressed in one of the outfits Gwen had conjured for her—jeans, running shoes, and a blue denim shirt—and gone in search of her friend.

She'd found her at the Ladies' Club, the sprawling Mediterranean-style restaurant where the Majae took turns providing the meals.

It had taken a certain amount of guts just to walk in the door, because Morgana had known perfectly well everyone would sense her utter lack of powers. Between that and her collar, the stares and questions had driven the two women into a secluded corner half-hidden by huge plants and a statue of Aphrodite.

Morgana looked up from her excellent veal parmesan to find Gwen studying her. "So what do you think about the idea of Percival sharing you with Cador and Marrok?"

She managed a casual shrug, despite the ball of heat that ignited low in her belly at the thought. "Well, considering I initially offered my Oath to all three of them, it's obviously not a distasteful idea."

Gwen snorted. "You don't fool me, Morgana le Fay. You find the very thought hotter than hell."

"Maybe." Morgana grinned and asked in a teasing tone, "And how is *your* arse today?"

"I'd be sitting on a pillow if I hadn't already healed myself." The blonde's smile turned downright feline. "Arthur can be such a bastard . . . especially when I go out of my way to make him jealous."

"Why would he get jealous? You two are Truebonded, for Merlin's sake. He knows you're not going to cheat on him."

The minute the words were out of her mouth, Morgana controlled a wince. Gwen *had* cheated on Arthur once. Never mind that it had been fifteen hundred years ago, or that both she and Lancelot had been under the influence of Merlin's Grail. The wizard's cup had transformed them into Magekind, but a side-effect of the potion was a savagely heightened sexual desire. To make matters worse, Lancelot, having just transformed, had been in a state of animal lust, with no idea who Gwen was at all. Gwen was in little better shape.

Things had gotten thoroughly out of hand. And Arthur had damned near killed them both.

"Yes, well, luckily, the wounds from that particular adventure have long since healed, so I can get away with teasing him," Gwen said dryly. "All I have to do is dwell artistically on the way some knight swings a sword . . . And voila! I get exactly what I'm after."

"A sore arse?"

Her friend grinned. "Among other things."

"Slut."

Gwen raised her wine glass in a toast. "Absolutely."

Chuckling, Morgana returned the gesture and took a sip of the light, sweet Riesling. Putting the glass down again, she began, "Speaking of drinking . . ."

"You need some way to heal yourself during Percival's Super Bowl party. Be a damned shame to pass out from blood loss just when things got interesting."

"To put it mildly."

"I've actually been thinking about this," Gwen said. "I think I could attach a healing spell to that collar of yours. Besides, considering how much magic it's diverting, it would probably be a good idea to burn some of that energy off."

Morgana considered the idea and nodded slowly. "Yes, that should work. I was going to suggest my mission ring as an anchor for the spell, but you're right, the collar would work even better."

So, trying to ignore the flare of heat at the thought of her team's revenge, Morgana went to work helping Gwen compose the spell.

It was past midnight when Morgana lay curled in bed, fighting the impulse to masturbate.

Percival wouldn't like that.

Unfortunately, the memory of her Oath Master's cock savaging her arse was ferociously arousing.

Then there was the thought of that damned Super Bowl party, and being at the mercy of Percival and his brothers. Feeling their fangs and cocks penetrating her, getting revenge for everything she'd ever done to them.

Slow, ruthless, deliciously erotic revenge.

Oh, Horned God. She bit her lip and snatched her hand out from between her bare thighs. Dammit, she shouldn't be turned on by the idea of being used as a fucking *party platter.*

Percival obviously intended the experience to be humiliating and demeaning, and she knew he'd make sure it was exactly that.

Thing was, she'd always secretly found Cador and Marrok almost as deliciously sexy as Percival himself, especially once she'd learned all three men were sexual dominants. She'd had more than one nasty fantasy of being at the mercy of the three men—of feeling their cocks sliding into her mouth, pussy, and arse simultaneously.

She . . .

"Morgana? I'm at the front door. Let me in."

She jumped at the familiar mental voice, her eyes widening. *"Soren?"* She frowned. *"It's late. What are you doing here?"* Though the collar blocked Morgana's magic, it didn't block Soren's, so the dragon was able to communicate with her mind to mind.

"I wanted to discuss the hunt for your human-killing dragon. It isn't going well, and I thought you might be able to suggest where we might look. You know Mortal Earth better than I, after all." He paused. When he spoke again, his tone was cooler, harder. *"I have also been reliably informed you let that vampire knight of yours enslave you."*

She winced, remembering the gauntlet of stares she'd walked past earlier tonight. The gossip mill was already grinding. *"He didn't enslave me, Soren. I took an Oath of Service to obey him for the next year. And since he wouldn't like you being here, I can't let you in. I think it will be all right to discuss the dragon mentally, though."*

"So you fear him that much?" There was a note of acid sarcasm in the ambassador's mental voice.

"I don't fear him at all. He would never harm me." Hurt, yes. Harm, no. Unfortunately, the difference between enjoyable erotic punishment and physical abuse was not a distinction the dragon would understand. *"But I also will not violate my Oath."*

"Then I will seek him out and discuss this with him instead."

And that was definitely a threat. *"Dammit, Soren . . ."*

"Let me in, Morgana. Talk to me, and I will leave afterward."

"Let me get dressed."

"Now. I am not feeling particularly patient."

Swearing, Morgana rolled out of bed, grabbed the first robe that came to hand and shrugged into it, and ran down the marble staircase and jerked open the door.

The man who sauntered in was tall and deliciously athletic in black slacks and a black dress shirt open at the throat, elegant and casual. His handsome face was narrow, with an angular bone structure and a long, jutting nose set off by an intensely erotic mouth. His head was perfectly smooth and bald, calling attention to the pale blue tint of his skin. His iridescent gaze flicked over her body in the thin robe, one blue brow lifting with obvious male appreciation. Dragon or not, Soren loved Mageverse women. "Hello, darling."

Morgana gave him a tense smile. "Hello, Soren."

Percival wasn't going to like this visit by her shape-shifting dragon lover one bit, but there wasn't a damned thing she could do about it now.

Soren eyed her silently, deliberately allowing an uncomfortable silence to develop. Percival, it seemed, wasn't the only one whose temper she had to contend with. She sighed. "You said you wanted to discuss the search for the killer?"

"Oh. Yes, right." The anger in his eyes faded into worry. "We've found out who he is, at least, and the news isn't good. His name is Huar, a dragon of great age and, accordingly, great power." He began to pace the foyer, striding back and forth past her restlessly. "I had feared it was him based on your description of the killer's coloring and size. It seems I was correct, for Huar has vanished from the Dragonlands." He ran a hand over his gleaming head with its faint blue scales. "In truth, I wasn't surprised he's the one who has begun killing your people. Huar is one of those who detests humans with a bitter passion, remembering the days when we warred with the Sidhe. I believe his mother was killed in a raid, or some such." The ambassador shrugged. "Too, dragons as old as he have a tendency to become mentally unstable."

"Oh, just lovely," Morgana growled. "A mad elder dragon with great power and a grudge against humans. Just what we need. What are you doing to find him?"

"I've been searching Mortal Earth for draconic magical signatures, but he seems to be blocking me somehow. I will, of course, continue to scan for . . ."

The house's front door opened, and Percival stepped inside. His eyes narrowed as he saw Soren. "Ambassador," he growled, "What are you doing here?"

Percival was not exactly thrilled to walk in and find Morgana's lizard Lothario paying her a visit. His temper didn't cool when he saw how close together the pair stood. His fangs lengthened with possessive male jealousy. *She's crazy if she thinks I'm going to turn a blind eye to that scaly fucker sniffing around her skirts.*

Skirts that presently consisted of a diaphanous silk robe that displayed most of her luscious anatomy. She looked so tempting, his fury blazed higher, stoked by lust.

"Ambassador," Percival said, fighting to control his rage enough for civilized conversation,"you're not familiar with our customs, so I will explain. Morgana has given me her Oath of Service—which means it's her duty to obey my orders without question for the next year." *In other words, get the hell out, you draconic fucker.*

"So she has explained—repeatedly. At length." Soren curled his lip in contempt.

Morgana squeezed her eyes shut as if grappling desperately for patience. "Gentlemen . . ."

Percival shot his witch a frigid glance intended to communicate just how little he appreciated finding Soren here. He fully intended to punish her for letting the bastard in the door. "Morgana's Oath, being a matter of her honor, takes precedence over whatever . . . relationship you had. In other words, she can no longer continue to see you."

The dragon shifter rocked back on his heels as he eyed Percival. "That would, of course, be your right—if you had forced her to submit in proper mating combat." Soren took a step toward him as those iridescent eyes began to glow with a hellish orange light. "But that's not what you did, is it?"

Well, hell. Soren's at least as pissed off as I am, Percival realized. *Good.* He was in the mood to kick some scaly arse, and it wouldn't be as much fun if Soren didn't fight back.

Soren narrowed those glowing orange eyes.. "You don't have the power to fight Morgana with magic. So instead, you blackmailed her into donning that abomination of a collar in order to turn her into your powerless slave." He jabbed a furious finger at it.

She didn't wring her hands—quite. "No, Soren, it's not that way at all!"

"Shut up, Morgana," Percival snapped. There was just enough truth to the dragon's accusations to sting. "I don't need you to defend me from your *ex*-lover."

"Don't you?" Soren gestured, and what looked like a glowing bull-whip coiled from his hand to writhe and hiss on the floor. "Perhaps you shouldn't be so quick to reject her protection, vampire."

Percival drew his sword from the scabbard that hung down his back. He never went anywhere without the great blade, because all too often in his long life, he'd needed it. This appeared to be one of those times. "If you want to dance, ambassador, I will be more than happy to oblige you."

"Oh, for God's sake!" Morgana snapped in raw frustration. "Would you two calm down? This is absurd!"

"What I find absurd is you wearing that thing," Soren said, indicating her collar with loathing. "I thought the idea of all this was for me to teach you how to control your powers . . ."

"Soren . . ." Morgana snapped, her gaze flicking toward Percival, as if the dragon had just revealed something she didn't want her Master to know.

"But how can I teach you anything when you've rendered your magic inaccessible, simply so you can accommodate *his* appetites!" He cracked his whip and circled to Percival's left.

The knight pivoted with him. Tall, blue, and scaly was *done*.

So frustrated she wanted to scream, Morgana watched the two males stalk each other. You could cut the testosterone with a knife.

And that was just Percival's contribution. Soren, for his part, was just as busy pumping out whatever the draconic version was. Which was probably why he'd almost blurted out the very secret Morgana didn't want Percival to learn. She'd had it with both of them. "That's enough!" Morgana thundered, in a roar she usually reserved for the battlefield.

It worked. The two men stopped and stared at her, startled. In her best icy tone, she snapped, "Ambassador Soren, please leave."

The dragon stared at her, his expression first stunned, then, to her surprise, hurt. She hadn't thought his feelings for her ran that deep.

Her tone softened. "Soren, I appreciate everything you've done for me. You've taught me so much about the control and use of my power. But as I told you, Percival is my Oath Master, and he's quite right that . . ."

It was evidently the wrong thing to say; fury flooded Soren's gemstone gaze again. He curled a lip at Percival, baring a mouthful of inhumanly sharp teeth. "He's not fit to be your master in *anything* . . ."

"Yes, Soren, he bloody well is!" She stopped to wrestle her temper until she was able to continue more calmly. "I was not *forced* to give him my Oath. I had the option of going to another team, but I wanted Percival." She took a step closer to Soren, and for once, let her true emotions show. "I wanted Percival, and he accepted me. You've been a good friend, and I hope our friendship can continue. But we can no longer be lovers."

Soren stared into her eyes, and for a moment she felt the sheer weight of his inhuman intelligence, age, and power. Then he nodded and straightened. "I see." He rested a big hand on her shoulder. "And of course we will remain friends. But when your year of service is done, do remember . . ." He gave Percival a long, level look." . . . I will be here."

Directing a courtly bow at Morgana, Soren turned and swept out. Automatically, she moved to close the door behind him.

A brawny arm blurred past her face and hit the door, slamming it so hard it rattled in its frame. At the same moment, Percival's hard body hit her from behind, flattening her against the closed door.

"Are you in love with him?" the vampire knight spat.

Morgana's first startled impulse had been to send him flying with a spell, but of course nothing happened. Genuinely confused, she asked, "Soren?"

His free hand wrapped around the front of her throat from behind and tightened. Not quite enough to choke her, but the don't-fuck-with-me message was definitely there. *"Are. You. In love. With him?"*

Morgana struggled for patience. She'd never have dreamed that Percival and the Dragonkind ambassador would lock horns like a pair of elk in rut. "No, I am definitely not in love with Soren."

"Don't play with me, Morgana," Percival snapped, still holding her pinned against the door, his groin pressed pointedly against her arse. His erection made her sore anus twitch, reminding her of his ruthless possession earlier that evening. "You and that lizard have been lovers for a decade."

"We've been fucking—infrequently—for a decade," she corrected him impatiently. "We have never been 'lovers.' Soren just enjoys screwing mammal girls, you know that." Given the chance, Soren would happily bed a different woman every night.

"Yeah, he certainly acted like a man who isn't your lover when he challenged me to a fucking duel just now." Percival leaned into her even harder. His cock felt like a steel bar against the small of her back.

"I have no idea why he acted like . . ."

"Why in the fuck did you let him in?" He leaned down until she could feel the heat of his breath on her ear. "Especially dressed like *that?*"

She knew better than to explain she'd done it to keep Soren from going after Percival. And she couldn't try to come up with a more palatable explanation, because he'd smell the deception in her scent. Which left her with no way to defend herself against his suspicions. "I told him he couldn't come in, but he insisted. He also refused to wait until I was fully dressed, so I grabbed the first thing that came to hand. Which happened to be this."

All of which had the advantage of at least being the truth.

The hand around her throat tightened almost to the point of pain. Percival's angry gray eyes narrowed. "You're talking around something you don't want to tell me. What is it?"

Goddamn it. She couldn't refuse to answer without violating her Oath. "He threatened you. He told me if I didn't let him in, he'd come after you."

"Then you should have let him. What were you going to do, fuck him to keep me safe?" The rage in his voice made the hair lift on the back of her neck.

"Don't be absurd."

He stepped back until he could spin her around and glare down into her eyes. "I am incredibly tempted to take off my belt and give you such a flogging, you'll think I used a single-tail. Fortunately for you, I never discipline a sub when I'm this pissed." He curled his lip in a snarl. "Any damage I do to you is going to be intentional." Opening the door, he stormed out.

Leaving Morgana shaking in his wake.

* * *

I hate to say it, but she actually had a point," Marrok told Percival when the three men met at Cador's Tudor mansion later that night. "You're good, but nobody's good enough to take on a dragon single-handedly with no magical backup. Soren would have handed you your head."

"That wasn't her decision to make," Percival growled. "She shouldn't have come to the damned door."

Cador eyed him. "I see why you're ticked off—you're her dominant; it's not her job to protect you. But getting in a pissing match with a dragon isn't the smartest thing you've ever done. I think this thing with Morg is screwing with your head."

"He's right," Marrok agreed. "When's the last time you let me tag you in practice?"

"Look, I was worried about her, all right? I fed pretty hard last night. It occurred me that she might have failed to show up at sunset because I'd taken too much blood. Distracted me for a minute . . ." They were both staring at him as if he'd grown a third eye. Irritated, he snapped, "What?"

Cador eyed him in unabashed horror. "You're falling for Morgana le Fay."

If Marrok had said something like that, Percival could have dismissed it; his friend had a romantic streak as wide as a woman's. Cador, however, was as far from being romantic as it was possible to get and still have a pulse. "Oh, bullshit."

"Fuck," Marrok groaned. "I was afraid of this."

"I am not in love with Morgana!" Percival said through his teeth.

Cador started ticking points off on his fingers. "You talk about her so incessantly, we're sick of hearing about Morg's pussy, tits, and arse . . ."

"Something I never thought I'd say . . ." Marrok muttered.

". . . You lost focus while worrying about her *in the middle of practice* and got yourself knocked cold. That's aside from almost ending up in a duel with a dragon. If all of that doesn't add up to a dangerous level of obsession, I don't know what does."

"Yeah," Marrok agreed, his expression resigned. "You've got it bad, brother."

Put that way, it did sound pretty bad. Percival glowered at his friends. "Not as bad as all that," he growled, and told them of the plans he had for his Super Bowl party.

"I can't believe I'm actually saying this, but are you sure that's a good idea?" Cador looked uneasy. "As much as I'd love to get my hands on Morg, our partnership means more to me than pussy."

Hell, no, he had no desire to share her with them, friends or not. On the other hand, he also knew that sometimes a warrior had to confront the thing he least wanted to do. Otherwise, he'd end up giving whatever it was even more power over him than it would have otherwise had.

"Not only do I wish to share her with you, I want you to help me punish her for her actions with Soren." Percival bared his teeth. "After which we will give her a fucking she won't forget."

His friends exchanged a quick look, but Percival ignored their obvious doubts. He was bloody well going to reestablish control over himself where Morgana was concerned.

On Sunday evening, Morgana made a point of presenting herself at Percival's house fifteen minutes before the time he'd given her.

She walked in dressed in the long leather trench Gwen had given her. Percival swept a cool glance from her black stiletto heels to the gleaming dark crown of her head, then gestured. "Drop the coat."

Nervousness clenched her stomach, but she tilted her chin and extended her arms to let the trench slide off. Glancing up at him from under her lashes, she waited for his reaction.

The black lace merry widow just barely veiled her curves, revealing the rose shadow of her nipples and the dark delta of her sex. Lace stockings clipped to a satin garter belt.

Percival's gray eyes heated with predatory lust, and his lips curled in a dark, hungry smile. "Very nice. But I think you're . . . overdressed." He crouched and drew a thin bladed dagger from his boot.

"This is what you told me to wear!" Morgana protested as he stood, taking a step back in a futile effort to defend her already miniscule wardrobe.

"I changed my mind." Hooking a forefinger into her bodice, he tugged it away from her breasts, then sliced the thin lace in two. The blade was so sharp, and Percival was so outrageously skilled with it, he didn't even scratch her.

Until he did. The knife's point traced a slow path across the top curve of her breast, spilling a thin line of crimson. She drew in a breath at the sting. "You did that deliberately." Her voice sounded tight, hoarse with thrumming desire.

The knight's gaze flicked up from her breasts to meet hers. One corner of his lips curled in a feral half-smile. "After fifteen centuries using a blade, anything I cut, I always cut deliberately."

His big hands gripped the sliced lace of her merry widow and ripped it like a man tearing into a birthday present. Then, with a deliberate flash of his knife, he severed the ties of her thong, leaving her helplessly creaming pussy bare.

Percival dropped the shreds, hooked one arm around her waist and the other around her arse, and lifted her off her feet to haul her against his body. His erection felt huge, a meaty length bulking behind the button fly of his jeans. Morgana gasped at the erotic threat of it pressed against her bare pussy.

The vampire knight bent over her breast, his gray eyes hot on hers. "For the record," Percival growled, "you're mine for the next year. No other man will touch you unless I allow it. That includes my brothers." His eyes narrowed, taking on a metallic gleam as he bit off the next two words. "You're. *Mine*. Is that understood?"

She swallowed. Her mouth felt dry, but everything below the waist seemed to be liquid, melted like chocolate by his demanding male stare. "No other man will touch me unless you will it." His eyes narrowed, and she quickly added," . . . Lord Percival."

He lowered his blond head over her desperately erect nipple. His tongue traced a hot, wet path along the length of the cut he'd inflicted, neatly licking away the blood.

His eyes lifted to her face, his gaze possessive, demanding, and very male. *Mine*. He didn't say it again.

He didn't have to.

Percival led her down to what Morgana privately thought of as his lair, with its massive U-shaped navy blue sectional couch and oak coffee table. A flat-screen television occupied most of one wall next to the barrel-shaped bar he'd stocked with pricy liquor and micro-brews.

The knight strolled over to the marble-topped coffee table and lifted it as though it didn't weigh roughly as much as a compact car. He put it down on the opposite side of the sectional, and ducked into a walk-in closet to the left of the bar.

"Morgana, get over here," he said from its depths.

Licking her dry lips, she clicked after him in her high heels, acutely aware she was naked except for the stilettos, lacy stockings, and her garter belt. Which, come to think of it, was the same nonexistent costume he'd reduced her to the last time he'd taken her in this room. Apparently he was a heels-and-stockings man. She grinned.

"Morgana." The growl from the closet sounded distinctly menacing.

"Yes, Master," she muttered, the last word a touch sarcastic, and stepped in after him.

"Did you seriously think I wouldn't hear that?" One strong hand seized her left shoulder as he whirled her around and jerked her back against his thick erection. "You just added another five to the halftime flogging I owe you." He lowered his voice to a rumbling growl. "Cador and Marrok are going to enjoy themselves thoroughly."

Oh, shit. "I'm sorry, Lord Percival," she gasped.

"Not yet, but you're going to be." Something jingled as he started buckling a leather restraint around one of her wrists. After checking the fit to make sure it wasn't too tight, he attached the matching cuffs to her other arm and both ankles. He checked to make sure the three cuffs weren't tight enough to cut off the circulation, then leaned in until his hot breath gusted against her pussy.

Morgana froze, her eyes going wide as Percival's tongue slid between her labia in a long, seductive lick. She damned near fell off her stilettos.

The knight grabbed her hips, steadying her, and laughed. The sound was just slightly taunting. Leaning in even closer, he traced a figure eight around her clit and the opening of her sex, once, twice. Three times.

She gasped in helpless arousal and caught his massive shoulders to keep from falling.

At last Percival drew back from her by now desperately creaming pussy and looked up at her, flashing his fangs in a wicked grin. "The scent of wet cunt was driving me mad. I had to see if you taste as good as you smell."

He pivoted on his knees and picked up something that rattled, then rose and handed it to her. Accepting it, she discovered it was a wooden chest, its curving top carved with what looked like some kind of sterilization spell.

Which meant the box was probably full of sex toys. The Magekind were immune to sexually transmitted diseases, but clean was clean. Judging from the sigils carved into the lid, you could put a toy in the box, and five seconds later, the spell would ensure it was sterile enough to use in an operating room.

Percival bent and picked up what looked like a long bench, before giving Morgana a carnivorous grin. "Well, Party Platter, it's time to get you ready for my *very* hungry guests."

Oh, Horned God.

TWELVE

I'll give you one thing, Percival," Cador drawled. "You do know how to put on a spread."

"Jesu, yes," Marrok rasped, lust raw in his voice.

"By the way, Morgana made arrangements with Gwen to add a regeneration spell to that collar of hers," Percival told them. "She assures me she could feed all three of us, and the collar would heal her blood loss."

Cador straightened, his gaze sharpening. "Well, now, that's convenient."

Percival didn't blame them for the heated anticipation in their eyes. Just looking at Morgana was enough to make his own cock buck hungrily behind his jeans' button fly.

The witch lay draped over the padded bench like an erotic offering to a dark god. The light spilling from discreet ceiling lamps made the pink, fragrant flesh glisten between those well-toned thighs.

"God, she's wet," Marrok muttered. "I can smell it."

So could Percival. The maddening scent of her need had been teasing him since she'd walked in the door, already so hot for him it was all he could do not to throw her down and fuck her in mindless animal rut.

He would have expected her to be anxious, knowing how utterly she was at their mercy. Especially considering the way she'd tormented them for so long.

There was a dark satisfaction in the sight of her naked and bound to the bench he'd built. Those gorgeous breasts rode her delicate ribcage, bare and pale and full, plump nipples flushed dark rose, seeming to beg for his lips, his tongue . . .

His fangs.

He studied her hungrily. The bench was built in four sections that could be raised or lowered to position the submissive's body according to her dominant's whim. It was currently arranged to raise her breasts higher than her head, which was thrown back to rest on a padded section, forcing her throat into an elegant and tempting arch. Her black hair spilled to the floor in a gleaming mass of curls. Her legs were bent and spread wide, then chained to the bench's stirrup-shaped footrests, which jutted at an angle to either side. Her arms hung down, wrists clipped to ankle-cuffs.

But that wasn't all he'd done to enhance her sense of vulnerability. A blindfold covered her vivid green eyes, hiding half of her face even as it drew attention to the lips she'd coated in glistening scarlet lipstick.

He'd been having repeated fantasies of plunging his cock into that crimson mouth, watching her suck him with that wicked skill of hers. Skill that perversely infuriated him with the thought of the men she must have practiced it on.

He'd never in his life felt this primal possessiveness for a woman. Though he supposed that was no surprise. Morgana had been his obsession for so many centuries, no other woman had ever really registered on his consciousness. He'd fucked them, punished them, fed from them, shared them with his brothers.

And dreamed of Morgana, naked and pale and at his mercy. Only to wake alone, gasping and frustrated, with a puddle of come cooling on his belly.

Now, at last, he had her. He'd fucked her mouth, pussy, and arse, drank from her pale swan's throat and delicious nipples. The obsession should have started to fade by now. It hadn't. He still hungered for her with such intensity, he was beginning to suspect it might take the entire year to burn off this gnawing need.

Look at the trouble he was having with the idea of sharing her with his brothers. These were the men he'd fought and bled and damned near died beside more times than he could count. How many times had they shared fantasies of taking her, about the grip of her body and the taste of those gorgeous nipples. They'd gotten drunk more than once speculating about what it would be like to punish and fuck her.

But now that the moment was here, all he wanted to do was sweep a blanket over her, hiding her from their lusting eyes.

Mine. My mate. Mine alone.

No, Percival told the primitive wolf in his head. *She's just a submissive, like all the others I've shared with Cador and Marrok. The only difference is we've waited longer to have her.*

The wolf snorted in disdain, but he ignored it to saunter toward the sectional arranged around Morgana's exquisite body, bound to the bench, ready for their pleasure.

Percival gave his brothers a determined smile as Cador and Marrok sank down on the couch, staring hungrily at Morgana's delicious curves. "Anybody want a beer?"

Morgana could almost feel their eyes on her bare breasts, her stiff rose nipples, and the arch of her throat and spread of her thighs. She wished she could see them, but she was blindfolded.

The length of soft leather not only covered her eyes, it bound her head in place to the padded bench. Between the strap around her head and the cuffs at her wrists and ankles, she had never felt more helpless.

Before he'd covered her eyes, she'd noticed the bench was a surprisingly beautiful piece of furniture, exquisitely carved with writhing female nudes, chained and lush and tangled together until it was difficult to tell where one woman left off and another began.

Like Morgana and her painting, most members of the Magekind had hobbies of one sort or another. Percival's hobby, he'd cheerfully informed her, was building and carving bondage devices like this one.

He'd certainly done a good job with it. Percival had designed the bench with a dominant's obsessive attention to his submissive's comfort. Its padding was thick and soft, its sections just wide enough to support her bound body.

Across the room, the enormous flat-screen television came on, filling the room with the cheers of the stadium crowd and the jovial commentary of the game's announcers.

By rights, of course, the set shouldn't be able to get any kind of signal in the Mageverse, but an elaborate system of enchanted devices picked up satellite signals on Earth, then transmitted them to Avalon, where they were bounced to all the city's residents. *And why the hell am I thinking about magical satellite feeds when my team is about to fuck my brains out?*

"God, you're hot," Cador said. Male fingers closed over one nipple, tugged, tightening right to the bright edge of pain. Percival had ordered Morgana to keep her mouth shut, so she said nothing as she instinctively arched her back to relieve the pressure. "She does have sensitive tits, doesn't she?" He captured the other nipple, began to give it the same delicately sadistic treatment. His voice dropped into a sinister purr. "I just love long, rosy nipples with a low pain threshold. There's so much you can do to them . . ."

Her cunt tightened with another juicy spurt of heat. Cador's erotic cruelty made her want to squirm.

Meanwhile, in marked contrast to his partner's sensual sadism, Marrok began to explore her with slow, sweeping caresses, his fingers gentle on the sensitive skin of her belly, the rise of one hip, the straining tendons of her spread thighs. "Her skin's so soft," the knight murmured, more to himself than Cador. "For such an ice bitch, she feels like warm silk."

An *ice bitch*? That stung more than Cador's torment of her nipples. Though thinking about the way she'd always treated the knights, she supposed it was a fair assessment. *I was afraid to let you get close*, Morgana thought. She didn't say it. She was vulnerable enough to them as it was.

She heard the click of Percival's boots on the hardwood as he returned with the beer, then the clink of bottles as he passed them out. Leather sighed as he sat down on the sectional.

Something icy settled between her thighs. She jerked with a startled gasp.

"Thought that hot pussy needed cooling off," Percival told her, dark amusement in his voice as he rolled the beer over her labia. Bits of ice slid down the crack of her arse, melting in her heat.

"You're one lucky bastard, you know that?" Cador told him, and paused. She heard him swallow, presumably a sip of his beer. "Getting to keep her for the next year. A whole year to fuck and punish the pretty slut." Judging by the lilt in his voice, he was grinning that sadistic fox grin of his. "If you run out of ideas, I can give you a few suggestions."

Percival snorted and removed the icy bottle from between her legs. "I'm sure you could, you vicious son of a bitch." He inhaled deeply. "God, smell that pussy. Scent of it's all over my beer."

"Maybe we should punish her for that," Cador suggested wickedly. "Getting her Master's bottle all stinky."

Percival snorted. "'Stinky' is not exactly the word I'd use, Cador. And I doubt you would either."

"Hell, no, but we don't have to tell *her* that."

"As I've told Morgana, I don't need an excuse to beat her pretty arse." He swallowed a few sips of his beer deliberately. "Though she has given me some very good reasons lately. Which is why you'll probably like my idea of a halftime show."

Cador laughed, the sound nasty. "Can't wait."

Morgana, listening to this predatory conversation, had to fight the impulse to roll her hips in need.

"Poor little slave," Marrok crooned to her in a dark whisper. "At the mercy of such a nasty pair of blackguards." His mouth closed over her nipple, still aching from Cador's rough treatment. He sucked, nibbled, licked, sending sweet ribbons of delight from her breasts to her creaming pussy. "You'll find me a much kinder lover."

His free hand brushed between her thighs, one finger stroking her clit on the way to delving between her creamy labia. When he stroked deep, she had to suck back a gasp and fight down the impulse to squirm.

She'd always secretly considered Marrok as deliciously sexy—so damned big, so powerfully built and impressively endowed.

So capable of bloody, appalling violence when he went berserk.

And yet he could also be sweetly tender. Of all of them, Marrok was the one who dealt with the traumatized victims they encountered far too often. Survivors—whether of terrorist attacks, natural disasters, war, or even torture—seemed to find something soothing about Marrok's low, warm voice and kind eyes. They somehow sensed they were safe in the protection of his massive frame. Morgana didn't have that ability to comfort without being overcome by a victim's pain.

Now as he stroked her pussy and suckled and tongued her nipple, she sighed at the keen delight.

Only to draw in a startled breath when he caught her nipple under the tips of his fangs. He didn't quite bite, but the promise—and threat—was definitely there.

A cheer came from the direction of the television, and the

announcer crowed, "Touchdown!" in such triumphant tones, you'd have thought he made the play himself.

"Where's your toy box?" Marrok asked Percival over inane color commentary from the TV.

"Here you go." It rattled from her left to overhead as if the knight had handed it over. The lid creaked open somewhere on the right. Morgana's mouth went dry during the pause as she wondered exactly what Marrok was looking for. Anticipation tightened her muscles, and she felt herself growing steadily wetter.

"Let me see that when you get done with it, would you?" Cador asked Marrok.

Rattle. Thump. Rattle. "Have at it."

"Thanks." Rattle. Pause. "Oh, now *that* has potential." A soft click. The hiss of a wick catching fire, the faint smell of smoke.

Another, louder click, and something began to hum. A boot heel scraped on hardwood, and the hum traveled around her body to between her thighs.

"And the field goal's good!" the announcer shouted over the crowd's delirious cheers.

Morgana tensed. She had a pretty good idea what Cador planned to do with that candle. The only question was why he hadn't done it yet . . .

The humming tip of Marrok's vibrator found the opening of her pussy and pushed deep in a single juicy stroke. Which was when Cador, with diabolical timing, spilled a stream of molten wax squarely over the tip of her nipple. The burning heat jerked her back into an arch. "Shit!"

Percival growled in a voice ripe with arousing menace, "Unless you want to add even more strokes to the punishment session I owe you, you'd better keep that luscious mouth shut."

Knowing her dominant meant that threat, Morgana set her teeth as Cador started painting wax over her right breast like a sadistic

Jackson Pollock—curves and splashes and a vicious swirling pattern she suspected was his initials.

She tried to divert her attention to the vibrator Marrok was thrusting in and out of her cunt in long, maddening strokes. Unfortunately, the pain was just too intense for the trick to work.

At least Cador seemed to know what he was doing. You could inflict some nasty burns with molten wax if you dropped it from the wrong height or used the wrong kind of candle. No surprise the sadistic fuck seemed to be an expert; the wax was definitely unpleasantly hot, but not to the point of injury.

Vibrator, Morgana reminded herself. *Concentrate on the vibrator.* While she'd been distracted by Cador and his wax, Marrok had buried the toy in her pussy and left it there.

Clothing rustled. She thought the big knight was preparing something, but couldn't quite identify the sounds over the roar of the game.

Boots clicked briskly on the floor. Ice rattled. Footsteps returned.

A second hum joined the first, the sound pitched just slightly higher. Sounded like a . . .

Another stream of wax splashed over her left nipple. She clamped her teeth over her yelp, just managing to swallow it back.

The yelp broke loose anyway as Marrok plunged a thick vibrating buttplug up her arse. Even so, it didn't hurt as much as it could have; he'd done a good job lubing the buzzing toy—that must have been what he'd been up to in that long pause—and she hadn't known to tense, being blindfolded and distracted by Cador's wax play.

Even so, the pair of vibrators, each buzzing vigorously, stretched her pussy and arse right to the edge of pain. She felt utterly stuffed as they vibrated against each other through the thin wall of flesh between them.

The combination of pain and pleasure—and the more concentrated blaze of Cador's wax—made her toes twitch in helpless reaction.

"Damn, Marrok, I didn't know you had a sadistic streak," Morgana gasped without thinking.

"That," Percival breathed in her ear, "adds two more strokes to the fifteen I already owe your arse." Then he pressed a handful of crushed ice against her desperately erect clit and hot, stuffed, swollen pussy. The contrast with the hot wax made her entire nervous system vibrate like a tuning fork.

Her stream of curses shot the swats her Master owed her all the way to twenty.

By halftime, the vampires had abandoned the pretense of giving a damn about the game. They marched her down to Percival's dungeon room, where they chained her up as he had the night he'd accepted her Oath. The blindfold came off, letting her get the full effect of being surrounded by horny vampires.

Once again, her Master began with the deerskin flogger, painting a stinging pattern across her arse and upper thighs. A glance over her shoulder revealed the men watched her like a trio of cats eyeing a plump canary. Morgana tried to keep from giving them any really entertaining jerks and twitches. As Percival's smacks grew harder, she kept her mouth stubbornly closed against the urge to yelp.

She did have some pride, after all.

After five blows, Percival put the flogger away in the enchanted sterilization box before turning to his wall of toy shelves. After a nerve-wracking pause, he chose something that looked like a Ping Pong paddle from his collection. Swinging the paddle with idle revolutions of his wrist, he sauntered over until he was close enough to murmur in her ear. "Do you really think I'm going to let you get away with playing *macho* with me?" He put such sneering emphasis on "macho" that she winced.

Definitely a miscalculation.

He drew back and let fly. Despite Morgana's grim determination to remain silent, the first impact shot her up on her toes and tore a cry of startled pain out of her mouth.

"Well," Cador drawled to Marrok, "she definitely felt that."

The big knight laughed. It was not a kind sound at all. Percival echoed that laugh with one even nastier and proceeded to tear into her with four more blows that had her bouncing in place like a paddled four-year-old. She managed not to scream again, though.

Just.

Finally handing the paddle off to Marrok, Percival stalked over to lean against the dungeon wall beside Cador.

Shooting a resentful glance over one shoulder, Morgana saw all three men had really impressive erections. Though her arse blazed like a Samhain bonfire, she found herself intrigued.

Percival expected Marrok to take it easy on Morgana, given the hiding he'd just given her himself. Turned out he'd underestimated his friend's nasty streak.

The big knight didn't go after her at anything close to full strength any more than Percival had—he'd have broken bones. But his five swats definitely made her dance on her toes, hissing in pain between her teeth. In lieu, presumably, of yelping.

The little witch really had more pride than was good for her. If she'd let herself yowl, Marrok might have taken pity.

Cador, of course, wouldn't have held back even if she'd screamed the house down. The redhead took his time with the paddle, landing his five with unpredictable pauses between them, careful not to let any kind of pattern develop as he swatted that pretty, bright red bum. Like Marrok and Percival, he was cautious with the force he used, making sure he didn't hit her too hard. Morgana rewarded him by squirming deliciously as she gasped, tears rolling in a stream down her flushed face.

Even so, she smelled of aroused pussy, delicious masochist that she was.

Jesu, she's hot. Her lovely breasts bounced as her arse-cheeks quivered delectably until Percival's cock jerked hungrily into his button-fly. He wanted to fuck her so badly, his back teeth ached.

He wasn't the only one, either, judging by the wood his friends were sporting. His possessive inner cave wolf didn't like that one bit. It still wanted to drag her off to enjoy in greedy solitude. *Down boy.*

The whole point of this exercise was to teach his inner possessive White Fang that Morgana le Fay was most definitely *not* his mate. His Oath Servant, yes.

Mate, *hell* no.

If he even gave her so much as a hint she had that kind of power over him, she'd be leading him around by his dick for the rest of his immortal life. *No, thank you.* He was, by the Grail, going to keep the upper hand in this relationship if it killed him. He was the Oath Master. Morgana was the Servant.

Period.

Cador tossed aside the paddle. Giving Morgana a slow, lustful grin, he ran a hand the length of his jeans-clad erection and cupped his balls at her.

White Fang growled like a chainsaw.

Morgana felt like a human dish of Crêpes Suzette—as if some sadistic chef had spurted liqueur all over her arse and lit it on fire. The pain was a bright, furious heat that made her want to fight her chains, despite the pride that demanded she hide any vulnerability from the hungry, watching men.

They had paddled her like an errant schoolgirl until it had been all she could do not to scream. But though she'd avoided that humiliation, at least, she hadn't been able to do a damn thing to stop the flood of tears that rolled down her cheeks in helpless reaction to the pain.

But the thing that truly infuriated her was how bloody arousing the whole experience had been. Even as that paddle hit her arse in solid jolts that drove her onto her toes, some perverse part of her thoroughly enjoyed the way they watched her. Those thick, predatory shafts straining behind flies, so long she half-expected cockheads to pop up above the knights' belts. Hot eyes focused on every twitch and flex of her body with stark masculine lust.

Especially Percival, who visibly battled jealousy. Marrok and Cador might be his brothers, his partners, and his dearest friends, but it was obvious he absolutely hated watching them touch her. The conflict in his eyes blazed like a torch burning in a dark room.

Yet the men had shared women before without jealousy. In fact, judging by the way they talked about it afterward, Percival usually joined in his partners' wicked male joy without reservation.

This time was obviously different. As if she was different—something more than just a submissive toy, an Oath Servant he could fuck and punish however he chose.

Don't be stupid, Morgana, she told herself. *You're nothing to Percival but his latest piece. Forget that, and you'll be left broken when he walks away at the end of the year.*

She was concentrating so hard on her dark thoughts that she hadn't even noticed that Cador had started freeing her, beginning with her ankle cuffs. Her knees buckled when he released the chains holding her wrists over her head.

"Hey." He scooped an arm around her waist and pulled her upright, a frown between his auburn brows. "You okay, Morg?"

"Fine." She straightened, vaguely aware that Percival halted his strides toward her as she steadied herself. He still looked worried. "I'm fine."

"Yeah, right." Cador swooped down and caught her under the

knees, then lifted her into his arms with effortless vampire strength. "I think you need a bed." His teeth flashed in a wolfish smile. "Come to think of it, I wouldn't mind one either."

He swept her through a doorway. Morgana blinked. The promised bed took up damned near every inch of the available space—and it wasn't a small room. "Horned God, you could land fighter jets on that thing. It's huge."

Cador laughed as he put her down on the mattress. "Well, it's designed for four . . ."

"Or more," Marrok added.

"I can see that." Its massive brass frame gleamed like gold, set with rings obviously intended as attachment points for chains. "And you could tie them all up, too."

Cador displayed his teeth in his best evil smile. "And frequently have."

As the two knights joined her on the bed, Morgana glanced around for Percival. He was still standing in the doorway, his massive shoulders bunched, hands curled in fists, gray eyes stormy.

A warm hand caught her chin, turning her head and angling it up. To her astonishment, Cador's mouth came down on hers in an impassioned kiss. Morgana froze.

She would have expected any kiss of Cador's to be nakedly carnal, maybe even vicious, with a great deal of pressure and teeth, maybe even a deliberate fang-rake designed to draw blood.

This kiss was nothing like that. It was slow, almost . . . tender, asking rather than taking, with a teasing stroke of tongue and lips that intrigued her into opening her mouth for him. He grew more forceful then, but in a way that suggested passion more than savagery. His warm, strong hands cradled her face, his mouth feathering over hers, his tongue playing in tiny strokes and smooth swirling caresses. It was a delicious kiss, ripe with need and sensuality—the kind of kiss that could effortlessly seduce a virgin or tempt a more experienced woman into bed against her better judgment.

Fifteen hundred years, after all, gave a man a long time to practice all kinds of useful skills. Percival, too, knew his way around a woman's mouth, when he was in the mood to seduce instead of demand.

And yet . . . and yet. Luscious and tempting though it was, there was something missing from Cador's kiss that she always felt even in Percival's roughest conquests of her mouth.

Every time Percival kissed her, she always sensed some fierce emotion, some deep hunger that somehow told her that not just any woman would do for him. As if Percival needed her as much as she needed him, little though either of them wanted the connection. Though, of course, she knew better.

Cador's kiss, skilled though it was, held none of that need, not even reluctantly. Not even the illusion of it.

Finally, he drew back. She stared blindly up at him, still absorbing the realization that there was something real and intense between her and Percival. Some mutual need she really didn't want to name even in her deepest heart.

Cador glanced away from her. Morgana followed his taunting gaze.

Percival had moved closer to the bed until he stood over them. Rage flamed in his eyes, a reaction to both the kiss and that sneering glance Cador had just shot him. Morgana sucked in a breath. *Is Cador* trying *to set him off?*

"I think we could all use a distraction," Marrok murmured, moving between her legs. Pushing her thighs apart, he settled on his belly between them. Two fingers parted her labia as he lowered his head and gave her a long, juicy lick that ran from her perineum to her clit.

Morgana jerked and gasped in startled pleasure.

Which was when Cador palmed one breast and sank his fangs into her throat. Delicately tugging and stroking her nipple, he began to drink in deep swallows.

Percival's growl could have come from a rabid werewolf.

THIRTEEN

Morgana stiffened in alarm, rolling her eyes to watch Percival where he stood tense in the doorway. But with Cador drinking from her and Marrok swirling circles around her clit, it was hard to hold on to that sense of danger.

Both men were really, really good at what they were doing.

Which in Cador's case, seemed to be deliberately trying to piss Percival off. The big knight moved, stalking closer to the bed, his gray eyes as frigid as a sleet storm. He stopped dead, one fist half-cocked as if he battled violent impulses.

Morgana stared up at him, uncomfortably aware of Cador's lips moving on her throat as Marrok licked and fingered her pussy with delicious skill.

Perversely, she found Percival's possessive rage somehow added to her arousal as much as it scared the hell out of her. For a long moment, she and the gray-eyed knight stared at one another as if balancing on a knife blade. Something told her that a blink at the wrong time would spill him into rage.

Instead, he reached for the hem of his black T-shirt, jerked it off over his head, and sent it sailing across the room as he went to work on his belt. Its buckle jangled as he unbuttoned his jeans and bent to jerk off his boots. Any other man would have had to hop around awkwardly to perform that maneuver, but he got them off without a hitch. Stripping out of his jeans, he kicked them aside.

And straightened, so magnificently naked, Morgana had to catch her breath. His cock jutted at her, angled upward in silent testimony to his lust, long and ruddy and delicious.

The rest of him was just as stunning, a big, scarred warrior who'd never lost the tan he'd had when he'd become a vampire. Muscle worked and flexed in tight plates over his body as he bent over her where she lay on the bed. His mouth found one erect nipple as his right hand caught the other, forcing Cador to surrender his hold.

Stretched between the three knights as they used their mouths and hands and teeth on her, Morgana felt deep inner muscles begin to clamp. "Let me come!" she gasped to Percival, feeling deliciously helpless, deliciously submissive. Half-expecting he would deny her.

But he lifted his head and growled, "Come, then. Come hard."

He bit her, sinking his fangs into the breast he'd been teasing. The merciless blend of bright white pleasure and stabbing pain fired her over the edge like a dried pea from a shotgun. The arousal the knights had built all day with a combination of dominance, pleasure, and calculated cruelty exploded like a piñata.

Morgana screamed, jerking like a seizure victim with the rolling pulses of her climax. The men pinned her in place as they continued tormenting her. Crying out, she hunched her hips against Marrok's face, mindless and lost.

A moment later, he turned his head away from her pussy. She felt his cream-smeared lips against her upper thigh, then he, too, bit deep, taking her femoral artery.

Around her throat, the bespelled collar heated, making the skin tingle as Gwen's spell went to work healing the blood loss while the three men drank.

By the time they drew away, Morgana lay utterly boneless, floating in lassitude.

"So she's merely your Oath Servant," Cador said to Percival, his tone cool. "Nothing but another piece of pussy. Was that why you just looked at me like you wanted to gut me?"

Morgana's eyes widened. What did he mean by that? Was Percival motivated by simple sexual possession, or something more? Something deeper?

The blond knight froze, staring at him. Then, at last, he spoke, his tone hard and chill as a blade. "Are we going to fuck her or not?"

The pain of dashed hope made Morgana squeeze her eyes shut. Bitterly, she wished Cador had kept his mouth shut.

Cador and Marrok stripped quickly, Cador folding his clothes neatly and piling them on a chair while Marrok tossed his into a corner.

Morgana, surrounded by handsome, naked vampire Knights of the Round Table, indulged her curiosity shamelessly. Marrok was massive everywhere, with a sheer muscled power that put her in mind of a warhorse. He had some truly horrific scars, reminders of the strikes he'd suffered from arrows, knives, and swords in his mortal days. One white starburst pattern over a brawny thigh she remembered as being the result of a mace blow that shattered the bone. Though she'd been Camelot's healer then, he'd owed his survival more to a miracle of God than her skills. What feeble magic she'd been able to command before she drank from Merlin's Grail had been of little use against that kind of blood loss and infection.

So to Morgana, all those scars didn't detract from Marrok's nude beauty. They simply made it clear what kind of man he really was. A hero to the marrow.

A very well-hung hero, at that. His cock, Merlin help her, was in proportion to the rest of him: big. Very big. And thick, as it swayed over his heavy balls.

Cador, though shorter than his teammates, appeared almost as powerfully built proportionally as Marrok. He could have modeled for Michelangelo or da Vinci with all that elegant sculpted muscle, his red-fox hair spilling to his shoulders in a gleaming waterfall of silk. His cock didn't look quite as thick as Marrok's or Percival's, but its length was every bit as impressive. And she knew just looking at it that it was more than thick enough to feel delicious when he drove it into her.

No doubt about it, she thought. *I'm in for one hell of a ride. I may not survive, but I'll die smiling.*

The three had apparently shared women often enough to have it down to a science. Marrok stretched himself out on the bed and fisted his intimidating cock-stand. "Come here, darling," he purred, in a tone she'd never heard from him.

Licking abruptly dry lips, she crawled across the mattress to him, swung a leg over his hips and began to lower herself gingerly down on that very big cock. Fortunately, she was still thickly creamy from her orgasm, and the sensation of his slow, sliding entry made her catch her breath. He didn't try to thrust, but let her set her own pace, evidently knowing just how intimidating his organ could be. So she was able to relax as she took more and more of him, stuffing herself in a delicious downward glide.

Still, by the time her bum touched his thighs, she felt full to the throat with cock. She knelt astride him, eyes wide, trying to get used to the stretch of his width, not to mention the sheer spearing length of his shaft. He smiled at her lazily and reached between her legs to tease her engorged clit. Morgana gasped in pleasure.

"That's it, relax," he purred. "You can move when you're ready." He gave her a slow, lazy smile. "I'm in no hurry. I'm happy just where I am."

Percival grunted. "To put it mildly."

Marrok's thumb teased over her clit, back and forth, then in slow, lazy spirals. Each tiny stroke sent another sweet jolt of delight through her nerves, making her shiver and gasp. Need rose, intensified. Finally she could stand it no longer and began to straighten her legs, rising slowly, carefully off the massive shaft.

Up. And up. And up. She could feel the contours of his cock teasing the walls of her cunt. And Horned God, it felt good. It seemed the big shaft twanged pleasure centers she hadn't even known she had. Head falling back, she began to sink again, letting him fill her centimeter by centimeter, raking over sensitive nerve endings until her awareness of the ruthless stretch began to fade. Or at least, seem a hell of a lot less important than the glorious delight.

Something moved in Morgana's peripheral vision. With a lazy sigh, she turned her head in that direction.

Percival stood by the bed, a tube of lube in one hand as he used the other to slowly rub a glistening layer of lubricant over his broad cock. His gray eyes, heavy-lidded, were locked hungrily on her face.

Cador, meanwhile, knelt on the mattress near her head, watching her just as intently, lust hot in his eyes.

A wave of heat rolled up her torso, making her face burn as her mouth dried out. The idea of all three of them buried deep in mouth, pussy and arse was intimidating. Yet that anxiety only intensified her arousal.

"Mmmmm," Marrok purred, rolling his hips to shaft her slowly. "I think she's ready, boys."

"Well?" Percival lifted a brow at Morgana as he squirted more lube into his palm and slicked it over his cock. "Are you?"

"Yes," she gasped, rising off Marrok's meaty erection and sinking down again. Meeting Percival's burning eyes, she swallowed, arousal clawing at her. "God, yes!"

He gave her a feral grin as he climbed onto the bed. "Bend over him." Breath coming fast, she obeyed as he straddled Marrok's thighs. "Don't tense."

She drew in a deep breath as he stroked his fingers over the tight, sensitive pucker between her cheeks. He pushed past the tight ring slowly, carefully, greasing the channel with deliberate strokes. "Merlin's Balls, I love your arse."

She caught her breath as his strong fingers played against Marrok's stroking cock through the thin flesh of her rectal walls. The extra stretch stung, yet there was something darkly seductive about it too.

Marrok drew out in a slow, silken slide, paused at the mouth of her cunt. Waiting for his partner to enter.

Percival pulled his fingers free of her anus, replacing them with the smooth crown of his shaft. For a moment both thick heads filled her side by side, and pain bit her, tearing a gasp from her mouth.

"Shhhhhhhh," Percival crooned in her ear. "Let go. Just open to us."

Marrok's index finger stroked another tight circle around her clit. The juicy chime of delight rang through her, and she shivered. *Both of them,* she thought, caught between pain and pleasure, fear and raw lust. *Both of them in me.* Morgana's eyes drifted closed at the unbearable eroticism of it. *Ooooh, yes . . .*

Slowly, carefully, Percival pressed his long prick deep, making her gasp at the stretching sting, the sense of being taken so hard, so ruthlessly, in such an unaccustomed way. When he finally, finally reached his root and began to slide out again, Marrok began to press in.

Morgana cried out, feeling for a wild moment that they were going to rip her in two. But as she panted helplessly, Marrok's fingers busied themselves again with her clit, and Percival's sword-callused fingers found one nipple, began to pluck and play. His other hand fisted in her hair, pulled her head around. His teeth found her ear in a gentle, arousing bite. Straining, she managed to turn enough to find his mouth. They kissed, hard and famished, as the knights' cocks edged past one another, raking her delicate tissues with every stinging pass.

With her senses so thoroughly overwhelmed, she was only distantly aware of Cador moving across the bed to kneel by her head as she crouched between his partners. "I'm feeling neglected."

She drew away from Percival's demanding kiss to find Cador's rosy cock bobbing beside her face. She eyed it as he held its thick base. "Now, Morg." With a sigh of pleasure, she swooped in to suck its head between her lips. It made a fine distraction from being stuffed like a Christmas goose.

The logistics of being fucked fore and aft while simultaneously giving a blowjob almost defeated Morgana for a moment. But as she paused in confusion, Cador began thrusting gently into her mouth, falling into effortless rhythm with his partners. Which probably told her more than she really wanted to know about how many times they'd shared a woman like this.

So she let her eyes fall closed and concentrated on suckling him as the three men cradled her between them, shafts sliding in and out. The pain of Marrok's and Percival's possession began to fade away, leaving only the hot pleasure of their cocks and skillful fingers hitting every bundle of nerves she had.

Until it began to seem she was floating in sweet euphoria, only vaguely aware of Cador's murmuring hot, obscene orders about what to do with her tongue and teeth. Knowing nothing except the feeling of hard, hot bodies rolling against hers, thick shafts stroking, stroking . . .

Until the fire blazed up, and she screamed, the sound muffled by Cador's cock . . .

Morgana convulsed against Percival's chest as he braced over her, shafting her in long, delicious digs. Her rectum clamped on his cock, a hot rippling sensation that almost tipped him over into climax, but he paused, determined that he would, by God, be the last to come.

With a strangled roar, Cador pulled out of her mouth to shoot across her cheek and down her chin. Eyes closed, obviously lost in erotic euphoria, she didn't appear to notice.

"Oh, Merlin's balls!" Marrok gasped, rolling his hips up so hard he almost threw Percival off-balance. One thrust, two, and the big knight threw his head back and bellowed. The feeling of his cock sliding past Percival's through Morgana's thin flesh ended any hope of control.

Snarling, Percival ground in to Morgana's exquisitely tight arse, thrusting with such force that she had to grab Marrok's hips and hold on to brace herself.

Fire blazed up from his swinging balls and tore up his shaft in spurts that made stars flare in front of his eyes. He roared, freezing there, his cock buried in her to the root, pressed tight to Marrok's in her pussy.

For a long, long moment, there was no sound beyond deep, desperate breathing as they all fought to recover.

"Jesus, that was hot," Cador gasped, breaking the silence. "I can't believe I gave Morgana le Fay a pearl necklace . . ."

Percival shot him a glare, and he snapped his teeth shut, losing his grin. Sharing her *had* been incredibly fucking hot, but that didn't mean Percival had to like it.

Carefully, he started sliding his softening shaft out of Morgana's no-doubt tender arse. He swung off Marrok's thighs and half lifted her off the big knight, turning her to face him as he lay down, cradling her as he panted. She looked dazed.

"You know, I think she flew," Cador gasped. He'd fallen onto his back, arms flung wide. "Her eyes definitely had that subspace glaze."

"Yeah, I thought that too," Marrok agreed. "She was starting to look a little vague right about the time you stuck your dick in her mouth."

"It looked that way to me, too." It wasn't the first time he'd sent a woman into subspace—that euphoria born of a combination of endorphins and adrenalin submissives sometimes experienced following a hard session of punishment. For many subs, flying was their primary motivation for playing in the scene to begin with. Making a sub fly was generally considered an accomplishment for a dom, since it took considerable skill.

"How are you feeling?" Percival asked Morgana.

She made an incoherent humming sound that somehow managed to communicate pleasure. The others were right; those green eyes were definitely vague, their pupils dilated.

"High as a kite," he grunted, and drew her against his chest. Looking at Cador over the crown of her head, he said, "Get us a blanket and a bottle of water, would you?"

Cador might be a bit of a prick at times, but he understood a dominant's responsibilities as well as Percival did. He nodded and rolled off the bed without complaint to go rummage in the small refrigerator that crouched in a corner of the room. Emerging with a bottle of cold water, he tossed it to Percival and ducked into the walk-in closet.

As Percival coaxed a dazed Morgana into drinking the water, Cador joined them to wrap a soft chenille throw around her bare shoulders. She gave them an incoherent murmur and wrapped her arms around Percival's waist, cuddling into him like a child. A reluctant smile tugging his lips, he wrapped the blanket more securely around her and settled back onto the bed with the witch in his arms.

He was only distantly aware of Marrok and Cador collapsing onto the bed too. God knew it was more than big enough to accommodate all four of them, and anyway, it wasn't the first time they'd all dozed off after an exhausting foursome.

Still, Morgana was staying in *his* arms; none of the others were touching her. His possessive inner wolf subsided with a soft mental growl.

At first Morgana thought it was the nightmare again, that dream memory of being trapped at the mercy of someone intent on torturing her simply because he could.

But then the pain sharpened, spiraled, became a flaming agony too intense to be anything but reality, paired with the sense of strength being siphoned away to feed the appetite of a killer.

She came off the bed screaming, writhing in the torment the victim felt, the helpless, hopeless sense that death's great wings shadowed her, about to bear her away. It took her a moment to hear Percival's voice calling her, feel his hands containing her struggles as the others called bewildered questions.

"*SOREN!*" Morgana screamed, but the dragon's telepathic grip fell away, leaving her shaking with horror and abject fear for her friend.

"Morgana!" Percival shouted, and she got the sense he'd been shouting her name for a while now. "What's happening? What did you see?"

"Christ, Percival, she had a nightmare," Cador growled in disgust, throwing himself back on the bed. "Thanks for giving me a fucking heart attack, Morg."

"That wasn't a nightmare," Percival snapped. "Morgana, what did you see?" He gave her a slight shake, then steadied her when she almost fell at his feet as her terror-weakened knees betrayed her.

"Soren," she gasped. "Huar has Soren and four women. He's woven a Death Magic spell around them, and if we don't get to them, he's going to trigger it."

"What?" Percival exploded. "I thought Kel told Arthur he and the rest of the lizards were going to hunt the bastard down!"

"And they've been working on it, but Huar stopped going to clubs and started just snatching people." Morgana shuddered, picking through impressions, snippets of information Soren had managed to communicate. "Huar's used Death Magic to kill more than fifty people in the past four days."

The knights stared at her, horrified. Death Magic was a type of spell that drew its power from torture and murder. They'd become all too familiar with its evil a few years ago, when demonic alien creatures called the Dark Ones had attempted to use it to invade the twin Earths. The Magekind had fought them off, but they'd lost a lot of good people, and too many innocent mortals had been murdered.

"How did you manage to have a vision wearing that collar?" Cador demanded. "I thought that thing blocked your power."

"It does. This wasn't a vision." Morgana wrung her hands and began to pace as she explained, "Huar tortured Soren to force him to contact me. The ambassador's hurt badly—he and the four hostages Huar used to trap him. They won't last long if we don't get to them—and fast. Percival, you've got to take the collar off. We have to go save them."

"That goes without saying." He bent to examine the collar. "How do I remove this thing?"

She touched the intricate engraving that covered the collar's lock. "Put your fingers here on the front clasp, and say 'Release.'"

Percival's warm, calloused fingers brushed her skin. She hid a shiver of reaction as he spoke the trigger word. Although the sound of the click was tiny—the results were anything but.

Power stormed over Morgana's skin in a painful, tingling jolt like an electric shock. She shook off the sensation, dragging the collar from around her neck as she called her magic. Energy swirled over her and the three knights, a shimmering wave of sparks that solidified into their armor and weapons a heartbeat later.

Percival drew his sword, checking the blade for nicks. "This time, dammit, we're calling Kel. Along with every other knight, vampire, and witch who's available."

"We can't. Soren told me Huar swears he'll kill them all if anyone comes but the four of us."

"Fuck, it's a trap," Cador growled in disgust.

"Of course it's a trap," Percival told him impatiently, then frowned at Morgana. "But why go to all this trouble just to trap us?"

"We beat him," Morgana said, her mind on the spell she was going to have to cast to find Soren, his captor, and the rest of the hostages. "Here we are, creatures barely more than apes as far as he's concerned, yet he narrowly escapes us with his life."

Cador swore viciously. "This is beginning to sound more and more like a suicide mission."

"I've been working on a spell that will amplify my abilities just as the collar nullified them," Morgana told them. "It's the same basic theory, only in reverse." Which was true . . . in a sense. More or less. "As we gate in, I'll shift to dragon form and take to the air to draw him off. When he comes after me, that's when you free Soren and the victims from that Death Magic spell. I'll give you something you can use to disrupt the spell. Once they're safe, you can call in reinforcements from Avalon and the Dragonlands."

Marrok scowled. "That still leaves you trying to go toe-to-toe with Godzilla until reinforcements arrive."

"Exactly." A muscle rolled in Percival's jutting jaw. "You do know the definition of insanity is doing the same thing over and over expecting a different result? This bastard is almost twice your size in dragon form. He'll kick your pretty arse again, just the way he did the last time."

She gave him a smile she hoped showed a lot more confidence than she actually felt. "My amplification spell will take care of that."

"Uh, huh." Percival's hard stare warned her he didn't entirely buy it. Fortunately, he also didn't have time to try to find out what she was stretching the truth to get around. Instead he said, "You are fucking *not* going to leave us this time, or I'll . . ."

"Don't be absurd." There was no way in hell she could take the chance of leaving the team behind. If her plan backfired, Percival, Marrok, and Cador might well be the only ones who could stop her.

Even if they had to kill her to do it.

Morgana frowned, realizing that she could no longer take the risk of keeping the team in the dark. Not when the odds were she was going to have to risk Mageverse Fever in order to defeat the dragon. *Oh,* she thought, *Percival's going to be furious.*

Didn't matter. She couldn't let the team walk blindly into such a deadly situation . "Look, there's another aspect of this I think I'd better make you aware of."

Percival gave her a narrow-eyed stare that held entirely too much perception. "Why do I get the sudden feeling I'm not going to like whatever you're about to tell me?"

"Because you won't." She sighed and hesitated, groping for words. Explaining this was going to be touchy as hell. "Look, almost all Majae have unconscious limitations on how much power they can draw on from the Mageverse. That's a good thing. Human minds—even the minds of witches—can't survive full contact with infinite power like that. "That's why so many young Majae go insane from Mageverse Fever."

"We know that, Morgana." Cador glowered at her, impatient. "If you've got a point, get to it before somebody dies."

"I don't have that unconscious limit." Approaching Percival, she stared up into his eyes. "I never have. Nimue told me once she thought it was from trying to draw on Druid healing magic from the time I was a mortal child. It's so difficult to reach the Mageverse's magical forces from Mortal Earth, I destroyed any unconscious barriers I ever had."

Percival stared at her, searching her face with worried eyes. "And that's not a good thing."

"No. It's not." She raked her black hair out of her face and looked away. "Because if I try to draw too much, if I drop all my conscious mental barriers, I could end up just as insane as any new witch with Mageverse Fever."

Percival froze, staring at her. After a moment, he said, "But why didn't you get Mageverse Fever fifteen centuries ago? Why did Nimue let you drink from the Grail if you had the potential to go insane?"

"Nimue was concerned about that after I passed her test, but she believed I'd be needed even under the circumstances. She decided to take the risk."

"Why the fuck haven't you mentioned this before? Christ, you've had fifteen fucking centuries!" Cador demanded. "I mean, this strikes me as the kind of shit Arthur would have liked to know."

"Because it never seemed relevant before." She turned to start pacing again. "Look, up until recently, we've never had to fight anything but plain vanilla humans. Yeah, they were tyrants, terrorists, communists, anarchists, whatever—but they didn't have *magic*. The power I had naturally was more than enough to deal with them." Morgana sank down on the bed, feeling suddenly weary. Which was just too damned bad. "Then things got . . . complicated."

"Geirolf and his cultists, you mean," Percival said, referring to a demonic magic-using creature from another universe. "And after that came the Dark Ones and the werewolves and Warlock."

"Exactly. There've been a couple of times in the past decade when I've had to get a little close to the edge, and things . . . happened."

"What kind of things?" Percival asked quietly, a muscle rolling in his jaw.

Morgana swallowed as bloody memories rose. "Remember when Warlock invaded Avalon with his werewolf army? It was daytime, and I was alone. He sent four of his wolves to get me. They're immune to magic, of course, and when they attacked, I . . . panicked. I knew throwing magical blasts at them was a waste of time, so I pulled on all the power of the Mageverse and cast a spell on myself to increase my physical strength."

Cador blinked. "You can do that?"

Percival ignored him. "What happened, Morgana?"

"I don't know." She glanced blindly around. "The next thing I remember, there were . . . pieces in my foyer. Blood and fur and chunks. Somebody's leg. Bones." She gave Marrok a fleeting smile. He didn't smile back. "At first I thought you'd gone berserk and saved me, but then I looked outside and saw it was still daylight. I had to have done it, but . . ."

"You had a blackout." The muscle in Percival's jaw ticked faster, and his gray eyes grew hot. "You went berserk, had a blackout, and ripped *four* eight-foot werewolves apart. And you never mentioned it to me." His voice began to grow louder. "You've been going out on missions with my team to fight supernatural creatures you knew you'd have to use magic against, and *you never mentioned the possibility it might drive you insane?"*

FOURTEEN

I didn't completely ignore the danger, Percival," Morgana protested, though she flinched at his rage. "That's why I started working with Soren to begin with. He began teaching me draconic magical techniques to help me learn to maintain control. I can manage far more power now without losing my grip. Yes, there are limits, but . . ."

"Limits?" The word was practically a hiss of fury. "But you *never* said a word to me?"

Morgana's shoulders slumped. "I was afraid of your reaction if you and the team thought I might go mad. I was afraid you'd reject me, that Arthur and the Magekind would think me untrustworthy."

"Hell," Cador exploded, "you *are* untrustworthy! You . . ."

"Cador, shut up!" Percival snapped.

"Look, I thought that even if we ran into another Warlock, I'd have so much backup from the rest of the Majae, I wouldn't have to draw on a dangerous degree of power. Except that now . . ."

"Except now," Percival finished grimly, "if we don't show up to fight that fucker Huar alone, he'll kill four innocent women and the Dragonkind ambassador. And you're afraid you're going to have to draw on so much power to fight him, it'll drive you insane."

"Yes." Morgana's voice was barely audible even to her own ears. Taking a deep breath, she added, "You may need to kill me, Percival."

At those words, fury blazed in the knight's gray eyes as he stared down at her—fury and fear. For her?

"Don't be a drama queen, Morgana," Marrok growled, his tone scornful. "They've never had to kill me, and I've been known to cause as much destruction as an F3 tornado once I get going."

"Yeah, but the kind of damage Morgana could do would be more along the lines of a thermonuclear bomb." Percival's gray eyes blazed, coldly furious. "Not just buildings blown apart but craters the size of Manhattan filled with molten lava."

"Yes," Morgana admitted, her voice barely audible.

"Tell me straight, Morgana. No lies, no bullshit. If you really did go mad—*Could* we kill you?" Even as he asked the cold question, there was anguish in his eyes.

She swallowed. "I . . . don't know. But once I take care of Huar, you'll be able to call in Arthur and the rest of the Magekind. With enough magical backup, you could do it. Probably."

Cador buckled on his sword belt and snarled. "Fuck me. Fuck us *all*."

"That's enough, Cador," Percival snapped.

The knight glowered, but subsided at last, evidently recognizing that his team leader had been pushed too far.

Percival stalked over to Morgana to stand looking down at her, his gaze conflicted, torn. She stared up at him miserably, all too aware of what she might do to them all if the situation went bad.

To her astonishment, the knight's expression softened. His hand lifted, stroked a black curl back from her cheek. "Okay, do it. We'll be there for you."

Her eyes stung, forcing her to blink hard. "You always have been." Her voice sounded rough-edged.

From the corner of one eye, she saw Cador and Marrok exchange a "*We're definitely fucked*" look.

Knowing she'd have to go in as hard as she possibly could to save Soren and the others, Morgana began drawing on as much power as she dared, dragging in great psychic torrents of it. Now so much magic filled her brain, it felt as if a swarm of bees buzzed inside her skull until she wanted to jitter in place like a hyperactive toddler.

Even if she managed to pull this off, Morgana knew the fallout would be devastating. Her relationship with the team would never be the same; she doubted they'd ever trust her again.

But if she thought things would be easy given all the power she'd inhaled, Morgana quickly realized otherwise. Just reaching Soren through the remnants of their psychic connection had been far more difficult than it should have been. Huar obviously intended that she be able to establish only enough of a connection to track the ambassador, not communicate with him.

Morgana, of course, wanted to know more about the trap the draconic fucker had obviously set for them. Despite the monster's magical defenses, she'd managed a quick scan of the death spell and Huar himself. She hadn't liked what she found.

Horned God, the fucker was terrifying. The last time she'd sensed an aura of black magic that strong had been when the Magekind had gone to war against the demon Dark Ones. She could still beat the bastard—Death Magic had its limits—but the price she might pay to do it scared the living hell out of her. If she wasn't careful, she'd end up killing everybody she was trying to save. Including Percival and her team.

As if that wasn't enough, she had to figure out how Percival was going to free the hostages from Huar's death spell. Lacking the time for anything else, she'd cobbled a counter spell around the collar, since it had already been designed to nullify magic.

She dared take no more than a moment or two to cast the spell, making up for the lack of the precision spellcraft by pouring as much raw power into the collar as she could.

"Morgana!" Soren's weak voice said in her mind just as she finished. *"Huar says if you don't arrive in the next twenty seconds, he's killing one of the women."*

"Fuck!" Morgana snarled, and thrust the collar into Percival's mailed hands. "Grab your weapons and prepare to jump. He's about to start killing women."

Magic boiled from her hands, pouring into a point in the air and instantly expanding into a wavering doorway, revealing a clearing in the midst of Mageverse trees the size of redwoods. She moved to leap through the minute the gate was open, but a hard hand thrust her back. Percival lunged in front of her, Cador and Marrok leaping in to join him on either side.

Morgana bit back a curse and clawed more magic from the Mageverse as the four of them charged, forming it into a hemisphere of dancing golden energy before them.

Huar's first blast hit the shield the instant they were through the gate. The spell barrier held against the eye-searing explosion of sparks, but just barely.

Desperate, Morgana dragged in yet more Mageverse energy until it felt like her skull was on the verge of detonating like a suitcase nuke. "Horned God, that fucking dragon might be stronger than a Dark One!"

"Shit."

"Yeah. I'm shifting. Get the hostages." She blasted toward Huar on a wave of magic, feet leaving the ground as she flew at her foe like a cannonball. Not something she'd usually chance doing, but she needed to get the hell away from the knights so she'd have room to shift. Otherwise she ran the risk of accidently crushing them as her body became thirty feet of dragon.

"Don't goddamn get killed!" Percival bellowed after her.

"That's the least of my worries," Morgana muttered, and began to shift as she flew toward Huar, who charged to meet her with an ear-stunning roar.

Percival watched, breath held, as the smaller black dragon slammed into the scarlet beast. Huar looked even bigger than he had the last time they'd fought him. The dragons roared in overwhelming blasts of sound, their bodies thudding together.

Worse—much, much worse—was the sense of raw, greasy evil the dragon emanated like a roiling stench. Adding to the malevolent effect, twisted black shapes writhed over Huar's crimson scales, evidently draconic magical symbols.

At first Percival thought they were some kind of paint, but a moment later he realized they were actually inscribed into the scales as if branded there.

"Big, Red and Scaly is definitely up to his horns in Death Magic," Cador said, staring at the sigils, his lip curled in revolted horror.

"We have *got* to kill that creature," Marrok growled. "We can't let him get away this time."

"Don't worry, he's dead." Percival dragged his eyes away from Morgana and her desperate battle with Huar. They had to free the dragon's victims and get help if she was going to survive her suicide mission. "This time tomorrow we're all going to be wearing dragonscale boots." He managed a crooked grin, despite the fear for her that tied his gut in knots. "Or in Morgana's case, dragonskin stilettos."

But when he turned and got a good look at what waited for them in the center of the clearing, Percival forgot the attempt at humor in sheer, frigid outrage.

Soren, in dragon form, lay imprisoned by a swirling green lattice of glowing draconic symbols shaped roughly like an egg. Women surrounded his painfully contorted body in four pitiful, bloody heaps. They lay unmoving, not even appearing to breathe.

Morgana bugled a draconic battle cry. Percival looked up, his heart leaping into his throat. Above his head, the two dragons dove at each other in a raking pass of claws.

"Fuck," Percival growled, and hurried toward them, pulling the collar out of the belt pouch Morgana had conjured for it. "Soren? Ambassador, are you conscious?"

Though the ambassador didn't lift his head, his eyes opened. His pupils, normally reptilian slits, were dilated into huge circles in thin rings of iridescent irises.

Though Percival had been ready to duel Soren the last time they'd spoken, he felt only pity for his rival now. Huar had cut magical symbols into the ambassador's scales with some kind of blade, perhaps even his claws. So much gore ran from the snaking cuts that blood loss could well have been responsible for Soren's obvious disorientation.

But Percival knew it was more than that. The Death Magic spell itself was responsible, draining the life force from Soren and the women and feeding that elemental energy to Huar.

Who meant to use it to kill Morgana. The idea that the creature would dare hurt her filled him with a rage more intense than anything he'd ever felt, even when his brothers had been endangered.

It was then the knowledge hit him like the blow of a battle ax: he loved Morgana. Arrogant, powerful, maddening though she was, he had loved her for centuries. That was why he'd wanted her with such desperation. And deep down, he wasn't even surprised by the depth of the love he'd denied so long. Though he'd always told himself his hunger for her had been born of frustrated desire, he'd secretly known better. If it had been a matter of sexual obsession, he'd have eventually gotten over it. After all, he was surrounded by beautiful, seductive women who were eager to submit to whatever he cared to do.

But none of them had been his Morgana. No one else would ever do.

Above them, dragons roared. This time Percival knew he didn't dare look up. He couldn't let himself be distracted by his own chilling fear for his witch. He had to pull it together, do his duty by Soren and the four women. For one thing, breaking the Death Magic spell would deprive Huar of at least some of his magical strength—which might help Morgana survive. Squaring his shoulders, he started forward.

"Stay back," Percival snapped at Cador and Marrok, even as he walked right up to the swirling, lethal energies. The lattice spun faster as he approached. He swallowed, hoping Morgana was right that the collar and its counter-spell would protect him. "You don't want any kind of contact with the bastard's Death Magic at all."

Then he drew back the collar as if it were a circular blade and sliced it through the nearest whirling strand of magical energy. The strand parted like wet spaghetti hit with a meat cleaver, except with a hiss and a puff of stinking smoke. Any sense of triumph Percival might have felt was blunted by the wave of nausea and weakness that promptly rolled over him. He wanted to think it was just an effect of that god-awful reek, but he knew better.

He'd felt the aura of the spell brush across his knuckles. That slight contact had almost sent him to his knees.

If this feels that bad to me, what would it be like inside the spell with no protection at all? Soren and those women would be in agony even if they hadn't been tortured.

Yeah, Huar needed killing—with extreme prejudice, if not outright glee.

Two massive bodies slammed together overhead with a meaty thud.

Morgana roared in furious defiance. He looked up, heart in his throat, to watch her wheel and rip at her foe, then dart away.

Dragging his gaze away from the witch he loved, Percival shook off the waves of weakness from the Death Magic spell and started working his way around the spell's egg-shaped boundary, taking the collar to it in long, ripping strokes. Each pass destroyed more and more of the dancing green symbols, but with every swipe, he grew sicker.

Finally he took a step and his knees gave. The collar seemed to weigh more than his broadsword at the end of a two-hour duel. He lost his grip on it. A hand grabbed his shoulder before he could hit the ground, a beefy arm sliding around his waist.

"Percival, what the fuck?" Marrok growled in his ear as the big man steadied him. "What's wrong?"

Cador bent and scooped up the collar. "It's a Death Magic spell, 'Rok. It's like fucking around in a radioactive field. He's probably considering puking on your boots right about now."

Then Cador, cheerfully whistling, went to work on the spell himself with long swipes of the collar. If he started turning green a moment later, it didn't seem to stop him.

When Percival's stomach was finally under control again, he recognized the song his friend was whistling: "Puff the Magic Dragon."

Huar's great jaws opened, and a blast of flame that looked like the product of a thermonuclear explosion boiled out of his mouth and shot directly at Morgana's head.

Knowing the blast would blow right through her shield, she opened herself to the Mageverse and let still more power rush in. A heartbeat later, she sent it roaring out again to slam into Huar's attack.

The two spells collided, swirled together in a vicious storm of opposing forces . . . and canceled each other out, dissipating back into the Mageverse.

"Human bitch," Huar hissed, his forked tail snapping in fury as he winged in dizzying bat-like circles around her. "I am going to rip the beating heart out of your mate's chest and eat it before your very eyes. Then I'll set the other two aflame so you can listen to them scream while I rape you."

Morgana knew the threat wasn't hyperbole. The dragon's great orange eyes blazed with madness, and raw evil swirled around him like sewage around a drain.

So yes, he'd do it. Hell, he'd done worse. Would do worse to her if she let him.

But even as her blood went cold, she laughed in his face. "All that Death Magic you've been using has rotted your wits," she hissed in the draconic tongue. "You're the one who'll burn like a torch. Fit payment for your filthy crimes."

That threat *was* hyperbole. Morgana was tiring, and the power she had to keep drawing from the Mageverse hurt almost as badly as Huar's attacks. *Which is actually a good sign,* she told herself. *I'll be in trouble when the magic starts feeling good.*

Morgana knew the sequence, had experienced it before. First pain from drawing too much power, then numbness, then a wild pleasure turning quickly to euphoria. Then . . . She didn't remember what came after that.

And it was that which frightened her most of all.

Marrok worked to banish the last of the green Death Magic symbols with grim swings of the collar, though he looked as if he'd fall on his face at any moment.

As his friend worked, Percival shot a glance skyward, painfully aware of the sound of lethal combat in the air over their heads. Morgana fought for her life—and theirs—while he was trapped down on the ground, unable to help her, unable to save her.

Finished at last, Marrok dropped the collar in sheer exhaustion. It took Percival and Cador together to steady him.

Lifting the spell had an immediate effect. Soren raised his great head and blinked at them in confusion. He said something in the hissing language of his kind before switching to English. "Sir . . . knight? What . . . ?"

"You were kidnapped by Huar, the dragon you were hunting," Percival told him, as Marrok straightened away from his steadying hand. The big knight was still pale, but his color was rapidly improving with the last of the spell gone.

Soren's head snapped up on his long neck, and his iridescent eyes went wide. "Huar! Egg-sucker . . . trapped me . . . cut a cursed Death Magic spell . . . into my scales!" His teeth bared, his head swung in search of his foe. "I'll have . . . have his blood . . ."

"I don't think you're up to it right now," Percival told him. "That spell has been funneling your life force to Huar. You need to concentrate on healing yourself."

"Yes . . ." Great dragon eyes blinked slowly, their pupils dilated and dazed. "I need to . . . heal."

"While he's doing that, we'd better check on the women," Cador said, shooting Marrok a concerned stare. "Are you up to it?"

"I think so." Marrok braced his tree-trunk thighs apart. "But we need healers. There's not a hell of a lot we vampires can do for these girls." He looked at Percival. "Have you tried calling Avalon yet?"

"I'm about to. You and Cador go check on the other victims."

"You won't be . . . able to get through," Soren said in a voice that sounded so uncharacteristically weak, it was hard to hear him over the roaring blasts of the combat overhead. "I just tried to reach Kel again . . . been trying . . . for hours now. Huar erected a spell around this clearing to keep us from calling for help. It's still there."

Percival pulled the enchanted iPhone off his belt and tried anyway, only to discover the dragon was right. The phone might as well have been a brick. "Is there any way you could open a gate so one of us could go for reinforcements? Maybe if you heal your injuries first?"

"The spell blocks any gates but those he . . . chooses to allow," the dragon said in that breathy, fading voice that was so uncharacteristic for him. "As to healing . . . I fear I am too weak. Perhaps after I rest . . ."

Percival wanted to snap that Morgana might not have that much time, but under the circumstances, even he wasn't that big of a dick. He bit it back. Instead, he and Soren watched the battle taking place overhead.

"Oh, Morgana," Soren breathed. "Don't draw any more power. You'll destroy yourself . . . and Cachamwri knows who else . . ."

His heart in his throat, Percival stared up at the battling dragons. "She may not have a choice."

Morgana no longer felt the pain. Not from the burns where Huar's blasts had penetrated her shield, not from the wounds he'd inflicted with claws and teeth.

She knew he was beating her, but the thought seemed distant, despite the chilling knowledge that once she was dead, he'd slaughter Percival and his team.

They'd die in agony.

Yet instead of the terror that thought should inspire, all Morgana felt was a growing euphoria. Every time she raked her claws across Huar's muzzle, pleasure rang through her like a great dark bell.

Huar might be winning, but she was hurting him. Making him pay for those women and Soren and her knights. And every moment she fought him was a moment he wasn't attacking those she loved.

And if some part of her knew this giddy pleasure was very, very bad, all she wanted was to bleed him. She thirsted for his blood like water in the desert heat.

Huar juked in midair, avoiding the spell blast she sent roiling at him, his huge sword-length teeth bared in draconic rage and frustration. "Human bitch! I'm going to rip you apart and feast on your steaming guts!"

"Big talk, lizard," she snarled.

Glowing orange eyes blinked and narrowed, trying to rid themselves of the blood that seeped into them from the bite she'd inflicted on his head. "Then when you are dead, I'm going to shift and fuck that mate of yours until he dies in blood and agony!"

At the threat, her wings lost their rhythm, and she faltered in the air.

Huar struck. His huge body slammed into hers, forelegs and rear claws snapping around her as he sank his jaws into the back of her neck just behind her skull. Her body twisted, trying to break his hold from sheer spinal reflex, but her mind . . . her mind . . .

She balanced on a stool on the tips of her toes, her hands bound in front of her, spots dancing in front of her eyes. She couldn't draw breath for the pressure of the noose around her neck, its rope taut, looped over the hook in the ceiling of the priest's cottage.

When the beatings hadn't made her admit to the perverted sins he described, he had decided to give her a taste of hanging.

The dragon's forelegs raked along her ribs . . .

She'd been sure—so blindly sure—he wouldn't actually dare kill her because he wouldn't be able to explain it to the bishop. And she'd known that if she did sign that disgusting confession, the Church would hang her as a witch.

"You will sign!" Bennett shouted, and stormed from the room. "You will confess your crimes!*"*

Her blood went icy in her veins as a five-year-old boy screamed. Bennett dragged Mordred into the room, jerked the struggling child to the floor in front of the stool she balanced on, and started jerking his tunic up. "Sign it!" Bennett shrieked. "You will sign it now!"

Huar's teeth tightened their grip on the back of her skull. She heard his teeth grinding into bone, the pressure vicious . . .

Morgana's hands flew up to grab the tight rope looped over the hook.

With a scream of mingled defiance and terror, she leaped straight upward with all the strength she had left, taking the tension off the rope so she could flip it forward. The stool fell with a crash.

If she'd misjudged her leap, she'd have hanged herself. Instead, she successfully flipped the loop off the hook.

Morgana hit the dirt floor on her backside with bruising force. She heard Bennett shout in angry astonishment, rising from her shrieking son . . .

Just as she jerked up the stool in both bound hands and swung it, slamming it hard into the side of Bennett's head. Then she hit him again. And again.

And again.

When she'd told Arthur that Bennett had died of plague, she'd lied.

Any second now, Huar's teeth would punch through her skull and into her brain, and she'd be dead. And she knew—*knew*—he'd carry out his threat to rape Percival to death. It seemed she could hear her lover's bellow of agony, the sound blending with Mordred's high-pitched child shrieks . . .

Morgana ripped away the last of the barrier that protected her mind from the Mageverse and let the infinite flood her brain like a tsunami hitting a sandcastle.

Percival heard Morgana scream, and terror froze his heart in his chest. He heard Marrok and Cador curse in unison with his own horrified "No!" Soren hissed something, the fear in his tone needing no translation.

The dragons fell, tumbling earthward in a tangle of desperately beating wings and lashing tails.

"Morgana!" Percival bellowed, and began to run toward the direction of their fall, terror for his woman gripping his heart. Cador and Marrok ran with him. He had no fucking idea what any of them would do when they got there.

A fall from that height would surely kill even a dragon.

The crash sounded like an explosion. Chunks of wood flew through the air, forcing them to duck and throw up their arms to protect their heads. Droplets pattered down like rain, hitting Percival's arms and shoulders and rolling down his face. He swiped at one runnel with his palm as he ran, threw a downward glance at it. It was a dark violet.

Dragon's blood.

A quick, frantic scan showed him no sign of red blood.

Then he looked up, squinting against the sudden wind, and saw why Huar's blood covered the ground. The great dragon had fallen into the trees, breaking and crushing several huge trunks like weeds.

He counted at least five shattered trunks impaling the creature like stakes. There was no sign of Morgana's body, though it had looked like the two had fallen together.

Percival looked upward, blinking against the wind, his heart frozen in his chest . . .

Morgana spiraled downward, landing on a shattered trunk impaling Huar through the back. She worked her way down the broken tree's length, her tail lashing.

Percival bent forward and braced his hands on his knees, heaving in breaths of sheer relief. She must have somehow pulled out of the fall at the last second and flown clear. "She's all right. Thank Jesu, she's all right . . ."

"No," Cador said in a voice rough with horror, "I don't think she is."

Percival glanced up. And froze.

Morgana was ripping into the dragon's belly with her jaws. As he stared in horrified disbelief, she swung her head up in a thoroughly inhuman gesture and gulped down a chunk of something that shone violet and wet in the moonlight.

"What the fuck . . ." Cador breathed. "Why is she doing that?"

"Because the . . . Mageverse has her," Soren wheezed, collapsing on the ground behind them in exhaustion, "and she's lost."

Percival hadn't even known the desperately wounded dragon had followed them. He wondered how the ambassador had found the strength.

Cador whirled on the blue dragon. "What do you mean, the Mageverse has her?"

"Let me try to heal . . . myself . . . first, and I will . . . explain. With Huar dead, I'll . . . be able to . . . repair most of the damage." The dragon closed his eyes and began to hiss a chant. Green energy began to swirl over his massive body, finding the bloody cuts and erasing them.

Tersely, Percival explained what Soren had told him while his partners had checked on the women—who by some miracle were all still alive. That was something, anyway.

Reminded of the human victims, he turned toward Cador. "Get on the phone and call the healers. Now that Huar's dead, his shielding spells will have collapsed. We'll be able to call out."

As Cador moved to obey, Percival looked at Soren. "What do we do? How do we bring her back?"

"I don't know if we can." The dragon's voice sounded much stronger now. His scales looked clean and whole, but something in the way he'd collapsed on his belly suggested the effort had exhausted him. Now he watched Morgana eat her dead foe with a kind of horrified fascination. "We'll be lucky if she doesn't go after us next."

FIFTEEN

Half afraid of what horror he'd see her performing now, Percival glanced around at her.

She had begun to glow. Her black scales shimmered with dancing waves of energy in a thousand shifting colors. As he watched, the glow grew brighter with every second that passed.

"What the fuck?" he breathed. "Soren, what the hell does that mean?"

"She's becoming an elemental."

Cador dropped his phone. He had to scramble to catch it before it hit the ground. He clipped it blindly on his belt as the three knights stared at Soren. "What, like Cachamwri and Semara?"

Cachamwri was the godlike being the dragonkind worshipped; Semara was his equally powerful mate. If Morgana was gaining that kind of power, if she went mad—and it seemed she was halfway there—she'd be able to kill every last one of the Magekind, the Dragonkind, and everything else on Mageverse Earth.

And she'd be lost. Morgana le Fay, the woman he loved, would be as dead as if Huar had killed and devoured *her*.

The realization that he loved her didn't startle Percival, barely made him even skip a thought. He'd always known in the core of his soul how he felt about Morgana. He just hadn't wanted to admit it to himself, because he'd feared she didn't return the emotion.

Now he simply didn't give a damn whether she loved him back or not. All he wanted to do was save her.

Percival straightened convulsively as a wild idea surfaced in his consciousness. "A Truebond! If I mind-linked with her, formed a Truebond, could I bring her back?"

Soren considered the idea a moment, watching Morgana feast. Finally, reluctantly, he shook his head. "It's more likely she would drag you into madness with her."

"I'm no stranger to madness," Marrok said suddenly. "What if both of us Truebond with her?"

Despite the desperation of their circumstances, Percival's inner cave wolf sent up a growl of protest. "Three people can't form a Truebond, Marrok."

"Actually, they could," Soren said thoughtfully. "Kel, Gawain, and his wife Lark formed one briefly in order to free Kel from that sword." After Kel's uncle had trapped him in sword form, he'd served as Gawain's talking enchanted blade for centuries. "But I'm still not sure your sanity would survive."

"What if all three of us Truebonded with her?" Cador turned to Percival. "It wouldn't be permanent—just long enough to bring her back. Then Marrok and I could back out of it and leave you two alone." He grimaced. "Believe me, I have no desire to have Morgana le Fay in my head for the rest of my life."

Soren paused a long, nerve-wracking moment. "With three of you, and given Marrok's experience with being a berserker . . . Yes, it's possible." His tail lashed, the gesture agitated. "But it's still no guarantee. You all may end up mad."

"Yeah, well, we've always been willing to die for each other," Marrok said. "This is no different."

"Oh, yeah, it is," Cador grumbled. "I don't want to end up eating people who piss me off."

The man had a point.

But despite the grim battle they faced, a shaft of warmth shot through Percival like sunlight. He'd always said his brothers were willing to follow him into hell. Now it seemed they were willing to prove him right.

"The problem is, you're going to have to convince Morgana herself to open the mental link," Soren warned them. "You can't force a Truebond."

"Shit," Cador growled. "How the hell are we supposed to talk her into anything? I mean, look at her . . ."

It was a damned good point, Percival thought, as Morgana ripped another hunk of meat from the corpse. Maybe if they could get her to shift back to human form . . .

An idea made his eyes widen. "Take off your armor," he snapped. "All of it." He seized one of his gauntlets and dragged it off his hand. "Strip down to your leggings."

Cador stared at him. "You've got to be kidding."

"If she decides to kill us, all the armor on the planet won't stop her from doing it." Percival pulled off the other glove.

Marrok exchanged a look with Cador and shrugged. "In for a penny . . ."

Grumbling, Cador went to work on his own armor. "I'd feel a lot better about this if she wasn't busy eating the last guy who pissed her off."

Just getting to her wasn't easy. Huar's plummeting body had knocked down and shattered trees, which had in turn uprooted and broken others. The three knights had to climb over or around the snapped trunks, while avoiding jutting spears of ragged wood. Their knee-high armored boots provided some protection, but they still had to move carefully.

Finally they found a spot left clear by a group of trees that had somehow remained standing not thirty feet from the red dragon's impaled corpse. And Morgana, still busy ripping it apart.

Looking up at her, Cador grimaced. "Now what the hell are we supposed to do?"

Percival took a deep breath and blew it out. "Get her attention."

Marrok laughed without real humor. "Are you sure we want it?"

"Probably not, but that's not the issue." He lifted his voice. "Morgana!" When she didn't look up from her meal, he shouted in a deep, harsh bark, "Morgana le Fay, leave that alone and come here!"

Cador stared at him, wide-eyed. "Are you trying to dom a thirty-foot dragon? A crazy, *cannibalistic* thirty-foot dragon?"

But she'd stopped to stare at them. Her muzzle shone wet and black in the moonlight. Even Percival was surprised when she leaped down off Huar's corpse like a cat leaping off a counter. She moved toward them, weaving between some trees, pushing others aside with a thrust of her neck.

Merlin's Balls, she was powerful. But was Morgana still . . . there?

Percival felt sick. Had he lost her so soon after finding her?

She stopped about fifteen feet away, studying the arrangement of trees that had fallen to form a rickety pyramid. "Could fall," she rumbled, and began to push them off to the left and right. One of the trees started to tip toward them, but before the knights could jump back, Morgana's head shot forward. She caught the trunk in her jaws and twisted her neck, uprooting it and turning to put it carefully aside.

Percival blinked, realizing that she was trying to make sure the knights weren't injured by falling timber. Once the trees were clear, she moved a few feet closer and settled down on her belly. Glowing eyes focused on them intently with what looked uncomfortably like . . . hunger.

"Morgana?" Soren rumbled behind them. Wood crunched and splintered with loud cracks as the big dragon moved toward them.

Morgana's head jerked up, and she half rose, her huge wings curling forward to mantle the three men. Her lips back from her blade-length teeth in a snarl. "Mine!"

Everyone, including the ambassador, froze at the stark rage on her inhuman moonlit muzzle.

"You'd better get back, Soren," Percival said with tight, careful control.

The ambassador spoke in a low voice, "But Percival, I think you're in danger."

Morgana hissed in rage, her tail lashing as her big body tensed in obvious preparation for an attack.

Percival swallowed, looking up at the figure towering over him. "We're in more danger if you don't get the hell back."

The dragon grumbled something in his own language, but began to back reluctantly away. Percival didn't dare take his eyes off Morgana long enough to look around at him. She glared after him, then finally settled down again, the fury fading from her inhuman gaze. She turned her eyes to them. "Am here."

"Yes." Percival's heart pounded in his chest, knowing if she chose, she could kill them before they even knew what hit them. Particularly since he'd decided they should leave their swords behind.

A man did not, after all, talk to a lover with a weapon in his hand. If they treated her like a potential enemy, she might well act like one.

But if he treated her like a submissive . . . "Shift," he ordered. "We want to talk to you."

"Talk?" She tilted her head and eyed their half-naked bodies with that unnerving hunger. "Or fuck?"

"Only if you brush your teeth," Cador muttered.

Her shimmering eyes narrowed; she'd obviously heard him. "Huar ate women." Her lips peeled back. "So ate Huar."

"She's got a point," Marrok murmured.

His tone unbending, Percival ordered, "Shift, Morgana."

Magic flared in her draconic eyes, bursting into a blinding blue-white swirl of sparks. Percival blinked the dazzle from his eyes to see her standing there in human form, lovely and completely naked. His shoulders slumped in relief.

Only to stiffen again as he abruptly realized her skin shone with an unearthly glow. And her eyes, normally a deep and verdant green, blazed with the same swirling blue iridescence they'd had in her dragon form.

Oh, that's not good. He exchanged a quick, dismayed glance with Cador and Marrok.

She moved toward them, barefoot as a nymph, lovely in her lithe nudity. He glanced down in alarm as he imagined the kind of damage all that jagged wood could do to her bare feet. Yet she strode toward them without evident hesitation. There was a reason for that; as she stepped on the splintered wood, it instantly burned to ash. Surprisingly, the ground litter beneath did not catch fire, despite the burning footprints she left behind.

Percival's gaze flicked back up to Morgana's face. Normally that kind of magical effort would have shown clearly on her face, if only as an expression of concentration. Yet she didn't even seem aware of it at all, as if her magic was eliminating threats without her conscious volition.

But as terrifying as he might find that, he couldn't let it matter. He had to be her dominant if he was to save her. He moved to meet her, coolly determined. She looked up at him with a hint of challenge, her eyes swirling with that strange blue iridescence. Percival reached out and cupped her face between his hands. Something hot and tingling invaded his fingertips, like an electric charge.

Ignoring that, he tipped her head up, and kissed her, making it as deep and possessive as he could, his tongue sweeping around hers, stroking over teeth and lips. For a moment she stiffened, and it crossed his mind to wonder if he was about to get very dead.

Then she relaxed, melting against him, kissing him back. As he concentrated on making love to her mouth despite the way her power burned him, he sensed Marrok and Cador step up on either side.

The two knights began to caress and kiss any part of her they could reach. One of them grunted softly in discomfort, reacting to the alien lash of her power.

By the time he drew back, they were all breathing in rasping pants, and his cock was beginning to press against his fly. "Truebond with me."

"Truebond with us," Marrok corrected.

Cador nodded. "With all three of us."

Morgana looked up at Percival with those alien eyes, then at his partners. "Truebond . . ." For a moment she appeared to struggle, frowning. "Only two . . . in Truebond."

Cupping her face between his palms again, Percival hardened his tone into a dominant's demand. "With all three of us, Morgana. Truebond with us all. Now."

She blinked up at him, confusion in her gaze. "But . . . It could destroy you."

"*Now,* Morgana." He used the inflexible tone that had always worked on her before.

And it worked again.

Her eyes widened, magic whirling and sparking in her gaze. The blue glowed brighter and brighter, seeming to grow until he had the sense of tumbling headfirst into that cobalt storm of energy.

For a moment he was aware of the familiar mental touch of Cador and Marrok—but not Morgana. He reached out, groping for her, trying to find her in the ripping winds of magic and light.

The sparks striking his skin began to burn with such intensity, he feared he'd actually burst into flame. He sucked in a breath, instinctively fighting the pain. It did him no good. Fireworks pelted him, flying into his consciousness faster and faster until it seemed he stood in a hurricane of energy.

Desperation growing, Percival fought to shield himself, but he didn't have the power to do it. Instead the sparks beat against him like sand in a sandstorm, shredding his flesh, his very consciousness. He realized it would eventually erode him away until there was nothing left.

And he had no idea how to stop it. Even worse, he'd dragged Cador and Marrok into this. They'd be destroyed too—and for nothing. He'd never managed to even touch Morgana, much less bring her back to herself. As despair raked him, something tightened around his throat, digging in, cutting off his breathing.

A noose. *There was a noose around his throat.*

He balanced on his toes on a stool, on the verge of hanging, fighting to breathe as a little boy screamed in pain and utter terror.

A man in a priest's rough robe dragged the struggling dark-haired child in front of Percival, and pushed the struggling child to the floor. As the knight watched in helpless horror, the priest began trying to jerk the child's tunic up. "Sign it! You will sign it now!"

Rage blinded Percival, but his hands were bound, and the noose strangled him into helplessness. There had to be a way . . . He looked up at the rope, gathered himself to leap . . .

Instead he fell into a fist the size of his entire head. The impact detonated stars in his skull, and a high, childish voice cried out in pain. Another fist hit, and then another, beating him viciously. He heard the distinct wet snap of a bone breaking . . .

Voices rose, shouting, cursing, a confusing babble of rage. A few sentences cut through the cacophony.

"Weakling!" a man's voice spat. "You disgust me, you weakling! You're no blood of mine!"

"It's no more than you deserve. After all, you let that priest do it to me, didn't you?"

Pain shattered his jaw. A woman's voice screamed. "Tom, stop! You're going to kill him!"

A noose tightened around his throat, cutting off his breath, making him wheeze. A child's voice screamed.

"Take the contents of your cursed womb, and get from my sight!"

"Tom!"

"Da! Please, Da!"

Light detonated behind his eyes with the bright agony of his nose breaking.

Claws raked across his skin as the werewolves closed in, their eyes glowing orange with bloodlust . . .

Pain and guilt and shame ripped at him, spun him, seared him.

"Weakling," the man's voice growled. "You're nothing. You're no one. No son of mine. Not fit to be my heir . . ."

"When Arthur's dead, you'll be at my mercy," another voice purred, somehow seductive and sickening at once. "No one will care what I do to you. They'll be too busy seeking my favor . . ."

Then another man's voice spoke, strong and sure and calm. "You're a leader, Percival. Lead."

Even after so many centuries, he knew that voice. It was his father.

"Weakling. You're nothing. You're no one. No son of mine. Not fit to be my heir . . ."

"Fear strengthens," Percival's father said, drowning out the other voices with his calm strength. "Pain feeds courage. Use them to fuel your fire. Use them to drive those who follow you."

Yes. Yes, his father had been right. Fifteen centuries of war had taught him the power of pain and fear in the battles he'd fought with Cador, Marrok, and Morgana beside him.

He knew them. Knew on some level what motivated each of them, even when he didn't know it consciously. He knew whose pain was whose, knew who feared what, knew the secret guilt, the seeds of suffering planted centuries before by those who should have known better, by the very ones who should have strengthened them, equipped them for life's battles.

Percival reached into the swirling chaos of anguish and guilt, ignoring the acidic burn of it against his skin. Searching through the storm, he found Cador, whose father had mocked and criticized until the boy had been easy prey for women who had echoed their lord's contempt.

"I need you," Percival said, infusing his voice with hard strength. Cador needed to be needed, needed to know he was strong no matter what he'd been taught from the time he was a child. "Lend me your strength. Help me save them."

And despite the sense of failure that still dogged him when he let it, Cador came through as he always had. Percival felt him reach deep, drawing on the strength his father had discounted.

The strength Percival had always been able to count on.

They drew together, and the stinging burn of the Mageverse faded. Not enough, nowhere near enough, but any relief from that ferocious pain was welcome.

"Now," Percival told Cador, "now we get Marrok."

Fused, strength blended so each reinforced the other, they plunged into the chaos together.

Directly into the blow of a fist. Into the cold fear of death at the hands of an implacable enemy. The crunch of his nose breaking with a familiar blinding agony he'd felt before . . .

A woman's scream, high and piercing. The crack of a fist hitting a face. Another scream, this one weaker, followed by another thudding blow and an even weaker scream.

"Mother! Mother! Da, stop!"

Marrok knew what it felt like to watch someone he loved die. When his father drank, he raged. And when he raged, his children bled. Died.

Marrok had watched his father murder two of his brothers and an infant sister with those huge, merciless hands. He knew too well the sight of broken bodies, covered in blood and bruises.

So when he walked in from the fields to find his father beating his mother, he did not sit by. He was bigger than he'd been when his brothers and sister died. Not a man grown, not yet, but big enough to fight back.

Big enough to defend his mother. Big enough to rage when his father began to beat him too.

Big enough to go berserk for the first time.

As he hit the bigger man, he felt the vicious satisfaction of striking out against someone who deserved to suffer. Deserved to die. He hit his father again.

And again.

And again.

It was the first time he regained his sanity to find himself surrounded by broken bodies—his mother's, dead at his father's hands, and his father, dead at his own.

He'd sat there, numb, lost in pain and guilt, until he realized he had no more reason to stay. He'd buried his parents and left their small holding, wandering aimlessly until he enlisted as a soldier in Arthur Pendragon's army. Fighting, after all, was the one thing he knew how to do.

During the training Arthur demanded of his men, he met Percival and Cador, and discovered the love he'd never known. The love of brothers in arms.

"We need you," Percival shouted over the roaring blast of the Mageverse storm. "Without you, I can't save her."

But Marrok didn't hear him. He'd already cycled back to the moment he'd watched his mother die. "Mother! Da, stop!"

Percival gathered his will even as Cador poured on his own reinforcing strength, and shot the combination like a crossbow bolt through Marrok's pain and guilt. The burst of will jolted the knight from his poisonous memories. They sensed Marrok's dazed awareness through the pelting slap of magic. "Percival?"

"We need you now, *Marrok."*

"I'm coming!" The big knight asked no questions, just answered Percival's call, joining his strength to theirs with an almost audible click. Wills melded into one iron unit, just as they'd always been one throughout fifteen centuries.

Then, together, they plunged into the hurricane of magic and madness that surrounded Morgana le Fay.

"Mamma!" the boy shrieked. "Mamma, help me!"

"It's no more than you deserve. After all, you let that priest do it to me, didn't you?"

"You may as well admit your crimes, witch. We all know what you are, what black perversion you hide beneath your beauty . . ."

Claws raked across her skin as the wolves closed in . . .

". . . When you are dead, I'm going to shift and fuck that mate of yours until he dies in blood and agony!"

"Enough!" Percival thundered, drawing on the power and authority he'd built over hundreds of years, using that dominance to cut through the black swirl of Morgana's memories.

"When Arthur's dead, you'll be at my mercy. No one will care what I do to you. They'll be too busy seeking my favor . . ."

"ENOUGH!" This time the three knights roared as one, their blended voices ringing with the furious strength of dominants.

Morgana responded.

They felt her turn her attention from the pain and madness, the power and the guilt. Percival took advantage of that moment. "You're mine, Morgana le Fay. You belong to me, not to some collection of ragged ghosts. I love you, and I will not share you with them any longer." He felt his words reverberate through Morgana like the tolling of a great bell, backed by the steely strength of Cador and Marrok. "I love you."

Three words he suddenly knew she'd never expected to hear from him. Words she thought she didn't deserve. "But . . . How . . . Why?"

"Do you doubt me, Oath Servant?" he demanded. "Do you call me a liar?"

"No," she said, her voice faint, broken. "I just don't see . . . why." Not when so many voices echoed with contempt and hate in her head.

"Take the contents of your cursed womb, and get from my sight!" "We all know what you are, what black perversion you hide beneath your beauty." "It's no more than you deserve."

Those voices were destroying her. For years, she'd contained them, ignored them. But now, with the power of the Mageverse ripping at her psyche, its energies eroding her emotional shields to dig at her with the sly, vicious words she remembered too well . . .

He was losing her.

Percival bared his teeth. Not very damned likely. *He wasn't going to give up on his witch,wasn't going to allow her demons to rip her apart with her own power.*

Cador and Marrok mentally rumbled assent, echoing his determination. "She may be a bitch," Cador said, "but she's our bitch. We've got to bring her out of this."

"But how?" Marrok asked.

Percival's eyes widened as a sudden thought struck him. "What if we use magic?"

"Vampires can't use magic," Cador pointed out.

Marrok smiled. "Morgana can. We could reach it through her."

"Yes . . . yes, that might work." Testing, Percival closed his eyes, reached out to the swirling forces that tore at them. And turned his will on Morgana.

At first she fought, bucking against his control, sending painful jolts through all three of them. "Morgana!" he snapped. "Stop that, Oath Servant. You will use your power as I command."

Her mental voice breathed, "Yes, Lord Percival."

Percival opened his eyes, withdrawing from the psychic stage he'd occupied with his lover and his friends. Once again, the four of them stood surrounded by the jagged shapes of fallen trees impaling the corpse of the dragon under the moon. His gaze fell on Morgana, standing slim and gorgeously naked in the silver light. Her face looked pale and beautiful—and intensely alien.

If I don't get her under control, she'll kill us all—and herself. He envisioned what he needed—what he'd last seen lying on the grass beside the bloody bodies of four women and a dazed dragon. Reaching out his will, he called it to his hand with her borrowed magic. As the nullification collar appeared in his palm, his fingers curled around it in a hard, instinctive grip. "Morgana le Fay!"

She opened her eyes then, and looked at him with those burning blue irises. He could feel the dark emotion that seethed in her, a fury that seemed far outsized for her fragile body.

Morgana looked at the collar in his hand, and her eyes widened. "I didn't even . . . think of that."

"Likely because you couldn't think. Not once the madness kicked in." Percival studied her face. "Kneel, Morgana."

She bit her lip. He felt her struggle to control the madness that clawed at her. "Without my magic . . . I won't be able . . . to sustain a Truebond."

Percival frowned. Now that he had bonded with her, he didn't want to lose that connection. "Can you add a spell to the collar to maintain the link?"

Morgana considered the idea. "I . . . Yes, I think so. Maintaining a Truebond doesn't take . . . much power." He felt her struggle to concentrate past the savage blasts of Mageverse energy. With an effort, she managed it. Her voice steadied. "I had always intended that the collars be able to allow varying amounts of magic so the Majae could learn to manage it." She shot Cador and Marrok a look. "Especially if you two don't want to remain part of the Truebond."

The knights exchanged a look. Percival tensed as his inner wolf suddenly awoke with a possessive growl. "I think we accomplished what we needed to," Marrok said.

Cador nodded. "Like you said, Truebonds are supposed to be for two." He grinned. "Not a psychic orgy—not that I don't enjoy the occasional orgy."

"Then I will do as you wish." Morgana gestured. Magic swirled around the collar. Gracefully, she sank to her knees and looked up at Percival.

He leaned down to take her mouth in a searing kiss, letting his tongue swirl around hers, then sucking her lower lip into her mouth for a slow, sensual nibble. "You're mine, Morgana. By your Oath. By my love."

She met his gaze. "I love you, too, Percival. I always have."

Warmth seemed to burst through his chest at the words until it seemed his ribs couldn't possibly contain it. He smiled at her brilliantly as he opened the collar, settled it around her throat, and snapped it closed.

And the burning, vicious power that had battered them simply . . . winked out, along with the connection to Cador and Marrok. All four of them sighed in relief.

Cador sank down on his haunches, raking his hands through his braided hair. "Thank Christ."

"That's putting it mildly." Marrok leaned a shoulder against one of the broken tree trunks. "Ahhhh—how are we going to get home?"

"I should be able to help there," a familiar voice said.

They looked around and found Soren standing behind them in human form. He'd evidently been busy while Morgana, Percival, and the team had Truebonded. Four women stood around him, looking whole, healed, and more than a little bewildered. More than likely, he'd not only healed them, he'd also altered their memories so they wouldn't recall the horrors they'd suffered at Huar's claws.

The ambassador jerked his chin at Morgana's collared throat, giving Percival a smile. "An elegant solution to the problem. I should have thought of it myself."

"As I told Morgana, we were all a little distracted."

"That's putting it mildly," Soren said with a snort. He swept the knights a level stare. "You saved me from a particularly horrific death, gentlemen. Any thanks I can give are pitifully inadequate, but I assure you, I will not forget."

Percival dipped his head in a bow. "No thanks are necessary, ambassador."

Cador grimaced. "We're just relieved we were able to pull it off. Huar was a nasty fuck." He slanted Morgana a look. "Who got what was coming to him."

Morgana suddenly looked distinctly green, her eyes widening as she covered her mouth with her hand, as if swallowing back bile. "Oh. My. Goddess." It had apparently just hit her what she'd done to her foe.

"Like Cador said, he had it coming." Percival slipped an arm around her waist. "If you can return us to Avalon, and these ladies to wherever they belong . . ."

"And we need our armor," Marrok added. "We left it all back that way."

"That will, of course, be no problem." The ambassador gestured, the sweep of his hands sending a swirl of magic through the dark woods. A moment later, the three knights were garbed in their armor and weapons again.

Another gesture created a dimensional gate. "Thank you, ambassador," Percival said.

As they started toward the portal, Morgana stepped over to her friend, rose to her toes, and pressed a platonic kiss to his cheek. "Thank you, Soren. We would have lost without you."

The ambassador smiled at her. "And I would have died without you." He stepped back, as though aware of Percival's jealous tension. "I will not forget you, my dear. Be happy with your knight."

Her smile was so dazzling, Percival's jealousy subsided, "I will be."

With that, the four of them stepped through the gate into Percival's living room.

"Morgana," Cador asked, frowning thoughtfully, "the next time you call on your powers, will it be like . . . that?"

"You mean, will it drive me mad?" She shrugged. "No. I drew on too much power because I had to in order to defeat Huar. I lost control of it, but the collar returned me to equilibrium, exactly as I designed it to do. I just have to be damned careful never to do that again."

"Believe me," Percival told her grimly, "I'll make sure of it."

SIXTEEN

Cador looked up at the grandfather clock ticking in the foyer. "Looks like we've got an hour and a half until dawn." He turned to Marrok. "Want to hit the Lord's Club? I don't know about you, but I could seriously use a drink."

"After the night we just had?" The big knight snorted. "I could kill a case of Jack and barely take the edge off."

Morgana flinched a little, knowing that she was a big part of the reason the night had been so rough. She opened her mouth, about to announce her own intention of going home and going directly to bed, but a big hand landed on her shoulder. She glanced up at Marrok in surprise.

The knight's handsome mouth curled into a smile. "Remember this, Morgana. You may be his . . ." He jerked his chin toward Percival. "But you're also ours."

Cador smiled. "Yeah, you're one of the team now. Merlin help you."

Further flustering her, the two knights pressed kisses on her cheek—Cador looked as if he was considering giving her one far more intimate until he caught Percival's sulfurous glare—then headed out the door.

As their deep, laughing voices receded toward Avalon's cobblestone streets, Morgana turned toward Percival. "I'd better be getting home myself . . ."

He folded his arms and looked at her calmly. "You *are* home."

She blinked at him, as the Truebond informed her of the stony determination behind his words. *"There'll be no more barriers between us, Morgana. Especially not the ones you erect to keep me at a distance."*

Morgana gaped, realizing he didn't intend that she leave at all. Ever. "But . . . I've got that house . . ."

"We can live there." She heard the next thought, though he hadn't intended her to. *But I'd rather live here.* He hated her house.

Morgana sighed. He had a point—it was pretentious as hell. And anyway, what was she trying to prove? To whom? Percival's home was somehow much warmer. Besides, it came with its own dungeon . . . "I'll give the house to some young vampire. I'm sure somebody's looking for a place to live."

He gave her a slow, warm smile that made cream gather between her legs, rich and wet. "Thank you."

Morgana slid her arms around his neck. "Now that that's settled . . . What next?"

He eyed her. She felt the brush of his thoughts against hers. "Considering the way your back's aching, how about the spa?"

Morgana smiled happily. "You've talked me into it."

Five minutes later, they sank naked into pleasantly hot, bubbling water in a spa the size of some swimming pools. Inset in the ground of Percival's back garden, the spa was an irregular, curving shape that was reminiscent of a natural pool. Flowering plants and bushes, all the blooms in shades of cream and white, heightened the effect, clustering around the spa's ceramic tiles and filling the air with sweet floral scents. White and cream roses blended with night-blooming jasmine and other pale blooms designed to look their best in moonlight—that being, of course, the only time the vampire owner could view it.

Percival handed her a glass of champagne and drew her down between his powerful thighs. She sighed in pleasure at the heat of the bubbling water and the hard strength of his body. He picked up a tube of massage oil, poured it into his palm, and began slowly working it into the slim muscles of her back. Finding a knotted muscle in the top of her right shoulder that hurt with a gnawing kind of pain, he dug in a strong thumb with a perfect degree of pressure—not too much, not too little.

Oiled hands explored the length of her back, seeking out every painful lump, then working it until it came unknotted.

By the time he was done with her, she sank back against his chest, warm water bubbling around her waist, feeling boneless with relaxation.

As she sighed in pleasure, Percival's warm, oiled hands came up and around her torso, finding her breasts, cupping their tender weight, teasing their nipples to tight erection. "Mmmmmm," she purred into his ear. "That feels incredible."

Still tugging the rosy points, he flashed a wicked grin, his eyes hot and burning with masculine hunger. "Yeah, I know."

And he did, she realized. Thanks to the Truebond, he shared every pleasure he gave her. His smile lushly sensual, he teased one breast with slow milking strokes as he reached down her body with the other hand, sliding between her legs, finding the plush petals of her sex.

"I always wondered how that felt," he murmured in her ear.

"And I've always wondered how this feels." Reaching behind her back, she stroked two fingers up the length of his erection, bobbing in the bubbling water. Her eyes flew wide, and she gasped at the starkly powerful pleasure, alien and intense. "OOOoooh. Like that . . ."

"Yeah. Like that." With a low growl, he caught her shoulders and turned her in his arms. His mouth came down over hers in a kiss that made her head swim like a slug of pure grain alcohol as his lips moved over hers, tongue swirling, thrusting.

Groaning, she kissed him back, losing herself in the hot male intensity of his passion, his need. "Horned God, I love you."

He drew back and smiled slowly into her eyes. "And I love you. I don't know why it took me so long to admit it."

She gave him a small, wry smile. "Probably because I didn't exactly make it easy on you. Too busy hiding too many secrets—and using sheer bitchiness to do it."

Percival's smile turned wicked. "Well, *that's* sure as hell over."

"And I'm not going to miss it a bit." She reached up, traced her fingers over the angular rise of his cheek. "I always knew you'd find a way to save me from myself. And you did."

"Well, I owed you. You saved us often enough."

Her smile vanished as she remembered the insane howl of the Mageverse. "I also came far too close to killing you tonight."

His eyes narrowed and went cool at the reminder. "Yes, you did. And I believe I owe you a punishment for hiding those blackouts and just how close you were to Mageverse Fever."

"Ah." Her eyes widened, and she swallowed, deciding that it behooved her to speak formally. Otherwise, he was likely to take a deerskin flogger to her arse again. "I am sorry, Lord Percival. I shouldn't have done it, but I wasn't sure how to tell you."

"You mean you didn't trust me." He didn't smile when he said it, either.

"I . . . No, sir, I suppose I didn't." The submission came automatically—and it had nothing to do with the collar. He was her Master, on some level deeper than even the Oath of Service. Looking into those cool gray eyes, she saw that he was aware of her need to submit to him. To yield to him.

And yet, he was also right when he said she hadn't trusted him—

or Arthur, for that matter. She'd feared how they'd react if she'd told them the truth. "I was wrong, Lord Percival. I could have killed us all."

"Yeah, you could have. We all got lucky."

She took a deep breath. "That wasn't luck. That was you, dominating the hell out of me. Making me want to yield to you even in my madness. Not from fear or force, but because of the nature of who you are."

"Flattering." His lips curved into an evil smile. "But it's not going to save you." Despite the menace in his tone, Morgana could sense the warmth and affection beneath it. He knew her, knew exactly what heated her blood—and his own. And he was fully capable of donning a cold dominant's pose if that made her hotter, more eager. "You deserve punishment, and I'm going to make sure you get it." He reached between her thighs with oiled fingers, sliding between the soft petals of her pussy, then pulled out to circle her clit. Pleasure spooled through her, making her shiver under Percival's predatory gaze, his dark male smile. As he worked her sex with one hand, the other found her breasts, tugging with oiled fingers until she threw back her head and panted in lust. Cream and heat flooded her cunt despite the bubbling water that surrounded her.

"Mmmmm," Percival purred. "You like that, don't you?"

She bit her lip and closed her eyes in delight. "Do you really need to ask?"

"No, but I do like to hear it." He caught her jaw in a hard grip, jolting her out of her quivering pleasure. "Oil my cock. I'm going to fuck that little pussy hard, and you don't have quite enough lubrication in all this water."

Morgana blinked up at him. "Yes, Lord Percival." The words emerged as a hoarse whisper of raw need. She reached for the bottle on the side of the pool, poured her palm full of the oil and reached for his cock. He felt so thick, long, and delicious as she began to stroke his length. One hand didn't seem enough, so she started using both, up and down, spreading the oil, enjoying the combination of that crowbar hard core and warm velvet skin. She flicked her thumb over the sensitive rim, heard his low growl of pleasure and warning, then slid a hand down to his heavy testacies, weighing and rolling them in her hand.

"Horned God, you feel good."

"So do you." He gave her a hot smile as his oiled fingers tightened on one nipple, tugging and milking. Simultaneously, the fingers of the other hand thrust deep in her juicing core. "Are you ready for cock?"

The rough note in his voice made her eyelids dip as she shuddered in lust. "Yes. Oh, yes."

He released her nipple and pulled his hand out of her cunt, caught her under the arse, and lifted her. Holding her backside in one hand, he used the other to position the head of his cock against the opening of her pussy. And thrust, sliding slowly into her, filling her pussy with his width and heat.

Morgana gasped at the feeling of being so incredibly stuffed. And met his fierce, triumphant gaze as he entered deeper and deeper, taking his time with her silken impalement.

The sensation was starkly delicious—and so was the pleasure he felt, echoing through the Truebond, feeding her blissful desire. As he supported her arse, he strummed the tips of his fingers back and forth over her clit. Each hot touch, each sweet thrust vibrated through her body, shimmered in the Truebond, adding to his sensual satisfaction, which added to hers, which added to his. Around and around in a tightening spiral, desire building to white-hot lust, pleasure to ecstasy more intense than anything she'd ever felt.

He snarled in animal rut and began to fuck her in hard, jarring thrusts that tore a scream of overwhelmed delight from her throat. Supporting her arse with his left hand, he brought his right up to seize a fistful of black curls. He dragged her head back, arching her throat, and bent to sink his fangs into her carotid just above her collar. Still fucking her furiously, he drank in lusty swallows.

The pleasure of it, the orgasmic feedback of his building climax pouring into hers, driving it higher and higher . . .

Morgana shrieked, convulsing, flying apart into light. He catapulted after her into orgasm, releasing her throat to roar.

She came back to herself slowly, feeling stunned and limp. Her fingers combed through his silken hair, down to the strong muscle of his throat, then along the broad line of a powerful shoulder. He released her with a reluctant groan, then levered himself out of the spa. Morgana took his hand and let him pull her out, staggering on weak knees to collapse with him on a wide, thickly padded chaise.

"I love you," she told him, as he wrapped his arms around her and pulled her against his body.

"I know." Percival grinned wickedly. "And in case you can't tell, I love you too."

Morgana grinned back. "I know." And she did. She could feel his passion and need, just as he could feel hers.

"But just for the record," he told her, "you're still my Oath Servant."

She licked her lips at the hot images that flashed through his mind of things he wanted to do to her, ways he wanted her to submit. "I wouldn't want it any other way, my lord Percival."

His eyes narrowed, heated. "And no, it's not going to be over in a year."

"Of course not." Morgana smiled and stroked a curl back from his eyes. "I'll be yours forever, Oath Master."

Percival smiled. "And I'll be yours."

BE CAREFUL WHAT YOU WISH FOR

When Jim Decker walked into Bottoms Up that night, you could almost taste the testosterone. Or vamposterone. Or whatever.

Decker worked his way through the Saturday night crowd toward our table, attracted either by me or the opportunity to yank Beau Gabriel's chain. The two had hated one another since Deck's vampire slayer days; the fact that I'd since made him one of us hadn't blunted the hostility. In fact, it had probably made it worse, because now they competed over me.

Beau had made me a vampire two memorable years ago. He'd read *Shadowmaster,* one of the string of vamp horror novels I'd written as Amanda Carlton, and decided I needed a bit more . . . research. I hadn't minded a bit. He'd seemed the cowboy embodiment of all my demon lover fantasies, like a cross between Dracula and a young Clint Eastwood, and I'd fallen for him hard.

I also found myself sharing his enemies, particularly Jim Decker, who in those days had been on a mission to avenge the sister he thought Beau had seduced and misused. Knowing Beau's effect on women, it probably hadn't taken much seduction, and no misuse had been involved. But big brothers need their illusions.

One night I'd been caught in the crossfire of one of their battles, and Decker ended up capturing me. To save myself from a staking, I'd tempted him into sex. Making him my blood lover had taught him we weren't the undead murderers he'd believed, but in the process, I'd become a lot more emotionally involved with him than Beau liked.

But really, it was inevitable that I'd be attracted to Decker. He had far more going for him than AB negative, no matter what Beau thought. I enjoyed his intelligence and sense of honor and deep love of everything female, not to mention the fierce sensuality that made him such a glorious lover.

Besides, I've always had a thing for big men, and like Beau, Decker qualified. Six-foot-four and powerfully muscled, he had broad bull shoulders, narrow hips, and the rippling musculature of a professional athlete. Even better, his was one of those sensual, hawkish faces that make women think of rough, fast, really good sex. Yet his lips looked like God had designed them for slow kisses in the moonlight.

Now, watching him saunter toward us on those long legs, I swallowed, remembering what it felt like to fist both hands in the black silk of his hair while he used that mouth to drive me mad.

As long as Deck had been merely human, Beau could tolerate the relationship by pretending the other man was nothing more to me than a blood supply. But when I'd decided to make him a vampire, Beau had been furious. So furious, I'd had no choice except to cool off the relationship with Deck or risk losing my demon lover.

As Decker stopped beside our table, his hot blue eyes swept over me in a hungry stare that spoke of longing and frustration. Today he wore a pair of beige slacks and a cream Oxford cloth shirt, tie loosely knotted, with a dark brown trench coat that reminded me of a film noir detective. "Amanda," he purred. His gaze flicked to Beau and cooled. "Gabriel."

Of the two men, Decker looked more like a vampire with those dark, European good looks, while Beau was blond and all-American, with broad, high cheekbones, a narrow nose, and a flashing grin. One look at that face, and you pictured him taking his best girl to a square dance. Which wasn't that far off, except that afterward he'd bend her over the trunk of his T-Bird and fuck her to a screaming orgasm, burying his fangs in her throat just as she came.

God knew he'd done it to me often enough.

"Deck," Beau drawled, a chilly smile stretching over that Sundance Kid face. With one forefinger, he pushed up the brim of his black Stetson. "Screw any werewolves lately?"

Ignoring that sally, Decker lifted a brow at him, pointedly scanning Beau's black Levis and western shirt. "The *Urban Cowboy* thing went out thirty years ago. Or hadn't you noticed?"

"Hell, after the first century or so, all the decades blur together." Beau crossed his cowboy-booted ankles and laced his big hands on his flat, muscled belly. "Anyway, urban I ain't."

Ah, no. Beau had actually *been* a cowboy, back 120 years ago. At least until he met a certain vampire dance hall girl who decided he looked tasty.

Decker opened his mouth, but before he could get down to some serious slander, a female voice interrupted.

"Oh, Jim! Thank God!" A pretty brunette shot through the bar's front door and across the length of the room to fling herself into Decker's arms. He caught her, and I felt a wave of jealousy at his utter lack of reluctance to find his hands full of overenthusiastic bimbo.

Then I made out what she was babbling and felt a little more sympathetic.

"God, Decker, don't let him do it to me again!" she gasped, her voice soggy with threatening tears as she clung to his big body like Spanish moss draping an oak. "I couldn't stand going through that again—and not being able to break the spell . . . ! Oh, please! You've got to help me!"

He stroked a hand through her hair as she quivered. "Calm down, Lynn. What's going on?"

"It's Jeffrey!" Lynn wailed. "He said if I don't go to his house and agree to—he said he's going to turn me back into a werewolf. Permanently!"

Well, *that* stopped conversation for a radius of about thirty feet. In the ensuing dead silence, I eyed the sobbing girl's back. "Maybe we should go somewhere else and discuss this."

"Oh, yeah, let's," murmured Beau. "My curiosity is killing me."

So we all trooped out of the bar and around the corner out into the parking lot. The other customers stared at us avidly as we left. Beau wasn't the only one dying to know what was going on.

I already knew part of the story. Right after Decker had become a vampire, he'd picked Lynn up in a bar, planning to fuck her brains out and sip a pint or so she'd never miss. But she had an even bigger surprise in store for him; as the full moon rose, she'd turned into a werewolf and pounced on him.

Deck, naturally enough, thought she was trying to kill him, and the result was a nasty little brawl. Eventually she managed to communicate that all she wanted was some of *his* bodily fluids; she'd been cursed by a wizard, and the only way to break the spell was find a man to make love to her while she was in werewolf form. He'd happily cooperated, and Lynn no longer had to dread moon rise.

Only now it seemed the wizard in question wasn't happy. And that could be a problem, because Jeffrey Copperstone wasn't the kind of man a wise woman wanted to piss off. He'd cursed Lynn in the first place because she wouldn't put out after he'd met her through a computer dating service. Now he was evidently at it again.

Some guys just don't know how to take no for an answer.

Out in the parking lot, we listened as she blurted out the new twist on her tale. Copperstone had been furious when he'd discovered Decker had broken the spell, but she'd made herself so scarce he'd been unable to retaliate. She'd even quit her job and moved to another city. But he'd eventually tracked her down anyway and started harassing and stalking her again. Yesterday he'd given her an ultimatum; return to Atlanta and present herself at his house the next evening prepared to give him what he wanted, or become permanently fuzzy. Fearing what the psychotic bastard would do to her one way or another, Lynn had wisely decided to hit all Decker's favorite haunts in hopes he could save her again.

While she quavered her way through her story, I kept an eye on Decker's face. He'd always had a chivalric streak, and I wasn't surprised to see that Copperstone's behavior royally pissed him off. His blue eyes began to spark and burn with vampire fire, and his fangs lengthened, all signs of one of us on a tear.

"Go on home, Lynn," he told her, as she burst into tears at the end of her story. "I'll take care of it."

"But he's a really powerful wizard, Jim! What if he does something to you?" She sniffed. I dragged a tissue out of my purse and handed it to her. She took it with watery thanks and blew her nose. "Maybe . . . Maybe I should just give him what he wants. Maybe he'll be satisfied if I just. . . ."

"Guys like that are never satisfied," I told her. "If he's this abusive now, what's he going to be like later?"

"Do what Decker says, Lynn," Beau said. "We'll take care of him."

At first I was a little surprised that he'd offer to help Decker out with anything, but on second thought, I should have expected it. Fangs notwithstanding, Beau had a very old-fashioned sense of the proper treatment of women, so it was only natural that he wanted to give Copperstone a badly needed lesson in manners.

Decker, oddly enough, didn't protest. He just gave us a grin that glittered in the moonlight. "Looks like we're off to see the wizard."

Beau's return grin looked more like a wolf's bared fangs. "To rip out his fucking throat."

Having both of them that ticked off didn't bode well for Copperstone. So why did I feel something icy creep down my spine? "How?"

I asked. "Like Lynn said, this guy is pretty powerful. What's to keep him from putting a whammy on us?"

Beau's green eyes narrowed. "Me. I haven't been a vampire for one hundred and fifty years for nothing. By the time I get through using my psi on that bastard, he won't be able to pull a rabbit out of a hat."

I certainly hoped not anyway.

Copperstone's house was located in an Atlanta suburb that must have been truly the sticks when the house was built. We parked Beau's T-Bird a mile away and slunk the rest of the way in the dark, vampire quiet. Sometimes I wish I really could turn into a bat.

Eyeing the sprawling two-story Victorian as we approached, I snorted softly. "Being a college professor must pay better than I thought."

"Actually, Lynn said Copperstone told her the house has been in his family since it was built," Decker said, his voice so soft a human couldn't have heard it. "Evidently they're old money."

Beau curled his lip. "Carpetbagger." Catching Decker's questioning look, he shrugged. "With a name like Copperstone, his people must be Yankees."

Yeah, three or four generations ago. Then again, to a man who'd fought in the Civil War, that was yesterday.

We split up to circle the house, using vampire senses to determine how many people were inside and what security arrangements Copperstone had. My attention was caught by the garden in the back—not flowers or vegetables, but neat rows of strange little plants, the majority of which I didn't know the name of. I wondered if he used them to cast spells.

He also had a pen full of goats and a chicken coop. Since Copperstone didn't strike me as the kind of man with an interest in animal husbandry, I started picturing blood sacrifices under a full moon. Which could just be my overactive writer's imagination, but somehow I didn't think so.

I met the boys on the other side of the house in the deep night shadows where no human eye would be able to see us. "He's upstairs in the attic, and he's alone," Decker said.

"Doesn't seem much worried about security." Beau frowned. "He's got no alarm system. Hell, the front door is unlocked."

"For Lynn, probably," I said. "The bastard doesn't expect her to stand him up."

I knew we were all thinking the same thing: *it couldn't be this easy*. This guy was a wizard. Either he was stupidly overconfident, or he had good reason to believe he could handle anything that came at him.

We looked at each other and shared a simultaneous shrug. It really didn't matter. We were committed to this. We were, in fact, probably the only ones who could stop this creep from abusing Lynn or anybody else he wanted. Assuming Beau was right, and his psi was stronger than the bastard's magic.

What the fuck. We had to try.

So together, moving with the speed and utter silence only our kind can manage, we headed up the porch stairs, through that unlocked door, and into the house.

Copperstone's decorating taste ran to Victorian kitsch—here a stool shaped like an elephant, there a lamp with long silk fringe around the shade, over there a tiger skin on the floor. All dark and tacky and ugly as hell. I was just as glad I had no more than a glance around the front room as I climbed the sweeping staircase at the boys' heels, heading for the source of the low chanting.

But when we hit the top of the staircase, we could still hear that voice coming from the ceiling over our heads. Decker glanced at Beau. "Must be another set of stairs somewhere."

I grimaced. "Probably behind a hidden panel."

I was right. It was in Copperstone's bedroom, set in one wall and camouflaged behind ugly flocked velvet cabbage rose wallpaper. Beau found the trigger to open the hidden door by zeroing in on the scent left by Copperstone's fingers.

While he sniffed the wall looking for it, my appalled eyes locked on the huge painting hanging over Copperstone's king-sized bed. It depicted some Roman emperor and a dozen well-hung Praetorian guards doing anatomically unlikely things to three naked female captives.

His attention caught by my revolted stare, Decker looked at the painting and sneered. "Little prick seems to like the idea of using force, doesn't he?"

I gave him a cheeky grin full of all the fang and bravado I could manage. "Yeah, well, I think it's time he finds out what it's like being on the receiving end. I feel a case of the munchies coming on."

"Uh huh." Deck wasn't fooled. Concern darkened his blue eyes. "Amanda, maybe you should go home. This could get rough."

"Not a chance," I told him, stung. No way was I going to stand by while the boys fought some creep who turned people into werewolves. "Did Dorothy blow off her buds just because of a green bitch and some flying monkeys? I think not."

Beau glared over his shoulder at us. "Could you hold it down? I'd rather the Wicked Dickhead of the West didn't hear us coming." He thumbed one of the rose petals. The panel slid silently aside, revealing a narrow staircase.

Decker lifted a brow. "Break and enter much, Gabriel?"

Beau smiled tauntingly. "Hey, you pick up all kinds of skills in a century and a half."

I barely resisted the impulse to comment on his talent for entering. Probably best not to get into that topic just now.

While I resisted temptation for one of the few times in my life, we slipped into the dark opening one by one and headed upward. The air filled with the sound of chanting. The voice was deep, masculine, and the words sounded vaguely Latinate. A glow that looked like candlelight provided just enough illumination for our vampire night vision as we climbed a stairway barely wide enough to accommodate the boys' shoulders. When we reached the top, we all flattened ourselves on the stairs while we checked out the situation.

A tall, thin man in blue silk robes stood with his back to us, both hands raised as he chanted in ringing Latin. He held a knife in one hand. On an altar in front of him lay one of the goats, hogtied and bleating softly.

I really hate it when I'm right.

He appeared to be praying to a three-foot statue of a naked horned figure with a truly ridiculous phallus. If the idol had been man-sized, its cock would have been two feet long. It was flanked on either side by black and red candles that burned with a scent like rotting meat. I decided I really didn't want to know how he'd gotten *that* effect.

As we watched, Copperstone drew back the knife, readying it for a downward stroke. The goat bleated.

"We'd better do something," Decker said softly. "I've got a feeling once that goat dies, Lynn's going to have a serious problem with unsightly hair."

Beau grunted. I saw the boys gather themselves to spring. I grimaced; from where I lay behind them on the stairs, I'd be the last one in.

The next instant, both vampires launched themselves out of the stairway and across the room. I scrambled to join them as Beau grabbed Copperstone and Decker snatched the goat away, snapped the cords, and turned it loose. It shot off toward the stairs, bleating, its little hooves clicking frantically on the polished wooden floor. I barely had time to sidestep it as it galloped out of sight.

"When a woman tells you no, you son-of-a-bitch," Beau snarled at the astonished Copperstone, wrapping both big hands in his robe and hauling him onto his toes, "you *drop* it!" I felt his power blast out of his mind in a wave so black and dark it sucked the breath from my lungs.

Baring his impressive fangs, Decker grabbed a fistful of the man's thinning blond hair and jerked his head back. "You're about to find out just how it feels to. . . ."

Then the power field Beau had thrown over the room suddenly cracked like an egg. For a moment, it seemed a hot red light spread over us all. "Enough!" the wizard roared, and spat out a series of tongue twisting consonants. Suddenly I simply couldn't move. What's worse, the boys froze too.

Oh, hell. We'd underestimated the little prick.

With an affronted huff, Copperstone jerked himself out of Beau's grip and straightened his robe with a twitch. He twisted his lip as he eyed my lovers' identical frozen snarls. "Vampires. Huh. I gather one of you is that friend of Lynn's. Little bitch. I suppose I should have anticipated this."

He sauntered around the room, eyeing us. I felt as though I'd been dropped in a vat of peanut butter; I realized I could probably move, but only after a long, hard fight. Setting my muscles, I began to strain. I knew the boys were probably doing the same.

That was good. Dickhead might be too strong for us, but we were too strong for him too.

Copperstone jerked, his long, homely face taking on a harried look. He bit his lip. "I'm not going to be able to hold you long, am I? You have powers of some sort . . . psychic, I think. It would take a major spell to stop you. But perhaps . . . a delaying action. . . ."

He looked at me, and his eyes lit unpleasantly. Turning, he looked at the two men, their big bodies tensing as they fought his magical hold. Copperstone glanced back at me again and grinned. I instantly decided I didn't like the look in his eyes.

The wizard sauntered back to my lovers. "I know just the thing to keep you busy and teach you a little lesson. And it will work like a charm, because you've already got the seeds of lust and anger in you." Leaning close to Beau and Decker, he said sweetly, "Why don't you two forget about me for the time being. You'd much rather fuck your tasty little friend." He bared his teeth. "Do everything you've secretly dreamed of. Let's see *you* stop when she says no. "

You vile little prick! I thought in fury as he strolled toward the door. Stopping beside me, Copperstone leaned down to whisper in my ear. "You know, I rather envy them. I wouldn't mind feeling those long legs wrapped around my hips." Then he turned and hissed a waterfall of Latin, his bony hands describing lines in the air. With a self-satisfied smile, he passed out of my line of sight. I heard the door close and the lock click. . . .

The spell holding me broke. I whirled and shot toward the door in a fury. If the stupid creep thought a hardware store lock would hold three vampires, he had another thing coming. I grabbed the knob, about to jerk the door right off its hinges. . . .

A big hand shot past my head and slapped against the door, holding it closed. I looked at those long, broad fingers spread over the wood, and my mouth went dry. Cautiously, I slowly turned around . . . .

Decker and Beau loomed over me, broad shoulder to broad shoulder. Two pairs of eyes glittered, predatory and hot, while two sets of fangs glinted in nasty grins. Glancing down, I saw a pair of bulges that would shame *My Friend Flicka*.

"Uh," I said. "I guess this is about that fuck spell."

"Looks that way," Decker purred.

I swallowed. "Luckily, there's something Wizard Boy forgot to take into account."

Beau licked his fangs hungrily, his eyes dropping to my breasts. "And what would that be?"

I grinned. "You can't force the willing. In fact, you can't even seduce the eager." I slipped both arms around Decker's neck and pulled myself up so I could wrap my thighs around his waist. "But you're welcome to try."

"Oh, we'll try," Decker said, with a low rumbling laugh as his powerful arms encircled me and plastered my body so tightly along his I could feel his thick hard-on rubbing my belly through his trousers.

"And we'll succeed." Beau stepped in behind me until I could feel every crest and hollow in his muscular body, his cock a steely ridge against my bottom as one hand slid around to cup my pussy.

And I didn't mind a bit. A ménage à trois with the boys had always been my favorite fantasy, but given their unrelenting mutual hostility I'd figured it would never happen. Now the Wicked Dickhead of the West had made my kinky little dream a reality.

Maybe he wasn't so bad.

Decker's mouth swooped down on mine, kissing, licking, sucking at my lips, his tongue dancing a wicked dance around mine. I sighed in happy pleasure and kissed him back, savoring the taste. Loving the feel of him against my breasts, my belly, pressing between my thighs. While Beau slowly rocked against my ass, one big hand slipping around my chest to find a tight little nipple through the fabric of my dress.

Hell, maybe I'd send Dickhead roses, I decided, as two pairs of strong, skillful hands began to explore and torment. Decker's long fingers squeezed and rolled my nipples as Beau reached under my skirt. My silk panties didn't have a prayer against his greedy rip. He dropped the lace rags on the floor and started delving between my soft lower lips.

Decker drew back and looked down at me, his eyes blue and hot. I saw his male delight at having me in his hands again, felt his hunger at the thought of thrusting hard into me. He swooped his head down and captured my gasping mouth in another long, liquid kiss. Beau bent his head to the curve of my neck, the points of his fangs delicately raking the skin, making me whimper against Deck's lips.

Meanwhile, Beau's rope-roughened fingers swirled around the creaming opening of my cunt. He slipped one of them in up to the knuckle, and I writhed against Decker's muscled torso at the sensation. Rumbling a laugh, Deck swirled his tongue inside my mouth and palmed my entire breast, squeezing slowly and rhythmically.

Maybe I'd put Dickhead on my Christmas card list.

Both men were rock hard. Slowly, they rolled their hips against mine, grinding in slow circles as if in the grip of such deep lust they had to satisfy it somehow. The feel of those two thick ridges, one pressing against the notch between my legs, the other nudging between my cheeks . . . *Oh, God.*

Beau added a second finger to the one in my cunt, then a third, slipping into my buttery heat easily, twisting his wrist to screw them in. His fingers filled and teased, building the heat between my legs to a blaze. I gasped as he licked the pulse on the side of my throat, not biting, but obviously headed in that direction. Decker left my mouth and began kissing his way under my chin, nudging my head back. I let it fall on Beau's shoulder as both men licked and suckled my neck. I suspected I was headed for major blood loss, and didn't really give a damn.

Decker grabbed the low neckline of my dress and jerked it down further, exposing more of my breast. Because of the cut of the neckline I wasn't wearing a bra, so he managed to cup my flesh and push it up until the nipple peeked over the fabric. Hungrily, he attacked it, nibbling and sucking, setting off hot, breath-stealing sensations in the delicate pink tip. I squirmed, pressing my bare, wet cunt against the rough fabric of his trousers, even as Beau's demanding fingers impaled me mercilessly.

With a growl, Decker ground his hips against mine. "God, I'm as hot and hard as the tailpipe on a Harley," he said, drawing back to look down at me with feral blue eyes. "How the hell are we going to decide who fucks her first?"

Beau lifted his head from my neck and laughed in my ear, sounding more than a little sinister. "We don't have to decide. She's got this really tight, tiny little asshole I've been dying to ream." His fingers slipped out of my cunt. Before I could do more than squirm, he'd slid a long forefinger right up my anus.

"Hey!" I jerked, arching my back at the startling sensation. It was both painful and shockingly erotic.

Decker—my sweet Boy Scout Decker—gave me a cruel, glittering grin. "Looks like you're gonna get double-stuffed, darlin'."

"Like an Oreo." Beau laughed that Marquis de Sade laugh again. "God, Deck, she's soooo tiiiight." He slid the finger out of my butt, then entered it again.

"Beau!" I gasped, squirming, instinctively trying to escape, but one of Decker's strong hands clamped over my thigh as Beau pinned me by wrapping an arm from the curve of my waist to my shoulder. "Stop that!"

"But it feels so gooood." As I twisted my head to glare at him, Beau gave me a dark, evil grin.

When he withdrew his finger, Decker put a hand down. And as Beau entered me again, I felt a second thick digit joining his, stretching my anus painfully open. Shocked, I snapped my head around to stare into Decker's handsome face, seeing a menacing lust in his eyes I'd never seen before. "Oh, yeah," he purred. He smiled slowly, partially withdrawing his finger as Beau thrust his even deeper. I felt the two digits twisting my delicate inner tissues as they slowly screwed my butt. "I wouldn't mind reaming that tight little ass myself. Is she virgin?"

"Not for long." Beau lowered his head and nipped the side of my throat, not quite drawing blood.

"Now, hold on just a damn minute!" I exploded, enraged. "You can take turns or I can suck one of you off, but we are *not* having anal sex!" Not as well hung as they were, anyway. I'm ambitious, not crazy. "We've talked about this before, Beau."

"And you've always said no." He pressed his finger deep in my ass, then began to slowly withdraw as Decker drove deeper. "But you know, somehow I'm just not in the mood to listen tonight." And he forced the finger in again.

That's when I remembered what Copperstone had said when he'd cast that damn spell. *Do everything you've secretly dreamed of.*

Hoo boy, I was in trouble—*big* trouble. In his right mind, neither man would dream of taking me in a way I didn't want. Yeah, Beau had made jokingly seductive attempts to introduce me to anal sex, but when I'd laughingly objected, he'd backed off. True, I was a little intrigued by the idea, and I'd probably allow myself to be talked into it—eventually.

But allowing Beau to gently initiate me when he was in his right mind was one thing. Being double penetrated by two ensorcelled vampires was a whole different kettle of KY.

Unfortunately, at the moment I was pinned between them with my feet off the ground, in the worst possible position to defend myself. Yeah, if they'd been human, I'd have had no problem getting away. Hell, with my vampire strength, I could fight off a dozen men without breaking a sweat. But Decker and Beau were supernatural too, and because of their greater size, they were several times stronger than I.

Plus, Beau has been a vampire for more than a century, so his power was that much greater than mine. What's more, since he'd made me a vamp he had a certain amount of power over me. If he chose, he could make me do any damn thing he wanted. I wasn't sure why he hadn't already tried it, but I decided I'd better get the hell out before he did.

Luckily, the power thing works both ways. After all, I'd made Decker.

I reached for Deck's mind, determined to use my own power over him and force him to turn me loose. Instead I got a nasty shock. The lust he felt was a solid wall of heat and aggression I instantly realized I couldn't penetrate. His thoughts were too filled with burning memories—my breast in his mouth, his cock in my cunt, the hot pleasure of riding me hard. My mind skittered back from his raw, incoherent lust with a purely female panic.

As I jerked my gaze away from his, shaken, I met Beau's narrow green gaze. He smiled slowly, and I knew he'd sensed my attempt to establish control over Decker. He sent me another image—me, my cunt and ass filled full of thick, surging cock, the long shafts grinding deep, my delicate body caught between two massively built males in full rut. "You always wanted us both," he rumbled, his voice deep, menacing. "Now you've got us."

Decker rolled his hard-on into the cradle of my hips. "What's the matter, baby? Afraid your eyes are bigger than your . . . stomach?"

"Let's take her to that bed downstairs and find out just how big she is," Beau said.

I didn't struggle while he kicked the door open and they started down the stairs with me. I wasn't scared anymore.

I was pissed.

All of this was thoroughly out of character for the guys. It was the work of that wretched spell, and I was damned if I'd let the wizard get away with it. For one thing, I knew both men would be horrified when the magic wore off and they realized what they'd done. Anything they did to me I'd recover from, but I wasn't sure they'd ever get over the guilt.

However, at the moment I was a lot more concerned about my immediate problem: getting through the next hour without getting my asshole reamed.

They carried me down into Copperstone's bedroom. Listening closely, I could make out no other heartbeats in the house than ours; apparently the wizard had taken off. Smart of him, though I wondered where the hell he went.

As they laid me down on the thick scarlet coverlet, I made no effort to struggle, carefully giving my best imitation of defeated submission. Despite my limp body and lowered eyes, I was busy calculating the distance to the bedroom window. It'd be a two-story drop to the ground, but that was nothing to one of us. The trick would be getting a head start on the guys sufficient for my escape.

And I quickly realized that wasn't going to be easy. Beau knew me too well to let me go; he maintained a hard grip on my shoulder as he crawled onto the bed with me, then swung one long leg over my hips and straddled me. Despite myself, I was intrigued by the picture he made as he knelt astride me stripping off his black shirt. His cock was a long, hard ridge behind his fly, and the muscles in his powerful torso shifted and rippled as he tossed his shirt aside.

Decker meanwhile let the trench coat fall off his broad shoulders, then jerked his tie off and unbuttoned his shirt with rough, impatient fingers. His body was a bit more brawny than Beau's leanly muscled frame, but both men made mouth-watering scenery.

It really was a damn shame this was nothing more than a spell.

They'd freed my hands so they could undress, and I stroked the tough fabric covering Beau's muscled thighs, then cupped him through the fabric, smiling seductively.

His eyes lit with approval. "That's more like it," he murmured, one big hand going to his zipper. He tugged it down, and I reached into the opening to trace a finger down the smooth line of his cock, straining against the plain white fabric of his briefs.

Gloriously naked, Decker crawled onto the mattress with us. Beau slid off me so he could shed his jeans. I curled a long leg up as though reaching for the buckle of my high-heeled sandal—and instead uncoiled it with a snap, meaning to kick Beau right in his muscled chest in a blow that would slam him into the bedroom's back wall.

Instead, one big hand flashed out and clamped around my ankle with such crushing force I yelped and swung at him. He caught my fist just as Decker came down on top of me, grabbing my shoulders with ruthless strength. I cursed and began to struggle in earnest.

Snarling in rage, Beau tightened his grip on my ankle, bearing down. Pain shot up my leg in a wave of heat and agony, and I knew that despite my dense bones, he could easily crush it. I drew back the other leg, prepared to batter at him to get free.

"Amanda, don't!" Decker gave me a little shake. Wild-eyed, I snarled up at him.

Only to see such naked desperation in his eyes that I stopped in mid-kick. "When you fight, it makes the spell worse!" he said hoarsely. "Please! I'm afraid we'll hurt you."

My gaze snapped to Beau's. For just an instant, the rage on his face lifted, and I saw the agony behind it. "Please," he said, his voice rasping, begging. "Let us make love to you."

I stopped dead. On some level, my lovers were still aware, still present. Which meant if I surrendered, I could trust them to retain control. But if I fought, they could lose it altogether, and all bets were off.

Besides, I really didn't have much choice. The only way I could escape was by injuring one of them badly, and I had no desire to do that.

Too, our hurting each other was what the wizard wanted. If we turned this into steamy passion, Dickhead lost. And I really, really wanted to beat Copperstone at his own game.

Even if it meant exploring variations I'd never tried before.

My eyes tracked from Decker's big naked body to Beau's, clad only in jeans. Their eyes burned with heat and fraying restraint.

"What the fuck," I said with a choked laugh. "Call Nabisco—I guess I'm an Oreo."

Beau grinned in sheer relief before his instant of sanity was lost behind another wave of lechery. "And I want to lick your creamy center." With a mock growl, he released my ankle and pounced, diving headfirst between my legs. He fisted his hands in my skirt and pushed it up, then gave my cunt a long, slow stroke with his tongue. I caught my breath as pleasure stabbed right into my skull. He looked up at me over my pelvis, then wrapped both strong arms around my thighs and dragged me to his mouth. Hungrily, he shoved his tongue straight into my cunt.

"God, Beau!" My back arched at the incredible sensation as he started licking my folds, obviously determined to get me as hot as he could as fast as possible.

Decker sat back on his heels, his thick cock jutting between his muscled thighs as he watched my face with predatory satisfaction. His gaze slid to my breasts. My nipples hardened under his stare into taut points of arousal under the thin fabric of my dress.

Decker reached down a big hand and wrapped it in the material, preparing to rip it from my body with one savage jerk.

"Deck!" I objected. "I'd rather not have to walk out of here naked."

He gave me a slow, dark smile. "But you look so good naked." Still, he slowly released his grip and caught the hem of my dress instead. That hint that he was still more or less in control comforted me.

But that control was growing shakier by the second, I saw, as he tugged my dress up, his eyes locked on my naked body as it was revealed inch by inch. I rolled my hips upward to let him pull the fabric out from under me. The movement raked Beau's tongue over my clit, and my knees weakened at the wet heat. He rumbled at me and circled the little pink bud with his tongue, shooting delight straight up my spine.

Even as Beau tormented my creaming cunt, my eyes caught Decker's shimmering blue gaze. When the dress slid up over my breasts, the shimmer leaped into a bonfire. He tugged the dress the rest of the way off and tossed the wadded red fabric across the room without breaking his ravenous stare at my body. I watched his dark head descend toward my hard, pointed nipples and moaned in anticipation.

The only thing hotter than the feeling of a male mouth feasting on your cunt is the sensation of a second male mouth simultaneously devouring your breasts. I damn near catapulted into orbit as the boys' tongues flicked and stabbed and circled. Teeth raked my most delicate flesh in almost bites, while big hands stroked my skin, squeezing my breasts, twisting whatever nipple wasn't being sucked. I wrapped the fingers of one hand in Decker's dark hair and reached down to grab a fistful of Beau's blond silk, writhing in the grip of real magic.

Something slid into my juicy cunt as Beau began finger fucking me while his mouth worked wicked spells on my clit. A second finger slipped up my ass, the sensation dark and erotic, a delicious counterpoint to the mind-blowing pleasure of what they were doing to me. Slowly, deliberately, he screwed the fingers in and out, rotating his wrist to tease and stretch both my channels.

Adding to the heat of the moment, Beau telepathically sent me an image of what he saw: my dark pussy, slicked with juice as he explored and plundered it. Below it, my small, puckered asshole sucked at his finger as he finger-fucked it. I pulled in a breath as that image changed in his mind, and the fingers became two huge cocks, one withdrawing while the other thrust deep.

The full psychic force of his lust slammed into my mind; his hunger to use my tight ass, to hear my whimpers and moans as he took me in long, relentless strokes. Decker built that telepathic fire by adding his own need to feel my creamy cunt clasping his cock, my nipples brushing his chest as he rode me, grinding deep.

I writhed, breathless, Beau's hot tongue dancing across my clit as Decker feasted on my nipples. Driving me insane. I could feel myself shooting toward my peak, about to come. I gathered my breath for a scream. . . .

And they stopped.

"Not yet," Beau whispered. I felt his lips moving against my labia as he spoke. "I'm not going to let you come until my cock is in your ass."

"No!" I gasped, as frustration washed over me. "For God's sake, don't stop!"

"Oh, we won't stop." Decker leaned over to give my nipple a long lick. "Not even when you beg us."

And both of them hit me with another blast of psychic male heat that burned right through me. Catching me on fire.

I wanted them to fuck me, cunt, mouth, ass—hard and deep and NOW. I didn't care if it hurt, I didn't care about anything but being fucked. "Please!" I whimpered, writhing.

Beau laughed, a deep, triumphant rumble. He rose from the bed with an easy male flex, leaving me with my legs spread and aching, my wet cunt chill.

But it didn't stay cool for long. Decker rolled off me onto the mattress, simultaneously grabbing my hips and pulling me over on top of him.

"Yes!" Eagerly, I spread my legs and rose until I straddled his brawny thighs. He grabbed his thick, hard cock and pointed it skyward as he caught a handful of my black hair with the other hand, gently guiding me toward it. I rose to my knees and positioned myself, then sank downward, spearing my cunt on his massive erection. The sensation of his width sliding into my creamy, desperate pussy made me yowl in pleasure. He bared his teeth and slammed upward, ramming to my depths.

I threw back my head at the deliciously brutal invasion.

Decker let go of my hair to capture one breast, twisting and thumbing my nipple with a roughness that might have hurt at any other time. Just then it spurred me on. I rose up his shaft and took it deep again as he ground up to meet me. Growling in animal desperation, we fucked each other.

I looked over to see that Beau had stripped off his jeans and briefs and was delving in a drawer in Copperstone's night stand. I barely had time to wonder what the hell he was doing when he pulled out a small white jar and turned around. He unscrewed the lid and scooped out a handful of thick, white cream, then began slathering it over his jutting erection.

His back arched. "Damn, that's cold," Beau growled, looking over at me as I rode Decker, fucking him in hard, fast strokes.

Beau scooped up another handful of cream and smoothed it over his shaft, his green eyes fixed on mine, hard, menacing lust glittering in them. I looked at that big cock as I rode the one stuffing me, and wondered how the hell I'd ever take them both. I knew it would hurt like a bitch—but I wanted it. Wanted them deep, needed it desperately. . . .

Slowly, Beau smiled. And I knew he'd read my thoughts.

He moved toward the bed, stalking me. Decker's strong fingers curled into my hip, dragging my thrusts to a stop. Reaching up, he fisted the other hand in my hair again and tugged me down over him. Giving Beau access to my ass.

My eyes flew to Deck's hot blue ones and widened. He grinned, showing every inch of his fangs. "Brace yourself darlin'," he purred. "Here it comes."

With a moan of helpless lust, I bent lower, reached back with both hands, and spread my cheeks for Beau's cock.

"Ohhhh, yeaaah," he growled, as the bed shifted under his weight as he crawled up behind me. "I always wanted to see you do that."

Quivering in a maddening combination of arousal and fear, I waited, stuffed with Decker's shaft. I felt Beau's fingers brush my tight little anus, which twitched. Slowly, carefully, he inserted one slick finger, easing it inside, joining Deck's dick in my body. The sensation of fullness it gave me sent a helpless shudder up my spine. He slipped it out, then in again, this time two fingers, stretching and readying me.

"Oh, God," I whimpered, trying to writhe on Decker's impaling cock. But his hand tightened on my hip, holding me still.

A third finger, working its way deep, sliding against the thick prick in my cunt, stuffing me so impossibly full. I'd never be able to take Beau's shaft, I thought wildly. Too big, too much . . . .

"Too bad," Beau rumbled. "You are going to take me. Every last inch." He withdrew his fingers.

I moaned, knowing what was coming. But I didn't let go of my cheeks.

He sent me an image just then—my little pink virgin asshole, tight and puckered over my cunt, which strained so wide around Decker's cock. The broad, flushed head of Beau's shaft approached my tiny opening, looking much, much bigger. I felt the first brush of its slick, greased tip and jerked, closing my eyes.

Decker caught my breast in one hand and began to play with my nipple again, sending a welcome flood of pleasure to give me something else to think about. The other big fist was still buried in my hair, silently telling me I wasn't going anywhere.

Then Beau began to enter. An enormous burning pressure, forcing my delicate tissues to spread. He sent me another image—the sight of my asshole flowering open around the rapacious head of his prick. Wider and wider, straining to take him. I arched my back at the pain of his entry—and felt how it felt to him, deliciously tight, clamping over the sensitive tip, yielding slowly as he forced his cock inside, inch by slow, torturous inch. I writhed, overwhelmed by the mix of sensations, his and my own and Decker's.

The two men could feel their cocks sliding past each other through the thin membrane separating my cunt and my ass, the stimulation hot and wicked and alien, a dark, nasty pleasure. I released my cheeks and grabbed desperately for Decker's muscled torso, holding on, a whine forcing its way past my teeth. Stuffed, utterly stuffed with cock, overwhelmed and helpless. I made a pleading sound.

Decker reached a big hand down between our bodies and found my clit with his thumb, caressing it gently as Beau completed my impalement.

Finally both men were in to the balls. I threw back my head and keened.

"Shhhhh," Decker whispered, and started squeezing and rolling my nipples with one hand as he stroked my clit with the other. At the same time, Beau eased out almost to the head. I braced myself over Decker, leaning forward just enough to give him room to move. He pulled out gently just as Beau pushed inside.

Then, slowly, ruthlessly, they began to fuck me.

I had never felt anything like it. It seemed my entire being was focused between my legs, on my cunt and asshole being conquered by those two huge cocks. And Decker's hands, coaxing pleasure from my overloaded nervous system, strumming and stroking nipple and clit. I could feel Beau's body covering mine with his hard muscled strength, his powerful arms brushing mine as he rolled his hips, his shaft tormenting my anal tube with every stroke, even as Decker's cock massaged my cream-filled cunt.

By slow degrees, pleasure began to grow through the pain of their possession. I could feel their hot male enjoyment of me, of my tight, slick body, of my soft skin and full tits. So small, so helpless between them, so lush and female as they plundered me.

Their lust stoked mine, until I began to move under them, feeling one nipple brushing Decker's chest while he squeezed the other. Teeth clamped in my lip, I made short little thrusts back and forth between them. The pleasure grew, in my cunt, in my clit, in my ravaged asshole, spurring me on. Until I felt ravenous for the next delicious double stroke, the next twist of my flesh between those two big shafts. The men picked up the pace, stroking harder, Decker's thumb rubbing my clit, spiking the pleasure higher.

Finally I found myself grinding hard against Beau's hips, taking his cock all the way up my ass, then jolting forward to feel Deck drive to my depths. Growling as they growled, lust burning me until I felt mad with it, wanting more, wanting it all, back and forth and in and out and. . . .

I screamed as the orgasm shot through me in a river of fire, scalding every synapse. "Oh, GOD!"

"Yeah!" Beau rammed all the way in, up to the balls, jolting me forward onto Decker's cock. Doubly impaled, I shook, only dimly aware of Beau's roar of triumph, of Decker's gasping groan as my orgasm triggered theirs in a psychic cascade of pleasure. I felt both hard cocks jolting, shooting my ass and cunt full of come. My climax surged higher and higher until it seemed my senses couldn't take any more of the overwhelming explosion.

Until it all went black.

I woke sandwiched between them. "Beau?" I groaned, wiggling. He lay over me like a hot, heavy blanket. "Decker?"

Neither answered. Looking into Deck's face, I saw his eyes were closed, his breathing deep. Twisting my head around, I saw Beau's face. His head rested on my shoulder, eyes closed.

"Hey, guys?" Damn. Both of them were out cold. I stirred, my body's aches making themselves known with a vengeance. Groaning, I rolled Beau's heavy body off mine, wincing as his cock slipped free of my ass. He collapsed beside Decker.

Sitting back on my heels, I gazed at the deliciously naked men and frowned. Something was wrong here. They should not be sleeping like this.

Oh, hell. Copperstone's spell. It must have been designed to put them out after they were through with me. Leaving them helpless.

Damn. The little shit had something in mind. I rolled off the bed and looked for my dress. Finding it in a corner, I scooped it off the floor and shrugged into it, suspecting I did not have much time. He'd be back any moment.

I was lucky he hadn't bothered to include me in his sleep spell; apparently he didn't consider me a threat. Just another piece of ass, like Lynn. Something to be tormented.

He was about to find out how wrong he was.

I took a moment to clean up in Copperstone's bathroom. Just as I threw down the washcloth, I heard the rumble of an approaching car engine. I flew to the window and looked out.

As I watched, Copperstone got out of his Honda Accord. He'd

changed out of his robe into black trousers and a shirt. And in his hands was a crossbow. A quiver filled with wooden bolts rode across his shoulders. I knew he meant to stake all three of us as the boys slept.

"Oh no you don't, you little fuck!" I snarled. Whirling, I made for the stairs.

I was waiting when he opened the door. It was dark in the house, and Copperstone's merely human eyes didn't see me as I crouched beside the door.

With a soundless growl, I pounced, wrapping one hand around his mouth, my fingers digging into his jaw so hard he grunted in pain.

After watching him in action, I knew the way to keep him from using his magic was to keep him from talking.

"You even try to say a spell, and I'll rip your fucking head off," I snarled in his ear, jerking him to his knees. He tried to kick back at me, so I straddled his back and gripped his hips between my thighs, bearing down until he yelped. "Thought you said you wouldn't mind being between my legs." I squeezed again. He groaned. "It's like I learned today—you really should be careful what you wish for."

I pulled his head to one side, arching his throat. He stiffened, knowing what I intended. "Now, listen up, schmuck, while I tell you what we're going to do. First. . . ." I ran my tongue over the banging pulse in his throat. ". . . I'm going to have a little bite. Then we're going to discuss how you will never, ever hurt anybody again. You'll never stalk anybody, you'll never rape anybody, and you sure as hell will never turn anybody into werewolves." I paused to rake him with my fangs, just barely drawing blood. The taste was delicious. "Then we'll go upstairs and break that sleep spell you put on the boys. If you're very, very good, I'll even convince them not to kill you. Got that?"

He gave a defeated whimper and went limp in my arms. I pulled him up into a more comfortable position—for me—and sank my fangs right into his pulse.

* * *

The bite allowed me to establish a mind link with him, which I used to make sure he'd be a good little wizard from now on. Then we woke the guys, who definitely were not happy with him. Both felt incredibly guilty about how close they came to forcing me, and they held Copperstone responsible. It took some fancy verbal footwork on my part to talk them out of killing him.

It helped that, guilt notwithstanding, the sex had been pretty damn outstanding.

I'd love to try it again, only this time without the guys being under the influence. I've been trying to talk them into it. Both of them have rejected the idea every time I've brought it up, loudly and with great enthusiasm. After all, they still hate each other's guts.

But, you know—I think they're tempted.

And temptation is one of my best things.

THE BLOODSLAVE

June 4, 2459 AD

When Captain Julian Bender started climbing the cliff, he fully intended to cut the sniper's throat. Assuming it had one, of course.

Firing from concealment behind several boulders at the top of the mountain, the alien son of a bitch had picked off half a dozen of Bender's allies with well-placed blasts of a Beamer rifle. Since the Jeranth weren't exactly built for stealthy cliff scaling—what with their six legs and massive bodies—it fell to Julian and his crew to go up after the shooter and stop him.

Once that was done, they should be able to wrap this up and get the hell off this planet fairly quickly.

God, said Dominic telepathically, bitching as usual, *I'll be glad to put this ball of rock behind us. I'm sick of synthblood. I can't wait to drink from something that squirms.*

Julian didn't answer, too busy digging his fingers into a handhold on the cliff face. Besides, they'd had this conversation before. It had been months since any of them had even seen a woman, and they were all eager to return to human space. They hadn't had a decent meal since they'd left.

Synthetic blood might keep a vampire alive, but it didn't wrap its legs around you while you fed. And it didn't come when you took it, pumping hot energy into your mind.

If the ship hadn't been so badly damaged, Julian would never have agreed to take this mission so far from human space. But they'd needed the money for repairs, and the Jeranth paid exceptionally well. Even among aliens, vampire mercenaries were renowned for their sabotage and assassination skills, and the Jeranth general had wanted their services badly. With the money he'd paid, Julian had been able to get the ship repaired in record time.

Unfortunately, Julian and his men then had to earn that money by spending six months out here on this godforsaken rock, among aliens so alien even their emotions tasted wrong.

In the act of reaching for another handhold, Julian stopped dead, his mind picking up a stray psychic wash from the sniper.

Despair. Grief. Rage. But not the alien versions of those feelings they'd come to know so well from the minds of their T'tcha Ker enemies.

Automatically, Julian glanced over and met his second-in-command's wide brown eyes. Clinging to the rock face, André lifted his brows and projected his thoughts: *Captain, our sniper's human.*

Hell, Julian, thought Dominic. *It's not just a human. It's a woman.*

As one, they all looked up the moonlight-washed cliff.

And grinned.

She was going to die today. Verica Sher aimed her rifle down at the detachment of Jeranth in the valley below and fired off another blast. Her alien target staggered and fell, all six legs waving in the moonlight. Her weapon vibrated between her hands, a signal it was running out of charge. And when the last of its energy was gone . . .

It would be over. Over for her, as it was for all the other members of T'tcha Ker who had been picked off one by one fighting this interminable war. Verica forced her mind away from that thought, forced herself to ignore the aching grief. It had been twelve years since her father had dragged her out here, as far from human space—and her mother—as he could get. To support them, Jonas Sher had joined the T'tcha Ker's mercenary unit, only to get himself killed five years later. Though the big, furry tripeds hadn't been even remotely human, they'd taken her in, trained her to fight and treated her with love and respect.

Now they were all gone. Gruff Itka and motherly Ch'fa and Garsh, her best friend, all dead, killed in this disastrous battle. And once her rifle's charge was drained, she'd be dead too, so far from human space the beings who'd kill her wouldn't even know what species she was. But in the meantime, she was going to take as many of the enemy with her as she could. Verica Sher would not die alone.

Plucky little thing, isn't she? André asked, watching the girl draw a bead on the aliens below.

A little too plucky, Julian thought. *She's got maybe two blasts left in that rifle, and I don't want her using one of them on herself.*

And she might, if she realized she was about to be captured by vampires. Some vamp mercenaries had such dark reputations most women would do anything to avoid falling into their hands.

It was a different story with humans who realized they were dealing with Julian. The mercenary community was a relatively small one, and everyone knew he didn't abuse prisoners. True, female captives expected to end up on the menu, but there were enough titillating rumors going around that they were usually less alarmed by the prospect than intrigued.

Some of Julian's former victims had evidently done a little breathless gloating.

It also helped that the old myth about vampires draining their victims had died a well-deserved death. Vamps just didn't need that much blood—no more than half a liter or so, less if they could get a good psychic charge from their partner.

Like orgasm.

But there was no guarantee this girl would realize she was in danger of nothing worse than hot sex from her captors. And Julian didn't want her jumping the gun.

For one thing, it would be a waste. He couldn't see much of her, since she was lying on her belly with her back to them—they'd come up the cliff on the opposite side and slipped up behind her. But she filled out her blue unisuit nicely, between her narrow waist, long legs, and the lovely, sweetly rounded ass Julian badly wanted to explore. Plus, he liked the way her long blonde hair shimmered in the moonlight.

Just then she hit the trigger pad on her rifle again . . . and nothing happened.

Well, gentlemen, thought Dominic, turning to smirk at his fellow vampires with wolfish hunger, *I think I just heard the dinner bell.*

Shit," Verica growled, cursing her weapon in the Terran Standard of her childhood as her stomach sank like a stone. It was over. She was finished.

"Rifle gone dead?" a human voice asked in the same language. "Tough luck."

With a gasp, Verica jerked around to face the man who'd taken her so thoroughly by surprise. *He must have come up the other side of the cliff,* she thought wildly, looking up at the first human she'd seen in seven years.

Big. Much bigger than her father. And handsome, like the actors on Jonas's collection of pornographic vids—dark, amused eyes set in a sculpted, angular face with a sensuous mouth and short-cropped black hair. Too bad he wore the enemy's colors on his black unisuit. And it was a safe bet the rifle he held so casually was fully charged.

"Don't you think it's time you surrendered?" he asked, his tone polite and interested.

Verica threw herself into a roll that carried her away from the edge of the cliff and gave her room to bounce to her feet. As soon as she got her legs under her, she swung the dead rifle like a club, right at her enemy's dark head. "The T'tcha Ker do not surrender!"

The weapon slapped into a casually lifted palm. His jerk ripped it from her hands so hard her arm muscles screeched in protest. Moving deliberately as she gaped at his strength, the human swung his own rifle by its strap across his back, out of the way. "You're not T'tcha Ker, girl. Or hadn't you noticed?" He tossed her Beamer over the cliff edge.

She leaped forward into a hand-to-hand attack, throwing punches and kicks with every ounce of her strength. He blocked each blow with insulting ease, his big hands blurring to knock her fists and feet away.

"You know, she's pretty good," another male voice said.

"If he were mortal, he'd probably have his hands full," another agreed.

Jesus, there were more of them. Verica darted a look in toward the source of the voices. Two men watched her hopeless struggle, both almost as big and handsome as her opponent, one blond, the other with the darkest skin she'd ever seen. The dark one crouched casually on top of an enormous boulder higher than his head, while his companion leaned against it.

With a defiant snarl, she snapped to face her foe and swung her booted foot in a high, hard kick at his head. He caught her ankle. Shocked at his speed, she just stood there for an instant, balanced on one foot as he gripped the other. Then another pair of powerful hands clamped around her shoulders. It dawned on her she was well and truly caught.

"I'm Captain Julian Bender," her enemy said. "And I really think it's time you gave up, don't you?"

But Verica had been taught to fight as long as she was conscious, so she drove a head-butt back at the man who held her arms, simultaneously ramming her free foot toward Bender's groin.

Her head smacked back into a big hand just as Bender caught her by the ankle.

"Thanks, André," the blond man who held her arms told the third one, who wrapped his dark fist in her hair. "She might actually have caught me with that head-butt."

Bender, both her ankles in his hands, pushed them apart and up, then stepped between. Verica squirmed and cursed, but the three men held her effortlessly.

Slowly, the mercenary captain moved closer, lifting and spreading her thighs until her shoulders were forced into the solid, muscular body of the man behind her, her head held in an arch over his shoulder.

"You know," the blond said in her ear, "this is starting to give me a hard-on."

"Everything gives you a hard-on, Dominic," André told him.

Bender moved his grip to the bend of her knees and stepped fully against her crotch. Looking between her trapped legs, she saw something cylindrical bulking under his unisuit, stretching in a long thick ridge the length of his belly. The feeling of that alien rod pressing against her cunt sent a trickle of heat through her.

So that's what a cock feels like . . .

Bender's eyes widened. "What do you mean, 'That's what a cock feels like?'"

"Good God," André said, astonished. "She's a virgin!"

Verica felt her face heat at the horrifying realization they had somehow read her thoughts. But the only humans who could do that were . . .

Dominic purred out a laugh in her ear. "That's right, darling. We're vampires. Very, very hungry vampires who've been living off synthblood since we were hired to fight this wretched war. And you, my love, are an answer to some very dark prayers."

"And maybe we can answer some of yours." André cupped her breast through her unisuit. His thumb brushed one nipple, which instantly hardened, sending juicy curls of heat up her spine. Watching her face with calculating eyes, he caught the little bump and began to roll it. She caught her breath in astonishment at the pure, liquid pleasure he conjured with such a simple gesture.

Opening her mouth to protest, Verica discovered she couldn't bear to say anything to stop that delicious sensation.

"Not so fast," Julian snapped at André. "How old are you, girl?" Reading the answer out of her thoughts, he looked relieved, then puzzled. "How the hell does a twenty-five-year-old woman stay a virgin?"

"Shit," said André, on a tone of revelation, his hand going still on her breast. "She's been living with these fucking aliens since she was thirteen!"

Stung, Verica snarled, "Would you do me the courtesy of letting me answer your questions instead of just reading my mind?"

"Did it ever occur to you that a captive who's a hungry vampire's wet dream should keep a civil tongue?" Dominic growled back, tightening his grip on her arms in warning.

She started to tell him what he could do with his hunger, but before she could open her mouth, a waterfall of alien clicking filled the air. Her translator brain implant turned the voice into words: "I see you've captured the sniper. Good work, captain."

Turning her head, Verica saw one of the Jeranth holding a beam weapon in two of its six limbs as it clawed its way up the cliff, accompanied by a shower of rocks. "You're worth every cred the High Command paid you," it told the captain.

"Thank you," Julian said in English. Evidently the Jeranth had a translator of its own. "Luckily the charge ran out on her rifle just as we came up."

"Lucky indeed. But why haven't you killed it?" the Jeranth demanded.

Julian's hands tightened on her knees. "She's one of our species. We're taking her captive."

"Squeamish, eh? Would you like me to kill it for you?" The Jeranth scrambled over and put the muzzle of his weapon against her head. Verica's heart skipped.

With a growl, André grabbed the barrel and shoved it away from her skull.

"No!" Speaking rapidly, Julian said, "We have a use for her. She's valuable to us."

The Jeranth jerked and moved all its limbs in agitation. "It has killed a dozen of my soldiers! I want it dead!"

Julian lifted an arrogant brow. "Oh, she'll be punished, sir, far more thoroughly than any quick death."

"Yesss," Dominic whispered, his neat blond beard brushing her ear. "We'll punish her for hours and hours. In every single virgin orifice."

Verica's reckless temper snapped. "Shoot me, alien," she spat, glaring at Bender. "I'd rather die like a soldier than be tortured by the likes of these bastards!" She tried to kick at the vampire, but he controlled her effortlessly.

"Idiot!" Julian growled, tightening his grip on her thighs until she winced.

"It seems to find a beam in the head preferable to your company." The Jeranth produced a hissing sound the translator rendered as a laugh. "Keep it, then, if it dreads you so. In the meantime, Captain, my general wants to see you."

Verica swore and began to struggle, her body lashing between the vampires' unhuman hands.

"Cut it out," Dominic said, clamping down hard on her arms. Stubbornly, she kept fighting. He increased the pressure until she gritted her teeth. "You've pissed the captain off as it is. Calm down and be a good girl, or you'll regret it."

"Fuck you!"

"Oh, you will," Julian told her, then jerked his chin at the vampire who still had her by the hair. "Take her legs, André. I've got business with our employers. Get her back to the ship . . ." He flashed them a warning glare. "But keep your greedy hands, fangs, and cocks off until I get back."

Simmering with fear and anger, Verica twisted her hands, trying to get at the knot that bound her wrists together.

The vampire bastards had tied her to a chair.

"You're going to get rope burns doing that," André observed, not looking up from his poker hand.

She couldn't answer, though she ached to curse him. They'd gagged her with a length of silk.

It had been an hour since the two vampires had summoned their star runner to land on the mountaintop and pick them up while Bender completed his business with the vampires' employers. Since then, she'd been subjected to another losing battle with her captors they'd thoroughly enjoyed, then left to stew in her despair.

From their conversation, Verica gathered that the war was indeed over; the engagement with her unit had been the last of the mopping up. The Jeranth had won possession of the planet. And the Lochta, who'd hired her mercenary company, were already pulling out of the star system, leaving Verica at the dubious mercy of three vampires.

Once they'd bound her, Dominic had stepped back to look down at her as she glared up at him. He was just too damned handsome with those angular features, a neat blond beard framing sensual lips. In contrast to his elegant good looks, his eyes blazed with earthy lechery. "God," he said to André, "I'd forgotten how arousing it is to tie up a pretty victim."

"Yeah," André agreed, fangs flashing against his dark, hawkish face. "I can't wait to get her naked. She's incredibly responsive. You saw the way she damn near hit orbit just from a touch on one nipple."

"Makes you wonder how she'll react having a hard cock shoved somewhere tight. Which reminds me; we need to decide who fucks her where first."

André lifted an eyebrow. "Well, the captain's going to want her ass."

Verica's eyes widened and her mouth went dry as she remembered the size of that thick ridge pressing against her crotch.

"Which leaves her mouth and cunt for us," Dominic said. "But who gets to pop her cherry?" He sounded so matter-of-fact, Verica blinked in shock.

"Good point," André said. "We'll let a poker hand decide it. Best two out of three. It'll give us something to do while we wait for the captain."

After Dominic went back to his quarters for a deck of cards, the two vampires sat down on the bed to deal out the hand.

Ha, Verica thought, watching sullenly. *The laugh's on them. I don't even have a hymen anymore.* She'd disposed of that one evening during an experimental fuck with a hairbrush handle while watching her father's ancient cache of pornography. But it had hurt, and she hadn't tried it since.

What would it feel like when Julian . . .

"A hairbrush?" Dominic hooted, looking up. "You are a naughty girl, aren't you? Not that it matters. You still haven't had a cock."

"You know, if she had that much trouble with her hairbrush, she's going to have a hell of a time with us," André told him, concentrating on his cards. "None of us are exactly small men . . ."

"Mmmmmm," Dominic agreed, smirking at her, an evil glint in his green eyes. "I'm starting to look forward to watching you get it, whether or not I'm the one who gives it to you. You'll be begging behind your gag."

"Hell, wait 'til the captain does her." André rearranged his hand. "That always gets a reaction, even from captives a hell of a lot more experienced than she is."

"Oh, baby." Dominic flipped a card down on the bed. "When you feel that big prick start forcing its way up your little backside, you'll beg for mercy. Not that it'll do you any good. Julian just loves a virgin asshole."

André glanced up. "Have you ever noticed how he's got this sadistic little twist he gives his hips when his victims start pleading?"

Verica chewed nervously on her gag, acutely aware of the rope biting into her wrists. She was completely at the mercy of these men. They could fuck her however they wanted, and there was nothing she could do to save herself. If their captain wanted to sodomize her, very soon she'd be bent and helpless waiting for him to slide that monster cock up her virgin anus.

Dominic looked up and shot her a smile that showed every inch of his long, sharp fangs. "Now you're getting the idea. You're defenseless, darlin'. And you're ours."

Verica stared at him, her cheeks hot. They were really going to fuck her. All of them.

Everywhere.

Twenty minutes later, when Dominic hooted in triumph and André groaned, she was so preoccupied with dark images she barely noticed that the blond had won her cunt.

Dominic and André simultaneously threw down the cards they'd been idly playing after deciding her fate. She looked up, startled, as they advanced on her.

"Captain's coming in the airlock," Dominic explained with a nasty grin, "and he's pissed."

André moved behind her and snapped the cords holding her wrists to the back of the chair while Dominic freed her legs. She aimed a kick at him, just on general principles, but he ducked away and stood just as André snatched her onto her feet.

The blond stepped aside as Julian strode in, his face grim. Without hesitation, the captain reached out, grabbed the front of her unisuit, and ripped the tough fabric down the front. Cool air flooded over her breasts. Verica yelped in outrage.

Ignoring her curses, Julian snatched her away from André and flung himself down in the chair, then dragged her face down across his lap. Locking a big fist in what was left of her unisuit, he stripped it away. Instinctively, she tried to rear out of his lap, but he just wrapped a big hand around the back of her head and held her down.

"It's one thing to attempt escape," Julian told her in a low, controlled voice. "It's another to attempt suicide. It's a good thing the Jeranth is so fuckin' perverse, or you'd be dead now." His broad hand descended on her bare butt in a hard, stinging smack that startled a muffled yelp out of her. "You will *not* do that again," he told her sternly.

"Oh, yeah! Beat that little ass!" Dominic said as he and André grabbed a couple of chairs from a nearby table and dragged them over. Grinning, they sat down to watch.

Verica set her teeth against the next smack and barely managed to hold back another yelp. But the following blow was even harder, and the next, and the next. Though she managed not to scream, she couldn't seem to keep from squirming under the rain of blistering smacks.

Yet, as a fire ignited in her ass cheeks, she felt her pussy heat as well. *God,* she thought, appalled at herself. *How could I find this arousing?*

But she did. Being butt-up across a handsome man's thighs as he paddled her under the lecherous gaze of his crew, knowing they'd all soon . . . She gasped.

And she wasn't the only one turned on. As Verica squirmed across Julian's muscular thighs, she felt his erection lengthening against her side. Turning her head, she saw that both Dominic and André were just as hard.

Seeing the direction of her gaze, Dominic ran the long fingers of one hand up and down the outline of his own broad shaft through his unisuit. Cupping his balls with the other, he leaned closer and met her eyes. "Nothing's quite as hot as watching a naked blonde's ass go red under a good, hard spanking."

"Unless it's watching her asshole stretch around a hard cock," Julian growled, suddenly breaking off his ruthless smacks. "*My* hard cock." He reached between her thighs and sought the opening of her cunt.

"Why, gentleman," the captain purred, "our little captive's wet!"

"She's *been* wet," André said. "I could smell it."

Her back arched as Julian's thick finger slipped deeper, then slowly withdrew only to dip inside again. The sensation was hot, dark, breath-stealing.

"I think she's got a submissive streak." Eyeing her, Dominic stroked his hard-on again. "I wonder if we've captured ourselves a potential bloodslave."

"If she is, we'll find out." The finger withdrew from her cunt and lifted, then pressed against her anus. Verica sucked in a breath behind her gag as the long male digit began to enter a place that had never before been penetrated. The insertion felt both painful and strangely erotic.

"Oh, yeah," Julian said. "Hard-ass on the outside, sweet submissive underneath. Get the rope and the lube, gentlemen. It's time little Verica lost every last virginity."

Tying up Verica for her first fuck was the hottest thing Julian had done in decades.

They could have subdued her so completely she'd have been unable to bat an eyelash, but they ended up letting her writhe just so they could watch her do it. She looked so tasty squirming and fighting that the process of hog-tying her took about three times as long as it should have. By the time they were done, Julian's fangs were aching in his jaw and his dick was hard as a Beamer rifle.

Had she truly been terrified and unwilling, of course, he'd have taken a different approach. Their objective, after all, was to get her as aroused as possible so she'd generate the greatest psychic charge when she came. They'd all been at this so long they knew when a captive would respond best to gentle seduction or a rough mock-rape. And Verica, virgin or not, wanted to be subdued.

She had to know she didn't have a prayer against three vampires. Hell, if they'd just been human, she still wouldn't have had a prayer. They were too big, and Verica was too small. Too female.

Too delicious.

Her pink-tipped breasts jiggled as she squirmed, trying to kick with those long, muscled legs or land a small fist in a punch. Her silky blonde hair whipped around her delicate face, and her full, pink lips drew back from her teeth in a snarl as she fought to bite anything she could reach. All the while, she glared around at them with what she probably considered a ferocious expression.

It wouldn't have occurred to her that those big, blue eyes were better suited to pleading.

And Julian badly wanted to watch her plead. It was almost a shame to blindfold her, but he knew it would increase her feelings of delicious vulnerability. He promised himself he'd take off the strip of silk once she started whimpering.

Panting, he and Dominic stood back, trying to regain a little self-control while André forced a spreader gag between her jaws. A wise precaution, since they all knew without the synthrubber guard holding her teeth open, she'd try to bite his cock off the minute he attempted to use her mouth.

She still hadn't stopped struggling, even though she was blindfolded and wrapped so tightly in one of André's bondage specials she could barely move. Her arms were lashed behind her, tied together from elbows to wrists so her back was pulled into an arch that forced her full breasts out. A couple of loops of rope circled her tits, making them bulge and drawing attention to their stiff nipples.

Together the vampires had spread her ankles wide and tied them to a couple of magnetic clamps attached to the ceiling. A third clamp held the ropes that supported the rest of her immobilized body.

André had passed another loop around her forehead, then lashed that to her wrists, so that as she hung in her cradle of cords, her neck was forced into a tempting arch. They'd suspended her at hip height so she could be entered easily, but it would be equally convenient to pull up a chair and feed.

"You know, we've done some kinky things over the centuries," André observed after he'd secured the ring gag, "but this is a record."

"It's the virginity," Julian decided. "That, and she's so damn stubborn. You can smell how wet she is, and she's still fighting."

Dominic grinned. "I wonder how long that will last."

Julian grinned back. "Let's get started and see."

Breathing hard through the ring gag, Verica hung in her bonds. They'd tied her in a demonically uncomfortable position, and though she was blindfolded, she knew the arch of her spine and the wide splay of her thighs offered her breasts and cunt up to whoever wanted to torment them.

This situation should not be arousing her, damn it. Yet she could feel the cream trickling in her core, a humiliating testimony to the lust this ridiculous scenario had tapped. No matter what her pride insisted, some dark, animal part of her ached for the cocks of her captors, for their mouths and hands.

And fangs.

They'd feast on her, the bastards, sink those long, sharp teeth into her tender skin even as they sank their long, hard cocks into her cunt, mouth, and ass. They'd fuck her ruthlessly, ride her without mercy, pump her full of cum as they drank her blood in greedy swallows.

What the hell was taking them so long?

"All that sounds really good," Julian purred in her ear, "but I hope you don't mind if we indulge in a little foreplay first. I know you've been waiting twenty-five years, but some things should not be rushed."

Strong fingers caught one hard nipple and began to delicately twist. Pleasure radiated from the tormented point, and she writhed in the rope harness, gasping at the intensity of the sensation.

Then it began. Slowly, even gently. At first.

Fingers touched, stroked, squeezed. Here a hand swept down the delicate hollow of her belly, there another traced the angle of a hipbone, while yet another fondled her ass cheeks. Fingers circled her rock-hard clit, eased into her cunt, brushed the line of her throat, stroked her thigh. Six hands, Verica knew there couldn't be more than six hands, but it felt like more, all doing things to her she'd never experienced.

She'd caressed herself before, played with her own breasts, masturbated to orgasm, but it had never felt like this, so hot and ferocious and utterly overwhelming.

Somebody was taking his time with one nipple. He'd brush it with the pad of his thumb, then pull it out just enough to make her gasp. Twist it back and forth a few times while pleasure jolted her in repeated hot stabs. Then he'd start the whole sequence all over again until she began drooling helplessly behind her gag.

Simultaneously, somebody else was lazily exploring her pussy, slipping his fingers through slick cream and lust-engorged flesh, teasing and penetrating, then setting off little blasts of pleasure in her swollen clit as he circled and strummed it slowly.

Another hand busied itself with her ass, tracing the tense muscle of her cheeks, slipping a finger into the crease and stroking the tight flesh, spread so helplessly wide by her position. Finally discovering her anus, he circled it with an impudent fingertip.

Sliding slowly inside. Slipping in and out at a rhythm that matched the finger that stroked her cunt.

Deep inside her tormented body, the hard, deep clenching of orgasm began. Sensing her response, her captors grew deliciously brutal, twisting her nipples ruthlessly while driving up her cunt, her ass, two fingers, three, stuffing her until her spine arched in pleasure/pain.

That callused thumb flicked her clit once, twice, and Verica exploded, screaming, her voice strangled by the gag, her pussy and rectum speared on long male fingers.

Never, she thought, dazed, shaken, as she began to slide slowly down from the crest. *I've never felt like that.* The orgasms she'd given herself were pale, feeble things by comparison, completely unlike this merciless rapture.

"There's more," Julian whispered.

She whimpered an involuntary protest, but it did no good. Mouths now, on her nipples. Biting, licking, sucking both hard little points, spinning sensations along her spine she'd never experienced at all.

Delicate, feathery sensations so darkly intense they drove helpless moans from her mouth. Too much, far too much, she couldn't stand it . . .

Silken hair brushed the inside of her thighs. Someone began feasting on her sex. His tongue danced liquidly over her clit, laving, circling, lapping at her labia, sucking and nibbling. Fingers spread her cunt lips so that rapacious mouth could devour her wet, sensitive flesh until she keened in ravished pleasure.

Verica could feel her climax gathering like a storm, so intense it terrified her. Instinctively she began to struggle, squirming to get away from those greedy, demanding lips. Strong hands closed on her, holding her still for her captors' tongues. She thought she heard a low, masculine laugh . . .

Her second orgasm went off in her cunt like a bomb.

The spasms were still shivering through her system when someone snatched her blindfold off and a hard hand closed on her hair. The first cock she'd ever seen was right in her face, looking huge and dark.

"Four hundred years ago, when I was a slave in Jamaica," André said, his voice rasping, "my mistress had hair the exact color of yours."

Taking the big rod in hand, he aimed it for the opening in the ring gag and drove it deep into her mouth. Verica gasped and choked as the big rod hit the back of her throat.

"One night she ordered me whipped until the blood ran, then thrown into the fields and left for dead." Slowly, he withdrew, then thrust deep again. She struggled to accommodate him, knowing she had no choice. "Julian found me as I lay with my blood soaking the ground, and realized I could become a vampire. He changed me, saved me, and went with me three nights later when I took my revenge. We punished her thoroughly—and made her come again and again. How I enjoyed the sight of her, writhing in shame and pleasure as I fed."

Breathing hard through her nose, Verica fought her gag reflex while he used her mouth in long strokes. She felt his slick satin shaft pressing past her lips, moving over her tongue, the head sliding against the roof of her mouth. As she sucked in a desperate breath, his clean, male scent filled her head. Upside down, her head tied back, she watched his dark balls swing over the working muscles of his thighs as he fucked her.

"Mouthful, hmmm?" Dominic whispered in her ear, catching one of her nipples in his hand and twisting it slowly. "You know, you look incredibly hot having your mouth fucked. Julian . . ." He raised his voice. "Mind if I take your place between those pretty thighs?"

"Not in the least. I think I'd like to have a word with her anyway," the captain's deep voice rumbled. Long fingers released her spread pussy lips.

Julian had been the one licking her cunt, Verica realized, and was startled at the heat that thought sent through her. Helplessly she watched the swing of André's balls, swallowing hard as her mouth watered from the thick shaft stuffing it.

Dominic's hand brushed the length of her thighs, caught her butt and held her still. Something big and blunt brushed across her needy cunt and worked its way between her slick lips. The shaft brushed her opening, then began to slowly force its way inside. His cock felt huge, a massive, tunneling invader forcing her delicate pussy walls wide.

"Ummm," Dominic said. "Tight as a nun's ass."

Even without her hymen, even with the slick cream that filled her, she thought for a minute he'd split her open. She whined around André's cock, the pain distracting her from his use of her mouth. He paused his stroking, holding his prick just inside her lips while Dominic completed his invasion.

"Too much?" Julian asked softly in her ear. Gently he reached up to toy with her nipples until delight shot through her discomfort.

"Poor little virgin. Try to relax." He tugged the pink tip and rolled it with delicate, ruthless skill. "We're nowhere near done."

He rose from the chair someone had put beside her head and bent over her, directing an idle order down the length of her body. "Play with her clit, Dominic. I want her to come again."

The blond obeyed; she felt a light stroke against her button, then a gentle circling that sent pleasure swirling up her spine to compete with the pain of his penetration. An instant later, a hot male mouth sealed around one nipple, and she jerked in her bonds.

Verica felt utterly overwhelmed, her senses battered by too much feral eroticism. The long cock stroking inside her mouth, the big cock shuttling back and forth in her pussy, the stroking fingers and Julian's clever tongue . . . Assaulted from all sides, it seemed she'd been transformed into a creature of raw sex and sensation.

Unable to do anything else, she surrendered, relaxing her muscles, allowing them to use her as they would.

Julian smiled around her nipple, feeling the erotic submission flooding Verica's mind. They had her now.

Her responsiveness sharpened his hunger. He could almost taste the blood rushing through the sensitive breast under his mouth, and the urge to bite nearly broke his control. He fought it back. The pleasure would be sweeter, hotter, when she came, when the raw psychic energy of her climax rolled from her mind, a delicious meal for her vampire lovers.

Blood was never enough.

The hemosynther could produce enough blood to bathe in, but they also needed *this*—the sensual response of a woman in the throes of climax. And the more overwhelmed she felt, the more intense her orgasm, the more psychic energy she'd feed them.

Which made little virgin Verica utterly perfect. He doubted he'd ever had such a sweet feast.

And he hadn't even entered her ass yet.

He sucked and lapped and nibbled at each breast in turn as the energy grew, a field of delicious heat surrounding her, flooding his mind with her pleasure. He could feel how erotically vanquished she felt with André fucking her mouth and Dominic shafting her cunt. This orgasm would be the most intense yet. And he was going to make it even hotter.

He released her wet, pebble-hard nipple and straightened, then pulled the chair closer to her head. He'd sensed her response to him, and he knew he could use it.

A big vein thumped wildly in the taut, white arch of her throat. Looking down at it, he smiled slowly in anticipation.

"You do realize they're about to come?" Julian rumbled in her ear.

"Then it'll be my turn." He reached a big hand over her body to stroke and squeeze one breast. André's cock surging in and out of her mouth, she could only listen. "We could have all done you at once, but I don't want you distracted when I give you your first buggering."

His lips closed over the lobe of her ear and gave it a gentle nibble just as Dominic drove in a particularly hard thrust. The first flutters of her climax teased her, and she strained, trying to force herself against the blond's hips for that last bit of stimulation. But the ropes held her immobile, and she could only whimper.

"It will hurt at first when I enter, and you'll want to fight it, but don't," Julian said softly over André's gasps and Dominic's harsh growls. "You won't be able to keep me out anyway. Just concentrate on relaxing that sensitive little asshole. It won't be easy for you, as tight as you are, but really, you don't have very much choice." He gave one of the taut cords of her neck a tender lick. "I'm going to ream your little rectum, darling. But first . . ." Another lick. His lips moved against her banging pulse as he spoke. "But first I'm going to feed."

With a roar, Dominic rammed all the way in, a hard, violent stroke that tipped her over. Verica keened around André's cock as her climax hit her like a meteor, twisting her in her bonds. It went on and on, long, racking convulsions of pleasure deep in her womb as the vampires fucked her so hard, she swung between them in her harness.

The last spasms had barely begun to die when something hot and bitter flooded her mouth. Swallowing automatically, she realized it was André's come.

Then Julian's fangs punched into her throat, and she whimpered at the hot, stabbing pain. Quivering helplessly, she felt his lips moving against her skin as he drank.

Julian only allowed himself a few burning, intoxicating swallows before he let her go. He knew the others would need to feed, and he didn't want to take enough to weaken her.

Besides, his balls were heavy and swollen, tight against his shaft, and he wanted to take that final, ultimate possession. The one that would set the seal on her soul.

It was obvious she was the one they'd been looking for—the perfect combination of responsive submissive and fiery soldier. And he was determined that tonight her body would learn who her master was.

He knew quite well it would take a little longer for the message to reach her mind.

As André and Dominic reeled away from her to collapse on the bed, Julian started ripping down the harness with a few ruthless jerks. Dazed from their sensual assault, Verica barely stirred as he tore the cords from around her body and carried her to the bed to drape her across it. Reaching down, he plucked the ring gag from her mouth. She licked her lips and worked her jaw, but didn't try to speak.

"What did you do with the lube?" Julian growled at Dominic, who smirked at the heat in his eyes, scooped up the tube off the bedside table, and flipped it to him.

Ready to spread those pretty white cheeks, boss?

He snatched it out of the air and dropped it on the mattress. *More than ready.* Catching Verica's limp legs behind the calves, he lifted them and nodded to the blond. *Grab her ankles.*

Dominic stepped to the side of the bed, directly over Verica's head, and took each of her delicate heels in his hands. Slowly, he spread them wide and pulled them toward him until she was bent almost double as she lay on her back, her cunt helplessly open in offering. Verica opened vague blue eyes and blinked, still dazed from shattering orgasms and the hard use her virgin body had been put to.

Julian licked his lips at the helpless expression on her face and the wet, swollen flesh of her cunt, still smeared with Dominic's cum and Verica's own feminine juices.

Dominic pulled her feet a little further toward him so that the cleft of her ass spread like a peach, revealing the tiny puckered opening between them. The head of Julian's rock-hard cock jutted above it, thick and dark and much, much bigger. He felt it twitch in anticipation.

Picking up the tube, Julian looked at his second-in-command who sprawled on the bed next to her. "Grab her hands, André."

Reminded that she should fight them, Verica threw up her fists, but André gathered them both in one of his before she had time to launch an assault. Not that she had a prayer in hell anyway. Julian just wanted her to feel her helplessness.

With a thumb, he flicked the top off the tube, his eyes locked on her face. Verica stared up at him, her eyes wide with an arousing combination of fear and lust.

"That's a really tiny asshole, Julian," Dominic observed in a sadistic purr. "You sure you can get your cock in there?"

"I guess we'll find out, won't we?" He inserted the nozzle of the tube into the starfish opening and squeezed. Then, slowly, he began to force the tube deeper.

Verica's spine arched as she felt her anus strain to resist the tube before reluctantly spreading around it. She gasped as a fiery pain radiated from her abused opening, but Julian kept pushing until both the tube and his fingers were deeply embedded.

Finally he began to squeeze. The thick, chilly lube flooded her agonized channel as he withdrew the tube again, inch by inch. At last it was out of her and he tossed it aside. She didn't dare take a breath because she knew that monster shaft of his was next.

Breathless, Verica stared up at the trio of hard, hungry faces above her, the strong, muscled bodies and rigid cocks. The eyes of all three men were locked unblinking on her virgin ass. Looking up between her legs at Julian's sculpted torso and jutting prick, she swallowed hard as her own excitement rose. Being sodomized by that menacing organ would hurt like hell. What she didn't understand was why she hungered for it.

Julian met her eyes and smiled slowly. Verica scanned his handsome warrior's features and felt another jolt of excitement. There was a smear of her blood on the corner of his mouth. He licked it away with a flick of his tongue. "Ready to have your ass stuffed?"

She made herself sneer, hoping he couldn't read her desire and feminine terror. "Get it over with, you son-of-a-bitch."

Dominic laughed. "You have no sense of self-preservation, girl. Most women are more deferential to Julian—particularly when he's in the mood for a slow, sadistic butt-fuck."

Julian leaned over her to brace one hand on the bed as he used the other to aim his cock. "I just wonder how long she can maintain all that magnificent defiance."

The thick rounded crown touched her opening. Licking her lips, Verica hoped she didn't look as nervous as she felt.

The captain smiled mockingly into her eyes. "They usually start begging right about now."

She snarled. "I wouldn't give you the satisfaction, you . . . AH!" Verica managed to bite off the rest of the cry as the massive shaft began to slowly enter. Pain seared up her spine as her anus struggled to stretch around his thick, smooth width.

As she fought her whimpers, the three men observed her anal impalement with glittering eyes.

"You know, as many times as I've watched you do that, I never get tired of seeing it," André said to Julian. "It's hotter than hell, seeing you stuff a woman's ass like that."

But he wasn't done yet. Still he came, working more and more of his cock into her channel. Verica writhed helplessly, but she couldn't get away from the deep, brutal sensation.

"Give her your mouth, André," Julian growled, watching her expression. "She needs to relax."

Dominic pulled her feet further back to give the dark vampire room, and he moved over her until he stretched his head down along her body.

Then André began to lick. The luscious pleasure of his long tongue dancing over her clit provided a sweet counterpoint to the massive pain of Julian's invasion.

At last the captain stopped. Buried inside her to the balls, he waited as André stroked and nibbled and sucked at her sex. Despite the pain radiating from her violated ass, the dark vampire's mouth spun such pleasure over her cunt Verica couldn't help squirming.

Helplessly, she looked up into Julian's black eyes. They glittered with masculine satisfaction at possessing her so utterly.

As André's tongue flicked her clit, she realized Julian's cock in her ass made the pleasure even more exciting. The combination of pain and delight burned her senses. She sucked in a deep breath.

Slowly, Julian began to withdraw. The feeling of his shaft sliding out of her carried a dark, wicked enticement. She whimpered. He smiled into her eyes and pushed in again. "That's right, relax. Open. It's starting to feel good, isn't it? I knew you'd like it once you got past the worst."

Julian eased out again, then in, riding her slowly in long, careful strokes that twisted and teased her most delicate inner flesh as André's clever mouth drew hot runes of delight around her clit.

Later she was never able to pinpoint the moment when Julian's use of her anus became searing pleasure instead of searing pain. All she knew was that suddenly she was thrusting up against him, taking the big rod deeper, fucking it with her ass. Focused on the sensation of his cock, on the way it teased and pleasured her, she barely noticed that André had left her pussy or that Dominic had released her ankles so that her thighs now lay over Julian's massive shoulders.

André's dark hand slipped under her chin, tilting her head back. His lips touched one side of her throat as Dominic licked the skin on the other.

Julian drove his cock in hard in a single, brutal stroke. She convulsed, screaming, kicked over the edge of climax. Simultaneously, she felt a double-pronged stab of pain on either side of her throat as André and Dominic bit deep.

Verica's wide eyes met Julian's as he came down fully on top of her, ramming her ass as his shipmates drank her blood. The conqueror's enjoyment in his eyes sent her orgasm cresting even higher, a white-hot wall of sensation that slammed over her mind in a wave.

"You're mine now, Verica," he growled at her, fucking hard, his sweat splattering her face. "I own you, whether you know it or not."

The pleasure spiraled higher, blinding, until she keened, André and Dominic still feeding, Julian possessing her. Light flared in her skull and it seemed she touched him, touched his mind, felt his immortality and his power and his predatory intentions. And a surprising yearning, as if she was something he'd been looking for and had finally found. Somehow he drew her mind to him, closer and closer, until she felt she knew him as she'd never known another human. Wonder worked its way through the pleasure . . .

Just as everything went black.

Julian studied Verica as she lay sleeping under the regenerator in the *Nosferatu*'s small sickbay. Her color was better, improved since the unit had forced her depleted blood cells to regenerate over the past half hour. He let his eyes roam over her tender nudity, admiring the long, strong legs, the sweet creamy mounds of her breasts, the tumble of dark gold curls around her head. In sleep, her face lost its hard, stubborn lines, taking on a tempting sweetness that made his protective instincts rear.

When André and Dominic wandered in from tending the ship, he curled his lip in a snarl at them. "Her blood volume is back to normal—not that either of you will be getting any of it any time soon."

André ducked one shoulder guiltily. "Sorry, Captain. It had just been a little too long."

Dominic glowered. "I don't see what the problem is. Ten minutes in regen, and she's fine."

Julian let the blond feel the full weight of his disapproval. "The problem is that I told you how much I wanted you to take, and you did not muster the self-control to obey my orders."

He kept his voice soft, controlled, but Dominic flinched and bowed. "You are, of course, correct. Forgive my greed, milord."

That last "milord" was not mockery. A thousand years ago, Dominic had been his vassal—until a beautiful vampire had made Julian something more than mortal. And he, in turn, had changed his loyal knight.

Dominic straightened his shoulders. "So. When will she be out of regen?"

"She already is."

André blinked. "But I thought you were going to put her through the procedure."

"Not yet."

"Aren't we going to keep her?" Dominic frowned." From what you said to her . . ."

Julian made a dismissive gesture. "Regardless of my comments in the heat of the moment, the final choice is hers."

"But you fully intend to help her make up her mind," André guessed shrewdly.

Julian looked down at their sleeping captive. "Oh, yes."

"Good. I like her." André studied Verica, his gaze lingering on her breasts. "She's got guts and heart. Not to mention a truly outstanding mouth."

"And her ass isn't bad either, huh, Julian?" Dominic grinned wickedly. "I can't wait to try it myself."

Julian frowned, surprised at his sudden urge to flip a sheet over that sweetly naked body; he had never felt possessive about a woman before. "If she does agree, I don't want you getting rough with her."

The blond's eyebrows flew up. It was obvious what he was thinking; Julian himself had gotten pretty rough. But Dominic said nothing; they'd been together so many centuries, he knew when his commander was in no mood for an argument.

"Which reminds me," Julian said to André, "if I didn't know better, I'd think you were beginning to believe that sadistic Jamaican mistress scam yourself."

André's grin was unrepentant. "Well, it's such a good story—and the ladies love it so. Even the ones who have no idea what I'm talking about." He'd been a twentieth-century American college professor when Julian met him and realized he was one of the few that could survive the process of becoming a vampire. Slavery had never been part of the equation at all.

Dominic braced his hands on the foot of the regen bed as he looked at Verica. "You know, Julian, despite that delicious submissive streak, she's going to object to this, if only on general principles."

"Oh, yes." Julian's eyes flicked to the soft blonde bush between her thighs. "But I've got a couple of ideas about that."

Verica woke with that familiar sense of energy and well-being that meant she'd just spent time in a regenerator. She suspected she'd otherwise be rather sore. Not to mention weak from blood loss.

She stretched lazily and almost purred at the sensation of neosilk sheets against her skin. Opening her eyes, she found herself back in the quarters the vampires had first taken her to. She'd decided earlier it was the captain's stateroom, judging from its size and the huge bed she sprawled across. Rank, she knew, had its privileges.

Realizing she was naked, Verica wondered if she was one of them. She really wished she could be more outraged at the thought. Yet there was something about Julian Bender that got to her in a way the others hadn't. Remembering the look in his eyes when he'd entered her, she shivered. *"You're mine now, Verica. I own you, whether you know it or not."*

Had he meant that?

Not that it mattered, she told herself staunchly. She belonged to nobody but herself, and she'd tell him so the next chance she got.

The question was, what was she going to do after they released her?

With her T'tcha Ker family dead, she had no home and no money. She supposed she could try to get on with a merc unit, but the fact that everyone in her old unit was dead hardly constituted a sterling reference.

That, of course, assumed the vampires didn't kill her now that they were through with her. *If* they were through with her.

Verica examined the thought and realized she wasn't really worried about it. Somehow she didn't think Julian would hurt her. There'd been a moment when she'd come that he'd . . . touched her mind somehow. She had a sense of him now, of what and who he was. Immensely old, yes, so old and so powerful she'd known a moment's raw fear.

But he was also vulnerable. Lonely, despite the shipmates whose friendship he'd shared for all these centuries. And most astonishing of all, he actually needed what she could give. Sex, yes, but something more than that, something she sensed he'd been seeking for a very long time.

She'd been a responsibility to her father and considered one of the T'tcha Ker's immense family, but none of them had ever *needed* her with that kind of raw intensity.

Verica frowned. Such need was seductive, but that didn't mean she should let it make a difference to her. True, the pleasure the vampires had given her was so intense she doubted she'd ever find the like again. But they also hadn't given her a choice—they'd simply taken her, though she hadn't been willing. Not completely unwilling, either, but still, it had been damned high-handed of them.

"I can be a lot more high-handed than that."

Verica jumped, startled. Julian stood leaning against the doorway;

he'd entered so quietly she hadn't heard him. He was dressed in black trousers and boots, but his broad chest was magnificently bare.

Internal female sensors began jangling in her brain at the sight of him as he strolled toward the foot of the bed. She instantly suspected the effect was intentional. Forcing herself to assume a dry, amused tone, she said, "Yeah, I noticed that when you shoved your dick up my ass."

He grinned, his teeth flashing white. "And a very nice ass it is, too." The smile faded. "We don't plan to release you, Verica."

She went still. "You can't keep me."

"Can't we?"

Her mouth went cotton-dry. "You're pretty formidable, but I'm not bad myself. I'll find a way to escape."

He lifted a dark eyebrow. "I don't doubt it. But it won't be easy, and by the time you do, are you sure you'll want to leave?"

She lifted her chin. "As you may have noticed, I'm stubborn."

"So am I." He braced both arms against the bed's footboard and leaned his weight on them. The pose made the muscle ripple and flex. She knew good and damn well that was intentional too. "Have you noticed that your options at the moment aren't exactly overwhelming, even if we do let you leave? You have no money and no place to go."

She wanted to pace, but somehow she didn't want to do it naked. "A mercenary can always get work."

"An experienced one, yes. Trouble is, all your experience has been with an alien unit that has been rather thoroughly wiped out. Any merc captain is going to wonder just what role you did—or didn't—play in your comrades' demise." She wondered whether he'd read her mind yet again. "I, on the other hand, am willing to make you a member of the crew and pay you accordingly. How about . . ." He named a figure that made her eyes widen. "I doubt you'll get a better offer."

"But would I be shipping out as crew or provisions?"

He laughed, but heat sparked in his eyes. "Both."

Verica lifted her chin at him. "That's very kind, but my career aspirations don't include becoming a human buffet for a trio of vampires."

"You're more than blood to me, Verica." His voice made her heart skip—low, intimate, sensual. She cursed herself, knowing her utter lack of adult experience with men was working against her.

She shook off his spell. "I'm not the first woman you've captured and fucked. Did you make this offer to them, and if so, where the hell are they now?"

He straightened, the muscle in his chest shifting temptingly. She wished he'd stop doing that. "No, you're not our first captive, but I've never made this offer before. We always drop them off at a spaceport with enough money to get wherever they're going."

"So what's so different about me?" Remembering something Dominic said, her eyes narrowed. "Or is it just that you've been six months without pussy, and you decided you want to keep one on hand?"

He looked at her and his eyes heated. Verica realized the sheet she held around her had drooped, revealing the tops of her nipples. She drew it tight again. "That's part of it," he admitted. "But not all. There's a fire and sensuality in you that would make you a perfect . . ." He broke off.

"Bloodslave. Is that what you were going to say?" She'd heard of them. "If you think I'll willingly become an oversexed, genetically engineered half-vampire sex toy, think again."

Julian gave her a mocking smile. "Why, Verica—your father did have interesting tastes in smut, didn't he?"

She shrugged. "There's also a couple million dirty jokes. 'How many bloodslaves does it take to change a lighting unit? None. They like it better in the dark.'"

"The dark has a great deal to recommend it."

"You would think so, wouldn't you?"

"Did the jokes mention that your strength would be five times what it is now, that your reflexes would be faster, your hearing more acute? Useful, for a mercenary."

"We use guns now, Julian. Or hadn't you heard?"

He laughed. "That wicked tongue is one of the reasons I find you so attractive."

"You have no idea what I can do with my tongue. You had me tied up, remember?" She snapped her teeth closed, appalled at herself.

Those dark eyes glittered. "Are you flirting with me, Verica?" He moved around the bed until he loomed over her. "Would you like to demonstrate your skills?"

"Sure." She bared her teeth at him. "If you don't mind being thrown into a bulkhead."

"Those were not the skills I was referring to." He sank gracefully down beside her. Senses clamoring at the proximity of all that male brawn, she had to suppress the urge to edge away. "Since you bring it up, let's talk about sex."

"Let's not."

He ignored that, instead reaching out to trace a fingertip across the fist she held clenched in her lap. "After the procedure, your nipples would be far more sensitive than they are now. The number of pleasure receptors in your clit, cunt, and anus would increase geometrically, making sex even more pleasurable." He looked into her eyes, immersing her in a dark, sensual stare. "Considering how responsive you are now, that idea takes my breath away."

She lifted a brow at him, fighting the raw seduction of that starkly handsome face. "Given your collective appetites, we wouldn't have the chance to do anything, since I'd be in regen all the damn time."

He shook his head. "Verica, that's the whole point of the procedure. Infecting you with a modified form of the vampire virus means you'd gain our ability to regenerate cells. You wouldn't need regen for anything but catastrophic injuries. And you'd be practically immortal."

Verica blinked at that, caught by the idea of having most of a vampire's powers without the drawbacks of a liquid diet. But . . . she remembered the other things she'd heard. Bloodslaves were designed for sex—that's why the procedure's creators had modified the virus to force an increase in the growth of pleasure receptors. Those who underwent it were intended to give their vampire lovers the most intense response possible. The procedure even altered brain chemistry; rumor said they were perpetually horny. "I don't want immortality enough to become a slave of any kind."

He shook his head. "You won't actually become a slave." His lips twitched. "Or no more of a slave than you want to be. And not 'perpetually horny' either. At least . . ." The faint smile widened into a wicked grin. "Not after the first month or so. Once your body adjusts, you'll learn to control it."

Looking at him, remembering what they'd done to her, she had to admit there was a certain fascination in the idea.

Then Julian met her eyes full on, and suddenly all the breath left her lungs at the sheer, sensual power of his stare. Her nipples hardened as she remembered what his cock had felt like, buried to the balls in her ass, André's tongue flicking across her clit. André and Dominic, shafting her in searing unison as Julian fed from her throat. Taken, ravished, overwhelmed.

God, she wanted to feel that way again. And she could. Again and again.

Madness.

She lifted her head and forced herself to meet his eyes defiantly. "I'd be placing myself at your mercy. What's to stop you from abusing me?"

His eyes were so dark and deep she felt dizzy looking into them. "My vow. I will not betray your trust, and I won't allow my men to betray it either."

She fought the hypnotic pull of his will. "And I'm supposed to just trust you?"

"Yes. Because you can."

And she wanted to. That irritated her, made her wonder if she was being suckered. She stared at him, resenting the fact that she wanted him enough to take that kind of risk, while he took no risk at all.

Unless . . .

Julian lifted a dark brow. "You want me to prove myself to you?"

Verica squared her shoulders. "Yeah. You want me to put myself at your mercy? Put yourself at mine."

Reading the image in her mind, he grinned. "You want to tie me up?"

She thought about it, then remembered the way he'd snapped her cat's cradle of cords. "No, you could get free too easy. Forcecuffs." She met his eyes, her own narrowing in challenge. "I want you in forcecuffs."

Julian straightened. "You are serious, aren't you?" Looking at her, he tilted his head, his gaze calculating. Then he nodded shortly. "You want proof; you'll get your proof." He straightened to his full imposing height. "Command me then. I'll obey you."

Hot excitement flooded Verica at the thought of having such a dominant man at her mercy. She fought to control the thrill, decide what to do next. "Strip for me," she ordered, and licked her dry lips. "And tell one of your crew to bring those cuffs. I want them to see you at somebody else's feet for once."

His eyes flashed, and for a moment, she wondered if he'd obey after all. But then his big hands went to the fly of his breeches and opened it with a stroke of long fingers. Eyes fixed on hers, hot and heavy-lidded, he pushed his pants down over his narrow hips. His erection sprang free, long, thick, and hard. She shuddered, remembering the feel of it.

Julian smiled slowly and sat down on the edge of the bed. He kicked off his boots, then wormed the tight breeches the rest of the way off his muscled legs. Deliberately he stretched out on the mattress, extending his powerful arms over his head and arching his spine, rolling his hips upward. The head of his cock brushed his ridged abdomen. He reached a big hand between his thighs and cupped his full balls, then stroked his long, eager shaft, displaying himself for her.

The door slid open and Dominic ducked in carrying a handful of wide gold rings several inches across. "Forcecuffs, boss?" he asked, grinning. "Don't you think that's overkill when you could wrap her up in a ball of yarn . . ."

Julian rolled off the bed, naked. "The 'cuffs are not for her, Dominic."

The blond vampire froze in his tracks. His green eyes widened. "You're not actually going to let her forcecuff you?"

"Trust has to go both ways."

Are you insane? Dominic stepped in close to Julian, projecting his thoughts, his fingers white around the 'cuffs with the force of his grip. *She's a killer, Julian! What's to stop her from slitting your throat?*

She won't, and you know it, Julian told him, mind to mind. *She's a mercenary, not a murderer. I want her. And I'm willing to prove how much.*

Dominic's green eyes snapped. *Look, I want a source of available pussy and blood as much as the next horny vampire, but I'm not willing to risk you to get it.*

You touched her mind, Dominic. You know she's more than just pussy.

The blond turned and looked at Verica who still sat on the bed. Coolly, she met his gaze and allowed the sheet to fall, revealing the lovely globes of her breasts with their pale pink nipples. Blonde hair tumbled around her shoulders. Her full lips were parted under blue eyes that snapped with excitement.

Dominic tossed the cuffs on the bed and said in a fierce, low tone, "If you hurt milord, we'll fucking drain you. And it won't be quick." With a snarl, he stalked out of the room.

Verica looked at Julian, lifting a brow. "Milord?"

"We have a very long history together." He shrugged. "And if he really thought you couldn't be trusted, he wouldn't have left. Not without a fight, anyway." And since André would have joined in, Julian knew he'd have had his hands full. His crew was loyal, but at times their idea of loyalty could stretch to outright rebellion if they thought he was being stupidly suicidal.

Looking at Verica, Julian grinned. With any luck, he'd soon have three of them to worry about. "Where do you want me?" he asked in a velvet purr.

Feeling her nipples harden, Verica shifted on the bed. Damn, how did he *do* that—make her cream just with the tone of his voice and the look in his eyes?

It was some comfort to see his erection lengthening again; it had subsided during the conversation with Dominic. At least she wasn't the only one caught in this ridiculous lust.

"Verica?" Amusement lit his dark eyes.

She blinked, having forgotten the question. Oh, he wanted to know where she wanted to put him. "The bed . . . No, the chair."

Julian nodded obediently and walked over to the padded black swoop of synthleather. Verica snatched up the forcecuffs and went to join him as he dropped onto it.

His eyes roamed over her as she crossed the room, and she was abruptly aware of her nudity. Rocking back on her heels, she gave him the same sort of slow appraisal.

And swallowed. Even sitting down, he looked big, his chest broader than the back of the chair, pelted in silken black hair that trailed down over his muscled belly to that massive erection.

Lifting a brow at her, he held up one powerful wrist, biceps bunching. Verica licked her lips and moved to kneel beside the chair, slipping one of the forcecuffs over his hand. When she held the ring around his wrist, the metal band instantly drew itself tight to his skin. His arm went limp as the cuff cut off his control of his muscles. Moving carefully so she wouldn't wrench it painfully, Verica drew his wrist back until it pressed against the back of the chair. She released him and the cuff locked his muscles in place, holding his arm in the position she'd arranged it in. Forcecuffs couldn't be broken because the captive's own strength held him.

She repeated the process with the other arm, then both ankles, positioning them beside the chair so his thighs were spread, giving her easy access to that magnificent cock.

But she wasn't through yet; there was a fifth ring. Julian had evidently instructed Dominic to bring a forcecollar as well. She looked up from the circle of metal, surprised he was willing to take it that far. Julian lifted a dark brow at her and she wondered if she was being dared.

"I thought maybe you'd want to make sure I don't . . . bite," he said.

Verica narrowed her eyes at him. "Now that you mention it . . ."

She half expected him to object when he realized she'd really do it, but he didn't protest as she opened the collar and slid it around the strong column of his throat. Leaning over his lap, she took his dark head in both hands and positioned it to her satisfaction. When she let him go, his head remained rigidly in place. The back of the chair wasn't quite tall enough; his head and shoulders extended above it.

Leaning back, she saw that his eyes were focused on her hard pink nipples, heat and hunger in his eyes. Bound or not, he didn't exactly look submissive.

"Julian," Verica said, trying out her own velvety purr, "where do you keep your toys?"

He grinned, not in the least intimidated. "There's a panel in the wall beside the bed. I'd get 'em for you, but I seem to be rather . . . busy."

"Oh, I think I can find it." She straightened and turned toward the bed. For the first time in her life, she deliberately put a sway in her ass as she sauntered across the room.

Following his directions, she found the control for the panel and watched it slide open, revealing a deep recess in the bulkhead. Her eyes widened.

Inside were a whole collection of whips, nipple clamps, butt plugs, and dildos, all neatly arranged, along with several old-fashioned cuffs and chains. "You're a bad boy, Julian," Verica breathed, staring at them in shocked titillation.

He laughed, a deep rumble. "Oh, yeah. The question is, how bad a girl are you?"

She grabbed a flogger and a couple of clamps, and turned around. "Bad enough."

Most men would probably have felt a little apprehension, watching Verica stride toward them carrying that leather flogger. Julian merely smiled. She wondered whether he knew she wouldn't hurt him, or whether he hoped she would.

"What do you think?" he asked, reading her mind.

She looked into his strong, handsome face and shrugged. "You're not a masochist."

"And you're not a sadist." His eyes dropped to the flogger with its soft suede lashes. "But you are inventive."

Verica eyed his face as she moved to stand over him. "You're going to be practically impossible to surprise, aren't you?"

"Well, that's the problem of playing with a telepath." He rolled his broad, muscled shoulders, but his immobilized arms remained pinned behind him. "On the other hand, there doesn't seem to be much I can do about it." His lids lowered. "Though there's always revenge."

"In that case, I'd better make the best of my opportunities." Dropping the clamps on the floor, she flicked the flogger across his rock hard cock. It scarcely qualified as a blow, but she looked into his face anxiously to make sure it hadn't actually hurt.

"Usually," he rumbled, "I use that on my captives' tits."

"I'll keep that in mind." She flicked her wrist again.

* * *

Julian caught his breath and tried to jerk his head back, but the collar held him still. The flogger's light lashes didn't hurt, as gently as she struck him. But the soft leather wrapped teasingly around his cock, caressing the long shaft as the lashes hit and pulled away. He'd used it just that way on assorted pretty nipples, but he'd never realized how effective it could be on a man.

Pretty damn inventive for a woman who'd been a virgin a few hours before. But then, her innate sensuality was one of the reasons he wanted her.

Verica grinned wickedly at him and struck him again, her lovely breasts jiggling delightfully as she moved around him on those muscled dancer's legs of hers.

Slowly she increased the force she used, her eyes locked on his, her breath coming hard as she flicked and teased his cock with the whip until he found himself arching his hips as the sting built in his engorged shaft, his balls aching fiercely. He wanted to writhe, toss his head, but the cuffs held him motionless, unable to move anything but his torso.

Half mad with lust, he snarled, "When I get loose, I'm going to fuck you raw. Then I'm going to sink my teeth into that long white throat while I ream your little asshole."

"Not yet." Verica threw the flogger across the room, then reached down and hit a button on the side of the chair. Obediently, it reclined, pulling him back until he was stretched out flat, his feet still on the floor, his head extending beyond the back of the chair. "I've got another use for your mouth first."

She bent to pick up the clamps she'd dropped on the floor, then rose and swung a long leg across him. Setting her feet apart, she straddled his face and bent so she was head-down along his body. Surprised, he stared up at the wet, creamy pussy inches from his lips. Her scent flooded his head, musk and sex and heat.

Reaching down his length, she wrapped one slender hand around his balls and slowly squeezed. She stopped well short of pain, but the threat was there. "Lick me, Julian. I want to come riding your tongue."

He smiled slowly and stabbed his pointed tongue up into her cunt. Verica twisted over him as that hot, wicked mouth went to work.

Her memories had not done his skill justice; he knew just how to lick and nibble and suck to wring searing pleasure out of her pussy. It wouldn't take him long to have her begging.

But she wasn't ready to release control just yet. Surreptitiously, she slipped one of the clamps she still held onto her little finger. It pinched, but not cruelly.

The jaws aren't that stiff, Julian said into her mind. *I never use anything I haven't tested on myself.* He burrowed his tongue up her slick core. *Within anatomical reason, of course.*

She gasped as he began gently thrusting. "Does that include the butt plugs?"

I have to know what effect I'm getting. He gave her a long, sampling lick that caught her clit. *I scale it down, of course. I'm a big man, and being a vampire, I can take a lot more abuse than a woman.*

Verica licked her lips, quivering in pleasure. Some fragment of her mind still capable of rational thought was reassured. Any man who was that careful wouldn't take her further than she wanted to go. "Let's find out just how much you can take." She gently thumbed one of his tiny male nipples and caught the little bead between the black jaws of the clamp.

Julian gasped against her cunt in a warm puff of air. His cock jerked. Pleased, she toyed with the clamp, opening it and releasing it. With her free hand, she reached down to cup his tight, hot balls. "Don't stop licking, Julian. I haven't come yet."

With a growl, he obeyed, catching her clit between his teeth for a gentle nibble that made her back arch. She swallowed as her thigh muscles quivered, then forced herself to continue working the clamp, pinching and releasing the tiny tip. Simultaneously she slowly stroked his cock, enjoying the feeling of slick, hot satin skin under her fingertips.

There's a twentieth-century saying that leaps to mind, he thought, projecting into her mind. *Payback's hell. The next time I get you tied . . .*

She grinned. "Don't threaten Mistress Verica, Julian. She doesn't like it." Giving his cock another taunting squeeze, she released the clamp to attach the second one to his other nipple.

As the tiny jaws grabbed hold, Verica felt something sharp scrape her most tender flesh and shivered. "Uh, uh, Julian. No fangs." She stretched down the length of his muscled torso until she could lick the thick, flushed head of his cock. "Or I'll use my teeth too."

He jerked in his bonds and she felt his wicked tongue go still on her damp flesh. *That's not necessarily a deterrent.*

Verica laughed softly and licked him again. She had never given head before—André's forced fucking of her mouth didn't count since she hadn't actually done anything. Not sure how to go about it, she began to gently tongue him, figuring she couldn't go wrong there. Encouraged by a muffled groan, Verica slipped the head of his cock into her mouth and took him as deeply as she could.

Julian fought not to come as her soft, untutored mouth worked his cock. Oddly, the ache from the clamps seemed to intensify the raw pleasure she inflicted with that sweet tongue. He knew of the effect from using it on his captives, but he'd never experienced it himself. And that, combined with the scent of her wet cunt, was just about to drive him out of his mind.

He'd agreed to this thinking it would prove to Verica he could be trusted. He'd expected she'd be a little clumsy with no real idea what to do with him once she got him. But he'd underestimated her badly. She knew exactly what do to with him, and untutored or not, she knew exactly how to drive him crazy. It had to be instinct. God, what would she be like after a few decades of experience?

Slowly she eased her way deeper onto his cock, taking it further into her mouth, her tongue sliding along the veined shaft. He started wondering whether he'd survive her first century.

Verica filled her mouth with him again, loving the way his powerful body writhed under her hands. God, she was hot. Her cunt felt swollen, engorged with blood, so that every lick and nibble set it burning.

But this, hot as it was, wasn't enough. She wanted him in her, fucking her, filling her.

"Yes!" he growled, and gave her flesh a sharp, stinging nip.

Unable to take any more, Verica jerked upright and swung off his head, then moved around until she could crawl across his lap. Hands shaking with lust, she planted her knees on the seat beside his hips, grabbed his magnificent cock, and aimed it for her juicy opening. Meeting his blazing dark eyes, she began to sink onto the thick shaft.

She instantly realized she was still too new at this; the big head entered, but then lodged fast as her tight walls clamped around it. But she was also too hungry to care, so she forced herself lower, driving his cock more deeply inside her body, impaling herself until it was all the way in, thick and maddening.

Julian swore breathlessly. She writhed, desperate for her climax. "Fuck me!" he growled and she braced her knees on the seat and lifted herself, groaning as his length slid from her, tormenting her sex deliciously. He rolled his hips upward, meeting her as she slid down again.

Hot, desperate, they strove together, cock and cunt greedy, ramming one another hungrily. Each slick, silken thrust maddened her until she jogged against him mindlessly. The pleasure built and built, his shaft creating a delicious friction in her tight, wet sex, and she felt herself trembling on the edge of a searing orgasm.

"Verica," Julian gasped, begging. "Release the collar!"

Knowing what he needed, she reached up and dragged her fingers over the control on the gold ring around his neck. It snapped open. She draped herself over his chest, presenting her throat to his hungry mouth.

Raising his head, he sank his fangs into the soft skin of her throat and began to drink in long, greedy swallows, rolling his hips hard, grinding against her spread, starving sex.

Fire burst behind her eyes in a shower of sparks as her orgasm rolled over her. She twisted, convulsing with a cry. He growled against her neck and surged upward against her as he jetted into the depths of her cunt.

He was still feeding, Verica draped over him in exhausted pleasure, when the door slid open and André and Dominic stuck their heads in.

"Uh, Verica, we were wondering . . ." André began, sounding surprisingly diffident for a man who'd mouth-fucked her a few hours before.

"Would you mind doing us next?" Dominic finished, grinning at the sight of his captain, bound to the chair with their captive lying limp on top of him.

Julian lifted his head from Verica's throat and snarled. Both vampires prudently withdrew.

Out in the corridor, André lifted a brow and grinned at his friend. "Maybe later."

Keep reading for a sneak peek
at Angela Knight's
next erotic romace novel.
Coming soon from Berkley Sensation!

Alexis Rogers shifted on her high heels, nibbling her lower lip. Her mouth felt dry, probably because every drop of moisture in her body had taken up residence between her thighs. God, she'd never been so turned on.

Especially not from watching somebody else have sex.

And how the hell did Frank turn swinging a bullwhip into a sex act? Not just a kink act—something that aroused you if you had a little twist in that direction. Which admittedly, Alex did. No, he used the lash with sensual precision, as if he were eating out the blonde lying across the spanking bench. Plump, pretty, and naked, Tara merely groaned in woozy pleasure.

Thirty people surrounded the two in the basement dungeon, watching with rapt interest. One of them was Tara's husband, who leaned a shoulder against the cement block wall. Roy was a gangly dominant with thinning blond hair whose hazel eyes were fixed intently on his wife. Though he loved bondage and emotional domination, Roy couldn't bring himself to hurt his masochistic submissive. He often arranged for someone else to provide the impact play Tara craved.

Apparently, Frank had volunteered to provide them with the foreplay this time. And foreplay was all he'd be getting out it; Tara and Roy never had penetrative sex with anyone but each other.

That was okay. If all went as planned, Alex would make it up to the big dominant. Or maybe not; she'd have to see.

Still, the Captain—host of tonight's house party—had been talking about Frank for years. She gathered they'd served together in the Navy before Cap retired and left San Diego to come to Atlanta with his wife.

Now it seemed Frank had moved to the area too. Must have been recently. Alex had never seen the big dominant at any of the very private parties Cap and his wife threw for close friends among Atlanta's kinksters.

CRACK! The popper—the fringe at the very tip of the bullwhip—struck Tara's reddening ass. By rights, it ought to sting like a bitch, but Frank had Tara so high on endorphins and adrenaline, it seemed she no longer felt the pain at all. At least not judging by the moan that sounded far more like pleasure than pain.

Which was a testament to his skill as a dominant. He'd built the intensity slowly, starting with a spanking, then progressing through two different floggers—the first deerskin, the second with thinner tresses that made the submissive yelp at the sting. The blows he gave her were hard, but not too hard, letting Tara sink into the sensations and get properly turned on. Only then had he got out the bullwhip.

Between clusters of strikes, Frank gave her erotic caresses, stroking her pussy and reddening ass. The combination of pain and pleasure had sent her flying on her body's natural endorphins and adrenalin. Alex knew from experience that the high was similar to what some runners felt during a marathon—a floating, delicious euphoria. Pursuit of that erotic high was what drove subs like Tara—and Alex herself, for that matter—to seek out dominants like Frank. Skilled, a little sadistic, with a keen understanding of a submissive's darkest needs.

Yeah, Frank definitely knew his way around a sub's body, just as the Captain had said.

Now the overhead spotlight pouring down on the blonde caught the wet glistening of rosy vaginal lips. She lay with wrists and ankles cuffed to the bench's legs, the wedge shape of the custom-made bench raising her hips higher than her head. Offering up her curvy little ass to her sensual tormentor.

Pacing around Tara, Frank dealt out another set of carefully measured blows, watching her with an absorbed erotic intensity. He seemed acutely aware of every twitch of her full ass, flex of her fingers, and heartfelt sensual moan. He moved like a bullfighter as he swung the whip in practiced, hissing arcs, using a blend of athleticism and grace that was all the more impressive considering his size.

Frank was big. Really big.

Alex, who was good at judging height and weight—she had to be, given her job—figured him at six-five or six-six, maybe two hundred and forty deliciously muscled pounds. If there was an ounce of fat anywhere on the man, she couldn't see where. He'd pulled his shirt off in the dungeon's warmth, revealing broad, brawny shoulders and the kind of bare torso that rippled in interesting places. His long legs were clad in faded jeans tucked into polished leather riding boots.

God, she'd always had a thing for riding boots.

It was harder to make out the details of his face as he paced in the basement's shadows. Fortunately, he'd e-mailed Alex a photo a week or so ago.

His features had a kind of stark good looks, with a long, thin nose, cleft chin, and a pugnaciously broad jaw. He wore his black hair in a stern military cut that emphasized the stark angularity of his cheekbones. The total effect might have been forbidding, had it not been for his mouth. Wide, with a plump lower lip and a pronounced upper bow, it looked soft, deliciously kissable.

Alex had wanted to taste that seductive mouth the moment the photo popped into her e-mail.

Patience, she told herself. Cap had said he'd introduce them after the scene. And since the Captain was a notorious kinkster matchmaker, she knew he'd keep his promise.

CRACK!

Powerful muscle rippled along Frank's right arm and across his wide chest as he popped the whip against Tara's ass. The sub caught her breath, then let it out in a long, erotic groan.

"Rate it," Frank ordered, in voice so rich and deep, it seemed to tighten something in Alex's sex.

Tara didn't answer. He stalked around the bench, wrapped a huge fist in her cascade of blonde curls, and jerked her head back with a dominant's showy snarl. "When I ask you a question, you damned well answer. Talk to me!"

"Uh . . ." The girl panted. Her voice sounded slurred, barely coherent. "I don't . . ." Yeah, she was definitely flying. All those endorphins had rendered her barely coherent.

Frank glanced toward Roy. Tara's husband nodded and picked up the blanket and bottle of water he'd had waiting for this moment.

Crouching by Tara's head, Frank began talking to her in a low voice as her husband joined them.

"You can tell a lot about a dom by the way he gives aftercare," Calvin Stephens observed from Alex's shoulder. "He could have just let her husband handle it, but he's taking part. Point in his favor." The submissive turned to the man next to him. His narrow, clever face split in a grin that revealed teeth so white, they appeared to glow against his dark skin. "You've always been good at aftercare, Sir."

Ted Arlington snorted. He was a head shorter than Alex, between the heels she was wearing and the fact she was five-ten to begin with. Even so, his build was all muscle and power—and he knew how to use it. Any idiot who assumed he could kick Ted's ass because he was short soon learned otherwise. Beneath the brush cut he had a broad, squared-off, intensely masculine face, with a full-lipped mouth, a round bulb of a nose and a blond mustache. "You're just saying that because I always give you cock as part of the aftercare package."

Cal grinned wickedly, dipping his dark gaze to his dominant's zipper. "And what a nice package it is, Sir."

"Suck-up."

"But you like it when I suck."

"You're pushing it, subbie."

As the two went into their standard teasing routine, Alex's gaze slid across the basement in search of Frank.

He'd helped Roy unbuckle Tara from the spanking bench so the two men could wrap her in the blanket. As Alex watched, they helped her over to one of the couches that stood against the big basement's walls. Pulling what was probably a trail mix bar from his pocket, Frank sank down beside the couple to unwrap it for her. Meanwhile, Roy helped her with the bottle of water she couldn't quite manage on her own.

"I don't know about you two," Alex said, with a nod toward the trio, "but I'm impressed."

"That's not saying much." Ted folded his massive arms and braced his legs apart. His brush cut hair shone pale blond under one of the basement's recessed lights. "You were also impressed by Gary."

Alex forced a smile to hide the sting of pain she felt. "Well, Gary was very pretty."

"So's a coral snake. I still wouldn't fuck one."

"Sir, you do know gay men are supposed to be sensitive, right?"

"Sass me one more time, subbie, and I'll make you so sensitive you won't be able to sit for the next week."

"Oh, would you, Sir?"

"Keep it up," Ted growled, eyeing him with the expression of exaggerated menace he reserved for his dom act. Alex had seen his real menacing expression frequently in the course of the job. It was one hell of a lot colder. "As for you . . ." He turned to give her the same look he'd just given Calvin. "I want to talk to this Frank before you traipse off to scene with him, got me? I don't want you hurt by some Mr. Danger Dom. I worked too damn long to turn you into a good cop to lose you to an asshole."

Alex smiled, warmed by both the uncharacteristic compliment and her friend's gruff concern. "You know good and damned well the Captain isn't going to set me up with a Danger Dom."

"Unless I'm really, really mistaken, I somehow doubt the Captain has ever slept with Frank, much less subbed for him."

"You're not mistaken, Sir," Cal assured him. "Cap definitely doesn't bat for our team."

"And how would you know that, Cal?" Alex narrowed her eyes in mock suspicion. "Been flirting?"

"With the Captain?" The slender young man recoiled in mock horror. "God, no. He scares me. He looks like Captain Picard's bigger, meaner brother."

"You are such a nerd, Cal."

He put up both hands. "Hey, my mom's a fan. She raised me on reruns of Next Gen."

"Your *mom*," she drawled, pumping skepticism into her voice. "Riiiiiiight. Tell it to somebody who doesn't know you and your fanboy buddies. I've heard y'all argue about whether Captain Picard is cooler than Captain Kirk way too many times."

"That's self-evident," Cal said loftily. "Kirk is *much* cooler. Take how he handled the Klingons . . ."

"Look, this is serious, Alex," Ted snapped, before she could make a concerted effort to divert him with the Alex-and-Cal comedy hour. "Not that you've ever had the sense to be afraid—of anything—but this guy is big enough to hurt you no matter how good you are in a fight. Don't give him the chance."

"Don't worry, Dad, I won't."

"None of your lip." Ted glowered at her. "Just because I don't do women, that doesn't mean I won't whip your little ass as hard as the subbie's."

"And that's pretty damned hard," Cal put in.

"Yeah, okay, I hear you." Her gaze slid back toward Frank again.

Ted looked at Cal. "I just wasted my breath, didn't I?"

"Might as well try to blow out a forest fire like a birthday candle," Cal agreed. "She's completely under his evil spell." His voice turned dreamy. "His muscular, towering, evil, evil spell."

"I am definitely kicking your ass tonight."

Which, knowing Cal, was precisely what he'd had in mind.

The redhead was driving Frank Murphy crazy. Alex—they'd exchanged e-mails, but she hadn't revealed her last name yet—wore the proverbial little black dress that hugged some luscious curves. Throw in those lace-stocking-clad legs and skyscraper heels, and it was no wonder he was finding it impossible to concentrate. Which was unacceptable, especially when he was providing aftercare to somebody he'd just whipped right into subspace.

Focus on Tara, dammit. He'd told Roy he'd take care of her, and he'd do it if it killed him.

Be easier if he could throw a burqa over Alex though. Those legs . . . God, the Leg Fairy had been good to the girl. Endless as a Fallujah patrol, with long, lean muscle in thigh and calf that flexed every time she twitched a do-me heel. He'd bet his Trident—the Navy SEAL special warfare insignia—that she ran every fucking day. He'd love to have her wrap his ass in those legs while he ground in nice and deep . . .

No wonder he had a hard-on up to his navel.

Tara, dammit. Get your mind back on Tara. Discipline wasn't usually this much a problem. Between Iraq, Afghanistan, and his mother—

and all their respective IEDs, whether literal or not—Frank knew how to gut it out through almost anything.

Roy looked up at him over Tara's blonde head. "I can take it from here. Go talk to Alex."

He stiffened. Was his distraction that damned obvious?

"You done good, Frank," the man reassured him. "I've never seen anybody send Tara flying this high. It's going to take me an hour to pull her down out of orbit—assuming she stays awake that long. I only know about Alex because Cap's been talking about setting you two up since he heard you were moving back to the area."

"Ah. All right. Look, thanks for trusting me to scene with your wife." Smiling, he shook the other dom's hand and rose. "You're a lucky man."

"Don't I know it." Roy gave Tara a tender smile as she leaned against his shoulder. She sent him a slow, dazed blink in return. "See you later, Frank."

"Later." Pivoting, he looked around for his host, wanting the introduction Cap had promised him.

"Nice scene, son," a voice rumbled from behind him. "You flew that girl higher than any space shuttle ever went."

Frank turned with a smile. "You'd have sent her higher."

"Now you're just flattering an old man's ego." Captain Kyle Miller was a tall, spare man, wiry and tough, with a fringe of gray hair around his otherwise gleaming bald head. His intense blue-eyed stare had a way of making even Frank want to drop his gaze. The intimidation factor was increased by his hawkish nose and wide, thin-lipped mouth. The black golf shirt he wore with black slacks revealed biceps that were still respectable, though he was old enough to have done two tours in Vietnam as a Navy SEAL. He'd stayed in after the war, making the jump from enlisted man to Officer Training School, eventually working his way up to captaining a destroyer in the course of his forty-year career. But in his heart, he was still a Navy SEAL.

Not, all in all, a man to fuck with.

"Let's go get you properly introduced," Cap said, and turned to lead the way through the crowded basement. It seemed his kinkster guests were all setting up their own scenes, now that Frank's bullwhip demo was over. "Y'all made any contact yet?"

Frank shrugged. "Exchanged a few e-mails, a photo or two, chatted on the phone a couple of times. Enough to know our tastes are compatible and both of us have tested negative for STDs recently. I've been so busy getting all the requirements done for the new job—not to mention stuff with my mom—that I haven't managed to set up an actual date yet." He frowned. "She hasn't told me much personal stuff, beyond that she's not married."

Cap shrugged. "I'm not surprised. She's pretty far into the closet, as far as the scene goes. Most everybody at the party tonight is."

"Including me." Being known as kinky could get you fired or ostracized, especially in the socially conservative, highly religious South. People had even lost their kids over being in the scene.

Which was why, as in the movie *Fight Club*, many kinksters never publically discussed anything they'd done, where they'd done it, or who they'd done it with.

The price of running your mouth could be entirely too high.

As his attention focused on Alex, Frank put out a hand to stop his friend. "Who's the guy glaring at me from beside her? The dom that looks like a blond fireplug standing next to the black sub in the harness. I thought she wasn't involved with anybody." The man wore the black leather pants and black T-shirt that constituted a popular uniform for dominants everywhere, just as that leather thong and artistic arrangement of straps was a common costume for male submissives.

The old SEAL laughed. "That's Ted—he and the black kid are a couple."

"So what's with the glare? They in a ménage with Alex?" Frank was the last man to poach. Not after what had happened a year and a half ago.

"That'd be damned near incest, the way Ted is about that girl. And no, they're not related—you'd just think he was her daddy, he's so protective." Cap grimaced, as if at an unpleasant memory. "Ted absolutely hated her last dom, not that you could blame him. That one was such a prick, he should have worn a condom over his face as a warning to the rest of us." Correctly interpreting Frank's wary expression, he added, "Don't worry about Ted, I'll deal with him. You concentrate on Alex."

Frank frowned, wondering if all that was an indication the sub was going to be more trouble than she was worth.

Then Alex turned, pivoting on those incredible legs, gleaming red hair curling around her shoulders, that black dress hugging bra-challenged breasts and curvy hips. When she saw him headed toward her with Cap, a smile lit her pretty face.

On the other hand, what's life without a little trouble?

Good God, he's huge, Alex thought, staring up at Frank Murphy as Cap introduced them with a flourish. She wasn't used to being towered over, especially not in heels that had her scraping six-one. *If he got drunk and disorderly on me on the street, I'd have to shoot him. Otherwise he'd kick my ass.*

Of course, if she did shoot him, the rest of the female population would probably rise up en masse and lynch her. If anything, the man was even more mouth-watering up close than he'd appeared from across the room. His chest alone seemed to take up her entire field of vision. And she definitely approved of the view.

"It's a pleasure to meet you at last, Alex," Frank said, engulfing her hand in a big, scarred palm.

"I can definitely say the same." His eyes were deep and gray, staring into hers in the kind of hypnotic dom stare that made her want to give him anything he wanted. Especially if what he wanted was her. She suspected her smile looked besotted. Her nipples had drawn into tight points. His eyes flicked down to the tight silk bodice of her dress, then flicked up again, darkening hungrily. She swallowed. "Impressive flogging demo."

"You do seem to know your way around a whip," Ted observed coolly from her shoulder. His tone indicated some skepticism that Frank's other skills were as well-developed.

Frank laughed, a dark, lovely rumble that made her pussy tighten. "Thanks. I sacrificed a lot of pillows to the bondage gods to learn how to use a lash." Dominants were often told to practice learning how to use a whip by practicing on pillows and stuffed animals.

"Got any references?"

"Yes, and I already checked them," Alex told Ted tartly, not for the first time. He was deliberately trying to yank Frank's chain, and it was starting to annoy her.

Cap moved up behind Ted and clapped a hand on the shorter man's beefy shoulder. "Come on, Ted, I'll get you a beer."

"I don't drink when I'm sceneing," the cop replied shortly, his gaze still locked on Frank's in challenge.

"Then I'll get you a Coke." The SEAL pulled Ted away. Cal rolled his eyes, gave Alex a wink, and followed them.

One thick, dark brow lifted, Frank watched them head for the refreshment table set up beyond the bondage gear. "Protective, isn't he?"

Alex sent a smile after her friends. "Can't seem to break him of the habit."

A woman cried out, the sound halfway between pain and pleasure. Someone else shouted, the sound ringing over Jim Morrison's throaty croon demanding that someone light his fire.

Alex had to raise her voice to be heard over the snap and whish of a flogger and the yelps of its target. "Want to step into the other room? We can't exactly talk in here."

"That depends. Will Ted feel driven to defend your honor?" Frank grinned, but there was no malice in his gaze as he looked toward the corner where, judging by his expression, the SEAL was attempting to reassure the blond dominant.

She slid an arm through his, enjoying the warm play of his bare biceps under her hand. "I'll protect you."

"Well, if you promise. . . ."

Alex laughed. "Pinky swear."

"Got a deal. Want something to drink? I'm dry from that flogging."

"Sure." She followed him over to a cooler and took one of the canned soft drinks he handed her. Neither of them reached for a beer. Ted was right; only an idiot sceneed when he was drinking. BDSM was dangerous enough when you were playing stone sober. Besides, the whole point of kinky games was the pursuit of a different kind of high.

Rising to her tiptoes, she said into his ear, "Want to head for the gym? I don't think Cap'll mind. It often gets used as a spare scene room for these parties."

Frank nodded. "If it's avalable. It's for damn sure we can't negotiate if we can't even hear ourselves think."

The Millers' basement was huge, running the whole length of the house. They wound their way through the dungeon with its bondage gear and party furnishings and across a short hall to the home gym.

Frank flipped on the light, revealing a treadmill, a wall-hung flat screen, and a set of free weights. A couple of thick padded mats probably did duty during yoga or self-defense practice. Or, knowing the Millers, sex.

Best of all, the room had a door. Alex didn't hesitate to close it, cutting the noise. Frank was right; there was little point in negotiations if neither of them could hear what they were agreeing to. And once you were bound hand and foot and a big guy was standing over you with a whip, it was a bad time to discover you didn't have the same thing in mind.

The skirt of her LBD was just loose enough to let her lower herself down on the stacked mats. Frank sat next to her, stretching his long legs out and crossing his booted feet at the ankles.

"I really was impressed with the way you helped Tara find subspace." She popped the top on the Coke and took a sip. After she swallowed, she added, "Wasn't surprised, though. Both those subs had a lot of good things to say about you." She might be an adrenalin junky, but Alex wasn't stupid; she'd called his references. It wasn't a good idea to play with someone you hadn't checked out, since BDSM did attract its share of assholes. God knew she'd found that out the hard way. "They said you play responsibly, push just far enough without going too far, and have a chivalrous streak that's surprisingly wide for a guy who likes using a whip. And judging by the way Cap sings your praises, you may be his favorite person on the planet—except for Mrs. Cap, of course."

"Cap's a hell of a guy. He taught me the ropes when I was just starting out on the scene." Frank eyed her over his Mountain Dew. "He thinks a lot of you, too."

"Really? Cool." She leaned back on her elbows, and didn't miss the way his gaze skimmed the length of her legs. "What'd you think of my limits list?" The question didn't sound quite as casual as she would have liked, though she hoped her tension didn't show. The list enumerated everything she was—and was not—willing to do during a scene, from bondage to flogging to sex.

He grinned, flashing white teeth. "I'm shocked—shocked, I say—by your kinkitude."

She grinned back. "Smart-ass."

Some doms might have been offended by the cheerful insult, but judging by his chuckle, Frank obviously didn't take himself that seriously.

She liked that about him. A lot.

Sobering, he brushed the back of her hand with his thumb. "Our tastes do seem to align pretty well."

She'd thought the same thing when she'd read his list of hard limits—things he absolutely wouldn't do, soft limits—things he'd consider doing, and fantasies. It had read a lot like the one she'd written about her own tastes.

On the other hand, she'd thought she was a good match with Gary, too.

He studied her thoughtfully, as if sensing the battle between her doubts and her desire. "Why don't we see how this evening goes?"

Alex blew out a breath. "That might be wise."

He started to lean toward her, only to stop. "May I kiss you?" A polite dominant never touched a sub without permission.

Her heart began to pound. "Yes." She swallowed, cleared her throat. "I'd like that."

Hot approval flared in his eyes, and he lowered his head toward hers.

His lips felt just as soft as they looked, tasting of Mountain Dew and masculinity. One big hand came up to cup her cheek, his fingers long and strong and warm. His broad body curled around hers, making her feel sheltered, protected. It wasn't a sensation she was used to. She was surprised at how seductive it was.

She reached for him, feeling the hot flesh of his ribs under her palm.

And sighed, melting into him.